Praise for Marie Myung-Ok Lee's *Somebody's Daughter*

Somebody's Daughter is that rare book, that rare page-turner, the one you cannot put down, the one you will suspend washing the laundry for or cooking breakfast for. It is the novel you will open and read in one urgent breath as you take in the storyteller's compelling tale of lives felt long after the book's end as you turn off the light to sleep.

> LOIS-ANN YAMANAKA,
> author of *Wild Meat and the Bully Burgers*

In a time when Asian adoptions are more and more commonplace, Marie Myung-Ok Lee's *Somebody's Daughter* hits an important and unique chord: the POV of the adopted child, now grown up and searching for her lost roots. Lee manages to be both comic and frank in this story of one girl's journey back to Korea, and her lost mother's own journey toward redemption.

> ANN HOOD, author of
> *The Ornithologist's Guide to Life*

Lee's story of one young woman's search for self in Korea will resonate equally with both adult *and* young adult readers— a remarkable achievement.

> MICHAEL CART,
> author of *Necessary Noise*

In this moving portrayal of an adopted girl's search for her biological mother, Marie Lee gives voice and validation to a segment of the Korean American community that has been overlooked too long and too often. *Somebody's Daughter* is a gift for those forgotten, for the thousands of Korean children adopted by white parents, for those who search and yearn for a sense of home and self.

> NORA OKJA KELLER,
> author of *Comfort Woman* and *Fox Girl*

With a pen dipped in deepest longing and grief, Marie Myung-Ok Lee has written an affecting novel of an adoption.

JACQUELINE MITCHARD,
author of *The Deep End of the Ocean*

Sumptuous and emotionally stunning ... Once you begin this novel, you won't be able to put it down, infused as it is with our fragile sense of self, the search for natural parents to anchor one's identity, and Lee's elegant, imagistically sinuous prose that continually stabs the heart.

SAM COALE,
Providence Journal

Be prepared to put yourself in the adoptee's frame of mind. It is written from our viewpoint, and it's a keeper.

EUN MI YOUNG,
Adoptive Families

Her colorful characters crackle and pop off the page ...
A grown-up gem of a novel where joy mingles with sorrow, and heartbreak is laced with hope.

ALLISON BLOCK,
Booklist, starred review

Somebody's Daughter

Also by Marie Myung-Ok Lee

Finding My Voice

Saying Goodbye

Necessary Roughness

Somebody's Daughter

Marie Myung-Ok Lee

BEACON PRESS
BOSTON

Beacon Press
25 Beacon Street
Boston, Massachusetts 02108-2892
www.beacon.org

Beacon Press books are published under
the auspices of the Unitarian Universalist
Association of Congregations.

09 08 07 06 8 7 6 5 4 3 2 1

This book is printed on acid-free paper that
meets the uncoated paper ANSI/NISO
specifications for permanence as revised in 1992.

Text design by Bob Kosturko
Composition by Wilsted & Taylor Publishing Services

Library of Congress Cataloging-in-Publication Data

Lee, Marie Myung-Ok.
Somebody's daughter / Marie Myung-Ok Lee.
p. cm.
Summary: Adopted and raised by Scandinavian-American parents in Minnesota,
a Korean teenager returns to her native country to find her mother.
ISBN 0-8070-8389-5 (pbk. : acid-free paper)
[1. Mothers—Fiction. 2. Adoption—Fiction. 3. Korea—Fiction.] I. Title.

PZ7.L5139So 2005
[Fic]—dc22   2004025757

Portions of this novel have appeared in slightly
different form in: *The American Voice,* no. 39,
1996; *American Eyes* (Henry Holt, 1994);
*Making More Waves: New Writing by Asian
American Women* (Beacon Press, 1997).

To Grace Koom-soon Lee and in memory of Dr. William Chae-sik Lee
and to
Jason,
whose courage inspires me, every day

"*If I bear witness of myself, ye will say my witness is not true.*"
—JOHN 5:31

How can you claim to know the taste of watermelon
when you have only licked the rind? —KOREAN PROVERB

Prologue

The dream unfolds as it always does, light goes to black, then back to color again. The last sensation from the awake-world is my limbs seizing like a jerked marionette as I pass into the deepest stages of sleep.

But this time, the dream is different.

This time, I'm dreaming I'm her.

She is sitting in a slow-moving trainlike vehicle, maybe the Small World ride at Disneyland. Her neck is craning like crazy; she's going to meet someone, but is seized by a sudden anxiousness that she's gotten the time or location wrong.

Another train is going the other way. In it are two girls, who catch her eye and wave.

"I'm Sarah," says one, in a Barbie-doll voice.

"So am I," says the other. The two are holding hands, looking like paper-doll cutouts.

She turns to face them. "You can't both be Sarah."

"Why not?" says the Barbie-doll voice.

"After all, we've got two mothers," says the other.

"You've only got one mother, ONE," she says. She decides she will break the chain of their hands and then everything will be logical again.

The trains jerk, beginning to pull them in opposite directions. She jumps off to pursue them. But try as she might, the girls' train pulls away too fast.

First one, then the other laughs, all mouth and teeth.

GET BACK ON THE RIDE, YOU!

I wake with a gasp. When I was little, I once did jump off one of the rides at Disneyland—I wanted to go live with the Pirates of the Caribbean. My friend Ashley beside me had been scared of them, but not me. I knew I'd be happy with those pirates, daggers in teeth, skin stained the same walnut brown I turned in the summer.

It takes me a second to recall the larger contours of my dream. When I remember that *she* was in it, I moan. Why didn't I think to look in a mirror? In the other dreams, her face is always hidden in shadow.

The tears come, another gasp escapes like steam. This chance to see what she looked like, gone. I stopper my mouth with a pillow, praying Christine won't wake and come running, face earnest and dutiful as a volunteer firefighter, hands soft, murmuring words of comfort. *You had a bad dream, sweetie?*

I can't bear to have her touch me.

❁ ❁ ❁

Where she is, it's day, not night, she's just woken from her afternoon nap.

Usually she sleeps light as a cat, whiskers alert to catch the slightest change in the air. But this time, her limbs had felt pinned as if by stone or thick ropes. Someone might have even said, "*Chuh-gi,* excuse me, but I really would like to make a purchase—ahem," and she wouldn't have been able to move a muscle.

While her body lay helpless, some other part of her had flown like a blown leaf all over the known world. From Korea to America, perhaps even beyond. So far, in fact, that when she wakes, she finds herself surprised that she is, well, herself.

She is reminded (though she is Christian) of the beautiful Buddhist koan: Am I a person dreaming I'm a butterfly—or am I a butterfly dreaming I'm a person?

PART I

SARAH
Minneapolis
1993

When I was eight, they told me that my mother's death was preordained. She had been murdered.

One Sunday after service, our minister, Reverend Jansen of the Lutheran Church of the Good Shepherd, bent down in a cloud of Aqua Velva to explain. We had been learning in Sunday school about Heaven and Hell, and in the middle of class I had fallen into a panic, wondering how I would recognize my Korean mother when I saw her in Heaven—or in Hell, if perhaps she and I both sinned too much.

Not to worry, I was told.

"God called your Korean parents home so that you could become the daughter of your mother and father," he said, his eyes sliding sidewise, for just a second. His breath smelled vaguely of toast.

"It was all part of His plan—you see how much your mommy and daddy love you? When the time comes, if you're a very good girl, you, your mommy, daddy, and your sister, Amanda—the whole Thorson family—will be in Heaven together, thanks to the Lord's wonderful and mysterious ways."

"That's why we named you Sarah," Christine and Ken added. "Because it means 'God's precious treasure.'"

God kills, I thought then. The same God who brought us Christmas and the Easter Bunny—he murdered my mother.

Shortly after that Sunday, I brought up my Korean mother again, asking about the car accident, how it had happened, exactly—was it like Phil Haag's father, who fell asleep at the wheel? Or like our plumber's teenage son who drove into a semi head-on?

"Sarah," Christine said patiently, looking up from the chopping board, where she was slicing carrot discs for pot roast. "We really knew nothing about her. *I'm* your mommy. Let's not talk about this any more, it makes me sad." She made little crying motions, pretending to wipe away tears, the same thing she did when I was bad, to show how I had disappointed her.

❀ ❀ ❀

I had grown up in a house in which *Korea* had always been the oddly charged word, never to be mentioned in connection to me, the same way we never said "Uncle Henry" and "alcoholic" in the same sentence. It was almost as if Ken and Christine thought I needed to be protected from it, the way small children need to be protected from boors itching to tell them that Santa Claus is not real. The ban on Korea extended even to the aforementioned Uncle Henry, who was then deprived of his war stories at our Memorial Day weekend cookouts. Although he proudly wore his felt VFW hat with its flurry of pins, including ones from his tour "overseas," Christine or Ken would quietly slip him some of his favorite Pabst or Schlitz, and in return he'd set up residence in the lawn chair at the far corner of our yard, away from everyone.

Somewhere back in the fuzzy clot of my teens (now, I'm at the worldly-wise age of almost-twenty), the '88 Summer Olympics were held in Seoul. We couldn't buck the Thorson family tradition of watching absolutely everything (that winter we'd raptly watched curling, for God's sakes!). But I was aware that pains were taken to modulate voices, vocal cords twisted to an excruciating, studied casualness until *Korea* came out Korea, exactly the same way we'd say "Russia" or "Carl Lewis" or "Flo-Jo."

Then Bryant Gumbel invaded our living room with his special segment on how *Korea,* one of the four "Little Tiger" economic miracle countries, was so enterprising that it had even made an export product out of its babies. Since the Korean War, more than a *hundred thousand children,* Made-in-Korea stamped on their foreheads, had left the country, their adoption fees fattening the government coffers.

Top that, Singapore! Gumbel's cheery smirk seemed to say.

"Well, Sarah's really American, not Kor—," Amanda had begun, until the look on Christine's face—despairing, fierce—stopped her.

We invent what becomes us.

SARAH
Seoul
1993

The plane had finally approached Kimp'o Airport three bad movies and five shrink-wrapped meals after I'd left Minneapolis. The video monitors had shown a graphic rendering of our progress, a cartoon of our plane inching its way over the Pacific Ocean toward the Korean peninsula. As we descended toward Seoul, the white cartoon-plane veered from its arcing trajectory to fly directly over some dot in the Sea of Japan called Tok-do. The Korean people on board cheered.

The twinkly-eyed senior across the aisle turned and smiled. He and his wife, matching canvas Elderhostel totes, clutched gnarled hands over the shared armrest, fingers tangling like brush.

"Glad to be home, eh?"

It took me a second to realize he was talking to me. Another second to step back and see me as he did: Korean girl returning to Korea.

I wiped at the corners of my eyes, fuzzed by no sleep.

"Oh yah, you betcha," I said, in my purest Minnesota-nice accent. His wife, whose name would just have to be Effie or Jean, leaned forward out of her husband's shadow to beam at me.

"We can still turn around and just go back home—Daddy and I don't care about cancellation fees." Christine's last words to me at the mouth of the jetway. "Sarah, you don't have to do this to yourself."

She made it sound like I was off to get a tribal tattoo, or maybe to go do that Sioux sun dance where you pierce your breast with a sharp spike attached by rope to a pole and dance around the pole in the hot sun for days, waiting for a vision.

"I'm just taking my slightly belated graduation trip," I'd said. In the waning days of my senior year, I'd been promised "a trip anywhere you like" if I could get myself off the Hold list and back into that stream of graduating seniors.

An extra credit report on plate tectonics (Earth Sciences), plus a record one week of resisting the urge to bolt while sitting in every class except maybe Chemistry, earned me my prize.

However, somehow, that subsequent summer oozed through my fingers, and I was still snoozing in my bikini when dead leaves and Ken and Christine's insistence that I take a try at college came raining down on me. I lasted not quite a year as a Golden Gopher at the U of MN, Duluth. I never knew the shores of Lake Superior could be so cold.

So here I was, taking my trip just a little bit late. It was just that no one expected me to choose Korea as my final destination.

❀ ❀ ❀

My watch proclaimed it almost midnight, but a blinding sun was battering to be let in under the ovalette window shades, my tongue stung from the sugar-greased pastries and rank orange juice the stewardesses had foisted on us.

In the airport, the silver-topped heads of the Elderhostel couple acted as a beacon as I followed them to Immigration and waited behind them in the line marked FOREIGNERS. They seemed to know what they were doing. In line, the woman showed her husband something in *Fodor's Asia*. At the baggage claim, my things were among the last to arrive, and Effie and Burt, as I'd named them, went on without me. After that, the only Caucasian people I saw were a few shorn soldiers in camouflage fatigues and black boots that always looked too big.

The last set of opaque electronic doors spit me out, then hermetically sealed behind me. I found myself in an arrival area filled with clots of identically black-haired people leaning over metal barricades, as if at a parade. Grannies, children, every age in between. TV monitors placed overhead about every six feet—the scene of me standing bewildered multiplied about eight hundred times—occupied the attention of the people on the fringes of the crowd. It appeared that some dignitary, or maybe a movie star, would be coming through. But if I could read Korean, I would have seen the signs plastered throughout: *Because of the increasingly hazardous congestion at our beloved country's national airport, please send only ONE family member to drop off or pick up the traveler.* In actuality, the government had already secretly broken ground for an additional airport on the other side of Seoul, acknowledging how obdurate and unbreakable, the Korean custom of deploying the entire extended family to greet or send off a sojourning family member.

The travelers behind me grunted their impatience and so I moved on. At the taxi stand, the snoozing driver didn't respond when I tapped on the window. I opened the back door, feeling like I was breaking into his house. But he didn't object, he readily accepted the Korean directions the school had provided. He lit a new cigarette, jerked the stick shift, and we began to make our way down a drive snaking between two giant Coca-Cola and Samsung billboards, neon looking wan and strange in the light of day.

We were bound for open fields framed by a sky that seemed to go on forever. Low flames blackened the fields of dead stubble to our left. On the right, three solitary figures inhabited the landscape: a man guiding a primitive plow being pulled through the dirt by two women straining under ropes, towels and pink plastic sun visors wrapped around their heads. Behind them, a yellow billboard rose out of the earth: HYUNDAI — FOR BETTER LIFE.

As if entering Oz, the fields gave way to tile-roofed storefronts, clusters of office-type buildings, then glass-and-steel skyscrapers. A shiny Kia car dealership, a Printemps department store. A giant pagoda-like gate commanded its own concrete island as six lanes of traffic flowed around it (Seoul once was a gated city, like Troy). Taxis and sleek black cars, billiard-ball-striped buses jostled us for space. On the sidewalks, men in suits, women in designer outfits carried fancy ruffled umbrellas to shade their faces from the sun. How could this be? My teachers always said that Korea, despite parts of it being gussied up for the Olympics, was a poor country, one where people only had small fistfuls of rice to eat, where they ate dogs and cats.

And what about Nana, goading Amanda and me into eating mushy Brussels sprouts?

"Remember the starving children in KOREA."

Or had it been, *"Remember the starving children in INDIA"*? Both? A multistory Pizza Hut whizzed by.

The driver shot through a majestic stone arch that said CHOSUN UNIVERSITY chiseled in English, somehow managing not to run down any of the students placed like obstacles in the street. We passed Gothic stone buildings, drove through what looked like a miniature forest, looped up a long driveway, then came to a stop in front of a building that looked like a Howard Johnson's: efficient, cagelike.

INTERNATIONAL STUDENTS RESIDENCE, it said, in English.

The driver dug some wax out of his ears with a pinkie, pointed at the meter with that same digit. ₩ 23,000.

Then he left me there. I made my way into the International Students Residence, my luggage wheels squeaking and echoing in what I feared was a dark and empty building.

It had seemed, on the face of it, a clever plan to arrive a few days before the Motherland Program officially started (March 1, also the beginning of the Korean school year). The brochure had said the Residence would be open as much as five days before. But I was, indeed, the lone occupant of that dank building, save for the five-foot watchman who skulked around the halls like some Asian Quasimodo. From time to time, he experimentally lobbed some Korean my way, then muttered something like *aiiieesshh* when I didn't reply.

It hadn't occurred to me that most of my program-mates *were* already here in Korea, some had even come a full month early. But unlike me, they had Korean parents who had molded their young bodies with Korean hands, so that their hearts had a space for this place. They knew how to bow correctly, the polite way to receive a gift. They also had relatives who took them in, gave them comfortable places to sleep, and filled their plates at every opportunity.

I had gone a small ways into the neighborhood beyond the school's back gate searching for food. But each time, confronted with the sprawling signs, the hard, sticklike letters, my courage failed me. The days ticked off, one by one, until the third day had passed with nothing to eat but a single bag of airline peanuts.

By then, I even found myself longing for the baggie of tollhouse cookies that Christine had forced on me at the last minute, that I had left on top of a garbage bin at Kimp'o Airport. At the time it had been a kind of adolescent exuberance—I'm an ocean away from Christine! But now, dammit,

I was hungry. I didn't want to admit that maybe Christine was right, that having never been in a foreign country before (unless you want to count fishing in Canada), I was ill-prepared to be here in Seoul. *Korea is a Third-World country. Everything over there is very different than what you're used to here.*

"*Mwoy yah?!*" the crone screamed.

I had approached her, and her wooden cart displaying some kind of golden steamed bread, on tiptoes. She was squatting next to the cart, leaning against one of its battered wheels, eyes closed. I stared at her face, fissured with wrinkles. Her hair, thinning, greasy, shrimp-gray, was pulled back into a tight bun that looked like it was made out of wire.

She opened her eyes with an almost audible snap, as if she had always known I was there. Startled, I did what I always do when I'm nervous: I made a fist and chewed on my thumb as it poked out, I've-got-your-nose fashion, between my fingers.

"*Yah!*" she screamed again, her thin eyebrows converging like birds.

My head, bulbous and light above my body. The bread seemed a brighter yellow, as if lit from within.

"I'd like to buy some," I said loudly, motioning with my fisted thumb.

"*Mussen sori yah?*" The woman leaped to her feet and began to slap the air around her as if she were fighting off a sudden swarm of gnats.

"*Ga, Ga—GA!*" she yelled, dancing.

Some passersby—students in primary-color track suits, housewives carrying plasticized shopping bags stuffed with giant leeks—stopped to titter benevolently.

"A-me-ri-ca, *nambah wang,*" said one of the track suits.

"You like-u practice Ing-leesh with Korean mans?" queried his friend. His sweatshirt said CHOSUN UNIVERSITY in English over what looked like the Cadillac crest. LUX ET VERITAS.

"*Na-GA!*" the crone screeched again, now waving a rusty cleaver.

I considered grabbing a hunk of the bread and running like hell. But no, too Dickensian. Something a street urchin, a desperate *orphan* would do.

I walked back the way I'd come, smelling the strange, smoky air, noting a heavy blue sky that looked close enough to touch. I could scarcely believe it, that this place existed, and I was here.

SARAH
Seoul
1993

"*Neh* is the word for yes," said our teacher, Choi *Sunsengnim*.

She made us go down the row, the five of us, repeating.

"*Neh.*"

"*Neh.*"

"*Neh.*"

"Again, please," she said, when she got to me.

"*Neigh*," I repeated.

"Again."

"*Neigh.*"

"Again."

"*Neigh.*"

She stopped, flustered.

I have always had an affinity for languages. When I was ten and went to the weeklong Concordia Language Village, I learned Spanish so fast, Christine went around telling everyone I was going to be a simultaneous translator for the U.N. someday.

I had planned to pick up Korean just as quickly, and then leave the Motherland Program to strike off on my own. But this wasn't some camp in the north woods of Minnesota. And Korean wasn't Spanish.

I was at the bottom of eight levels at the Chosun University Elite Academic World Language Institute. Our class was referred to as *ill-gup,* as if we were sick. At the placement test, someone handed me a sheet of paper containing only the broken-stick Korean letters, not even anything as basic and familiar as NAME _____. When the teacher saw my befuddled face, she said something to me in Korean. Then louder. When it dawned on her that I didn't understand a single word she was saying, she announced in a braying and modular English that anyone who knew absolutely no Korean should report to the *ill-gup* room on the first floor.

I found myself in a cramped room, a chilly breeze seeping through a cracked window patched half-heartedly with duct tape. The floor was unspeakably grimy, the blackboard had its corner cracked off.

Eventually, two Korean-looking guys, one squat and thick-necked, the other better looking and wearing a Princeton sweatshirt, walked in. Then, a pretty, willowy Korean-looking girl appeared. I thought I was imagining it, but the three of them began speaking to each other in Korean.

We were joined by one more student, a thirtyish, solemn-faced woman in gray nun's habit, the kind that would have made her look like a hospital orderly if not for the black headscarf. Her eyes were the almost transparent green of iceberg lettuce. I was relieved that she didn't join in the Korean conversation—that would have been too much. I ventured a greeting, *Hi, I'm Sarah,* but she didn't respond. She seemed to think there was something fascinating outside the window, opaque with grime.

"Sarah-*ssi,* you never heard the word 'yes' at home?" Choi *Sunsengnim* said.

I shook my head.

"But what about your pah-rents? They never taught you any word? Not a one? Do you know *u-yu,* the word for milk? No? You never hear them talk, at least know the sounds?"

I shook my head, again, again.

"Your pah-rents never speak in Korean?"

I would be surprised and amazed if they did.

"They're not Korean. I'm adopted."

My classmates stared.

"Excuse?" said Choi *Sunsengnim.*

"I'm adopted. A. Dop. Ted."

"Oh-moh!" Sunsengnim put her hand to her throat. *"I-byung.* I have heard of those like you, but I have never before met—" She drew in air through her teeth. "So your pah-rents, they are, are—"

I was wondering if she was searching for the word for white. Honky. Gringo. Paleface, etc.

"Cock. Asian." The Princeton sweatshirt guy filled her in, sliding me a Bryant Gumbelesque smirk.

"Ah, yes, Caucasian," the teacher said with satisfaction. "So you think of these Caucasians as to be your pah-rents?"

I shrugged.

"But your Korean pah-rents, what happened to them?"

You're supposed to be teaching us *Korean,* I wanted to say. I wanted to learn. As quickly as possible.

No one moved.

"Your Korean pah-rents, what happened to them?"

I took a big breath.

"Dead. Car crash."

"*Oh-moh-moh-moh!*" Choi *Sunsengnim*'s textbook hit the floor with a hollow crash.

For the rest of the class, she eyed me, the way one does when passing a horrible accident. You look, but want to pretend you're not looking. You don't want to have it known that you are the kind of person who can be horrified, repulsed, and fascinated all at the same time.

My new classmates—Bernie, Jeannie, Helmut, Sister Marie-Thérèse—were walking toward the main campus gate. Maybe they were going to lunch. I began to follow them.

Then Bernie Lee, Princeton sweatshirt, turned and saw me, cocker-spaniel-eager to catch up. He sneered. Microscopic crick of the lip, but a sneer. I swerved back into the school building, walking busily, arms swinging, pretending to have somewhere much, much, much (much!) more important to go.

In the dark alcove, students pushing past me, I shook with hunger—and ridiculous pride. The same pride that had kept me from asking for help in the first place just because the program handbook had said:

Although the International Students Residence has no cafeteria facilities, Seoul has an abundance of restaurants, cafés, and food preparation services, so this should not be a problem.

On the contrary, most students find that the variety of food available can be almost overwhelming.

I was expecting, what—manna dropping from the sky?

I slipped out the back of the building, where I found another small gate in the massive stone fence that encircled the entire campus. Just outside it, four lanes of traffic hurtled by. A few blocks down there was a metal-and-concrete pedestrian overpass conveniently waiting.

On the other side I found a maze of alleys, promisingly crammed with businesses. Many of the storefronts had rice-paper windows and doors, keeping their trade a mystery. I passed some clothes stores, then not one but two prosthetic shops, artificial arms and legs wrestling in dusty bins out front. Another store had its paper door pushed open to reveal rows of women bent over at sewing machines.

A few doors down, a photo studio. In the display window, a group of portraits. A couple in Western wedding clothes, a stiff-posed family. The photo in the middle of everything was of a pleasingly fat baby in what must be Korean clothes: a silk jacket with rainbow-striped sleeves, shiny orange pants that were tied at the ankle, and—I suddenly noticed—cut away at the crotch to reveal a shy, beetlelike penis.

Then, in the reflection of the window, the marvelous vision appeared: a 7-Eleven sign beckoning from across the street. Could it be? I almost knocked over two old ladies in my haste to get inside, where it looked exactly like the 7-Eleven at home, down to the Slurpee rotating on its tilted axis, cigarettes behind the counter, a cold-food section in the back, racks filled with chips. They even seemed to sell booze, judging by the rows and rows of green glass bottles, one of which said "alcohol drink" in English.

I ran to the back and lost no time grabbing a sandwich, then noticed that next to it in the refrigerated case was a flattened, shrink-wrapped squid. The shelf above it had takeout trays of what looked like wheels of rice wrapped in carbon paper. The sandwich in my hand was white bread, sure enough, but holding a slurry of pimento-red filling of unknown provenance. The bags of chips had pictures of smiling shrimps and raccoons on their wrappers—could they possible be made of raccoon?

A skinny young man with John Lennon glasses and possibly illegally tight jeans, brushed by me carrying a styrofoam bowl. He peeled the lid off and filled it with hot water from a spigot, stirring it with disposable chopsticks. A most delicious, salted smell wafted up in the steam.

It was a foodstuff I recognized. And even liked.

Ramen! I was saved—for now.

KYUNG-SOOK
Enduring Pine Village
1993

Her parents had named her Kyung-sook, Virtuous Modesty, but by now, most villagers called her "Shrimp Auntie," or, on Sundays, "Esteemed Minister's Wife."

She was, of course, no longer young, no longer known for her thick, gleaming hair or her musical talents. Now, she drew her daily pride from her reputation as an honest merchant: she haggled out of habit, but never overpriced her offerings. The quality of her shrimp was unquestionable. And she had her cadre of faithful customers, whom she rewarded with a bit extra added to their orders, every time.

One of these regular customers was a girl, Small Singing, who was newly married. This girl couldn't even read the labels that declared "Special Product!" on the tins of salted shrimp, but she did have that kind of country common sense that Kyung-sook appreciated: she didn't dither on and on about whether the salted shrimp in this pile was better than in that pile. She brought the right amount of money so that Kyung-sook wouldn't have to run out for change.

The girl, however, always left the shrimp stall with a frown, even with her extra grams of shrimp and with Kyung-sook's polite language ringing sweeter than spring birdsong in her ears; Small Singing had grown up all her life hearing only the low language, just because her father's job was cleaning shit out of concrete sewers with his short-handled brush. In her childhood season, Small Singing's neighborhood nickname had been "stinkpot," despite how she always took pains to make sure she was scrupulously clean, scrubbing even between her toes and in the part of her hair with the pumice rock. Now she was a wife taking care of an entire household, but except for Kyung-sook the Shrimp Auntie who called her Gentle Customer, the other merchants in the market still subtly disdained her, addressing her only as "You, there."

No, her displeasure had to do with the fact that Shrimp Auntie had never acknowledged first, her moonlike pregnancy, and then, her precious baby boy. When she made her visits, Shrimp Auntie might amiably complain about the weather, ask about Small Singing's family, but never a word about Small Singing's bulging belly, or, when she showed up at the shrimp stall after the birth, about her beautiful baby boy. Even the most disinterested people found it fit to congratulate her on the success of her breath-holding exercises (done so zealously, they had often caused her to faint), her hundred continuous days of prayers to the Birth Goddess and the Seven-Star God, the bestowers of male children.

"Shrimp Auntie can be so cruel," Small Singing complained to Cooking Oil Auntie, whose bottle-lined stall was across the way. "Even when I presented her with the hundred-pieces rice cake for the baby's hundred-day anniversary, she didn't say a word. How can she be so cold?"

Cooking Oil Auntie made a clicking *tsk-tsk* noise in her throat, bent to adjust the seed presser so that the drops of thick oil didn't come out so fast.

"Don't be such a silly girl," she said. "Tell me, where do you see her children, the sons who will support her in her old age and provide her with grandchildren? Are they hidden in the barrels of dried shrimp?"

"Then she is like the thirsty calf looking down the well," Small Singing huffed. "She resents what she can't have."

"Now, who is the one being cruel?" asked Cooking Oil Auntie.

"It's not my fault that I am able to bear children. I did a hundred breath-holding exercises every day for a month. Shrimp Auntie married when she was long past twenty—and to an old man who's a cripple to boot."

Cooking Oil Auntie made the *tsk*ing noise again, mumbling about how the girl's sighs and cries as she performed those vaunted exercises could be heard far beyond her family's gate (and what was a few sessions holding one's breath compared with having wild mugwort burned onto one's bare stomach, as she had done to combat her own drawn-out infertility?).

Neither woman was aware that Kyung-sook the Shrimp Auntie herself was walking right behind their backs, returning from a delivery to the Gleaming Jade restaurant. Even though each merchant had his or her own patch of dirt, carefully marked off by wooden crates of still-flopping fish, fabric towers of ladies' panties, display cases of mirrors and scissors, or buckets of dried crickets, no one owned the market's air or the words that floated within it, so Kyung-sook, ears itching, had received every bit of that conversation as freely as if she had been standing next to them.

That girl, she thought, who did she think she was?

She watched Small Singing leave the cooking oil stall, heavy with groceries and the child strapped to her back by a quilted podaeki. She probably needed to add some meat to her load, or at least stop at the fishmonger's before trotting down the dusty road back to her in-laws', where she would wash, chop, peel, scale, and cook the day's dinner, laboriously feeding wood or charcoal briquettes into the stove, the whole time the baby on her back crying for milk, the mother-in-law wailing that she was going to die of hunger before her infernal daughter-in-law would have some food ready.

Once the endless dishes of seasoned vegetables, salted fish, steamed rice, several kinds of kimchi were laid out, the house would quiet as everyone except Small Singing ate their fill. Small Singing was known to be a fine cook, so likely when it was her turn to eat, alone in the cold kitchen, only some dregs of vegetables, perhaps a fish head if she was fortunate, would be left to mix with the grains of rice still sticking to the sides of the blackened iron pot. To clean the rice pot, she would pour a kettle of hot water into it, then drink up the rice-water to fill her stomach.

Her mother-in-law, who had always secretly envisioned her son marrying someone who looked like those sleek, big-eyed women she saw in the fashion magazines and not the snaggletoothed daughter of the night-soil hauler, would often interrupt even this rude meal. Between burps and tooth-sucking, she would complain that the seasoned bellflower roots, which Small Singing had scrubbed to whiteness with salt, then shredded painstakingly with a pin, had needed more hot pepper. In slicing the fruit for the last course, perhaps a bit of pale apple-flesh had been wastefully pared away with the skin. Small Singing would have to get on her knees, lower her eyes, and say, "Forgive me, Mother. I did wrong."

Later, Small Singing's husband, a filial son, would reiterate his mother's message with his fists.

The next time Small Singing came to Kyung-sook's stall, she would have a bruise under one eye, her lip would be swollen and split like a packed pig's intestine sausage. The baby on her back would be dirty and crying. The late afternoon sun would be slanting through the spaces between the plastic roof-tarps, so Small Singing would implore Kyung-sook to hurry and give her a *kun* of shrimp paste, which she would wrap into her carrying-cloth and go on her way.

That girl thinks she's better than I am because of that pumpkin-headed baby, Kyung-Sook would think with wonder, shaking her head.

SARAH
Seoul
1993

"Sarah-*ssi*—" Choi *Sunsengnim* sighed like a deflating balloon before adding, "What will we do with you? You are falling far behind in class."

"Thank God *Sunsengnim* finally said something," muttered Bernie Lee, sotto voce. "She's holding up the whole class."

Okay, I admit I had trouble remembering the word for "car," *cha-dong-cha,* and no one else seemed to have trouble with it. But it wasn't for lack of trying. I studied all night. It was just that Korean words were so damn hard to remember.

Bernie was staring at me. He was wearing yet another orange-and-black PRINCETON sweatshirt, as if he feared we might forget where he went to college unless he reminded us, every day.

"What are you looking at?" I snapped.

"You look Korean," he said. "But you sound *exactly* like a white person *trying* to speak Korean—it's the weirdest thing." His face was handsome in its own way: long, angular, hairless as a pear. I already disliked him.

"You're a Twinkie," he concluded. "Yellow on the outside, white on the inside."

"Ber-nie," Jeannie giggled. "That's so mean."

I rolled my eyes. He didn't know the first thing about me: in a taxonomy of Hostess junk-food cakes, I went beyond Twinkie, I was a Sno-ball, the coconut treat that's white to the core.

Some time after Rev. Jansen's mini-sermon on whose daughter I was, I became the *Fabulous Sarah Thorson*, the daughter with Ken's seaglass-blue eyes, Christine's creamy complexion, pale cornsilk hair.

But are you saying that you truly believe you have blond hair and blue eyes—despite what the mirror tells you? An unbelieving shrink, from when I was ten. *Is that why you keep trying out for* The Sound of Music *every year even though you must know they would never give the part to someone who looks like you?*

How could it be otherwise? With the arrival of Amanda (who eventually landed the part of Gretl, the youngest Von Trapp daughter), our family became the living embodiment of the Scandinavian phenotype. I wanted to be included.

True, an accidental pass by a mirror, a store window, the bright-polished side of a toaster might yield a glimpse of a girl with black, straight hair, eyes the shape and color of apple seeds, a light spray of chocolate-chip colored moles across her left cheek. But those fleeting images I disowned. That girl's Asian face was recognizable yet strange, like seeing your name writ large in an unfamiliar hand.

The lovely, fragmentary Fabulous Sarah Thorson was the one who explained away the dissonance of family pictures: Who—or what—was that dark stain in the middle of this American family?

Not the Fabulous Sarah Thorson: she comes from sturdy Norwegian- and Swedish- and German-American stock. Her speech is punctuated with Norwegianisms like *uff-da!*, and her Nana, who looks just like Grandma Moses, was born in Norway. At Christmastime the Fabulous Sarah Thorson stuffs herself with Swedish potato *lefse* and *spritz* cookies, even chokes down rubbery bits of lye-pickled Norwegian *lutefisk* herring, which will make her father, Ken, happy, for he is the Son of Thor.

I claimed stomachaches on school picture day. Christine despaired at the crooked parts in my hair, green balls of snot hanging from my nose. No matter what high gloss she could buff me to in the mornings, I acquired my own patina of gleet and ooze by afternoon.

"Sarah, don't you ever look in a mirror?" she would sigh, scouring my face with a spat-on hankie as I sat in the back of the car on the way to yet another classical music concert or Ibsen play at the Guthrie Theater. Even now, when I sit in the back seat of a car, that maternal musk revisits me, that same intoxicating Joy-parfum-lipstick-wax-Mommy-breath-Johnson's-baby-powder concoction I once discovered inside the bundles she mummified in yards of toilet paper, those white pillows hiding mysterious, rusty stains.

Yet, why did the spit-hankie never touch Amanda? Amanda with her blond curls neatly barretted off her face, scuffless Mary Janes; in the summer, she ran free under the radiant sun while Christine smeared me with a zinc-oxide sunblock the color of chalk. It was only those young summers when we rented that cabin out at Sand Lake that Christine let me enjoy the unadulterated kiss of the sun. That was back when Nana was still alive, when we still lived in that tiny house in Bliss Court, and when Amanda was still part of some cosmological future Ken and Christine couldn't even (pun intended) conceive of. By the time we moved to Inwood Knoll, within the environs of the Eden's Prairie Country Club, my hue had become her obsession. Thus the summers in whiteface, designated a nonsinging minstrel, the most useless kind.

But the Fabulous Sarah Thorson, I knew, tans a honey-gold, which makes her look even blonder, her seaglass eyes paler. I depended on her to get through the day. That time I had almost lost her made me realize that.

The last day of school in fifth grade. Our teacher had covered the back wall in brown kraft paper and told us to make a mural of our ideal summer vacation.

I drew myself as a stick figure, fishing rod in hand, sitting atop a crate (THIS END UP pointing down—humor where I lacked artistic talent). I was drawing in our Sand Lake cabin, when Merlin Gustafson muscled me aside.

"You need ching-chong eyes," he declared. He reached a sweaty arm across me and rubbed a black crayon over my figure's dot-eyes until they became a pair of heavy, horizontal lines.

Then, his encore: he pulled the corners of his eyes until the lids became razor slits, pulled until they turned inside out, displaying pink, moist undersides.

The Fabulous Sarah Thorson, exploding: blue eyes, creamy white skin, golden hair. Protoplasm splattering everywhere.

The bell rang. While my classmates streamed out into the larger world, I ran into the girls' room, sitting fully clothed on the toilet, trying to shut out the voices.

> *Chinese, Japanese, dirty knees.*
> *Ching-chong Chinaman*
> *Ah-so.*

Returning to the classroom, I dug through the Crayola box until I found the color I wanted: a deep, oceanic blue. Then I redrew my eyes as larger orbs, Merlin's horizontal lines the circles' diameter; when finished, my picture had eyes bigger than everyone else's, a drugged, dilated-pupil look that satisfied me.

In Korea, however, everything has reversed. This morning, in a crowd of people hurrying to class, I happened to glance at the giant mirror posted at the entrance of the school. For a giddy, vertiginous second, I didn't know who I was looking for, or who I would find. I had somehow smoothly joined this black-haired, dark-eyed crowd.

"So, iss dat why you never told us your last name?" asked Helmut, who came from Munich. The first day, the three students of authentic Korean stock had proudly rattled off their Korean names, surnames placed first in the traditional style: Lee Jae-Kwan (Bernie), Lee Jiyoung (Jeannie), and Kim Bum-Sik (Helmut). I just said, "I'm Sarah," a habit acquired after hearing "Thorson, that's a funny name for an Oriental," ad nauseum.

"Hey Twinkie, do you even know your Korean family name?" Bernie, working my nerves. "All Koreans should know their family names and their ancestral clans."

"My clan, *I-ssi*, is the Chunju Lees," Jeannie broke in, giving Bernie a significant look. If there was an "in" clan, that, apparently, was the one. Almost a quarter of Koreans shared the name Lee, but these particular Lees could claim lineage reaching back to the beloved King Sejong, the inventor of the Korean alphabet, whose picture graced the ten-thousand-won bill. Apparently, for each family there was some kind of official document, a family register that recorded all the births and deaths and marriages starting from when the first Koreans climbed out of the Primordial Ooze.

"Mein klan is the Cheju-do Kims," added Helmut.

Bernie looked at me with a cranky, hungry expression, as if suffering from some male version of PMS.

"Why are you even here?" he said. "It's not like you're going to go home and start talking in Korean to your *pah-rents*."

"You don't own Korea," I said, scratching my nose with an upraised middle finger.

"Ooh, I'm scared of you," he said. *"Sunsengnim!"*

"Lee Jae-Kwan-*ssi?*"

He spoke quickly in Korean, the only words I recognized were my name and "bad." He was obviously tattling that I had flipped him the bird; however, in his re-creation of my crime, he raised a fist—thumb poking out between the first two fingers. Exactly the gesture I had made to the old crone that day I tried to buy some steamed bread.

Choi *Sunsengnim* looked in shock from the thumb to me and said, *"Oh moh!* Sarah-*ssi,* please! We must show respect in our classroom."

"Bernie is the one who started the whole thing—" My voice involuntarily thinned to a whine. "He—"

"Please, Sarah-*ssi.* Of all the students, you have the most to learn. As I was about to be saying, you must have extra conversation practice. A friend of my brother's wants to make his English better, so you two can do a language exchange. His name is Kim Jun-Ho, and he's a student here at Chosun University, although right now he's doing his mandatory military service."

I opened my mouth to protest. This was the beginner's class, for Christ's sake, the class for people who don't know any Korean. But even the nun, from Paris, had studied Chinese from when she had been a missionary in Hunan province. A goodly number of Korean words were based on Chinese ones, so she already had a solid vocabulary. She, for instance, didn't have any trouble remembering the word for "car": *cha-dong-cha* was "moves-by-itself-vehicle" in both Chinese and Korean.

Choi *Sunsengnim* handed me a telephone number. She would brook no objections.

"I will wait to hear from him, Jun-Ho Kim, how it was," she said.

"Let's get *pudae chigae* for lunch," Bernie said, after class. Everyone else, nun included, seemed to think that was a splendid idea. No one turned to me and said, "Sarah, what are you doing for lunch? Want to come along?"

Sarah the misfit, even in her native country. How had it come to this, I wondered, that in the space of a single generation, I had become some kind of Darwinian reject, a fish with lungs, a duck-billed platypus. I wasn't Korean-hyphen-anything, for what was Korean in me had become vestigial, useless. But at the same time, ching-chong eyes prevented me from claiming any kind of race solidarity with the nun—or with my so-called family, back in Minnesota.

All I knew was that if someone were to invite me, I would gladly eat poo day chee-gay, even if it was literally made out of poo, I would allow Bernie Lee to classify me as any preservative-and-lard-filled cake he wanted to, just so long as I wouldn't have to eat yet another meal standing awkward and abandoned at the 7-Eleven counter.

The four clattered out without me.

KYUNG-SOOK
Enduring Pine Village
1993

Enduring Pine Village was Kyung-sook's official ancestral village, but more tellingly, because she still lived there, had lived there basically all her life, it was also her ko-hyang, her hometown. The best way to know a stranger, any fool knows, is to know their hometown.

Enduring Pine Village was situated within the southern tail of the sacred Diamond mountains, almost within sight of the border with North Korea. It was a place of wildrushing beauty intertwined with a melancholy history, just like in the sentimental song:

> *I remember my old hometown,*
> *a mountain valley where the flowers bloom:*
> *peach blossoms, apricot blossoms, and baby azaleas,*
> *what a colorful place it was ...*

Back in the Chosun dynasty, a geomancer had decreed that a new village should be erected "where the mountain peaks resemble a horse's ears, and where the valley is encircled by ancestor pines."

The horse-car formation was found next to a grove of long-needle pines, the kind that bore the pale nuts revered as a delicacy and whose parasol-like shape was a staple of classical paintings. The elders noted this auspicious sign and made sure that the first structure built in this new settlement was a shrine for San-shin, the Mountain God who had so generously inspired the geomancer.

The town became known as Enduring Pine Village for its abundance of long-needle pines, blue-green pines, and the stately white-bark fir. Farmers marveled at how rice planted in the mountain soil seemed to mature overnight. Pregnant women received the ultimate blessing from the Birth Goddess: sewn bundles of bright red chili peppers hung from almost every family's gate announcing the good news—sons.

And because the village happened to be situated at almost the exact midpoint between the capital to the south and the northern provinces, naturally travelers stopped at the village to meet and trade, and soon there was a booming business for Enduring Pine Village's wine houses, which became famous for the pungent local mac'oli rice wine as well as the most beautiful, most witty kisaeng hostesses in all of Korea.

The spirits continued to offer their protections even during the terrible Japanese colonial period. No villagers lost their homes. No women—kisaeng or otherwise—were taken to the rape camps set up for the Japanese soldiers.

Even on the fateful March First, 1919, when villagers pulled out their taegukis, the forbidden national flags, and cried "Korea will live a thousand years!," the Japanese did not retaliate with bayonets and murder as they did in other parts of Korea. When the Americans dropped their light-flashing weapons in Hirossi-ma and Naga-sagi, ending the war and the occupation, thousands of Korean slaves in Japanese munitions factories cried black tears and died in misery far from home, but none from Enduring Pine Village, such was its auspicious nature.

The villagers wondered later, of course, about the turn of Fortune's wheel. Had they grown too complacent, full stomachs forgetting what it is like to be hungry? During the colonial period, everything Korean was forbidden, but villagers had gone into their homes and done their rites to the Korean gods in secret and at great risk. Now, as free men, the younger magistrates had been known to neglect San-shin's shrine, especially during the period they were preoccupied with maneuvering Enduring Pine Village to become the county seat. Further, these same upstart magistrates, seduced by promises of education and Western-style medicine, welcomed the white missionaries, who openly declared their hatred of Korean gods; before anything else, the first thing the whitemen did to "help" the villagers was to destroy San-shin's shrine.

Starting on 6.25, bombs fell from the sky. The North Korean soldiers seized Enduring Pine Village's males—young and old—for their army, killing anyone who resisted, including sobbing mothers and grandmothers.

South Korean forces recaptured the village, but then the Communists took it again. The villagers were forced to flee once, twice, three times. During the Armistice, the Red soldiers retreated north through the village. What people came back to: at the village's east end, the Shim family—father, mother, sons, daughters, the lastborn five-year-old twin sons—were found floating in macabre poses, rag dolls flung against a wall. The elder Shim, hedging his bets, had assisted both the Communists and the ROK governments—depending on which flag flew from the pole in front of town hall—so no one was sure who had tied them to a fence and shot them. More corpses unburied themselves from a hasty grave behind the high school. Starving soldiers had even broken into the mission and murdered two of the white nuns.

War changes everything. Many others never returned—killed, frozen, or starved to death. Neighbors settled feuds by turning people in as Red sympathizers, real or not. Of the ancestral yangban families, only a handful remained. Enduring Pine Village's new inhabitants were refugees from the north or carpetbaggers—scoundrels and opportunists, or those with something to hide. No one knew, for instance, where Cooking Oil Auntie's family had come from. They had appeared at the village gates almost a decade after the 6.25 War, speaking with a strange, harsh accent even though they insisted, somewhat haughtily, that they were from Seoul.

What did the future hold? The rice production had dwindled so much that during droughts, rice had to be imported from other parts of Korea. Every year, the soil grew poorer, more oily chemicals needed to be applied to the fields (and washed out into the rivers during the monsoon rains).

A few years before, Korea's president, himself from a rice-growing village, came up with an idea to preserve Enduring Pine Village, like its neighbor, River Circle Village, as a tourist site, where the increasingly urban population might come to watch rice being grown the traditional way. The government had gone so far as to spread asphalt, six lanes wide, over still-arable land, to accommodate the tour buses and cars. But then a new president came into office, and the plans were scrapped. The expanse of asphalt sat abandoned, an immovable black sea on the southern end of the village.

Nowadays, many of the farmers left their farms and instead boarded a bus on the Days of Moon that took them to the battery factory in the new Satellite Suburb Village of Ho-Chun, where they would work for the week and return home on the weekends, carrying their chemical-saturated workclothes in drawstring sacks, their fingertips burnt clean of prints by the corrosives they handled.

As a child, Kyung-sook had been regaled with tales of the majestic courts, the educated literati of the old Chosun dynasty. She knew that her great-grandfather was buried in a special site at the foot of the sacred Horse Ear Mountain. She had been shown his headstone, a pagoda-like chinsa ornament marking his scholar-official credentials, the biography of his life—his schooling, his passing the Civil Service Exam, his government rank—all displayed in the gray stone.

This place was much more than just a random rice-farming hamlet, Kyung-sook's parents told her, it was once an important trade and governmental center. But stories of the past meant little to Kyung-sook.

"I saw the Five-daughter Kim Granny coming out of the rice cake shop," Cooking Oil Auntie remarked, sticking her head into Kyung-sook's stall.

Kyung-sook, small rake in hand, continued smoothing the mountain of salted shrimp before her. The tiny, curled bodies pressed against the lip of the barrel.

"Oh, goodness, I just ran in here without even a 'good morning,' didn't I?"

"Suit yourself," Kyung-sook said.

"Well, 'Good morning, Shrimp Auntie.' There. Anyway, you're not my superior in age are you? We can skip the formalities, don't you think?"

Cooking Oil Auntie settled her wide ongdongi onto the upturned apple crate Kyung-sook used for a seat.

"Now, did you hear me? The Five-daughter Kim Granny was buying ceremonial rice cakes."

"What's so odd about that? She was just over at the fishmonger's saying it's time for the yearly chesa."

"Oh, yes, Kim Granny makes a lot of noise about the ancestor offerings, but everyone knows the cakes are an appeasement for the last-one's spirit."

"The last-one?"

"The last-one, the fifth daughter of Kim the junkman. You must remember—he didn't even bother to learn his daughters' names, he just called 'em One, Two, Three, Four, and Five."

Kyung-sook almost jumped. A familiar name, unearthed like a forgotten kimchi pot.

"You mean—Yongsu?"

"Unh, Yongsu, the one with the boy's name." Cooking Oil Auntie nodded, eying a display of baby-finger shrimp, the kind you served with beer. "None of the daughters married very well in that wretched family, but Necessary Dragon—"

"She was my friend," Kyung-sook interrupted. "In my childhood season."

"Oh moh!" Cooking Oil Auntie sat up. "You don't say! Well, Pig Intestine Sausage Auntie told me that Alder Pass shaman told the family that her spirit demanded they hold a yearly appeasement ceremony."

"That's claptrap, a shaman wanting to make quick money," Kyung-sook said. "I don't think she's dead. There's never been any word."

"Of course she's dead. She left the village unmarried, and never came back to check on her parents, even for their hwangap, when they reached that most venerable age of sixty."

Kyung-sook started smoothing the next barrel's shrimp.

"What I would guess," Cooking Oil Auntie mused, "is that she froze to death as a beggar some winter. Or maybe she met her end with those Yankee soldiers on the army base—that was the direction she was heading when she left, supposedly. If that were my daughter, I'd do an appeasement ceremony, too: people who meet a bad end always leave behind restless spirits."

Kyung-sook wondered how many years it had been since she'd last seen Yongsu. Twenty? Thirty? Her childhood friend, the one she admiringly called Older Sister, would have fifty years on her now.

"Ai-gu," Kyung-sook sighed. "The spring breezes always make me sleepy." She moved as if she wanted to sit down.

Cooking Oil Auntie took the hint. On the way out, she pretended to be swatting at a fly and palmed a few sweet curls of the baby-finger shrimp. She hummed as she walked back to her stall, the heels of her slipper-shoes raising a cloud of dust.

Kyung-sook's hands suddenly started trembling. That memory, jumping out at her like that, over a chasm of so many years. It made her wonder, what else of her life had she forgotten—or made herself forget?

SARAH
Seoul
1993

"My name is Sarah Thorson," I said to the Korean man sitting across from me, strangely relieved to be speaking English. We were at the Balzac Café. The neighborhood bordering the huge main gate of Chosun University turned out to be home to a number of these trendy coffee-and-juice bars named after dead French writers: the Rousseau, the Rimbaud, and around the corner, Proust.

"I am very happy to be making your acquaintance. Please let me introduce Jun-Ho Kim." The man rose and bowed deeply from the waist.

My first Korean bow! I tried to reciprocate, but it was an unfamiliar motion that collapsed in on itself, and I ended up executing a slightly eccentric plié.

"*You* don't need a language exchange," I said. "You already speak English fine."

Jun-Ho Kim giggled, then lit up a cigarette. He had small, childlike hands, a 50s buzzcut. His oxford shirt was buttoned all the way up the neck, the kind of thing you see only in five-year-old boys mother-dressed for school pictures. I couldn't imagine this child-man handling weapons in the army.

"Oh, I thanks you for your compliment, but I have much to learn," he said. "I want to speak like the American."

The waiter set my kiwi juice in front of me. I'd ordered it because I liked the look of the black-dot seeds suspended in brilliant green slush. In my mouth, it made my teeth feel squeaky, like when you eat raw spinach, and the tiny seeds stuck in my gums.

"We can commence in English?"

I nodded, not knowing he was going to use words such as "homolog" and "ontogenesis" for English practice. English was supposed to be *my* native language, but our exchange quickly took on a peculiar quality, like grabbing a 500-pound bull by its nose ring, as Jun-Ho led the conversation around the subjects of nuclear reactors in North Korea, his favorite American movies (anything with Meg Ryan in it), prostate cancer, dead French writers. From his knapsack he produced some ancient *Newsweek*s, their articles striated with fluorescent highlighter marks, and he asked me how to pronounce such words as "Buttafuoco" and "(Long Island) Lolita," "sphincter," and "epididymis."

"Lo-LEE-tah," I said.

"Okay, now we will commence with Korean?"

Jun-Ho asked me about my siblings. How many?

"*I am the younger sister,*" I replied. "*Her name is Amanda.*"

He paused.

"The way you say it, you are saying 'I am the younger sister.' I think you mean, '*I have a younger sister.*'"

After that, my mind went blank. I couldn't think of anything to say except "thank you," *komapsumnida,* what I habitually and automatically said to the 7-Eleven clerk after I bought my ramen.

Jun-Ho ventured more Korean, words that flew past my ears like bullets.

I toyed with my glass, empty except for a thin layer of aquarium-green slime at the bottom. I was tired. Jun-Ho was laughing.

"What's so funny?"

"I will speak some English, if that is okay to explain?"

"Fine, whatever."

"Your name in Korean, it can mean many things."

"My name?"

"Yes, in Korean, you are 'child for purchase.'"

"What?"

"You are 'child for purchase.'"

I had once heard Jeannie complain that discretion was not a Korean trait, that Koreans had no shame about demanding intimate details: How much money do you make? What's your blood type? It was apparently acceptable to admire a stranger's boy child by reaching into his pants and squeezing his penis, remarking on its heft and size. Choi *Sunsengnim* must have told Jun-Ho that I had been an "exported" child.

"'Murderous assassin child,' that is another," he said, giggles turning to guffaws.

"I'm sorry," I said. My hand clenched under the table. "I don't understand what you're talking about."

"Your *name,*" he said.

My name. Sarah. "God's treasure."

"Sal-Ah," he said. "*Sal* in the Korean vernacular means 'to-be-purchased' and *ah* means 'child.' Or *sal* in Chinese characters can mean 'assassin.' Assassin child, you understand?"

Choi *Sunsengnim* also pronounced my name as Sal-Ah instead of SAY-Rah, which I had attributed to the Korean propensity to tumble English r's and l's together. Now I wondered, was she also thinking of me as child-for-purchase?

Jun-Ho started speaking in Korean again.

"What?"

"I said, do you want to meet here at this location next week?"

Next week? I had planned to meet him only once to satisfy *Sung-sengnim*. I should have known better. It seemed like every person in Seoul was trying to learn English. Every time I opened my mouth in public, a crowd of people would materialize around me, saying "hello?" "excuse?" and shoving business cards, which I couldn't read, in my face.

"I will pay," Jun-Ho said, when the hour was up. From under his seat he pulled out a rectangular leather case with a wrist strap—a purse, in not so many words—and took out a wallet. Inside there were only some pink bills—dollar-bill equivalents. My kiwi juice had been at least six or seven dollars, American.

"I can pay for mine."

"Oh no. We are in Korea. We will do it Korean way." He waggled his eyebrows at me, so I wasn't sure he was totally innocent of the double entendre he'd just made. He returned from the cash register and, with a decorous bow, handed me a plastic-wrapped rectangle.

"A gift," he said.

A packet of toilet paper that said Balzac Cafè (accent *grave* instead of accent *aigu*).

"In your opinion, next week at the congruent time is okay-dokay?" he said, sliding his empty wallet back into his pocket.

What else do you say to someone who's just bought you a seven-dollar glass of juice and given you a present?

I said okay-dokay.

SARAH
Seoul
1993

I gulped, pretended not to listen, and strained to hear every word.

". . . and the guy, he died from eating too much RAMEN!!!" Bernie was saying.

Ramen, my daily bread, so to speak. Breakfast, lunch, dinner. When I was lazy, I crushed the noodles in my hands and ate them raw.

"This guy made instant ramen for all his meals because he was busy studying for his law exams—did you know Koreans are the world's largest consumers of ramen? No shit, I was surprised when I heard that, too—Koreans eat more ramen than all the people in China? Anyway, turns out the noodles had been fried in *industrial waste oil*. The company did it deliberately, too, to increase its profit margin. I guess they figured no one would eat only ramen for days on end."

"Oh, I saw the headline in the *Korea Herald*," Jeannie said, a hand sneaking onto Bernie's knee. "People are calling on the CEO to perform ritual suicide."

"Yeah, but it'll turn out he's some old high school chum of the President—he'll get off. There's no fucking accountability, look at that mall that collapsed in Pusan and killed all those people, not to mention the formaldehyde they put in the *soju* to give it an extra kick. I bought some at the 7-Eleven and it knocked me flat on my ass. I thought I was going to need to get my stomach pumped."

"By the way, what brand of ramen was that?" I ventured.

"*Horangi*," Bernie said with disdain. "It means 'tiger,' by the way."

Thank God. My brand was KONG BEANS, the only one that had any English on its label.

Choi *Sunsengnim* glanced at the clock, began to rise from her seat. Behind her, the classroom door suddenly opened, and a guy carrying our *ill-gup* textbook walked in.

We stared. It had been so long since I'd seen a white person—besides the nun—that the newcomer looked strange and out of place, like he'd just walked in from the moon.

"Who are you?" Choi *Sunsengnim* asked.

He stopped in front of her desk.

"Doug Henderson." His skin was an opaque white like school paste, and pocked with ice pick scars, suggesting he'd had bad acne as a teen. He was also a giant by Korean standards, over six feet, spindly like a houseplant that doesn't get enough sun. A military star winked from the collar of his frayed flannel shirt.

"Must be one of those fuckwad army guys," Bernie Lee speculated, as if the visitor wasn't standing right in front of us. "The Eighth Army pays for them to take classes here."

"I was sent down from Lee *Sunsengnim*'s class," Doug Henderson said.

"Lee *Sunsengnim,* level-three Lee *Sunsengnim?*" Choi *Sunsengnim* stared at him, the same way she had stared at me when she found out I didn't have Korean parents.

"Level-three Lee *Sunsengnim?*" she repeated.

"Sam-gup ae so nae ryunun dae yo," he said.

I could hear people's mouths dropping open with wet sounds, including my own. This guy spoke Korean. Really well. Maybe even better than Bernie Lee, who was the best in the class. I almost expected to see a Korean person emerge from behind as a ventriloquist. This was all a joke, right?

"*Oh-moh*, Mis-tah Henda-son," Choi *Sunsengnim* said in awe. "You speak like a Korean."

The guy shrugged and sat down in the only place that was open, the desk next to me. He didn't look at any of us.

At lunchtime, everyone ran off together as usual. I gathered my things, wondering what I could eat for lunch besides ramen. Take a chance on a sandwich with its frizzled red fillings? Pick the rice out of those paper-wrapped wheels? Take a risk on raccoon-flavored chips?

Doug Henderson remained, like a rock. Like he was going to sit there until it was time for class again tomorrow.

"How about some lunch?" I said, impulsively.

He looked sidewise at me, then unfolded himself from the seat. Wordlessly we walked out the back gate, across the pedestrian walkway, down the first alley to a crumbly beige structure with a corrugated metal roof. I'd passed this place daily on the way to the 7-Eleven, but because I couldn't read Korean, I had no idea the word meant restaurant.

We ducked the low doorway and entered the gloomy stucco shack. When my eyes adjusted to the darkness, the rest of our class materialized at a table in the corner. No one acknowledged us, except for the nun, who nodded in greeting as she chopsticked a clump of kimchi out of a bowl, holding the wide sleeve of her habit so it wouldn't dip into the hot, red kimchi juice.

We took a two-person table on the opposite side. The table was an odd, square shape, only a container of metal chopsticks and spoons, and a roll of toilet paper on top of it. The seats were low and plastic, like children's outdoor furniture. There seemed to be waitresses, middle-aged ladies in tight, unattractive perms, but no one had given us a menu. Doug was fixated on a peeling and stained piece of paper tacked up on the wall. It was all in Korean, the characters running up-and-down instead of side-to-side the way we'd learned them.

"What are you going to have?" I asked. In the kitchen, matrons with bulky arms that stevedores might admire were attending to rows of stone pots hissing on the blue-flamed gas range, or scooping rice out of a giant cooker. A sweaty waitress hoisted a tray of four bowls of stew, still boiling, onto her head, and plunged fearlessly among the clustered tables.

"I'm having *lar-myun*," he said.

Oh, what the hell. This would be an adventure.

"Make it a double," I said.

"*Ajuhma—lar-myun, dugae!*" He yelled at the waitress, the one unloading the tray of stews spitting steam. She glared, bowl in hand, callused thumb half in the soup, but then turned and shrieked in the direction of the kitchen,

"*Onni! Lar-myun, dugae!*"

Maybe five minutes later, she came back and set two bowls filled with —of all things—ramen in front of us.

She also unloaded tiny platters of lumpy things that collectively gave off a festering oceanic smell, like the beach at low tide.

I waited to see what Doug Henderson, the copper-haired boy, would do with these meal components. The waitress thumped another bowl in onto our table.

Kimchi: fermented spiced cabbage. Korea's national food, as I had learned from our cultural activities visit to the Folk Village. You packed the raw materials—cabbage, hot peppers, garlic, ginger, shrimp paste, salt—in these ceramic pots big enough to cook a missionary in and buried it in the ground, like seeds. But instead of sprouting, it came back pickled and spicy and pungent as old socks.

Doug speared a clump of the kimchi, smutty with burning-hot peppers, and ate. He huffed on his noodles and pulled half the bowl into his mouth, like the character in *The Five Chinese Brothers,* the brother who could slurp up the entire ocean into his mouth.

We had yet to say three words to each other. Instead of eating, I watched the dust motes writhing about our heads in the ray of sunlight suddenly let in by one of the waitresses, who had pushed open a sliding rice-paper window.

Doug picked from all the little side dishes as he ate, orchestrating the tastes together, the way Amanda and I used to play "breakfast smörgåsbord" as kids: place a forkful of scrambled egg inside mouth, insert half a stick of crispy bacon, add a blob of jam or marmalade or Mrs. Butterworth's, top with a bite of buttered burnt toast, close mouth and chew until the sweet-salty-greasy contents are all deliciously mashed together. Repeat until Christine tells you that what you're doing is disgusting.

I tried the ramen. Oily red broth, delicious and MSG-y, the way ramen is supposed to taste. From the little platters of stuff, I ventured a strand of what looked orzo pasta.

The taste, pleasant. Sprinkled with black pepper, but no pepper taste. I ate more. Sweet. Chewy. When I pulled a piece out, exactly two bits of pepper came with it. I looked closer, and almost screamed.

Eyes.

The pepper was eyes. This wasn't pasta, but some kind of worm or fish that had bifocal vision. Doug grabbed a bunch of them with his chopsticks, placed them in his mouth, ate a bite of noodles and raised his eyebrows to me as if to say, "good, huh?" He unrolled a few squares of toilet paper and wiped his lips.

When we finished—he didn't ask why I left most of my meal untouched—Doug paid and returned with two sticks of Lotte gum that warned on the label, FOR LADY ONLY!

Outside, we blinked in the bright sunlight. It wasn't quite spring yet, but one of the restaurant ladies, who Doug said are called *ajuhmas,* aunties, followed us out and set a pot of peonies by the door. The buds were still closed tight as fists. Christine kept peonies in her garden at home, and I knew that they needed ants to eat off the sticky glue before the globes could open. Korean ants must know to do the same thing. This thought cheered me.

I popped my gum into my mouth, hoping to get rid of the trace of some unpleasant metal-fish taste—from the worms?

Perfume exploded in my mouth. Without thinking, I spat.

"Shit," said Doug, returning from wiping his mouth. "What the hell kind of gum was that? I feel like I just ate a bar of soap."

I looked up from my own wad, glistening wetly in my palm, smelling chemically fragrant like room freshener.

"Ick, I assumed the FOR LADY ONLY thing was just the English gibberish they slap on everything," I said. My 7-Eleven face soap, for instance, had Meg Ryan's face beaming pixie-ishly from the wrapper over the bizarre brand name, SEXY-MILD.

Now talking, I continued to babble: "But I guess the wrapper was trying to communicate something real, like FOR HOOKER ONLY, YOUR FLOWER BREATH WILL ENTICE MEN LIKE BEES."

Doug Henderson stared at me, as if in disbelief, then turned on his heels, a military move. The next thing I saw was his back rapidly receding down toward the mini-highway. He wasn't looking back. If he did, he would have seen me standing among discarded green *soju* bottles, the pot of peonies, a broken plastic slipper, candy wrappers, and other jetsam and flotsam in the narrow alley, wondering if I'd already lost the closest thing I had to a friend in Korea.

KYUNG-SOOK
Enduring Pine Village
1993

Kyung-sook had been selling various kinds of shrimp at the market for almost twenty years. Her days had a reassuring sameness to them: up before dawn to prepare Il-sik's breakfast rice, warm and fresh, then attending to her father. Then to her market stall when the sky had lightened enough for her to see the wares she was arranging. After that, she would wait for her customers.

Under normal circumstances, Kyung-sook liked the late-morning at the market the best. At that time, the housewives would be out in force, strolling past the piles of winter melons, platters of glistening headcheese, bundles of wild leeks, and comic jumble of plumbing joints and implements. Sometimes, more for fun than for a need to attract customers, Kyung-sook would stand outside her stall and join the other merchants in trying to entice the passersby.

"Salted shrimp—best quality!" she might yell.

Today, however, she was distracted, could barely measure out the right amounts of dried shrimp, shrimp paste, give back the proper small-money. Her thoughts would not stay in the present, but instead kept circling back through the years, over and over, the way a tongue goes back again and again to prod a painful tooth—to see that it still hurts.

Images passed through her head: The Month of Steady Rains. Herself, as a twelve-year-old girl. Hauling tools and bundles of seedlings to the fields at first light. The knotted red string stretched across the rows. Spending hours, days lined up with the other workers, bent over sickle-shaped, transplanting endless rice sproutlets into the mud. The stories told, songs sung to make the work go faster. The leeches were the worst thing. People with relatives in Seoul begged them to send their old nylon stockings so the planters could wade in the mud protected from these vicious biting creatures. But Kyung-sook, like Yongsu, had no rich relatives. Once, Kyung-sook had seen a huge leech swim up to her and then disappear into her heel. Yongsu, her own legs covered with black lumps, pulled Kyung-sook to dry ground, put her foot in her lap, then dug deep with her fingernails, bringing bubbles of blood to the surface of Kyung-sook's skin, until she extracted the leech—like pulling a swath of shiny black fabric through a woman's ring—from an impossibly small hole in Kyung-sook's foot. Then, while Kyung-sook lay back in a faint, she threw the bloated creature on the ground and stamped on it.

The tiny rivulets of memories eddied together and began to flow as a river of time, gathering strength from its banks. The top reflected the clear, pure emerald green of a field of rice plants growing toward the sun. Underneath was contained the sand, the silt, the riverweeds, the occasional flashes of brightness from tumbling stones.

A line of women dancing and singing under a harvest moon. A bitter winter when all the oxen died. Gathering the rubbery stamens of the

Chinese-lantern flowers to make gum to snap between the teeth. The clack-clack of the taffy-maker's shears, children running into the dusty lane.

A flute at the bottom of a rice chest. A death. A disappearance. A lost child.

"Hello, Shrimp Auntie?" Small Singing stood just outside the square tins that marked the entrance to Kyung-sook's stall.

"Good morning, Gentle Customer," Kyung-sook said, shaking her head to dispel its ghosts. "Please come in."

"Actually, I'm looking for Cooking Oil Auntie—she wasn't at her stall."

"Well, she was here earlier, but not now. Wait, there—" Kyung-sook could see Cooking Oil Auntie's gourd-shaped form moving amongst the stacks of blue-green bottles.

"Oh, good. Madam Mother-in-Law is having special guests this afternoon, so she sent me for some dark sesame oil." In her right hand, Small Singing held a yellow rope of gulbi fish, eyes still bright and shiny as if they were still swimming in the ocean. With the left, she hoisted her other package, her infant, further on her back. He made bubbling noises and smiled an insipid pangool smile at Kyung-sook.

"Well, Cooking Oil Auntie makes the real thing. There's nothing like it, especially compared to that cheap perilla oil they try to pass off as sesame oil these days. The oil extracted from sesame leaves doesn't taste half as rich as the oil squeezed from roasted, high quality seeds, don't you think?"

Small Singing huffed a bit.

"Yes, that's true," she said. "Sorry to have disturbed your lunch. Goodbye."

Kyung-sook poked at the Chinese black noodles she had ordered for an early lunch. Usually she ate Korean hotpot or seaweed rice, but today she wanted jia-jia myun. She thought with a small laugh how she used to think Chinese food came from heaven. Now it was cheap stuff even the market-lady could order for lunch. How things had changed.

She put her chopsticks down, knowing she wasn't going to eat just yet. The current of memory carried her along, further, further. This time, she didn't resist.

SARAH
Seoul
1993

The watchman downstairs grunted and motioned me over. The respectful term to address a man his age would be *ajuhshi,* the male counterpart to *ajuhma.* He was known among Motherland Programmers as the Stamp *ajuhshi* because of his eccentric love of philately—he could spend hours gazing at our mail with its foreign stamps.

He handed me a DHL package, which I brought into my room. The return address was Lund, Markey & Bjornstrom, Ken's firm. The looped script on the label was Christine's. CONTENTS: *Care Package.* Inside, a novelty photo frame (the four of us as a *Time* magazine "Family of the Year"), gummy candies in the shape of Minnesota, fancy French lace cookies fractured in transit, a tiny plum-colored Lancôme lipstick, free with a fifty-dollar purchase. The letter inside was dated the day before I left.

That was so Christine, always planning ahead.

You have to have a plan, she had told me, when I dropped The Bomb. *You can't just go there with no plan.*

"There" was Korea. And operating with no plan was precisely the point.

My not-quite year of college had brought no answers other than that I definitely didn't want to become an occupational therapist. Fittingly, it was en route to the registrar's office to submit my withdrawal that I passed the International Studies department's bulletin board.

JUNIOR YEAR IN GENEVA. POLISH AT THE UNIVERSITY OF CRACOW. EL CENTRO BILINGUE IN BEAUTIFUL SAN MIGUEL DE ALLENDE. Further down, the magic board was shingled with even more opportunities:

LEARN GERMAN, SPANISH, NORWEGIAN, FINNISH, SWEDISH WITHOUT LEAVING MINNESOTA AT THE CONCORDIA LANGUAGE VILLAGE. YEAR ABROAD IN BRITAIN. NYU IN PARIS. SEMESTER AT SEA.

I dumped an assortment of the brochures—France, Mexico, and Poland—into my bag. Then I saw STUDY AND TOUR KOREA WITH THE MOTHERLAND PROGRAM. The brochure was fronted with a picture of a man in a smiling wooden mask that looked like the comedy half of comedy and tragedy. He was clad in flowing white pajamas and doing a dance against a backdrop of mountains. The mountains had caught my eye. Gray, granitic mountains, like the Rockies. I didn't get it. Rice paddies, temples, people wearing white pajamas and masks, all right. But where did the mountains come from?

I dumped it in my bag, along with SEMESTER AT SEA.

The Registrar accepted my resignation with equanimity. She even gave me a friendly and bored wave as I left, as if to reassure me that what I was doing was perfectly within the natural order of things. Christine would be a different story. She wouldn't be happy for the distinction among her friends as the mother of Eden's Prairie High School Class of '91's first college dropout.

In the parking lot of the U, I reached into my purse, fished among the brochures without looking.

What say ye gods? Pull.

Korea.

At my dorm, I grabbed my taciturn roommate's Magic 8-Ball.

The Future Looks Promising.

Korea instead of sunny Mexico or the Semester at Sea? I could hear the rolling of the cosmic dice.

All Signs Point to Yes.

When I arrived home, my Ford Escort squeezed to bursting with my things, Christine's eyes bugged out of her head.

Ken, at least, remembered to give me a welcoming hug. He turned to Christine and I heard him whisper, "Let's sit down and hear what she has to say."

At the kitchen table, the two of them sat on one side, facing me.

"I just couldn't take it anymore," I said. "My supervisor, Peggy, said that in the OT program, people either burn out the first year or they go on. I burned out. I couldn't take it, all those people and their injuries."

Christine didn't say anything. Ken's mustache twitched. I know that they both still harbored the ridiculous fantasy that I'd become a doctor just because some teacher once told them I had an aptitude for chemistry. With my grades, the biggest favor I could do mankind would be to do something else, anything else. I didn't tell them that for the first day of my OT practicum, when faced with a man whose skin had been burned to a shell of beef jerky, I had run away, knowing that I would vomit on his hospital-issued slippy-grip socks if I stayed.

"So what do you plan to do?" Ken asked quietly.

"Well, I—"

Amanda came into the kitchen, a good ten minutes after she'd been summoned. She displaced Christine's twin Persian cats off a chair, sat, and buried her face in her arms to signify her undying support and interest in my life.

"So, Sarah, what do you plan to do?" Ken repeated.

Amanda glanced my way, rankled that she was being forced to attend yet another family meeting about me, the prodigal daughter who'd irreparably ruined basically all potential avenues of rebellion for her—anything she did would inevitably be psychologized as merely copycatting. From the living room, Hubert, Christine's macaw, screamed.

"I'd like to take my graduation trip, go abroad and learn a foreign language at this language institute."

Christine and Ken looked bewildered for a second; they were obviously expecting I was going to announce I was joining the Branch Davidians, or something.

"So you'd be, in a sense, still going to school?"

"Oh, yes," I said truthfully. "The Institute gladly provides college credits." Amanda pretended to snore.

"And," I embellished, "the registrar at the U said I can always resume right where I left off, no penalties." I had no idea if this was true.

"A year abroad," Ken mused, stroking his mustache. "Now, that's the kind of mature thinking we were hoping we could get out of you. I always wished I'd taken some time to go off backpacking in Europe or something, myself, instead of rushing life so much."

He passed Christine one of his fuzzy-lipped see-sweetheart? smiles. She reciprocated with an icy glare. I was aware that she often blamed their bout with infertility on Ken's hemming and hawing over having children while her twenties spooled away. Her thirties brought years of painful fertility treatments and bloody miscarriages before she gave up and decided to adopt. Then she got pregnant just months after I arrived.

"So, Sarry, where are you hankering on going?" Ken asked. They both leaned forward, straining to hear, as if they were only going to be told once. Amanda rolled her eyes.

"Korea," I said.

No one moved. The air crackled. We'd suddenly been turned into a glassed-in diorama at the Natural History Museum.

AMERICAN (?) FAMILY, circa 1990.

Ken and Christine, frozen. The air was so iced over I could almost see the hairline fractures. Amanda was the one who moved, her head rising off the notches of her arms to regard me with shock and disgust, and behind it, a kind of unhinged admiration. Christine made a vaguely keening noise before she grabbed the treasonous brochure out of my hands. In the background, there was another sound, even higher. It was the screaming sound of cloth being rent, of the shoddily woven fabric of our family coming apart more easily than anyone ever imagined.

SARAH
Seoul
1993

I was surprised to find Doug Henderson waiting for me, just outside the classroom door. We walked to the restaurant in silence, a pattern we would repeat many times.

We sat at the same battered plastic table, ordered something called *kalguksoo,* safe, white noodles.

In class today, Doug had known the word *t'angol son-nim,* "regular customer," a word that Bernie Lee hadn't even known. This had sent Bernie spinning into a terrible mood.

"So how'd you learn Korean so well?" I asked, emboldened.

"My mother," he replied, just as it hit me. "She's Korean."

His hangdog eyes were the color of weak coffee, an acceptable Korean shade, but they were round as marbles, so the Korean in them was lost. His cheekbones—two swelling cliffs near his eyes—seemed somewhat Asian, but they were negated by an aggressive, pointed nose. His skin, the pale alabaster that I knew Koreans consider "good," the way blacks determine "good" hair, was all thrown off by his copper hair. Clearly, the American Doug had been formed first, and the Korean genes had had to scramble to fill in wherever they could at the end.

But now that I knew this about him, I was a little spooked.

"So you grew up in Korea?" I asked him.

"Till third grade. I grew up in a camptown near a U.S. army base."

I noted that star, which he was wearing again today on the neck of his T-shirt.

"So you came to the States after your dad's tour in Korea ended?"

"It was a little more complicated than that, but yeah. How about you? You were born here?"

I nodded without elaborating.

The waitress, bumping up the narrow aisle, knocked over our container of metal chopsticks and spoons, spilling them onto the concrete floor in a chorus of chimes. She paused to pick each one off the filthy floor and put it back into the container.

With a sigh of *"Ai-gu,"* she plunked the container back on our table, midway between Doug and me, in its former place. She walked away. Earlier, I had caught a glimpse of a waitress busily dumping diners' remains of the ubiquitous little side-dishes—kimchi, little dried minnows, seaweed dredged in salt—back into a communal pot that then went into the refrigerator for reuse. I had decided that what I'd been seeing was a mirage, a misreading of the situation that was a product of my paranoid Western imagination that immediately assumed that everything in the Orient was dirty.

"You're not hungry?"

"Um, my stomach's a little upset all of a sudden."

He laughed. "How can your stomach be upset? Korean food is the only thing that will settle my stomach."

"Uh huh."

Before we left, Doug returned with more Lotte gum. These came with a suspicious picture of a flower on the label, but they had a sweet coffee flavor that lasted about three chews before the whole thing became a tasteless wad. Outside, the peony globes were covered with ants, like moving black sprinkles on spumoni ice cream cones.

"Would you like to take a walk?" he said, when we were back on campus.

"Um, sure." I was realizing I hadn't done much exploring beyond the Language Institute, the 7-Eleven, and the Balzac coffeehouse. I kept forgetting that our school was just one tiny building occupying a corner of a huge university filled with Korean students.

Some of the Chosun Daehakyo students were passing us now. The girls walking arm-in-arm in tight jeans and platform shoes, the guys in sweater vests, hair greased back à la Ken's high school pictures, some also arm-in-arm.

We veered to a path that led behind a dingy building, test tubes crusted with frosty white precipitates airing out in the open windows. The dirt path ascended directly up a mountain—a random peak erupting in the middle of campus. In a few minutes of upward hiking, I could smell pine. I could also see smog padding the city below.

"Where are we going?"

"Yak-Su," Doug said.

A noise, like the cackling of chickens. From behind us, a dozen octogenarian Korean men and women gained on us. They were clad in some serious Sound of Music hiking gear—Tyrolean hats, wool pants held up with suspenders, knee socks with alpine patterns, hiking boots, gnarled-wood walking sticks. They were all carrying empty plastic jugs.

"They're going to Yak-Su, too," Doug said, as the group, amazingly, pistoned past us up the steepening slope, their happy chatter unabated. Soon, they disappeared beyond a bend in the trail.

Doug stopped where the trail continued up to the summit and another trail broke off to the left. He pointed to the sign.

Two simple syllables, no diphthongs, even. Yak and Su. 약 and 수.

"Oh, Yak-Su," I said. "We're here."

He nodded, then started down the left-hand trail, which ended abruptly at a lone metal pipe emerging from a rock. It was dribbling water into a rusty drain; a middle-aged Korean woman squatted like a frog next to it, alternately filling up a pink plastic dipper and drinking from it. By her feet sat a plastic jug, filled to the brim with water.

"The Stamp *ajuhshi* told me this is some of the best *yak-su* in the city."

"Oh, um, really?" I said, suddenly realizing that *yak-su* was a thing, not a place.

"You've never had *yak-su*?" I shook my head. From his voice, I felt as if I should have, or at the very least, should know what it was. I just stared ahead blankly.

"You know, 'medicine water,' the spring water that flows off the mountain."

"Oh, yeah."

The woman placed the huge water-filled jug on her head and began to amble down the slope, even singing as she went. Doug bent down by the dribbly stream, his body folding quite naturally into the lady's same squat. He picked up the pink dipper, which she'd left on top of a rock.

"You're not going to drink from that, are you?"

He looked at me, then laughed. "Of course I am. We're all Korean. We can share germs."

"But—"

"At home, don't you all eat from the same bowl? You see at the restaurant how the *ajuhmas* put our leftover kimchi and stuff from the tables back into the pot, right?"

I wish he hadn't told me that.

He took a draught and then handed me the dipper.

"I think I'll pass—I'm not that thirsty," I said, my tongue folding like cardboard in my mouth.

He shrugged. "Use your hands if you don't want to use the cup. I mean, we came all this way. And hurry, the hiking club will be coming back—they'll be here all day filling up their jugs."

As if on cue, a yell of *"yaw-HO!"* drifted from down the summit. Where did those old people get their energy? Maybe there really was medicine in the water . . .

I stuck my index finger in the stream, which was freezing. The water looked clear, but I knew that didn't mean anything. At the Motherland Program orientation, they had warned us about the water. More than half the country's people lived in Seoul, we were told, so the overtaxed, outdated water system was teeming with bacteria. They told us to buy the two-liter jugs of purified water and keep them in our rooms, even for brushing our teeth.

Don't drink water in restaurants unless you know for sure it's been boiled. Don't drink anything with ice in it, don't eat ice cream from a street vendor, no raw fruits or vegetables that aren't peeled, don't eat at a neng myun *restaurant unless you know for sure it's clean.*

"In July, watch out for *chang-ma,* too," Bernie Lee had added. "When it comes, don't open your mouth or let it fall on your head or you'll go bald."

Everyone had laughed in recognition and appreciation, except for me, who didn't know what *chang-ma* was. I worried that it was some kind of malignant animal that fell from the sky—a rain of Wizard-of-Oz monkeys that pulled out your hair. Only later would I find out that it was the monsoon rains that came in the summer. The black exhaust from the belching buses, the industrial smokestacks, all this stuff that gave Seoul its odd, sulfurous light was sent back to earth in this impure rain.

Who knew where this *yak-su* water was coming from, how much acid rain it had absorbed? Upstream, there could be any number of animals adding fecal matter and *E. coli* bacteria. And what about the microbial dangers, parasites? Amoebic dysentery? Even the thought of allowing benign but wiggling organisms—hydras, paramecia—into my digestive system made me feel woozy.

The voices drew closer.

"Man-sei!"

"Yaw-HO!"

I cupped my palms and drank. The cold water thundered down to my stomach, my fillings jackhammered into my jaw. I opened my mouth to gasp, and an *aaahhhh* sound—the same one Ken makes when he drinks a cold beer in August—emerged. I plunged in again, drinking until I thought my stomach would burst. The taste was pure, primordial, as if I was resting my tongue on a cool, clean slab of granite.

Further up the mountain, we sat at a bench, a split log.

A gazebo-like wood structure was perched on a cliff a few hundred feet above us. I saw no paths leading up to it. Painted in muted greens and browns, it looked like a part of the mountain itself. I wanted to ask Doug

Henderson if he knew what it was, but then decided I wanted to preserve my cover as a "normal" Korean for a little longer.

A warm breeze blew across us.

"So if you were born here, what's the deal with your Korean?" he said.

"What do you mean, 'what's the deal'?"

"You sound like you're completely unfamiliar with it."

I thought I had been getting better. The last time Jun-Ho and I had met, he had complimented me on my pronunciation. I had had a wild thought of henceforth telling people my name was Sarah Kim and trying to "pass." But reality was intruding.

"I'm adopted," I snarled. "It wasn't *my* decision to grow up in a white family in the fucking Midwest."

Doug fumbled in his little rucksack, so I couldn't see the reaction on his face—shock, pity, recognition? He handed me a *mok kehndi. Mok kehndi,* "voice candy," were basically just cough drops, but I loved their sticky, weedy taste. Doug ate them constantly, he said, because the pollution made his throat scratchy. They were only a chunwon, a dollar plus change, for a whole green tin decorated with pictures of Korean medicinal herbs. I took the candy as an apology.

A shrill cawing from above us made me jump. I expected something big and black, Poe-ish, but a dove-sized bird, blue and white colors clean as a school mascot's, landed at our feet.

"Do you know what that is?" Doug asked.

"A bird."

"It's a *kach'i.* They're a sign of imminent good fortune."

"How do you know all this?"

"I suppose my mother must have told me."

"It's funny." The last vestiges of my anger melted away with the *mok kehndi.* "I never cared about Korea before. When I was in high school, they had these summer camps for adoptees to learn about Korean culture, but I never considered going. I mean, what did Korea have to do with *me* and my life? But now I kind of wish I'd gone, learned at least a little about Korea."

"It's not too late to learn," he said. "That's why you came on the Motherland Program, right?"

"I'm not sure why I came. Semester at Sea was a close second."

"Well, here, I can teach you a song about the *kach'i*. No, wait, that's just for the Lunar New Year. How about *'San Toki'*?"

"What's that?"

"The little mountain rabbit song. Every single Korean kid knows it."

> *San to-ki, To-ki ya,*
> *O-di ro ka nyu nya?*
> *Kkang chung kkang chung kkang kkang chung*
> *ko geh ro . . .*

The third time, he asked me to join in. I tried, then stopped.

"What's up, don't you like the song?"

"I don't know what I'm singing."

"*San* is mountain and *toki* is rabbit."

"*To-ki,*" I repeated.

"*O-di ro ka nyu nya* is 'where are you going.' "

I repeated.

"Yeah. And *kkang-chung, kkang-chung* is the sound of the rabbit hopping."

"*Gang-chung.*"

"*Kkang-chung,*" he said. "Put a little more emphasis on the first 'kk' sound."

"*Ggang-chung,*" I gagged.

"Better."

He started again. Into my head came a picture of a rabbit hopping.

We sang together, softly at first, but then louder, finally with gusto, as if "Little Mountain Rabbit" were a sea chantey. The Sound of Music hikers stopped on their way to the *yak-su* to observe us, puzzled by two adults braying out a children's song. One of the old men, however, clapped approvingly when we finished.

O-di ro ka nyu nya?

I sat back on the rough-hewn bench, savored the breeze. So this was springtime in Korea, a place that was both polluted and beautiful, with the smells of industrial pollution mixing with that of a living earth warming, of flowers and fertile insects. I looked past the smog to the overhead sky: intense, Windex-blue, once again almost close and solid enough to touch. The sight of it set off an intense feeling of longing—but for what, I didn't know.

I glanced over at Doug Henderson, planning to make conversation to fill up the empty spaces. His face was also tipped up toward the wispy clouds. He was singing, silently, to himself and suddenly I knew he was no longer here, but somewhere far, far away. Had he, too, come to Korea to search for something? Was he like me and perhaps didn't even know what that something was and was hoping that in time, it would make itself clear?

KYUNG-SOOK
Enduring Pine Village
1993

The river of memory flowed on. Its sights and sounds became particularly vivid to Kyung-sook in the quiet of the late afternoon, when a kind of calm settled over the market. By then, the most serious customers had come and gone, so the merchants, stomachs heavy from their lunch of cold noodles or dried-cabbage-leaf stew, stretched out for a nap. Cooking Oil Auntie snored from a bench in front of her black-and-white TV. The medicine seller ducked behind a row of bottles in which obscenely forked ginseng roots floated in amber liquid. Others lay on stacks of burlap packing bags or nested in a pile of coats they were selling. Even the market's chickens and cats scrounging in the garbage seemed to stop for a nap.

Except for Kyung-sook.

Even as a child, you hardly ever slept, her mother had told her once. When we brought you to the fields, you sang with the birds, all day. That's why your milk-name was Chatterbox, my daughter.

She should have been a son.

There had been a son, born a year before the 6.25 War. Her parents had named him Jae-song, Having All the Brilliant Stars in the Sky. So overjoyed by his birth, they didn't even give him a milk-name, like Dog Shit, which would have hidden from the gods how very precious he was to them.

When the family had fled south, away from the onrushing North Korean soldiers, they, with a group of refugees from another mountain village, had had to ford the Glass River at night. It was rumored that the area was infiltrated with enemy soldiers.

Someone had procured a makeshift raft, and a dozen people clambered onto the listing platform, two men in the back carefully poling it through the water.

Halfway across, Having All the Brilliant Stars in the Sky began to cry.

Kyung-sook's mother attempted to give him her breast, but as she fumbled at the tie of her top-blouse, hands snatched the child away from her.

You want to get us all killed?

Keep the baby quiet!

Kyung-sook's mother had wanted to scream *Where is my baby?*, but there was no sound in the moonless night except for the *slup-slup* of the river against the banks.

A flash of light on the other side, a sharp report.

Soldiers were indeed there.

Someone shoved the child back into the mother's arms when the raft hit the opposite bank, the people scattering into the night amid gunshots.

Kyung-sook's parents hid among the trees as shadows of soldiers came within meters of them. Kyung-sook's mother kept her hand tightly over the child's mouth.

We can't all die this way, like dogs, she vowed.

Only later, under the safety and light of a refugee camp, did she see that Having All the Brilliant Stars in the Sky had been smothered. By her hand, or by another's on the raft, she would never know.

"Madame Shrimp Auntie, my mother has sent me to pick up half a kun of shrimp paste!"

A little girl in pigtails stiff as calligraphy brushes stood at the entrance of the stall.

"Come on in, Child," Kyung-sook said, getting up from her crate. She shook out the folds in her apron. "My aren't you chak-hac, a good girl, helping your mother with the errands?"

The girl bowed modestly, and Kyung-sook took advantage of her averted eyes. The girl's hair was dark as night, making the white sliver of a part look all the more tender and sweet. Her hands were grubby, but well formed, each fingernail an exact miniature of an adult's.

Kyung-sook measured out the shrimp paste, making sure to add in a little extra, and gave it to the little girl. Then she glanced at her unfinished lunch.

"Here, why don't you take this?" she said, palming her red-bean bun. She expected the girl to take an impulsive bite out of the sweet, as children were wont to do, but this girl received it respectfully with two hands, then placed it in her pojagi, which already had a bundle of Chinese chives sticking out of it. From a hidden pocket, the girl took out some crumpled bills and smoothed them before handing them to Kyung-sook.

"You're not hungry?" Kyung-sook asked, disappointed. The girl's clothes, she noticed, were slightly worn, but bleached clean and ironed. The bits of colored yarn tied to the ends of her braids attested to someone's love and care.

"I want to share it with my mother and my little brother," she said. "They like bread."

Kyung-sook smiled and bent down to the girl's eye-level.

"You're a good girl who'll have lots of good fortune, I can tell," she said. "I could have become a face reader if I didn't become a shrimp seller, you know—my readings are quite accurate."

The girl lifted her head, and her eyes met with Kyung-sook's for the barest second. A tiny, pleased smile played at the corners of her mouth before she again bowed modestly.

White-hot lightning shot through Kyung-sook's body, igniting her to the roots of her hair, making her jerk upright. She caught her breath. She fought to control her expression.

"I must go now," said the girl.

"Hm, oh yes, go along, Dear," Kyung-sook said, barely daring to breathe.

What was this feeling?

The girl bowed and said, "Goodbye, Shrimp Auntie," and Kyung-sook replied, as she did to all her customers, "Come again, would you?"

But behind her smile, her face still felt tight and hot. For the briefest moment, she found herself thinking what she would never let herself think before:

That girl could have been mine.

SARAH
Seoul
1993

"So how's your *yuhja chingu*?" Jeannie said to Bernie. Sneeringly.

The new daytime drama, *The Ill-Gup Class.*

It seemed just yesterday that the studio audience had been left with the image of the two of them, bottle of *soju* in hand, going off into the neon sunset, to one of the "love hotels" near campus.

"She's more than a *chingu*," Bernie replied, with a sneer of his own. "She's my *ae in,* my love thang."

"Yeah, right," Jeannie muttered. "She's obviously just trying to get a free ticket to the States, just like those skanky *yang kongju* who hook up with the GIs."

"Hey, watch it. Don't you know that the majority of the Koreans in the States can trace their way back to some Korean whore who hooked up with a GI, Miss High and Mighty?"

"So how fitting for you!" she spat back.

"*My* dad came over through the special provisions made for professionals, since he was a surgeon. You told me your dad has a *chang-sa*—a grocery, wasn't it?"

"That doesn't mean shit," Jeannie said. "He has an advanced degree in chemistry."

"But if he's stuck running a grocery, that sounds like a green card problem to me." Bernie began humming that horrible Phil Collins song, "It's No Fun Being an Illegal Alien." Jeannie turned livid.

"Hey, soldier-boy." Bernie, bored with Jeannie for the time being, looked toward Doug. Doug didn't move.

Bernie said something to him in his quick, fluid Korean.

Doug replied in equally rapid Korean.

Now Bernie looked frustrated.

Thankfully, just then, Choi *Sunsengnim* burst in, overloaded with books.

She wearily dropped her load on the desk, mumbled something about the traffic, and started to take attendance.

We were all here, for a change.

At lunch at the dingy restaurant (ironically named *Mujigae,* "rainbow"), we saw the rest of our class again. Bernie gave Doug the finger, American-style.

"Don't pay any attention to Bernie," I told Doug. "Did you hear him tell Helmut his haircut made him look like a Hitler Youth?"

"Oh, I can handle guys like him," Doug said. "I met a dozen Bernies in college. That was the first place I tried to 'come out' as a Korean, at the Korean club."

"Your college had a Korean *club*?"

"Yeah, but they wouldn't let me in it. The guy who ran it was this asshole, Pil-baek Bang. This guy drove a Mercedes, wore a suit and tie to class. First meeting, he says to me, 'Why are you here?' I said, 'Because I'm Korean.' And you know what he said to me?"

I shook my head.

"He said the club wasn't for the half-breed sons of Western princesses."

"Western princess?"

"Yeah. *Yang kongju,* a Korean woman who's hooked up with an American GI. It's a synonym for prostitute."

"Um," I said.

"In a way he hit the nail right on the head. My mother was a bargirl at a bar that serviced American GIs, and I am half white."

"So . . . Um."

"But unlike some bargirls, after *Umma* met Hank, my dad, she had sex with him exclusively—and they did marry."

I blinked. So casual, as if he were discussing something suitably public—a stock trade, maybe—not a trade in his mother's body.

"What led her to that, um, life?" I ventured.

You probably would have become a prostitute if you'd stayed in Korea.

He shrugged. "She was a peasant. She was really smart, but being the fifth daughter of the village junkman who called his kids One, Two, Three, Four, and Five and who liked his rice wine a little too much, being sent to school wasn't an option. Working the bar scene was."

"Oh."

"So how old were you when you were adopted?"

"Eighteen months, I think."

"Were you born in Seoul?"

"I guess. That's where my parents lived."

"What happened to your Korean parents—do you remember them at all?"

"They died in a car accident. I don't have any memories of Korea at all."

"Tell me about being an adopted Korean, then. What's that like?"

My metal chopsticks scraped against the stainless steel bowl, my rice a half-eaten, ruined sphere. Why had no one ever bothered to ask me that, until this guy Doug, two steps away from being a complete stranger? Why was my being in the Thorson family presumed, assumed normal, and anything else was not?

"What's there to tell?" I chewed and chewed until the rice disintegrated to liquid, my jaws clenching.

Sundays were our "family day." We went to church together, we hunkered down at home for a big midday meal, before which we said long graces about how grateful we were. Grateful that Ken made tons of money so we could have our nouveaux-Victorian palace in this place that had no sidewalks. Grateful that Christine could buy all this food at Lund's. Grateful. Full of grate. I hated that word.

Don't talk to your mother like that! Don't you know that when you first came, she stayed up all night, night after night, trying to feed you? You might have died, otherwise.

I was aware I refused to eat when I first came to America. But was that my fault? I was eighteen months old.

You don't know what it is you have, don't you know what your life would have been over there? You should be grateful.

Sundays. In Korea, that's the day families emerged from their homes. Saturday, still a workday, but Sundays, mother and fathers, sometimes grandmothers and grandfathers, accompanied children to parks, to Lotte World's skating rink and Bavarian Village, to museums. Sometimes they even outfitted themselves in identical clothes, say red-and-blue polo shirts, like some traveling athletic team. My greedy eyes would devour them.

The Motherland Programmers would also regroup. One girl always greeted a sun-browned uncle who drove a "Power Bongo" pickup truck filled with turnips or potatoes. Bernie Lee met a white-gloved chauffeur, one who had been known to wait for him for hours, wiping nonexistent specks of dust off the sleek black car with a feather brush. Sometimes even mothers and fathers visiting from the States arrived.

In the evening, everyone returned, logy from huge meals, toting shopping bags stuffed with persimmons, fried honey cookies, rice cakes, and boxes of canned fruit drinks with names like SacSac. As they said goodbye to family, ballasted by edible tokens of care and affection, I watched them, chin on my fists, elbows sore from being pressed into the windowsill for hours.

I realized then that I had been misguided in my envy of the people in Eden's Prairie, thinking it was merely their whiteness I wanted. No, it was their knowing their place in the world, a complacency the Motherland Program students shared. In Korea, Bernie Lee became Lee Jae-Kwan. Then he could return to America and Princeton and being Bernie, for he had parents whose faces mapped where he had come from, his life made perfect sense. So, too, the lives of Jeannie from Illinois, Helmut, the Gallic nun. They all carried with them the solid stones of their past in one hand, and bright, shiny futures in the other. For me, everything was vapor. I had to take it on faith that my past even existed.

"What about your Korean family?" Doug said. "You must have had relatives, an extended family, siblings maybe."

"I don't know."

"Your adoptive parents never told you anything?"

"I don't think they know much more than that, either."

"Well, now that you're in Korea, don't you want to find out?"

You're afraid to face your feelings of being different, said the social worker (the self-righteous one, for whom I decided that "MSW" stood for Minority Savior Woman). *And then you lash out at those around you, making quite a mess for everybody.*

Sparing Christine and Ken's feelings had never been foremost on my mind. I called them "Ken" and "Christine" (over their howls of protest) to show them I didn't fully consider them to be my "real" parents. But I couldn't fathom taking that next step, to consider being part of a *Korean* family.

And really, I needed to be pragmatic: knowing the past wasn't going to change the present. Some undiscovered nugget wasn't going to suddenly make me wake up white, or in a different house, in a different country. I would still be Sarah Ruth Thorson, American citizen, of 27 Inwood Knoll, U of M dropout.

"You were born here," Doug said. "In Korea. Your story begins here, not in America."

"Tell me something I don't know." Someone else's voice. Sounding snappish, juvenile.

I looked down at my hands. Not the white, slender, cerulean-blue-veined hands I used to see. But ochre-tinted, almost tanned, the yellowish cast making the veins look slightly green, blue-green like the salty sea.

His words had cracked something open. All my stated reasons for being in Korea scudded away, clouds unveiling a full moon of certainty. I had known all this time, hadn't I, the same way I had seen the sign 月 on a calendar and known somehow that it was the Chinese sign for moon. Bright, spare, unmistakable.

"Maybe I do want to try to find out what happened."

Me, Korean, for almost two years plus the nine months I was carried by my Korean mother. That made *years* of a history complete and separate from what I eventually became with Christine and Ken Thorson in Eden's Prairie, Minnesota.

"I especially want to find my mother." I was suddenly breathless. "I mean, I want to find out more about her." Had I ever consciously thought about her, talked of her, since that day I wondered if I'd see her in Heaven, or Hell?

But I was talking about her now. Christine and Ken, an ocean away, couldn't hear my treasonous words—nor I theirs. Amanda couldn't say, as she had that day, in awe and wonder, *Sarah, you're fucking disowning us! Thanks a lot!*

"Oh my God," I said. I looked at my watch. "I forgot that I was supposed to meet this guy, Jun-Ho, for our language exchange."

KYUNG-SOOK
Enduring Pine Village
1962

At last, the river of memory came to the flute, the taegum, which was where the story really began.

Kyung-sook was thirteen when she had found it lying at the bottom of an unused rice chest in the storeroom. Seeing this unexpected object, wrapped in brilliant, if crumbling, silk amidst a latticework of cobwebs and stray grains of rice, she had naturally picked it up, that knobby length of bamboo that felt strangely familiar in her hands. On a whim, she put it to her lips. And this is when her destiny changed.

Until then, she had merely lived her life, accepting its joys and hardships like a ship tossed about on a vast sea. She had never had, until that chance find, something to live *for*, a certain direction she wanted to follow. Now, all the necessary parts of her life—eating, sleeping, studying—became mere pauses before she would steal away again to the Three Peaks Lake to play this flute, eventually learning how to capture the quivering sounds of the wind and water, notes that filled her more deeply than any food.

At those times, in the place where the pines gave way to summergreen oaks and wild pear trees, Kyung-sook would feel she had held the flute in her fingers for only a minute—but then she would notice that the sun, which had been high over the three peaks in the mountain when she started, would be beginning its slow, somnolent descent over her westward shoulder. When she returned home, looking tired, her parents would beam at her and say, "Look at our Kyung-sook-ah, studying so diligently, a true Bae descendant."

Occasionally some grandmothers wandering for ginseng in the fall or tender fern bracken in the spring would be attracted by the sounds and they would stop to listen.

This music, that beautiful vibrating sorrow, is the pulse of us, they would say. We have seen two wars, so much destruction. Yet, we are still here, Korea is still here, and we hope some day we will be allowed north to visit the sacred Mount Paekdu, the way our people used to when our beloved country was one land. Oh, the beauty and sorrow of our han. You have somehow managed to capture this at such a tender age.

Her audiences showed their appreciation by leaving her with mung-bean pancakes, fruit, or rice balls from the grannies' own lunches as they walked away, sighing about what a shame it was that there weren't more young people who appreciated folk music nowadays.

One day, a woman appeared on the ridge. She stayed a distance away, listening, but then, when Kyung-sook was finished, approached her.

It was her mother.

Kyung-sook gulped, moved to hide her schoolbooks, which were scattered disrespectfully nearby in the goose-grass.

But her mother didn't scold her. Instead she set down the bundle of wild onion she carried on her head.

Music exists for the Huhr clan, she said, referring to her maiden family. It is in our blood.

It must be true, Kyung-sook thought. At every Autumn Harvest Moon Festival, people begged Kyung-sook's mother to sing. And when the women assembled for the kangkang sullae dance, it was her mother's true soprano that broke the first verse of the dance.

That taegum belonged to a great-great-great grandfather, Kyung-sook's mother said, looking at the ancient instrument. She did not ask Kyung-sook where she had found it, only settled herself more comfortably on the grass.

Back in the Chosun Dynasty, when the arts and letters flourished, this man was a court musician, so renowned for his music that whenever he played, people from all over the province would travel to hear him, she went on.

The musician's wife, however, had never heard her husband play a note. The man even practiced in a special insulated room that the governor had made, just for him.

When the wife complained that every peasant in the province had heard him play, and she had not, he answered, "Woman, how can I let you hear me play? You know that music is of a woman's world—are not the kisaeng all given musical training? I am your husband. I cannot have you see me that way."

The wife consoled herself by reminding herself that a musician made a good husband. He didn't drink because alcohol might interfere with the exquisite sensitivity of his lips; he didn't chase women because music was his only love.

Yet, every time her husband performed for an audience, she would hear about the heartbreaking music he produced, how even the rigidly classical songs rendered by his flute could make the strongest man break down and bawl shamelessly for his mother.

One day it was announced that an envoy from Japan would be visiting the Highest Order of the Provincial Authorities. The elders would be arranging different performances at court. Not least would be the woman's musician husband.

I simply must hear him, this once, she told herself. I'll just stay in the shadows, he won't even know I'm there.

The woman waited until her husband left that night, and then she stole away to the great hall. She was awed by the architecture, the silk tapestries that hung from the walls. She delighted in watching the court musicians play the traditional instruments: the silk-stringed kayageum harp, the tiny p'iri flute, the paired-string violin.

Her husband, last. He came out in a red robe decorated with gold leaf and a black scholar's hat. The wife had never seen him look so impressive, so imposing before. When some inner voice told him he was ready, he lifted the flute to his lips and began to play.

The woman cried, and cried openly. She was not particularly educated, but she had never heard such beautiful music in her life—autumn leaves falling into a rushing river, a maiden's longing for her lover across the Milky Way—and it was her husband who was creating it! She was so moved she stumbled out of her place in the shadows. When she realized her mistake, she slipped back in without him seeing. But really, she thought, why shouldn't everyone in the village see how proud she was of her husband?

That night, her husband, for the first time ever in his life, brought his beloved taegum home. He wrapped it in silks and carefully stored it away. The wife wanted so badly to talk about the music he had played, but she had to pinch herself, remind herself that no, she had not been away from the house.

The next day, when she went out to the well to get water for the morning meal, she found him. He was in his workaday white ramie clothes. Hanging from a branch of the sturdy pine tree just outside the door. The woman dropped her water crock, and, apparently raving mad, dove into the well, killing herself, too.

The children left behind were their ancestors, Kyung-sook's mother explained. They had passed the flute down from generation to generation, every one of the Huhrs too afraid of the musician's ghost to throw it away.

I won't scold you for digging into the chest, her mother said, but now you know about the curse that goes along with the Huhr clan's gift for music. I myself had been told many times I could become a famous p'ansori singer. But I thought to myself, where would that leave my family if I had to take to the road and travel? Each person in the family has a job to do. You, too, must put that taegum back where you found it, forget about it, and focus only on your studies.

Kyung-sook said she would. But at the very core of her being there was a tiny ember, growing ever brighter without her even giving it breath to fan it.

SARAH
Seoul
1993

I wasn't sure if Jun-Ho Kim would still be at the Balzac, forty-five minutes after the appointed time, but he was there at the glass-topped table, a smile on his face. I apologized, and apologized again, not quite wanting to admit that I had simply forgotten. He didn't press me for an explanation, instead, he seemed impressed that I was wheezing and gasping, clearly having run all the way over there.

After I sat down and gulped some water, he started our session by telling me that he had only three more weeks available for our meetings. His battalion was moving out to an army base called Camp Ozark in one of the northern provinces, and he was going to be a KATUSA —Korean Augmentation to the U.S. Army—working and living alongside American troops for his military duty. Since all young men had to go into the military for two years, the KATUSA program was considered to be a plush assignment—better food, a chance to improve one's English, a chance to wallow in beloved American pop culture—instead of living in a Quonset hut in the middle of some potato patch out in the country, where your superiors could beat you on a whim. You had to have connections or be very, very smart to be a KATUSA. I think Jun-Ho was the latter. His father was a low-level salaryman accountant, he'd told me.

I was happy for him, but even more, relieved for *me*. The end was in sight. I managed to gamely stumble on in Korean until it was time to switch.

"What is the interest in your life?" Jun-Ho asked.

"I'm going to try to find out about my mother—my Korean mother," I announced, feeling a bit of the giddy boldness of revealing secrets to a stranger on a train. In three weeks, I'd never see him again.

"But you said your Korean mother is dead?"

"She is. But I've decided to find out about her, who she was—about how I came to be adopted, see if maybe I can find some family."

"How are you going to do this, this research?"

"I'm not sure yet, but I know the name of the orphanage." I had once seen it on a mailing, even though normally Christine spirited such things into the garbage, right away. The adoption agency had been announcing a fundraiser for the "Little Angels Orphanage"—could someone come up with a more awful, euphemistic name? I remembered thinking.

"Then call on me if you have need for helps," he said.

"Okay," I said. "I'll keep it in mind."

Jun-Ho's face closed on itself, folding like those little pleated leather coin purses that you squeeze to open. "It isn't, I will keep it in *my* mind? I think you will need a possessive article."

"No." I was suddenly conscious that while he had always meticulously corrected my Korean, I'd been letting his most egregious mistakes parade on by. I parsed the sentence on an imaginary blackboard:

I'll keep it in mind.

I'll keep it in my mind.

It revealed nothing except that the English language could be utterly illogical and ridiculous.

"I don't know how to explain it, but it's just 'I'll keep it in mind.' "

He reached into his breast pocket and removed a small notebook. The pages, spiral-bound cards, neonatal kitten cartoons and photo-stickers of Meg Ryan on the cover—very seventh-grade-girl locker interior.

"I will . . . keep . . . it . . . in . . . mind," he wrote, letters slightly curvy and broken, as if he were writing in Cyrillic. I felt like advising him to ditch the Hello Kitty before going to Camp Ozark with the American yahoos, but I couldn't find the right words to explain why.

"I'll never learn English," he said with a chuckle, snapping the notebook shut. "It's too hard."

When the hour was over, I tried to pay, but Jun-Ho made a gentle scolding noise in the back of his throat.

"In Korea, the man always pay," he said. "The world belongs to man, so man must pay."

Korea is a man's world—that's what Bernie Lee said, gleefully, every time he described to us how his new girlfriend Mi-Sun—a genuine Korean-Korean—delivered home-cooked meals to the dorm, shined his sneakers with white shoe polish, did his laundry by hand.

"Okay, go ahead and pay," I said to Jun-Ho. "After all, Korea is a man's world."

"Korea is a man swirled?" Hello Kitty reappeared. "Is that a common expression in America?"

He didn't understand why I was laughing.

SARAH
Seoul
1993

It was as simple as that.

114, Directory Assistance, called by Doug, a number found for the Little Angels Orphanage.

The number, the secret code, the magic combination to the lockbox of my past. But for two days I stared at that slip of paper pinned on my room's bulletin board, paralyzed.

This was ridiculous. Gathering handfuls of silver won pieces, I went downstairs to the pay phone.

A woman's disembodied voice.

"*Agichunsakoahwonimnida.*" I reflexively hung up.

More coins, dialed again.

"*Agichunsakoahwonimnida.*" The same woman.

Panic seized me. Why hadn't she said *hello* the way we learned it in class, *yo-bow-say-yo*? Why didn't the Korean I heard ever leap and sing, *kkang-chung, kkang-chung,* like the song about the mountain rabbit?

A dwindling pile of won pieces.

"*Agichunsakoahwonimnida!*"

How was I supposed to answer that?

A pause.

The line, dead.

I clutched the phone. I needed to talk. The last of the won fed into the pay phone's maw.

"*Agichunsakoahwonimnida!!*"

"My name is Sarah Thorson," I choked. "I'm from America. I was adopted from the Little Angels Orphanage. I want to find out about my birth family, especially my mother. This *is* the Little Angels Orphanage, isn't it?"

She responded in loud Korean, irate words that drove away any clinging bits of the language in my head. I couldn't even remember how to say, *Is there anyone who can speak English?* or *Please help me.* I could only wait for her to finish saying what she was going to say. When she did, she hung up.

At lunch, I asked Doug if he could call for me.

"No," he said to my surprise.

"Why not?"

"I don't want such a huge responsibility. If you want to do it right, get a Korean native speaker. Why not ask Choi *Sunsengnim?*"

I cringed, picturing Choi *Sunsengnim*, fingers rifling through the helpless pages of my history, how she'd exclaim *oh-moh!* if she found something juicy.

"But Doug, I'm sure you'd do fine—you're the best speaker in the class."

"Sarah, I'm a Korean kindergartner who swears really really well. I don't know the word for 'adoptee'. I only knew 'orphanage' because my mother used to threaten to put me in one, when I got on her nerves."

"You could use the dictionary."

"A reminder, I can't read—that's why I was kicked out of Level Three. I wouldn't be able to write down what the orphanage people are going to say—I'd miscommunicate things. I'm sorry. I do want to help you."

"Do you?" Besides that day he taught me the song about the mountain rabbit, Doug would never practice Korean with me even when I risked embarrassment by venturing something in my horrible Korean first: when he showed up to class one morning with a ripped hole in his pants, I looked at his bloodied, exposed knee and said, *"Uh-tuh-kae?"*—how? He told me in English about going up to T'apkol Park at daybreak to catch a glimpse of the elderly men doing calisthenics together, of tripping on some stone steps. In contrast, when I had said, almost unthinkingly, to Bernie when he held the classroom's door open for me: *komapsumnida*, thank you, he—at least—had replied *kurae*, the Korean version of *de nada*.

"You always say you'll help—then you don't," I accused. "When Jun-Ho leaves, I won't have anyone to practice Korean with."

"I can't speak Korean to Americans," he said. "You're 'American' to me."

"What?"

"The way you speak Korean, your accent. Korean's always been dangerous for me—when I was growing up, my dad beat me every time he caught me speaking Korean to any Americans."

I caught my breath.

"He couldn't stand seeing me, his kid, open his mouth and have gook-speak come out. Once, I accidentally greeted one of the staff sergeants in Korean—that's how this happened." He gestured toward his left eye, the one that looked "sad." When I focused on it, I saw how it hung slightly lower than the other, a gem jarred from its setting.

Oh moh! I wanted to say. "I'm sorry, I didn't know," I said, instead.

He smiled the beginning of a wicked smile. "You've got to work on your accent. You sound like the goddam base chaplain who learned his Korean from Berlitz."

"You know," I said. "There actually is a word I can say with a proper Korean accent."

I knew he wouldn't believe me. My inability to correctly pronounce any Korean word had become legendary in the Motherland Program. The language turned like meat in my mouth, the sharp corners of the letters rounding, proper intonations breaking free of their moorings. What came out of my Americanized, hybridized mouth was both comic and grim, a Babelized language of loss that would cause Choi *Sunsengnim* to sigh in despair, Jeannie to giggle behind her hand, Helmut to say "Ach!" The nun, I hope, prayed for me.

But there was a word, *ddong*—the word for crap, merde, shit—that I could pronounce. I had few opportunities to say *shit* in class, but in the safety of my room, I would sometimes say *"ddong, ddong, ddong"* to the walls, wondering how was it that I could say *ddong* when I couldn't even manage the *dd* sound: in my mouth, the word *ddal,* "daughter," weakened to *dal,* "moon," or even further to *tal,* "mask."

It was only when I said *ddong* that the sound came from someplace else, from a Korean-run sound factory that produced that exact *dd* sound, the resonance of a church bell in the moment right after its tense and waiting surface has been struck. In this way, the word for "shit" stayed itself and didn't become the word for "East."

"*Ddong*." I said, expecting a laugh.

"You said that perfectly, you know."

He was deadly serious.

I shrugged.

"You must have memories," he said.

I shook my head. Where *ddong* had come from, I hadn't the faintest clue. Looking into my past was like looking into dark water. I wondered what Amanda's memories from eighteen months were like. But then it didn't matter: she had flash photos, home movies, eyewitness stories giving light and color and shape to the murk.

"Sometimes, I'm afraid I'm going crazy here," I told Doug. "I don't know what's real, what's not real, what's memory, what's pure projection. I have these flashes: *mandu* dumplings, I *know* these from somewhere. But if I really sit down and think, I know the dumplings from General Tsao's, this Chinese restaurant in Minneapolis. Same way, that day we were up on mountain, I had this flash—I've been here before—but we don't have mountains in Minnesota and I've never been out West to see the Rockies—isn't that crazy?"

"No, that's not crazy," Doug said.

My fingers, grown slippery with sweat, couldn't contain my metal chopsticks. They hit the table, then slid to the floor. The *ajuhma* glared when I reached over to the container for a new, possibly clean, set. Doug showed me again the proper way to wrap my fingers around them, his hand covering mine like a paw.

"So what are you going to do about contacting the orphanage?"

I bit my thumbnail.

"Do you think if I studied really hard this week, my Korean could get good enough to do the calling myself?"

His answer: a laugh.

SARAH
Seoul
1993

"You will pick an afternoon class for your elective," Choi *Sunsengnim* told us in English, to make sure we—I—understood. "You can choose between traditional music, tae kwon do, ceramics, or remedial pronunciation.

"*Sal-ah-ssi,* I think it would be best for you to participate in the pronunciation class," Choi *Sunsengnim* said, when the sheet arrived on my desk.

I felt my usual irritation at her meddling, but then I reminded myself: the orphanage was there, presumably with some real, solid information for me. By the time we started the elective classes, everything could be different. Maybe I'd find some of my family, and I'd start living with them. Once I began sleeping in a Korean bed, eating Korean food made by familial hands, everything Korean about me would come back naturally, I was sure. Maybe I'd even leave the Motherland Program, come back as the best speaker in the class.

I put my name under the pronunciation class and smiled agreeably at *Sunsengnim.*

KYUNG-SOOK
Enduring Pine Village
1963

This flute would take her out of the village.

She didn't know where, or when, but she sensed a larger future waiting for her beyond the craggy mountains, beyond their flowering valley.

Would she be like Yongsu and merely disappear?

More likely she would leave on her own two feet, in the light of day, as her imo had done before her. But unlike Imo, she would return in glory and acclaim after having grasped her singular destiny as a musician.

Kyung-sook's aunt, her imo, had been the first of the Huhr clan to ever leave the village, and she had never returned. She had been driven out because of her love for the whiteman's god, Christo.

Imo was the only Christo-follower in all the generations of a clan that had always worshipped the Lord Buddha, kept up the ancestor-worshipping rites, and—something they tried hard to keep secret—occasionally dipped into the shrouded crevices of shamanism.

In fact, when Kyung-Sook's mother was sixteen, she had fainted upon hearing some harvest-time changgo drumming. Suddenly, she had risen up and begun to dance wildly, foaming at the mouth and claiming in a guttural voice that she was the Sauce-Pot God. The local shaman, observing this, had remarked that she could become a shaman priestess, a mu-dang, if she allowed the gods to descend on her. Her parents were horrified. Most people thought of shamans as disreputable types who dwelled on the margins of proper society. Shaman priestesses were known to tear off their clothes or simulate sexual acts during a kut, they shamelessly extorted money from the sick, the desperate. Becoming a mu-dang was out of the question for someone from a respectable family.

From time to time, however, Kyung-sook's mother still experienced fainting spells marked by a strange voice muttering prophecies that people took careful note of—because they almost always came true. Sometimes when this happened, her parents would beat her or plunge her in water to make the voices stop. But when they did, her skin would bloom with an angry rash, as if the spirit were determined to come out somehow.

In an attempt to break this cycle, both Kyung-sook's mother and her sister, Imo, were sent to the missionary school, which had declared war against such earthy paganism and, as an added incentive, provided its students a free daily meal.

Of course, the main mission of Our Holy Father School was to convert children to become Christo followers. Kyung-Sook's mother easily ignored the gibberings of the ladies in black-and-white robes that only showed their rubbery faces. They showed her a picture of a whiteman and said in bad Korean, "This is Christo, your Father," and they slapped her when she laughed and said, "No, my father is the man out in the rice fields."

Sometimes the somber missionary man would come out and make her partake of acrid red liquid and dry crackers, saying, amazingly, that those foodstuffs were Christo's *blood* and *bones*. At other times, they forced her to stare at pictures of Christo, this time bloodied and hanging from two joined pieces of wood. One particularly ugly image was of his face, blood streaming from some sharp brambles on his head, eyes rolling upward, his mouth in the middle of a ghastly scream.

Kyung-Sook's mother remained unmoved as the nuns yelled at her in more bad Korean about this sulfur-smelling place called Hell where everyone who didn't follow Christo burned up in eternal torment. Then they tried to beat the stubbornness from her, but she was used to blows at home and took her punishment without expression.

Once, she was supposed to be praying in front of a man-sized statue of Christo on the cross-pieces. She dutifully murmured the meaningless words, her hands pressed palm-to-palm, elbows out, the same way she prayed at the Buddhist temple.

If I hadn't seen it with my own eyes, I would not have believed it, one of the nuns said.

The gilded, pierced body of Christo began to tremble and shake, even as Kyung-sook's mother continued to mumble, "Ow-er Hebben-ree Fad-dah . . ."

Then, the arms of the figure flew off and crashed to the floor.

The devil! the nun screamed. It could only be Satan who could manage such a thing. Kyung-sook's mother was banished from the school.

But Imo was different.

She loved hearing the stories of Christo, how he healed the sick, how he hated the tax collectors and other bad men yet welcomed the prostitute who came to him with a pure heart. Those bloody portraits of him caused her to weep when she learned how Christo had suffered on the cross—for her and all Christo-followers. During Communion, she would find her heart singing, expanding as the magic wafer melted on her tongue, and she thought of how through this suffering Christo became an essence, a pure light.

The Huhr matriarch, of course, was furious when Imo declared she was renouncing Lord Buddha and her venerated ancestors, even going so far as to declare that other members of the family should do the same. The matriarch had wanted to stop the shaman cycle, not have Christo-follower children. She immediately hired the local shaman to perform an exorcism. The mu-dang danced to exhaustion, shaking rattles and hitting gongs in front of Imo's face—to no avail. The mother then called in the more powerful River Circle shaman, one who, upon entering the house, immediately detected the presence of Christo, and without any preparation at all, fell into a trance and began beating Imo with her fists, shrieking at the spirit of Christo to come out. She sacrificed a pig's head, she danced in bare feet over sharp scimitars. But each time she tossed the divining fish, waiting for its head to point out the door, signaling that the spirit of Christo had left the house, it did not. It always pointed back at Imo.

When Imo left Enduring Pine Village, her own mother did not say goodbye to her. Imo traveled to Seoul with few possessions other than the Bible the nuns had given to her, the one that had her Christian name, Mary Rose, inscribed on it in gold powder, as she had been their biggest success.

Destiny, woo-myung, turns and turns on a cosmic wheel.

"We are prepared to send you to college," Kyung-sook's parents told her. "Because our family has no sons. If you pass the entrance exam, you may go. Your imo in Seoul, though long estranged from the family, has agreed to lodge you."

SARAH
Seoul
1993

Eureka! I had devised a system for conquering Korean, a system for memorizing words. French, at least, had cognates with English: *Liberté, fraternité, egalité*. And Spanish was cognate city. *Producto de México*.

So I created my own for Korean. *Oo-yu*, the word for milk, became (m)*oo-yu*. And so forth.

In class we had been asked to name a family member we liked. Bernie had shown off with *"I like my X"* (X, a long word I'd have to look up later, which turned out to be "mother's brother's wife"). At my turn, I said I liked my *harmony*. My grandmother. My perfect cognate.

Nana Thorson was the one who had taken care of me after Amanda was born. Amanda, milkweed fluff for hair, eyes that turned from transparent to a clear, devastating blue. The house had been packed with visitors, as if the Christ child had been born here.

At first, I was scared of Nana, of the way she looked at me—as if I had done something wrong. But she warmed up, and we had tea parties where she'd happily pretend to quaff the grass-clipping-and-dirt tea I'd made her. When my irritating Aunt Connie (a neighbor, not a true aunt), the one with the chicken legs, would come over, exclaiming over Amanda's "angel hair," saying "You can see whose daughter she is, that's for sure," Nana would call me over with a secret curl of her ring finger.

"Sarah," she'd whisper. "Did you know that your hair is the exact black-purple of a blackbird's wing?—I can't imagine anything more beautiful!"

She used to tell me how the lakes in Minnesota were formed in the footprints of Paul Bunyan's great blue ox, Babe. And she'd sing me to sleep with this nonsense song that sounded like *bya-bya, litten gurren*. It wasn't until she died and they put coins on her closed eyes and her frail white-haired friends came over to sing some hymns in a strange language that I realized she had been singing to me in Norwegian.

"Harmony is what you use in music." Bernie rolled his eyes. "*Harl-moni* is grandmother."

Some kind of cog in my brain slipped. I wanted to stand on my desk and release my rage. Nana, gone, just like my nascent, budding Korean tongue.

"Fuck you, Bernie," Doug said, his cold expletive turning my scorching rage into a manageable, tepid goo. "Sarah, you're doing much better—you just need a little time and practice."

At the Balzac Cafè, Jun-Ho ordered coffee. The waitress returned with the usual pot of hot water, a small paper tube of Maxwell House Instant, a larger one of Cremora. You mixed the two powders into a cylindrical glass, added the hot water, and stirred it with a long swizzle, as if the whole thing was a chemistry experiment, searching for the formula for the world's weakest coffee compound. I nursed a ginseng tea that I'd tried in vain to sweeten with three spoonfuls of sugar.

"What did you do this week?" he asked in Korean.

I stared back at him.

"What did you do this week?"

"I understood what you said." I was furious, again, but I didn't know at whom. All I could think was, if I could remember *ddong*, I could remember other words.

What did you do this week?

No Korean words came to mind.

"Korean food is spicy." I parroted a phrase I'd memorized from the lesson.

"Yes, it is spicy," Jun-Ho said, without missing a beat.

He said something else that I didn't understand. I cocked my head at him, pushed one ear forward, as if all my trouble was in the hearing, a physical impediment.

"What I said: all my life I want to visit to America to say hello to the big green lady."

"Big green lady?"

"You know, like this." He toasted me with his coffee, Cremora'd to a leisure-suit beige.

"What are you talking about?"

"The big green lady, the freedom lady. The independence lady."

"Oh, you mean the Statue of Liberty?"

"Yes, Statue of Lib-ah-ty." Hello Kitty came out again.

"Liberty," I said. Li-ber-ty."

"Libahty. Thank you, Miss Sarah. I am noticing some probulem with English words with facing consonants. Thank you for your helps."

"Actually, I need some helps, too."

"Okay, what helps?"

"Remember how I said I want to find out about my Korean mother? I called the orphanage, and I, um, don't think they speak any English."

"You want me to do the telephone?"

I nodded with relief. I gave him the piece of paper on which I'd written the number of the orphanage, my full name, Ken and Christine's names, our address, the year I was adopted, my birthday.

"I want to go there and look at my file as soon as possible."

He studied the paper.

"Okay, you wait." He made his way toward a bank of phones lined up like slot machines at the entrance of the café. I couldn't help following him.

From his wallet he extracted not coins, but a credit card that had a picture of Mickey Mouse on it. Almost no one used coins at public phones, I'd noticed. The card seemed much more convenient and advanced. *Everything over there will be very different than what you're used to here, much more primitive.*

He punched in the number, waited, said hello—which was accompanied by a half bow. I heard "Sal-ah Dor-son" and "Min-ah-so-tah," and then he lost me in a stream of native-speaker Korean. He kept on, five, ten minutes.

"What? What?" I said, even before he had hung up.

"I spoke to a Miss Park, the curator."

"What?" I said. "About what?"

"How to get to the orphanage, that kind of things," he said.

"But do they have anything, on me?"

"There are some records, yes."

"About my family?"

He nodded, slowly. "They keep a record of each child. But maybe not so much for to tell you about your parents."

"But *something*. I mean, you were on the phone for a long time."

He nodded.

"Can we go there right now?"

"Two weeks, that is the soonest someone can see you. That will be the last time we meet, also."

"Two *weeks*?"

"That is what the curator said."

I sighed. Jun-Ho's flash card system had the side effect of overcramming his brain with arcane and slangy words, churning his speech into a stew of malapropisms. When the hot coffee made him sweat, he giggled about his "respiration." When recounting Bernie's scorn at my attempt to say *harlmoni*, the word for grandmother, Jun-Ho pronounced that Bernie needed to see a "shrimp."

And earlier, he had been puzzled by my shocked look in response to him saying he was going to miss these afternoons of "intercourse" with me. Should I tell him that "curator" wasn't the right word for the orphanage lady? But suddenly, I couldn't think of what the right one would be. Curator now sounded strangely accurate, as if it had picked up new meanings as I pondered it.

I gave up. I was ready to give up on Korea. All I wanted right now were the answers to my life. How was I going to exist, child-for-purchase, for two more weeks?

SARAH
Seoul
1993

"Miss Sarah!"

Jun Ho's hair was now so close-cropped, it revealed the stark whiteness of his scalp, like the sun shining into primeval forest canopy. The Oxford shirts and sweater vests had given way to his army uniform, regulation camouflage. He was calling to me from a car, a kiwi-green hatchback.

"How about if we do something different?" he asked, out the open window.

He tossed me a grin as I slid in. Unlike your average scowly-faced Korean man, e.g., the Stamp *ajuhshi* or the unsmiling men who worked in the Institute's administrative office, Jun-Ho let his face melt with mirth or cheer when he felt it. I was beginning to think I might actually miss him when he was gone.

The car started with a hop and a chirp, and he pulled into the vortex of Seoul traffic. The car was his friend's. Borrowed, he said, so he could show me around a bit before he left. I was suddenly aware that I'd seen very little of Seoul besides the immediate neighborhood of the school, so I sat back, pleased.

"Next week is the orphanage," I said. "You're coming with me to translate, right?"

He cracked another grin. "Right now, we will have fun," he said. "We will talk only about fun things. We shall conversate in Korean, or English?"

"Oh please, I'm experiencing brain-lock," I told him, gazing at a plastic Tweety Bird ornament hanging from the rearview mirror. I wondered if his "friend" was male or female. A lacquered Kleenex box dripping with an elaborate fringe of fake pearls (Koreans seemed to never be without their tissues) in the back window also gave no clue.

"You have to speak to me in English if you want me to say anything at all."

"Aye-aye." He saluted smartly, before clapping both of his small hands back on the wheel to avoid a gargantuan bus tipping over the asphalt's solid white line, threatening to obliterate us.

"There, the U.S. Embassy used to be, before the Korean War," Jun-Ho pointed, as we passed a two-storied Western-style building, insignificant in the shadow of the Lotte Hotel across the street. Now, it was UNITED STATES INFORMATION SERVICE.

"And Lotte, you know Lotte?"

"Oh yes," I said. Lotte was a chaebol, a Korean conglomerate, probably one of the largest. Besides the hotel, there was Lotte gum, Lotte cookies, Lotte-burgers, Lotte shoes and Lotte sportswear, not to mention Lotte World, the Disneyland of Korea.

"*The Sorrows of Young Werther*. That is one of my favorite texts that I was introduced to in college."

"Oh?"

"Yes, Lotte, Goethe's great love."

"Oh."

Jun-Ho navigated the buglike car through the yellow afternoon light. I was surprised to see that all the road signs were in English as well as Korean, although a sign that said Yongduip'o (arrow, next exit) didn't mean a lot to me.

Jun-Ho explained that the signs were for the U.S. military—in case of an emergency, they needed to be able to get around. He also pointed out some huge, dolmen-like concrete structures, which he said were antitank barriers.

We were going to Yoido, Seoul's own Île de la Cité. Yoido, he told me, contained all the city's important buildings: the National Diet, the National Library, Korea's version of Wall Street, Korea Broadcasting, and the Six-Three Building, the tallest building in Korea.

As we crossed the bridge, the traffic slowed to a snarl at the nexus of bridge and island. But no one honked; this condition must be normal and expected. The pollution here seemed even worse than the rest of Seoul; the slanting sun gave Yoido an unnatural phosphorous glow. As we waited, I looked out onto the waterfront, bordered by dilapidated food stands, skeletal trees, and a concrete walkway along which mothers, children, and old men strolled, their faces pushed dreamily to the wind. The children's voices unfurled into the chemical air like colored kites, adding another layer of unreality to the bleak landscape.

Truly, Yoido, this showcase of the city, was barbaric. There wasn't enough room for all the vehicles trapped in the blocked and hardened arteries of the island. Besides the desiccated trees teetering precariously near the water, there were no other signs of sustainable vegetation. Everything on this island seemed faked, claustrophobic. It was someone's vision of a great, metropolitan structure, but it wasn't mine.

After measuring our progress in millimeters, we finally reached our destination, the Six-Three Building. It was called that because it had sixty-three floors, or was supposed to—I didn't count. In the late seventies when Korea wanted to show the world it wasn't just some backward country, Jun-Ho told me, it erected this. At the time, the highest building in Asia was fifty-five floors. The Koreans ascended to sixty and added on an extra three floors along with a cloud puncturing antenna just to make sure it was the tallest. The building had an impressive glimmery gold surface on its exterior that would make it look like a trophy in the setting sun.

We headed for the observation deck. In the elevator, a lady dressed in a stiff Jetsons-type uniform announced something in a soft voice and then pushed the buttons with a white-gloved hand. She was even taller than I was.

We walked out of the elevator into a round space that was covered by what I can only describe as a glass orb, almost geodesic, Buckminster Fuller-ish.

By leaning into the sides of the orb, we could command a panoramic view of the city. I would have expected the city to be obscured by Yoido's smog, but from our height, we could see past all that.

"Wow!" I said. "You can see *everything*." The scenery seemed to be shifting very slowly, but steadily. Then I realized that *we* were the ones who were moving; the round platform was turning, revolving-restaurant-style.

Jun-Ho grinningly nodded. "No one can hide from you up here, Sarah."

I pressed my face as close to the glass as I could manage. Now, I could see the mountains ringing the city again. When I'd first flown into Korea, I'd looked out the plane's window and seen those gray peaks; there had been the last little bit of snow remaining on their summits, as if the mountains had been inverted by the huge hand of God, their peaks dipped in sugar, then righted again. That sight had struck me, suddenly, as so familiar, so *home* for some reason, that this feeling had burbled over into tears. I sobbed—invisibly, I thought—behind a paperback book tented over my face. But the man next to me, a stoic Korean businessman who hadn't said a word to me during the twenty-hour flight, poked a package of tissues over the top of my book.

Beyond the mountains were more mountains. I came out of this place, somewhere. Where was my Korean family during that small, fleeting time? Were they north of the Han River? South? Rich? Poor? What was the name they had given me, and who named me? My mother? Had she been thinking of me those last seconds before the toothed glass and groaning metal devoured her tender flesh, leaving glass diamonds and glistening rubies of blood spangling the asphalt? Where had they been going, why had I not been with them?

Jun-Ho must have wandered away, for he was back, holding in his hand a small figurine that looked like a pair of warped, demented totem poles. At the top, each pole had a grinning monster head.

"Please receive," he said, proffering it respectfully with both hands. "A gift."

"What is it?"

"This is a replicate of the gateposts Koreans used to erect outside their villages to honor the Five Generals Who Hold Up the Sky. See here—" He pointed to some Chinese inscriptions carved in the bottom. "It says, 'General Scare Away Demons.'"

"So will it scare away my demons?"

"It might," he said. "You try."

Jun-Ho escorted me around the floor. A few times, we bumped accidentally. We'd never been this close physically, I was realizing—we'd always been separated by an expanse of glass-topped table. I was a good four inches taller than he was.

He stopped at an ice cream stand and bought us watery soft-serve cones. He devoured his in three sucking bites, as if he were eating a juicy peach.

"Jun-Ho," I laughed. "It's ice cream. You're supposed to lick it."

"That is American style?" he asked, curling his lip. "This, too, is American style to eat chicken." He pantomimed licking his outstretched fingers.

"Okay, true," I said. "We call it 'finger lickin' good.'"

"Not so good—very dirty," he said. "Koreans don't eat things you touch by your hands. Even fruit, we use toothy-picks."

I had to smile at him. His uniform was open at the neck, revealing a small triangle of gray undershirt and the tiniest bit of smooth chest, a child's skin. There was something vulnerable about that place, and I suddenly wanted to kiss it or touch it with my fingers as if it were a baby animal. But I looked down to see his black army boots galumphing on the floor, that idiotic purse dangling from his wrist, and then I wanted to laugh. How had it come to this, that I had become friends with this man from another country, who spoke a language I didn't know, and chewed soft-serve ice cream, ate fruit from toothy-picks?

We called the elevator, and the lady pressed the button for us, again—how could she stand such a job? She kept her eyes lowered, never once looking at us, her makeup so thick it looked like a mask. Perhaps she wasn't real; maybe she was a Stepford Korean. I felt no motion as we descended, heard no sounds, so when the door opened in the lobby, it was as if we'd been beamed in from another planet. The lady bowed mechanically and thanked us as we left.

"Thank you," I said to Jun-Ho, when he dropped me off at the Residence. Bernie, Helmut, and some of their friends were playing basketball at the dilapidated hoop out front. Even though it had grown quite cool, they'd taken off their shirts—possibly for the benefit of the girls hanging around the fringes of the court. Their skin glistened white as bones in the fading light.

"Americans." Jun-Ho chuckled, as if the scene confirmed some long-held theory of his. "I hope you passed your time enjoyably, Sarah."

"I did, thank you," I said. I had one foot on the concrete of the parking lot, the rest of me still in the car. Between the two bucket seats, a paperback textbook was wedged: *Common American English Slang, Idioms, and Vernacular.*

"And you'll be there next week—we'll go to the orphanage together?"

He nodded, but his face turned sad. I didn't want him to leave; I wanted us to embrace, to touch. But the insistent thunking of the basketball and the assorted cries of "Shit, man!" and "What the f-u-u-u-uck!" kept me from doing anything.

"Thank you, Jun-Ho," I said again, trying to put all my emotions and feeling into it. Maybe if I knew Korean I could say something that would show my gratitude for all the things he'd done for me. "Thank you" was inadequate, something you said to the elevator lady. But once again, I lacked the words.

Jun-Ho grinned and saluted smartly with his tiny hand, but the sadness remained, a glum residue. I watched as the green car (called a PONY GALLOPER in English), belching unhealthy black clouds, chugged back toward the road that would take him, now, to wherever he was going.

"Hey, good going, adoptee-girl," Bernie said, punctuating his words with the *thunk-thunk* of the pockmarked basketball. "That horny soldier show you a good time? You know it's customary for guys to go to prostitutes right before they get inducted."

"Shut. The. Fuck. Up." An unbidden rage curled my hands into claws.

"Bitch," he said, mortally offended. "You know, your mother must have been a whore or something—those are the kids that get put up for adoption. Normal kids are taken care of by the family."

I lunged at him, grabbing the ball out of his hands and smashing it across the bridge of his nose, his orbital bones flattening and fracturing under the blow. The girls in the background screamed, Helmut and the other players gaped, but didn't move. But then Bernie rose, blood on his face, and marched to the phone and called the director of the program, describing my transgression. I would be made to go home within the week, days short of my goal. As I saw all this in my head, I turned, leaving him untouched, and flew up the building's steps, up to my room.

SARAH
Seoul
1993

The next week, Jun-Ho was there, waiting, at the Balzac.

"Ready?" I asked, starting to shake slightly in anticipation, like a frisky horse.

"We should partake of something before we go," he said. Mildly irritated, I sat down. How could he be thirsty on this, the day of days?

The coffees arrived, in their usual bonglike glasses. He regarded his but didn't drink.

"Sarah," he said. "I don't know if this is, you know, an auspicious idea."

"What?"

"Trying to find out about your parents."

"What are you talking about?" My voice rose several octaves. "You said the orphanage has things in my file."

"Yes, some officious data. But not so much to help you find out about your family. I am sorry."

I jumped up. The sugar canister keeled over, the brittle sound of glass on glass. People at the next table openly stared. Jun-Ho, to my surprise, didn't look angry or embarrassed. He just had that sad, vaguely wistful look he had had last time I saw him.

"So this whole thing's been useless?"

He looked down at his hands. He informed me that he'd made the appointment for two weeks hence in the hopes that maybe I would give up, lose interest. To soften the blow.

"Perhaps that is the more advantageous way—for you, for your Korean family," he said. "Let the past become nostalgic."

"That's not for you to decide," I said. "How can you say you'll help me and then turn around and stop? You promised you'd help me."

Jun-Ho's hands, lying between his knees, flexed open and shut as if he were warming up to play some scales on the piano. He sighed.

"Okay," he said. "We'll go. *Kapsida*."

It took two subways and a bus to get to the Little Angels Home. The brick building was nondescript—there wasn't even a sign marking it. Inside, it was hot, the cries of babies and the smell of unwashed baby bottoms filling the stagnant air. I longed to smell some kind of strong-smelling disinfectant. Menthol. Pine. Anything.

A lady in a severely tailored Western suit, a Miss Park, greeted us. She seemed too old to be a "miss." She had a half-grown-out perm, straight on top, then crimped at random angles like a tangle of insect legs.

She sat us down in her cluttered office that abutted the nursery. An assistant, her own perm crispy-new and uniformly curly as ramen noodles, offered us Dixie cups of sugary coffee. Why was everyone trying to delay me with coffee? The chemical smell of it, mixed with the smell of urine and old formula, turned my stomach.

But a few minutes later Miss Park returned with a folder, and my heart jumped. In there, my life was in there. She handed it wordlessly to Jun-Ho. I expected him to tear it open. He just looked at me.

"Please," I said. "Please read what it says."

Two yellowing pages. He glanced at them, looked up again.

"Sarah," he said. "It doesn't say much. Just about your eating habits and so forth."

I gripped his arm, as if I needed to feel the veins, sinew, tendons to know he was real, to know we really were in this place from which I'd come.

"Read it to me," I said. "Don't skip a word."

He bowed his head, cleared his throat with a mucusy *haAAAARGH*.

" 'The baby did not eat for the first three days after she was brought to the orphanage,' " he read. " 'But after that, she ate some. She had very regular bowel movements. Dr. Bai determined her to be free of diseases. She cries a lot and does not sleep much some times but otherwise seems to be a happy baby.' "

" 'She was assigned to foster mother Kang Koom-Soon shortly after.' "

Miss Park, absently flipping through papers, looked up and said something to Jun-Ho. He nodded.

"He says Kang Koom-Soon is dead, he was an old lady."

I smiled. Jun-Ho was always mixing up the gender pronouns, a small but significant thing that still eluded him.

"Okay, then it says 'child was adopted at eighteen months by Christine and Kenneth Dor-son of Minnesota, the United States of America.' "

He took out the second page.

"Here is a copy of your passport," he said, handing it to me. "You were a nice-looking baby. Cute."

I grasped the page. It was a bad Xerox, all shadows. The child in the picture had a tragic expression, like she was posing for a WANTED poster. That was me?

Lee, Soon-Min, it said in English letters under the Korean. *The Republic of Korea.*

"My Korean name is Lee Soon-Min," I said in wonder.

"Unh," he said, taking the page. He put it back in the folder and closed it.

"Is that all there is?" I said.

He nodded.

"Are you sure? It seemed like there was a lot of writing on that first page—at least four paragraphs." I looked him in the eye. He flinched, ever so slightly. I stared at him until he opened the folder again.

" 'A name of Lee Soon-Min was bequeathed,' " he added. "They made a passport for you, and you got your special-entry status to America."

"Wait." The air was suddenly electric. "They gave me a name?"

"They gave it to you for your passport." Jun-Ho was sweating. "That is the system of doing so."

"What do you mean?"

Miss Park stared at me.

"Also, why did I go home with a foster mother—didn't my parents have any relatives?"

I tore the page out of his hands, but again, it was a maze of symbols that I couldn't wring the meanings from.

"Jun-Ho," I said, voice now dwindling to a whisper. "Truth, please."

"You were named Lee Soon-Min and sent to America," he said. "What of it is giving you confusion?"

"I was *named* Lee Soon-Min? I didn't have a name before that, is that what you're saying?"

"The orphanage did not know if you had a name."

"But why not? It doesn't make sense."

Jun-Ho paused. I could tell he was itching to light up a cigarette, but he could hardly do it in this place of babies. He twitched instead, waggled the booted foot perched on his knee.

"I won't leave until you tell me."

To make my point, I folded my arms like Sitting Bull.

Jun-Ho looked back at me, then back down at his boots. He looked, only, sad.

"There is another paragraph here. But if I read, it will cause you much hurt."

"Hurt?"

"Injury," he clarified. "The heart inside the chest will become sore."

The folder was open, like butterfly wings. I couldn't believe that I could just reach out and touch the mysterious framework of my Korean life.

"It's okay, whatever's in there," I said. "I just need to know. How would you feel if you didn't *know*? I'm Korean but I can't speak Korean. I was supposed to grow up in Korea, like you. I need to know why I didn't."

Jun-Ho took a deep breath. The folder trembled slightly in his hand, as if a breeze were passing through the silent air of the office.

" 'The baby has no known family,' " he read. " 'She was brought to the orphanage on September 3 as a girl infant who had been left on the steps of the Hoei-Dong Fire Station. There was not any kind of note left with her and she was officially declared abandoned and fit for adoption.' "

Oh my God. He looked up at me with worry, but I raggedly choked out that I needed him to go on.

" 'The baby appears to have been born in a toilet or some kind of commode. The umbilical cord was still attached, and he was covered in feces …' "

The tears began to fall. I had no hope of stopping them.

" 'We cleaned the feces off.' "

Ddong. It was becoming clear. A baby arrived covered in *ddong.* Not a baby who was part of someone's family. No, a baby that someone had shit out and didn't even bother cleaning up while leaving it like a terrible prank at the door of a fire station.

That baby was me. The cord that had connected me to my mother had been cut carelessly, left to dangle. My Korean mother had cut me off and run. She hadn't wanted me.

And September 3, my birthday. Mom and Dad Thorson said that I had been a child who was loved, whose birthday was celebrated with candles and cake and presents and whatever else Koreans did to mark that important day.

My fist had found its way in my mouth. I was biting down on my knuckles, sobs wracking my body in waves. Miss Park came forward, murmuring comfort, patting my arm. Jun-Ho had already circled an awkward arm around me as I cried into his shirt. The three of us remained in this makeshift huddle for what seemed liked hours.

"Let's go," Jun-Ho said gently. *"Ka-yo."* He led me outside where a pale blue cab happened to be parked. As I groped my way into the back, Jun-Ho placed his palm between my forehead and the too-low steel rim of the door just in time. He barked directions to the driver, a large, oily man who looked back at me, my tears and some stray hairs clogging my mouth. Jun-Ho barked something else, and he started the car.

"Where are we going?" I surprised myself by speaking in Korean.

"Home," he said, in Korean. "Back to where we came from." He reached behind me to a gaudily beaded box that contained—what else?—tissues, and handed me a bouquet of them.

I turned my face to the window.

On the street, the rows of tiny shops were pressed together so tightly they looked like one continuous, rickety storefront, except for the different signs in Korean writing. I leaned my head against the scratched plexiglass of the window as the car jerkily accelerated. Watching the signs blur, I could feel something of my old self being left behind, like when you're dancing, and the music abruptly changes; you're left abandoned, half-aware in this temporal space, sprawling valiantly, stubbornly, to something that now only exists somewhere in your imagination.

PART II

KYUNG-SOOK
Enduring Pine Village
1972

They unrolled the scroll of names ever so slowly.

"Goddam pompous officials," someone muttered, as the crowd pressed closer. The two men in shiny Western-style suits seemed not to hear. With each hand's-width of the paper they exposed, a shout of joy or a sob of disappointment could be heard. The two men with fancily oiled hair kept to their own rhythm, neither speeding up nor slowing down for the hundreds of names.

The results of the college entrance exam.

For months before the exam, her mother had stayed up with her, every night, pinching the tails off soy sprouts or sewing up the covers on the just-washed sleeping pads. Whenever Kyung-sook's head began to nod, her mother would bring her a bitter-smelling herbal elixir. Sometimes, she just pulled her daughter's hair.

"A person who sleeps more than four hours a night has no hope of passing the entrance exam!" She oftentimes shouted this famous proverb in Kyung-sook's ear.

The year before, a boy who had once been a *beggar* had achieved the highest scores on the entrance exam to Seoul National University, the best college in the land. Kyung-sook's mother had taken it as an example that even if you started with nothing, with enough studying, one could accomplish everything.

Even restore their family's yangban honor.

Kyung-sook's mother prayed every day. Once, she went up to the mountains and came back scratched and black-and-blue, with leaves and twigs caught in her hair. She mumbled that she had become possessed by a spirit while praying. Her husband quickly shushed her and brought her inside the house.

The spirit had told Kyung-sook's mother to keep Kyung-sook from eating slippery things, especially seaweed soup, lest her mind "slip" on the exam, and every morning, a dish of the day's first pure water from the well needed to be placed outside the door to remind the gods to make Kyung-sook's mind similarly lucid.

On the testing day, Kyung-sook's mother had waited outside the school all day, counting out prayers on her Buddhist rosary with one hand, pressing pieces of taffy onto the bars of the school gate with the other.

"I went to the market and bought the best kind of *yut* they had to entice the benevolent spirits," she recounted proudly to the neighbors.

Other mothers affixed pieces of taffy on the gate, too, to help the answers "stick" in their children's heads. But Kyung-sook's mother was extra-vigilant and made sure that a piece of hers was always on top of everyone else's.

The name Bae Kyung-sook came into view.

Her mother went home and immediately prepared a thanksgiving offering to the Grandfather Spirit and to a special spirit she called The Lonely Saint.

"It is all arranged: we will be sending you to Seoul," Kyung-sook's father said.

"Yes, to live with your imo," her mother confirmed. "Imo has agreed to take you in. Now, don't let her be filling your head with her absurd notions about Christo. Your job is to study as hard as you can so you can return as soon as possible and get married."

Married!

"Of course," her mother said, noting Kyung-sook's puzzled look. "We need to marry you off. Having 'college graduate' on your side will put you in an entirely different class with the matchmaker, as it should, considering our lineage."

Kyung-sook couldn't question her elders, but she didn't understand. Why bother to go to college when in the end it would all be the same again? The former beggar boy at Seoul National University would probably become an important judge, a member of Parliament. But what would happen to her—become someone's wife and mother, no different from the most illiterate woman in the village? Why be shown all the wonders that lay beyond the fields of rice only to have to return as a country wife? It would be like showing a hungry child a sweet, then giving her a bowl of stones.

I will find a way, Kyung-sook decided. I *will* become a famous musician—so famous that people will beg me to perform in front of important dignitaries, maybe even abroad. So famous that I will be able to support my parents in their old age.

The day Kyung-sook left, meager belongings stuffed in her travel bag, she walked stiffly and slowly.

Ah, my daughter is sad to leave her home village, Kyung-sook's mother thought. It was just like in the sad song, "Arirang": . . . *before you walk ten li away from me, your foot will ache . . .*

Kyung-sook bowed deeply to her parents before she boarded the train. In her bag were some clothes, a few new pairs of underwear, money for tuition and books.

Kyung-sook sat in her seat on the train, looked out the window at her parents, who waited, still as statues, as the train began to pull away.

They kept waiting, waiting, growing smaller and smaller until they were just two small shapes in the past.

Kyung-sook let her shoulders slouch a bit. From under her skirt she pulled out the flute and sighed.

SARAH
Seoul
1993

The phone lines from Korea to America run from continent to continent. Through all those miles of dark ocean—how? Did a plane fly its many hours, unspooling gossamer filament as it went? Did people have to work underwater, inch by laborious inch, in diving suits and anonymous masks? The cables certainly can't be buried—the ocean would be much too deep in places for that. So does it just hang, a clothesline in Atlantis, draped with its seaweed laundry?

I considered this as I stood in front of the phone, contemplating how a phone call needed to be made. There were pay phones all over the Residence, but the lobby had a special one where you could just press the button of your carrier, AT&T, Sprint, MCI, and you would be connected to an international operator who would answer the phone in good old American English, *hello?*

A transpacific call to Minnesota needed to be made.

All this time, there had been a reason. Some small piece of my brain had scavenged this truth, doggedly preserved it, perhaps sent it wraithlike into my subconscious: your Korean mother is still on this earth.

That's why for all those years I had refused, on pain of death, to say I-love-you to anyone, least of all Christine and Ken. It had been diagnosed as abnormal, a sickness, a "bonding disorder," "attachment disorder," by *their* hired guns: psychiatrists, psychologists, social workers. Normal kids tell their parents they love them, they said. My failure to meant there was something wrong with *me*.

No, the fault lay within the system.

No divine destiny, no master plan. Not even a heavenly homicide to explain things. Only a conspiracy of adults bending my hapless life into a mold of their own pleasing.

What right does anyone have to do this?

Now that I know the truth, I must tell them, Christine and Ken, have them know that I know. Catch them flat-footed, and see what their pathetic excuses are.

The air had grown uncomfortably warm in the booth, there was a line, three people long, the first person tapping her foot impatiently.

I pushed open the folding doors and stepped out, gasping, as the other girl stepped in. She didn't shut the door, probably to clear the funky air. As I walked away I heard her tell the operator the number, and seconds later, she said, "Hello, Mommy, *Umma? Na ya,*" in a voice that broke my heart.

I didn't know why I hadn't thought of this earlier: I would find *her* first. When I called Ken and Christine, I would push the receiver toward her, urge her to speak.

It would take them a moment to figure this out.

We can't understand a thing this woman is saying, Christine would complain. *She must be speaking in Korean.*

Korean, yes. Speaking. Alive.

That's my mother, I would tell them. *I found my mother here in Korea. A living ghost.*

SARAH
Seoul
1993

"Don't forget, this afternoon you start your elective classes," Choi *Sunsengnim* reminded us.

"Sarah-*ssi*," she said to me. "Please see me after class."

I walked out with Doug, then remembered. I sent him on to the Rainbow, went back into the school. Choi *Sunsengnim* was sitting at her desk in front of a styrofoam takeout container of *kimbap*—American cheese, SPAM, Korean pickles, and rice wrapped into seaweed rolls that she was poking with a toothpick. She was going to teach the advanced newspaper-reading class in the afternoon.

"*Sunsengnim?*" I said.

She tucked a half-chewed bolus of *kimbap* into her cheek when she saw me.

"There will be no pronunciation class," she told me.

"No class?" I said, slightly relieved.

"There are not enough students who have an interest. You should choose between tae kwon do, ceramics, and traditional music."

I sighed. I didn't have any particular interest in any of these. All I knew was that Bernie Lee was taking tae kwon do, so I told *Sunsengnim* I'd take music.

"I think you will learn a lot," she said, and she instructed me to show up at the rec room of the Residence at one o'clock.

"However," she went on. "I have regrets that there aren't enough students for the *parum* class."

"*Neigh*," I agreed. Choi *Sunsengnim* sighed.

KYUNG-SOOK
Seoul
1972

Arriving at her imo's, Kyung-sook realized that if you wanted to live in Seoul, you had to learn how to make yourself small. The city was all buildings and people and roads packed together, especially in this rundown section of the city by the old Japanese neighborhood. Imo lived in the room in the back of her store, Arirang. In this one room sat a butane burner, a one-person rice table, bedding folded in the corner. A single pot and a stirring spoon hung from nails on the wall. Imo owned only two pants-and-blouse outfits, one she was wearing, the other soaking in a bucket, waiting to be washed.

What took up the most room was another low table on which sat a picture of a bearded whiteman with long yellow hair—Yesu Christo—and a string of magic Christo beads that Imo would stroke long into the night, her body swaying, rocking, sometimes crying as she did so.

During the day, Imo sat on a worn cushion behind the store's small counter, reading her red-covered Christo book, the gilt long worn off by her faithful fingers. At night, she ate the barest meal of rice and kimchi behind the rice-paper door—but she was ever willing to slide it open and tend to anyone who came in saying, "Anybody here?" A few cents gained from some gum or soap powder would mean a few more cents for the church's coffer, no matter what it meant to Kyung-sook's sleep.

As Kyung-sook's mother had predicted, Imo immediately nagged Kyung-sook to abandon Korean gods and follow Christo. An unusually bright look passed through Imo's face as she explained how this man Christo was a king, so powerful that even after he was executed, he came back to life and was waiting for his followers in Heaven.

Kyung-sook wondered why the white people would want to kill their god in the first place, as she fought drowsiness to listen to Imo. Finally, a customer banged on the door. While Imo tended to him, Kyung-sook snuggled deeper into the bedcovers hoping for some sleep until the next interruption.

SARAH
Seoul
1993

"I thought Choi *Sunseng* wanted you to take pronunciation," Jeannie said when she saw me enter the rec room. I noted how she'd cheekily left off the honorific "nim" in *Sunsengnim*.

"She did. But the class was cancelled—lack of interest."

A tall and lanky woman walked into the room.

"Hello, class," she said in a barely accented English. Her name was Tae *Sunsengnim*, our music teacher.

"I'm a graduate student here at Chosun," she said. "I went to the conservatory at Oberlin College for violin, but then I decided I wanted to study Korean folk music instead."

She unzipped some nylon bags and took out an hourglass-shaped drum, a tom-tom-shaped drum, a mini-gong the size of a saucepan lid, and a wooden flute.

"This is the *changgo*," she said, holding up the hourglass-shaped drum. "It's a staple for farmers' music and *p'ansori*.

"This is the *puk*, the barrel drum, two striking surfaces. You can hold it like this, or strap it on.

"This gong is the *kaenguri*. The *kaenguri* player sets the rhythm for the others."

Last, she held up the flute.

"This is a *taegum*, the Korean transverse flute. Six finger holes, a membrane hole for the vibrato, the seventh hole just for show."

"Why is that hole there if don't you use it?" someone asked.

"Ceremonial value, for Ch'ilsong, the Seven-Star Goddess," Tae *Sunsengnim* said, as if she were a bored docent in a museum.

She spent the rest of the time scribbling music on the blackboard and teaching us rhythm patterns that we tapped out, *ta-ta-ta-tta-tta-tta,* with pencils. I knew nothing about notes or bars or measures or rests, while all the other students seemed to be mini Yo-Yo Mas. So intent on following the music, at least, that they seemed not to notice, or care, how lost I was.

SARAH
Seoul
1993

The communal phone in the hall rang, early in the morning.

The sound of flip-flops making a slap-squish slap-squish sound on the floor.

Jeannie's voice floated down the hall, *yobosayo?* When she spoke Korean, her voice turned soft, lilting, so *feminine* that she suddenly became a courtesan in a long-ago Korean kingdom, not the girl who had screeched expletives at Bernie.

In Korea, everything was changeable in the blink of an eye.

A knock.

"Sarah? It's the Stamp *ajuhshi* downstairs. He said there's an international call for you."

"For me? International?"

The Stamp *ajuhshi* handed me the receiver of the phone at the watchman's station. It was heavy, like a dumbbell, and smelled of hair oil.

"Hello?"

"Sarah, is that you? The connection sounds so clear!"

Christine.

"Yes, it's me."

"You know, Daddy and I have been trying to call you forever, but the person who answers the phone doesn't speak any English. We haven't known what to do for weeks!

"So this time, I just kept saying, 'Sarah Thorson, U.S.A., Sarah Thorson, U.S.A.,' and I guess we got through."

"Is Ken there, too?"

"No, your father's working late at the office. So are you okay, how is everything?"

"Everything's fine. It's early morning here."

"Are you liking the program? Learning a lot?"

"Yes," I lied.

"Are your accommodations okay? Are you finding things to eat? Do you need me to send you any more snacks?"

"Everything's fine," I said. "In fact, food here is cheaper than in the States—a chunwon can buy you ramen, a whole tin of *mok kehndi*."

"A what can do what?"

"Oh, a dollar. For a tin of candy."

"We've been so worried about you, sweetie. We didn't even know if you'd gotten there okay."

"I meant to call. It's just hard to figure out the system."

"You could write."

"I could."

"Are you okay, sweetie?"

No, I was going to say. I'm not okay.

"My Korean birth parents—" I said, half statement, half question. I thought I heard her suck in her breath. This wasn't the right time to let it slip, I had to hold back. But the questions still came.

"How did they die again, my Korean mother and father?"

"Sarah, are you okay? You're starting to worry me."

"How did they die again?"

"Honey, you know it was in a car accident."

"How did you find that out?"

"Oh, I don't know. I think it was in your file."

"So if it was in the file, did they have the names of my biological parents, or any relatives?"

Pause.

"I don't think so. When a child is given up for adoption in Korea, parents—even dead ones—relinquish all rights. So they don't keep a record of these things."

"Could I see a copy of the file?"

"Sarah, I just wanted to call to see how you're doing over there, not get the third degree. I'll look for your paperwork—but I'm not sure we still have it."

"This call must be costing a fortune."

"It's okay. I love hearing your voice. Are you sure there's nothing else I can send?"

"No, I'm fine."

"Well, I miss you."

"Say hi to Ken and Amanda."

"Daddy misses you, too. And Amanda."

Silence.

"Sarah, I love you."

An "awk!" in the background. Hubert the macaw must be on Christine's shoulder. His feathers would be glinting red like a new paint job on a sports car. I pictured his beak, two cashews coming together, gently nipping Christine's ear.

"Sarah? Sweetie?"

The Stamp *ajuhshi,* leaning back into his flimsy chair, staring dreamily at a package plastered with about twenty "LOVE" stamps, jerked his head up at the sound of the receiver crashing down on the battered body of the black phone.

I would later blame the cutoff on a bad connection.

KYUNG-SOOK
Seoul
1972

Maybe none of that tragedy would have happened if she had never left school. But Kyung-sook couldn't ever know for sure. In life, it was impossible to spin out all the possibilities.

She thought of the case of Pumpkin Grandmother. Her parents had been very poor, so they had sent her as a child to a house in River Circle Village. She went as a minmyunuri, a future daughter-in-law who would grow up in the household as a servant. Pumpkin Grandmother missed her family terribly and the house's owners worked her to the bone and made her sleep in the stable with the animals. But the worst indignity was to come years later: being married to the youngest son, the one with the gaping cleft palate and an even uglier temper. The first night after her hair was put up in a married-woman's knot, he filled up on wine and tore off her clothes—she was only thirteen.

After he blacked out from the cheap rice-alcohol drink, she jerked her clothes back on and fled. She had no bribe for the ferryman, but the man said he would take her across the river for free.

But it turned out the man was also an agent for the Japanese, one who earned a bounty for each young girl he kidnapped. Instead of ferrying her across the river, he took her to the local police station, where she was beaten senseless, thrown into a truck, and shipped to Manchuria where she was raped night and day by the barbaric Japanese soldiers. After the Japanese lost the war, they abandoned the "comfort station," and she had to make the slow, agonizing journey back to Korea on foot.

"If only I had stayed that night with my husband, as bad as he was," she sighed to anyone who would listen. "I probably would have had many children to comfort me in my old age."

Now she was an old woman with a useless arm from being broken so many times. At the bathhouse, one could see poxlike burn scars covering her back. Too ashamed to return to her own village, she had settled in Enduring Pine Village, where, without family to help her, she eked out her living by selling the pumpkins that grew on the roof of her small hovel.

Kyung-sook wondered what other course her own life might have taken had she not left school—would she have become a teacher in the village? But she had been bored by the classes. And her professors were aloof, her classmates snippy girls from Seoul who spent hours in beauty salons getting their hair permed and marcelled, the acrid smell of their wormlike hair sickening her.

Kyung-sook had wanted to talk about music, about her dreams of playing a san-jo in front of hundreds of attentive people. But no, these girls, intent on achieving the newest "beehive" hairstyle and little else, snubbed Kyung-sook, especially once they heard her country accent. One senior girl whose father was an important government official claimed that she could smell manure on Kyung-sook, and she called out "Hey pigshit!" whenever she saw Kyung-sook coming.

What could she do, then, except leave?

SARAH
Seoul
1993

The flute was coming into my hands.

We had been divided into four groups. Our group: another girl named Jeannie, a guy named Kevin.

Up close I saw the instrument was made of bamboo, its joints swollen and awkward, like an old person's arthritic fingers. Tae *Sunsengnim* had randomly handed the instrument to me, but the Other Jeannie reached past my open hands and grabbed it.

"This isn't like any flute *I've* ever played," she declared, after blowing out a flat *whoooooo* of a dysenteric owl.

Around us, *whump-whump*s of the drums, brittle *chang-chang-chang*s of the gong: crazed, shrill noises of some kind of orchestra in hell.

Tae *Sunsengnim* whistled with two fingers, piercing through the cacophony.

"We can't all play the instruments at once." She walked to the group with the hourglass drum.

"We'll try the *changgo* first."

She finally got to us.

"I'm going to play a *san-jo,* a solo piece in the improvisational style," she said, in her bored docent voice.

She pursed her lips and blew.

My scalp prickled. It was as if some physical presence had wrenched me off the floor, sending me floating toward this odd music, almost atonal yet unsettlingly beautiful. The notes dug straight for the marrow of my bones.

Tae *Sunsengnim* rolled the flute a degree away from her mouth, put more of her fingers on the holes, and the notes climbed higher, higher.

I thought my heart was going to burst.

The tiny bones in my ear were going to shatter into splinters.

She continued up the unorthodox scale until the notes teetered maddeningly on the edge of disappearing, like the exquisite urge to sneeze.

"Ugh, that sounds like the beginning of a kung fu movie," the Other

Jeannie commented. When Tae *Sunsengnim* handed the flute back to her, she passed it off to Kevin.

"What's this instrument called again?" I asked.

"*Taegum*," Tae *Sunsengnim* said. "Don't just sit there," she told Kevin, pushing his fingers onto the holes.

He blew, emanating a muffled, diluted whine. He whoofed again, and again. The flute began tipping to and fro as if he were playing on a pitching ship. Tae *Sunsengnim* made a face when he returned the instrument, an elastic cord of spittle stretching out between them.

She wiped the mouthpiece and handed it to me.

"Your turn."

The bamboo was thick, heavy-looking, but when I put the mouthpiece to my mouth, my arms felt like they were going to fly away with the *taegum*.

"Rest it on your left shoulder." Tae *Sunsengnim* roughly pushed on my shoulder to form a vise. "Reach around with your arms and cover the holes with your fingers."

My fingers, nail beds flat as spades, fit perfectly on the holes. Tae *Sunsengnim* nodded approvingly when she saw this.

"So remember, it's not a *ttu-ttu* blow like for a Western flute," Tae *Sunsengnim* said, then added with disgust, "that's spitting. For the *taegum* you make your breath a breeze that flows through the instrument. You manipulate this breeze with your fingers."

The breeze of my breath flowed through the instrument—then out of it, making nary a sound.

"Keep going," she said. "Keep a good, strong flow."

I blew. And blew and blew and blew. The air continued to flow out tracelessly, the same disconcerting feeling when you first learn to snorkel: you expect to feel the resistance of the water as you exhale, but there is none, so you try again, harder, harder, until you hyperventilate, the air in your lungs scrabbling for traction.

I started to feel dizzy, as if I were breathing nitrous oxide through this wooden tube. No sound. In desperation, I even resorted to *ttu-ttu* spitting. That did nothing, except make the mouthpiece wet and slimy.

Tae *Sunsengnim* grabbed the flute away from me.

"Maybe you'll do better with the gong," she said.

SARAH
Seoul
1993

Hallo Miss Sarah,

I hope you are passing time well. What's shaking? I am sorry I do not have my dictionery with me right now so I will create many mistakes. I hope you will forgive.

I like Camp Ozark and my soldiers friends. We have started joint exersizes. This is first time I meet the blacks. One guy here wears this net on his hair when he sleeps at night. He is a funny guy, always making jokes.

But American guys are not always liking about meeting Korean. Some of them like tae kwon do, but most are not too interested in Korea and of course none of them can speak any Korean like you can. Not even anyonghaseo. The American guys, they are not so joyful toward fraternizing with Korean, so I am not practicing my English as much as I liked, not even as much as when I used to meet with you.

I also have a question for my English. Some guys will be using this word, fagot. My dictionary says it is a word meaning 'bundle of sticks.' When I ask the American commander, he (she?) says she (he?) is not telling me what this word is going to mean. Is this something of American slang? Please explain when you write me the next letter.

I hope your Korean studying is going well and that you are passing your time enjoyably.

Very often, I keep you in mind.

Yours Truly,

Pvt. Jun-Ho Kim

Postscript: American guys here call me "Jim." You can call me that, too, if you like.

"How come I never see you on Sundays?" I asked Doug, over noodles at the Rainbow. "Does a little chauffeur guy come whisk you away, like he does for Bernie Lee?"

Doug shook his head.

"I chase ghosts."

"Ghosts?"

"Yeah, ghosts. Not *kwisin,* those flour-faced Korean ghosts, but ghosts of the living."

"Where do you find them?"

"Different places. But mostly the Yongsan Eighth Army Base. I have a friend I visit, and he lets me go ghost hunting."

"Was that where your father and mother were?"

"No, they were at Libertytown, north of here."

"So why Yongsan?"

He shrugged. "It smells like Libertytown. Reminds me of my kidhood."

"And what smells exactly?"

He shrugged again. "Fried food. I don't know. It just smells like a place."

Doug was slipping away again. Sometimes when we talked, I'd inadvertently say a word, make a joke about some experience we'd shared, and then all of a sudden, his face would blank out, and I could see him descending into some kind of toxic hell of memory. There was no telling what would trigger these moods, or what could be done to dispel them.

"Tell me about your kidhood—some good memories."

"Let me see." He gobbled a small mountain of kimchi.

"I went bowling once, with my dad. They had a bowling alley in Libertytown. I thought it was so funny to be wearing shoes on those pristine wooden floors—*and* someone else's shoes."

"Tell me more."

"Oh, I don't know. Dad would bring Mom stuff from the PX. American pancake makeup, some brand the Korean ladies were all nuts about—Cody? Nylon stockings, peanut butter, Marlboros—she loved to smoke—Johnny Walker Red. She used the whiskey as a bribe for me to get into a local school. If being mixed-blood wasn't bad enough, Hank technically wasn't my dad then."

I held my breath, waiting to see if he'd offer me any more of himself, his history. "For a few years, it was pretty good. They loved each other. Dad was this Polish-Irish punk who'd grown up in a tough black neighborhood in Queens. He decided to change his last name—Osciewicz to Henderson—and go into the army before he ended up in jail. And you know what my mom was. Not exactly Romeo and Juliet, those two. More like Bonnie and Clyde. She also married him because she knew we needed a ticket out of there, she didn't want me growing up in Libertytown. But being back here in Korea, it's making me remember, one by one, all the terrible things he did to her. I think if I ran into that bastard on the street, I'd kill him."

Doug looked out the window, even though the rice paper was blocking his view.

"Let's go there some time," I said suddenly. "To Libertytown."

Doug's hand, the one holding a cigarette, jerked. He looked startled.

"I don't know if we could get in," he said.

"Figure out a way."

He sighed. "You know, I've actually been thinking that I want to go back there. Just to see what's there, what's changed."

"So let's go."

"Why," he said, "do *you* want to go so badly? Are you thinking this is somehow going to help you with your own little identity search? If so, I doubt it. You're from a Seoul family. Your mother died in a car accident and with your *father*. Two decades ago, only upper-class people had cars in Korea. Going to the place where I grew up has got to be the farthest place to search for anything about *your* birth family."

How was I going to tell him that now, my mother could have been anyone?

"I just want to go," I shrugged. "I'm offering to keep you company, that's all."

"We'll see," he said, flipping his cigarette into his half-eaten bowl of noodles, where it extinguished with an extravagant hiss.

KYUNG-SOOK
Seoul
1972

The school refused to give her the tuition money back. Kyung-sook tried saying that her mother was sick and she needed the money for her hospital expenses, but the answer was still no.

Despite this setback, Kyung-sook decided she would still strike out on her own. There was no place for her to play her flute at Imo's. And Imo, between her harangues about Christo, would want to know what she had learned about pedagogy, and it was becoming harder and harder for Kyung-sook to make things up. That night, Kyung-sook bundled her things up when Imo was sleeping, and she set out, as usual, the next morning, as if going to school.

A job would be easy to come by for a hard worker such as herself, she thought, as she headed toward the city's center.

In the neighborhood by the Myung-Dong cathedral, she stopped in a Korean dress store that had a headless mannequin wearing a hanbok out front. She politely inquired about a job as a shop-girl. The owner shook her head.

She stopped next at a bookstore, the Chosun, named promisingly after one of the great old dynasties of Korea.

"I'm a hard worker," she told the owner, who was sitting amidst a pile of yellowed books, some with the covers torn off. A musty-pleasant smell, like sniffing in the corner of an antique chest, pervaded the entire place.

"I'm a college student and I know my han-mun Chinese characters well," she added. "I could help you with cataloging your titles."

The man looked at her with rheumy, mucus-beaded eyes.

"I'm sorry," he said. "I can't afford employees."

"I could work for very little."

"No one wants to read the classic texts anymore," he said, as if talking to a third person in the room. "You used to need to know a thousand han-mun characters just to read a newspaper decently. Now we have to carry those things—"

He gestured toward a stack of cheaply bound books by the door.

Goodbye, Weapons, it said in Korean, written by someone named Ehl-nest Hae-ming-wae.

"—and I can barely make my key money even carrying those. The newest Western translations are what people want to read."

Kyung-sook decided she wouldn't want to listen to the man complain all day, anyway. She liked books, but she could do almost anything.

Closer to the City Hall area, she came upon a row of Western dress shops.

She went into the one that said LIVE FASHION in English. A few store signs here and there appeared this way, so she was glad she had learned her English letters in school.

The first thing she noticed when she entered was how clean and un-cluttered the store was, not like a Korean dress shop. There were only a few dresses displayed, not packed as many to a rack as possible. There was soft Western music playing in the background, a tune so engaging, it would make you want to hum.

"What do you want?"

Kyung-sook was shocked at the saleswoman's tone, her use of the in-timate style of Korean.

"Well—," Kyung-sook began.

"You obviously can't afford these clothes." The woman set her jaw. "Please leave—we can't abide loiterers. And man-chi-jima!—don't touch!"

Kyung-sook tried to shake off her disappointment as she left, walking past all the dress shops. Their hard, glass façades all seemed to shout at her, "Don't touch!"

She wandered down an alley. It was a thread-alley, winding around and around until she found herself in an older section, not unlike Imo's neighborhood, where the houses had cracked roof tiles and red chili pep-pers or squash slices drying on straw mats right out in the dusty street.

After Kyung-sook had passed the same street a few times, a well-dressed woman who had been watching her wander about, suddenly stepped from the shadows of a doorway and approached her, asking her if she was looking for work.

"How did you know?" Kyung-sook asked, astonished.

She smiled. "I must be a fortuneteller, yes?" She said she was out seeking likely candidates for a position in her coffee shop as a "coffee lady."

Kyung-sook was intrigued. This woman in her vivid green-and-pink hanbok seemed to be rising like a phoenix out of this drab neighborhood. How difficult could work in a coffee shop be? She followed the woman down yet another thread-alley past Heavenly Real Estate and South Mountain Tailors, past a row of closed, gated homes, to the Spring Fragrance Coffee Shop. On the wooden door, a handlettered sign read "closed."

The coffee ladies worked for tips, the woman said, ushering Kyung-sook into the one-room shop. A few round tables crowded haphazardly in a corner, some with their legs pointing toward the ceiling. On the walls hung some old-time Korean paintings and gourd dippers; an electric gramophone sat in the corner.

The proprietress brushed by Kyung-sook to retrieve a pitcher that said "coffee." She poured some brownish liquid into a china cup that had a handle on one side, like an ear, and as she set the cup in front of Kyung-sook, she gave off a powerful, but pleasant scent, like flowers and ginger. Kyung-sook was excited: she had heard of coffee, but like most people in the village, had never had a chance to sample this exotic Western beverage.

The proprietress perched decorously on a stool, her shoulders forward, as well-bred ladies were taught to do.

"As I said, it's just tips, but most of the enterprising ladies I employ earn quite a nice living," she went on. And this was what most young women on their own in Seoul were looking to do, wasn't it?

Kyung-sook nodded eagerly.

All the job entailed was getting men to buy cups of the house's coffee. Each cup sold meant a few won for the coffee lady, but the real money came from the tips they received from their customers. Of course, if Kyung-sook was going to work there, the proprietress said, she might want to get a loan from her to go out and buy some jazzier clothes, and some makeup.

"You could start this very afternoon if you like," she offered. "I'll put your clothes and makeup on your tab."

Kyung-sook nodded vigorously again.

"But why," she wanted to know, "would the men pay tips for coffee?"

She was disappointed to find that the coffee tasted like brine-water, nothing special at all.

"Don't be coy," the woman said impatiently. "Do you think men come into these places to overpay for coffee that's mostly burnt barley? The smart regulars skip the coffee and just get their feel before they have to go back to work."

"Feel?" Kyung-sook ventured.

"Where in the world are you from?" The proprietress's face suddenly bent into an unbecoming sneer. "Hm, I should have known from your country-clod accent and awful clothes. This is a coffee shop, yes? Men come here to relax and have a nice conversation with a nice lady and feel her nice breasts, her titties, if you will. And no dating customers—we want steady customers, but not that steady."

Kyung-sook's mouth fell open, like a fish. She had never heard such language coming from the mouth of someone who spoke in such a respectable Seoul accent.

The woman was staring at her with cold eyes. Her lipstick looked as if she had spread red chili paste on her mouth.

"So do you want to start this afternoon, or not?"

Kyung-sook didn't know what to do. She had a strange urge to cry out, "Mother!" Without thinking, she grabbed her bundle and ran for the door, wondering why she hadn't noticed that although the shop was romantically named "Spring Fragrance," all the windows were completely covered in black paper and the entrance was hidden several paces off the thoroughfare.

"Hey, you owe me fifty won for that cup of coffee!" the woman roared, the intricate tasseled ornament on her silk jacket swinging wildly as she leaned out the doorway. "Come back here you devil-bitch! Thief!"

Kyung-sook ran and ran, veering up a different alley, then another, until she had run up the summit of a hill. There, she stopped, panting. Was anyone pursuing her?

She was in front of a decrepit dumpling shop in an alley that smelled of old grease and bean curds. In the hills a short distance beyond lay a shantytown. Amidst the mud shacks were a few opulent creations made of cardboard and flattened soda cans that glittered in the light, the cans no doubt scavenged somehow from the Yankee army base.

NOODLES + DUMPLINGS said the crudely handpainted sign propped outside the door of the shop.

A toadlike woman emerged and dumped some gray water into the dirt. Kyung-sook glanced over her shoulder, quietly asked the woman if, perhaps, they needed a serving girl.

The toadlike woman's answer surprised her.

"C'mon in—our regular girl ran off with some fuckin' bastard hoodlum this very morning." The woman identified herself as both the cook and the owner of the establishment. In her accent, a North Korean dialect was still perceptible.

Kyung-sook followed the woman into the restaurant, throwing one last, worried glance over her shoulder. She certainly hoped the coffee-shop owner had given up on her pursuit.

"Hm, but you sure you can do this work?" The cook-owner stopped to scrutinize Kyung-sook, reached out a water-wrinkled finger and poked her, as if testing a fish for freshness. "You look a little frail, your hands look like the hands of a schoolgirl."

"I am a girl from the country," she reassured her, exaggerating her country accent a little. "I have spent many seasons planting rice." Her hands had stayed soft and white because for the last year she had mostly studied while her mother's hands were exposed to the sun and wind and water.

"I admit, I went to high school," she told the cook-owner. "But I am also a hard worker."

"All right, Professor. We'll soon enough see what strength you've got in those limbs."

She motioned for Kyung-sook to follow her into the back room where she returned to a basin of uncooked rice on the floor. She squatted next to the bowl, a rosary of farts trailing out from between her thick thighs. Kyung-sook immediately bent down and helped her clean the rice, picking out pebbles, bits of straw, small black rice bugs, a few mouse droppings. The cook-owner poured a pitcher of water into the rice, swirling it around with her hand. The water became cloudy as the powdery talc rose to the top, her hand disappeared into the grains of rice the way Kyung-sook's feet used to disappear into the mud of the rice field.

When the water finally ran clear, the cook-owner rose and dumped the whole load of wet rice into the iron cooker.

Then she handed Kyung-sook a tray filled with heavy stone bowls. "Get ready to sling some fuckin' dumpling soup!" she yelled, her hot breath filling the air like boiling soy sauce.

By the end of the day, Kyung-sook couldn't even lift her hand to scratch her nose, her arms hung like weights. As the cook-owner banged the restaurant's sliding doors shut, Kyung-sook approached her and shyly asked her if she might have a place to stay, perhaps in the back of the restaurant.

"Yah! This is a restaurant, not a damned hotel," the cook-owner grumbled.

"I don't have anywhere to go," Kyung-sook's voice was barely a whisper.

The cook-owner sucked air.

"Great, I get rid of one headache and I promptly get another, curse you fuckin' gods and ancestors!"

"I'll have to sleep out on the street if you don't let me stay here in the restaurant."

"The police will arrest you if they find you on the street after curfew, especially these days—don't you know anything?" the cook-owner said irritably. She glanced at Kyung-sook's fingers, bruised from banging on the serving trays.

"Please," Kyung-sook said. "I beg you . . . Teacher's Wife."

From the look on the cook-owner's face, Kyung-sook knew that no one had ever addressed her by such a respectful title before.

"Well, lessee. On the other hand, I suppose if you slept in the storage space, you might drive the mice out."

In the closet in the very back of the restaurant, there was barely enough room to unroll a sleeping mat amid the bags of rice and flour and rock salt, but this was exactly the kind of thing Kyung-sook was hoping to find. It was quiet, and she could play her flute as much as she wanted. During the day she could palm a few dumplings or fingerfuls of rice when the cook-owner wasn't looking, perhaps take a few spoonfuls of anchovy broth off the tops of customers' soups, and thus save up for her career.

That night as she lay down in her new space, Kyung-sook found a needle of regret working its way into her heart. She was troubled by thoughts of her imo: she had spent weeks eating her imo's paltry food, sharing her threadbare bedding, and she had left her without a word of thanks, only a note saying she had returned to the village.

Perhaps if she had gotten to know her imo better, she could have explained to her about her plans and dreams, her hopes of becoming a famous musician. Maybe Imo, who had herself gone away from the village in order to pursue her destiny, would understand. Kyung-sook fingered her flute. She loved the way the wood warmed under her hand, until the instrument was like a living thing unto itself. She consoled herself with the thought she would indeed see her imo again someday. But right now, she had her year laid out before her, like empty bowls waiting to be filled.

SARAH
Seoul
1993

Doug said, "It's going to be a bit tricky, getting in there."

"In where?"

"Libertytown."

I looked to his face to see if an invitation was there. His eyes had that curious, blank look like those abandoned houses with boarded-up windows.

"My friend at Yongsan said he could help."

"Clever idea, going to him. Someone already in the army." I kept my voice noncommittal.

"He gave me this—and some other stuff." Doug showed me a military ID. His friend had blond hair. And glasses.

"At least your friend isn't black."

"It'll be dark when we go, also."

"We?"

"Don't you want to come?"

"Of course!" I found myself grinning, like I'd passed some kind of test.

"The best cover for you would be pretending to be my prostitute girl-friend."

"You're not serious," I said.

You probably would have become a prostitute if you'd stayed there.

"You don't have to go." The boarded-up look again.

I just needed to ignore the irony, I decided, treat this more like Halloween. Doug was right, of course: a Korean girl from a suburb of Minneapolis was going to be a lot harder to explain than a Korean ho from a nearby village. From my wardrobe I fetched a skirt whose waistband I could hike up, plus a CALVIN KLEEN tank top, purchased from a street vendor.

"After lunch," Doug said. "We'll go to the bus station together."

❈ ❈ ❈

The bus seats were capped with white covers, like dentist's chairs. People continued to clamber on and on. The combined exhalations of the passengers swirled a reek of digested kimchi into the air. A stumpy *ajuhma* boarded the bus carrying a bunch of dried squid impaled on a wooden pole. The squid were football-sized, squashed flat enough to fold and mail. A dozen hands extended chunwons, and soon there was a stuffy, fishy smell added to everything else, even as the loop of a recording told us in a breathy woman's voice (as Doug translated):

For the comfort of your fellow passengers, please do not bring strong-smelling food on the bus.

The bus lumbered into the street like a large animal waking. I pressed my face against the window. The Seoul bus station, not unlike the bus station in Minneapolis, was situated in a not-so-nice neighborhood. My eyes took in the buckling tin-roofed shops, people squatting in the shade of the few urban trees, slices of zucchini drying on rooftops, thousand-year-old men with wispy snow-capped beards spitting into the gutter.

This was the real Korea, devoid of white people, or even Korean Americans like Bernie Lee. She could very well be out here, I thought, in front of my face.

After unsnarling ourselves from Seoul traffic, almost like a dream, we were on the highway, open spaces rolling out before us. A few tiny shacks dotted the landscape, as if planted there by the hands of giants, but it was mostly rice fields. The fortresslike mountains around Seoul gave way to gentle hills, rock peaks softening to the shape of a woman lying on her side.

I turned from the window to say something to Doug, but he was asleep, oblivious to the roar of the bus's engine, the gay chatter in the seats around us. He seemed to be lost in that magical deep-sleep of childhood.

I rooted in the 7-Eleven bag, pulled out a CRUNKY chocolate bar, a cartoon of a smiling, big-lipped African with a bone through his nose on the wrapper. I wished I could nap, too, but I've never been able to. I'm not a good sleeper at night, either.

Back when I shared a room with Amanda, I always marveled at her ability to drop off to sleep the minute her head hit the pillow.

On TV commercials for Nytol, the wild-eyed insomniac was always a man or a lady, never a child. Children always slept peacefully, effortlessly. Some nights I managed to push myself down into a shallow dozing, barely skimming the tops of my dreams. But what I yearned for was to tumble into a thicket of logy black sleep, the kind where Amanda would sigh and giggle and snore and fart with abandon.

So while Amanda snuggled safe and secure at the foot of the Thorson family tree, I stared into the blackness for hours until I swear I could see atom particles bouncing to and fro.

Why am I I? I wondered, over and over, a fist of unease knuckling my stomach.

Until the morning light, when it was time to get up, wash, don the Fabulous Sarah Thorson face. At least during the day I had a role to play, and I knew the lines. At night, it was all chaos. Especially after I turned thirteen and started having The Dream, the one with her in it. After that, I wanted to sleep, and sleep deep, more than ever. This desperation, of course, kept me awake, a water-stiffened rope that kept me firmly moored on this side of consciousness.

We were approaching a town. Motorcyclists clad in plastic slippers passed us on the shoulder, stacks of toilet paper rolls on the back of their bikes towering over them like cresting waves. Power Bongo pickups, the size of riding lawn mowers, transported even more magnificent loads of cabbages, TVs, bed frames, and cardboard boxes held to the back by faith and straining black bungee cords.

I was wondering if I was going to have to wake Doug, but his eyes snapped open when the driver called our stop. He leaned over me and gazed out the window at the same scenes, in the dying light. If we stayed on the bus, we could go all the way up to the mountain seacoast resort of Sorak-san, which, by some whim of geography, was situated slightly north of the thirty-eighth parallel and therefore technically in North Korea. I guess that most of the Diamond Mountains, a chain of peaks that were sacred to Koreans, were in North Korea, but this tail end had somehow been left in the South, and the South Koreans had developed it as a national park. Jeannie had been there and described it as incredibly touristy—souvenir and ice-cream vendors no matter how high up the mountain you climbed—but also vaguely ominous, with heavily armed soldiers patrolling the fenced-off beaches, the tall machine-gun-equipped towers from which grim soldiers watched the expanse of sea for telltale traces of an encroaching North Korean submarine.

As we made our way up the aisle, there was an anonymous mutter of contempt that seemed to be aimed at Doug, his green uniform, his father's face. But he didn't respond.

In the bus station's bathroom, I exchanged my sneakers for heels, rolled the waistband of my skirt until I felt it swishing my thighs. Then I troweled on some makeup, although in the dim one-bulb light, I wasn't sure how accurate my painting was.

Doug donned some horn-rimmed glasses that made him look like Clark Kent. He pulled the cap tight over his hair.

"Nice," he said, looking at me, his eyes lingering a moment longer than usual. He stashed our civilian stuff behind a bench.

A lone taxi idled outside the bus station. The driver, back slumped against the door as if the car were a giant Barcalounger, fuzzily paged through a newspaper as high-pitched Korean folk music squeed through his radio. Doug leaned in the window, told him in English we were going to Libertytown.

The man turned to look at us. His gaze stopped on my bare, knobby knees. He spat, then gave us the universal "hop in" sign, a backward nod of the head.

Five minutes later he dropped us off in front of a compound, stone fence topped with razor wire. He opened his palm for a twenty-dollar fare, shrugged about his broken meter. The arch on the gate read WELCOME TO LIBERTYTOWN.

"Riberteeton," the driver cackled. He cracked open the door, as if to accompany us, but then I heard a faint trickling sound and realized he was peeing.

A Korean guy with an armband that said MP guarded the entrance. Doug saluted smartly and said some things about name and rank in plain English that somehow made him sound dumb.

The guard narrowed his eyes when he looked at me. I tried to smile back coyly. He barely glanced at Doug's I.D. and waved us on through.

As Suzy Bargirl, I tried not to gawk as we walked into the compound. Drunk GIs, red-white-and-blue faces, Nike T-shirts and Levi's jeans, stumbled in and out of neon-lit clubs with names like THE ALAMO, LAS VEGAS STYLE, HUBBA HUBBA, CHERRY'S. Farther inland, an electric sign rose above the low buildings, a familiar-looking red-pigtailed cartoon-girl's face aglow. Wendy's.

This was America, yet it wasn't. The gentle hills of the countryside weren't the same, the far-off smells of cooking fires made the place smell like Korea. Libertytown was a foreign version of America, a U.S.-land that they might have at an offshore amusement park.

"Which one's where your mother worked?" I wasn't supposed to speak English, but I couldn't help it.

Doug shook his head violently, didn't answer. He just tugged me along, a fish on a line. We headed down a dirt path, away from the lights, toward a row of corrugated tin houses.

I could see through their glassless windows: a bed, a mirror, maybe a dresser, and usually a canvas army-issue duffel. A few of the occupants were home. Under the light from bare bulbs, the women primped, skirts so short they made my thigh-high mini look like a muu-muu.

I began to imagine Doug's mother getting ready for work. The seducing followed by manipulating those pussy-whipped farmboys into raiding the PX for her so she could sell her goods on the black market for some extra cash. Doug, Du-sok, would be shooed away to play outside, or would cram himself into a far corner, shutting his ears to his mother's love cries.

Stop! I wanted to slap myself. I had no right to construct Doug's life out of whole cloth—as I did my own. I was the Korean princess, somehow abducted and sent out of the country by evil relatives. I was the treasured child of my mother, but she had died defending me from muggers. The car-accident story had never been enough, it was only a hurried, distracted mercy like the way they put stun guns to the heads of cows before they slaughter them. But now that I had kicked apart that flimsily constructed lie, what was underneath was much, much worse.

Doug looked at me. He reached over and gently touched my fingers, which had become numb and clenched around his arm. When I opened my fist, I felt better. We started walking back the way we'd come.

From the shadows between two lean-tos, a grubby little kid emerged. He was playing with a pink plastic sliding whistle. On closer inspection, I saw it was a tampon applicator. He put it down for a second to dig in his pocket. He held out a fistful of wilted Wrigley's Juicy Fruit.

"You wanna gum, sol-jah?" he said. Doug gave him a few coins, left the gum. The boy shrugged and resumed playing with his "whistle."

The streets were even more packed now: burly guys with no necks next to smooth-cheeked kids whose ears stuck out like dried apricots. Many had startlingly beautiful Korean women on their arms. When we passed another club called, not too subtly, AFRICA, I saw some Korean ladies who'd transformed their straight hair—somehow—into cottony Afros. Doug had told me that if a woman so much as accepted a single dance with a black soldier, that was it for her. She would have to start working the black clubs because white soldiers would reject her.

Doug pointed to HUBBA HUBBA, whose lights pulsed suggestively. I decided I was done with this place. It was time to go back to Chosun University. But how could I let Doug know this without blowing my cover? He wasn't looking at me anyway, he was entering the club. I had no choice but to follow him.

Inside the hollowed-out building, a strange kind of pink lighting gave everyone a hideous, irradiated glow. On the dance floor, a few tease-haired Korean women were slowly gyrating with soldiers, more stood waiting at the bar.

Doug purchased two drinks, one he handed to me. I sipped it. It was warm, tasted like canned Delmonte orange juice.

The woman next to me was exchanging meaningful glances with a GI, whose jungly eyebrows I could see from across the room. The woman sported a huge white cardboard badge on which her picture, a number, and her name, Mi-Ja Choi, were clearly visible.

Doug had explained the badges to me one night, after a few shots of *soju* (lemon-flavored, an improvement on the usual acrid formaldehyde notes) that we'd bought from the 7-Eleven. The badges were part of some system worked out by both the Korean and American governments for controlling VD outbreaks, a potential threat to the strength of the U.S. Armed Forces. When Doug's mother had worked, VD-infested GIs had to rely on their memory of whom they had slept with, which usually resulted in a virtual crowd of women with the last name Kim being sent off to the "Monkey House," a shack halfway up a mountain near the base, with bars on the windows and steel U.S.-military-issue beds lined up in a row.

Jungle-brow approached the woman, his eyebrows even more magnificent up close. She giggled, tipping a little on her high heels. He put his hand on her buttock, squeezing it like a bicycle horn.

She giggled again.

"You buy me drink, hunh?" she tittered, a little unsteadily.

He leered one more time, then bought her a Delmonte orange juice. Before she had a chance to take her first sip, he kissed her. I could see his sluglike tongue working its way into her mouth. She didn't back away, but her face took on its own abandoned-house look. When he disengaged himself, she laughed and then took a swig of the juice.

Something dry and scratchy landed on my arm, like an insect. A slightly cross-eyed GI had clamped a hand on my upper arm and was smiling crookedly at me, as if he'd just lifted a rock and found a coin.

"Juicy girl?" he said. His thumb reached out and brushed against my breast. I was ashamed to feel my nipple harden and push against my flimsy bra.

"She's with me." Doug's voice was deep.

"What's wrong with me buyin' her a little juicy, punk?" he sneered. "I don't see no ring, so she's here for alla us."

Doug stood up to his full height. As he grew, I shrank against the bar.

"Leave her alone." His eyes went flat. "I'll kill you."

The man sneered again, but took a step back.

"She's ugly. Too tall, too. There's lots prettier here."

As the man pushed by me, he took another look at my chest. I hoped against hope that my nipple had smoothed itself.

"Hey, where's your badge?" he barked, over the music.

"Where's your badge?" he yelled again. "Bet you're the one been spreading the clap to everyone!"

Doug grabbed my arm. We headed for the exit, me tottering on my ridiculous heels. People were following us.

"Shit!" Doug said. "Oh shit, come on!"

We made it out the door, where I tore the shoes off, my bare feet hitting the dirt.

"MP! MP!" the guy was yelling. "Over here!"

Outside it had become even darker, the light from the neon signs and outdoor lights canceling out the stars. For a second, we weren't sure which way to go, but Doug's head turned toward the compound's gate, sure as a homing pigeon. No matter how long he'd been gone, the landscape of his childhood was branded into his brain.

We grabbed hands and ran.

KYUNG-SOOK
Seoul
1972

It had, of course, been many years that had come and gone like guests at a funeral, but Kyung-sook knew she would never forget the cook-owner. A short woman, rounded as a soybean-paste pot, who swayed her hips from side to side as she walked about the restaurant. She told Kyung-sook she had been left stranded in Seoul as a thirteen-year-old at the end of the Japanese colonial period.

"We had no idea what was going on after the war ended," she said. "The Russians came in, and they seemed to be a better sort than the Japs—gave us food and medicine, let us speak Korean. But just in case, I started making trips south to peddle some gold things—our family was quite wealthy and my daddy wisely had buried most of our gold so it wouldn't go to the Jap war effort. It was dangerous work, of course. Once, I ran into a Ruskie soldier. My guide, who had been paid handsomely to see me to the other side, ran away, that bastard. I heard shots *pow!-pow!-pow!* from the direction he'd gone, so I ran the other way, swam through a creek, and hid in the woods. At daybreak I crawled out, came upon some farm lady tending a plot and I said, 'I beg of you, in heaven's name, where am I?'

"She said, 'You're in the South, dear,' and that's all I needed to know, I was safe.

"One day, on my way to the border town where I normally crossed, the man next to me on the train said, 'I hope you don't think you're going north, child.'

"Of course, I had no idea who he was—he could have been a Commie spy, so I just kept my mouth shut.

"'I can tell you are,' the man went on. 'You don't even have a little bundle—traveling light, yeh? Well, take heed: the Reds have sealed the border. If you don't believe me, go see. You'll see wire fences and big guns waiting to shoot right at your heart.'

"And it was a good thing I did do that," the cook-owner said. "If I'd tried to cross that night, I'd've met my ancestors."

Kyung-sook listened politely as she stuffed some dumplings. They were advertised as "hand" dumplings, that is, with handmade skins, but only the most naive customer would believe that. Real dumplings, like the kind her mother made for the Lunar New Year, had skins that were thick and irregular and bore traces of her mother's fingers and the taste of her hand. These premade skins were thin and perfectly square, tasteless as pieces of origami paper.

"So from that day on, I was permanently cut off from my family. How it kills me not to have seen my beloved mother and father into their old age—and now I don't know whether to do the chesa rites for them, because I don't know if they're alive or dead, and it's all because of those fucking Commies and Americans who sliced our beloved country in two!"

Kyung-sook made a compassionate *tsk*ing noise, but Sunhee, the other serving girl, rolled her eyes behind the cook-owner's back.

The cook-owner went on to recount how on her own, she elbowed her way into the Great South Gate Market, first selling heads of pickling garlic, then her own soft tofu that she made at night, squeezing out the bag of curds with her huge hands.

"I came from an aristocratic family, but I'm no weakling—I could carry a whole day's supply of the tofu in a giant soup pot on top of my head," she bragged. "I just had to move my hips from side-to-side like this to keep it balanced. See, I still walk that way, I got so used to it."

"Yah, so aristocratic, our yangban boss," Sunhee sniped, when the cook-owner went into the storeroom for more rice. "The reason she waggles her ass like that is to try to catch the eye of Old Bachelor Choi. He's filthy rich, owns the Jade Moon real estate office, but he orders the cheapest noodle dish here every day. Watch the cook-owner, she'll make sure to pass his table beating her breast—'Aiiii-gu, my poor parents! Aiiiigu, my poor husband killed in the Korean War!' Don't buy it for a second. She has a northern accent, but you can hear some southern Cholla dialect slip into it from time to time. Her story's not what she says it is."

Kyung-sook only smiled as she spooned some more filling into the flour square that felt dusty in her hands. She dipped her little finger in egg yolk, then spread it on the skin's edges as if she were gluing an envelope. She pressed and crimped the edges together until she made a crescent moon.

No one knew her true story, either. That was the wonderful thing about being in the city—you could be who you wanted, you merely had to spin out some story, and no one cared. Today she was a serving girl in a dumpling house, a rotten place where, when the wind blew a certain way, the smell of sewage from the shantytown reached their noses. But tomorrow she would be a famous musician, asked to perform for the President. Who could say?

"Aigu!" yelled the cook-owner, from the kitchen. Had she burned her arm on the stovepot again? Found another mouse-mess next to the rice? She stood framed at the door to the kitchen, staring at the front of the restaurant.

A Westerner stood in the entrance.

They all blinked. And blinked again. They all knew there were Westerners in Seoul—but how could this one have found his way to this place, at the end of a maze of winding alleys, channels so narrow and twisty that two people with handcarts could not pass going in opposite directions?

And their restaurant was just one of a number of shacks, marked only by a small sign in Korean, NOODLES + DUMPLINGS, not even DUMPLING SPECIALIST or THE KING'S DUMPLINGS—the name the regulars jokingly gave their little dump.

This man, he was the first paek-in, the first whiteperson any of them had ever seen for real. Kyung-sook could barely stifle startled giggles upon seeing the man's nose—it was like the prow of a ship. His eyes were strangely round and pale, his skin so pinkish it reminded her of the stupid pale skin on a dog's belly.

The man had to duck to enter the restaurant. He was wearing a soft hat, and the bits of hair sticking out from under it was black, the color of cooking coal. He pointed to an empty table and made eating motions, as if he wanted to be served some kind of stew that he would eat with his hands.

The cook-owner threw up her hands and looked at the sky.

"Okay, you fucking gods and ancestors," she bellowed. "What kind of joke have you got in store for me today?"

No one else in the restaurant moved.

"Kyung-sook-ah, make that creature sit down," the cook-owner ordered. "A foreign bastard, he must be rich."

Kyung-sook took a step, but then her feet wouldn't budge.

The cook-owner eyed Kyung-sook for a second, then came over and slapped her on the rump, as if she were a recalcitrant horse or ox.

"You're the only one here who went to high school, Professor. You expect anyone else here can understand foreigner-speak?"

The cook-owner shoved her, propelling her like those little eggshell boats they used to sail on the river on Lord Buddha's birthday.

The man didn't seem to know any Korean; he barked a command in English and pointed to the water-dumplings that Old Bachelor Choi was masticating with his ill-fitting dentures that occasionally slipped out of his mouth.

The cook-owner noted this, and perhaps to celebrate the arrival of the first Westerner to her diner, added an extra three "king" dumplings onto the plate of water-dumplings. Old Bachelor Choi yelled for more of their free mussel soup. Kyung-sook fetched it for him. Then she served the foreigner.

Looking at his sumptuous plate, the foreigner barked again and shook his head.

Everyone was puzzled. Even Old Bachelor Choi, delicately fishing around in his soup with two fingers, stopped to consider the scene, his mouth puckery as a mended sock.

"What's he waiting for?" grumbled the cook-owner. "Is he one of those Christo-followers? I heard they have to say all this mumbo jumbo around their food to cleanse it before they eat."

The foreigner stared at Kyung-sook.

"Not mine, not mine." His barking had turned to yapping, and she still didn't understand him—his English didn't sound anything like the English she had learned in school. He was pointing at the three fat dumplings. "I didn't order these. No order. No pay."

When Kyung-sook looked at the king dumplings he was pointing to, they seemed to rise before her eyes. They levitated a few centimeters, switched places as if in fun, then settled back onto the plate. English words then rose to the surface of her brain like bubbles in a pond.

"Eat," she said. "Please. For you."

"What are these?" the man said, pointing to the dumplings suspiciously.

"Whang man-du," she replied. "King. Eat. Especial for you."

"Oh, ho," the man said, beginning to smile. He ignored the chopsticks and instead picked up his soupspoon and balanced one of the dumplings on it like a weight. "So I'm a king—" He took an enormous, sucking bite of the dumpling. "Okay."

"O-kay," she mimicked back teasingly. She wondered if he could see in her face how repulsive she found him.

Everyone in the restaurant was still looking at the foreigner. Even Old Bachelor Choi, who had finally caught his teeth and was busily returning them to his mouth. He smiled, chimplike, as broth dribbled from the corners of his mouth.

The cook-owner removed the cover from a pot of boiling water, releasing a ghostly cloud of steam. She looked like she was laughing about something.

"Oh my fucking gods and ancestors," she said.

SARAH
Seoul
1993

We were being carpet-bombed. By cherry blossoms, whenever we went outside.

How great it was to be back amidst the cherry trees of the Chosun U. campus. I gave Bernie Lee such a wide smile that he narrowed his eyes and said, "You're freaking me out, Twinkie."

"Maybe I'm just happy to see you. I didn't see you all weekend."

His eyes narrowed further, to threadlike slits. "Uh huh. You go somewhere or something?"

"Maybe." I almost looked over at Doug, but I didn't dare. Instead, I just smiled again. How great it was that it was spring. How great, everything.

Outside, everything smelled pink. Pairs of college boys armed with cameras roamed the campus, cajoling girls to stand for photos under the clumps of blooms, the photographee often slipping a hand on a feminine shoulder or tender upper arm while the girl was immobilized under the camera's eye.

The next day, the cherry trees were just normal trees with leaves, not a single petal left. Then the weather turned hot, and azaleas and forsythia, blazing yellows and fuchsias, exploded from bushes, as if unleashed by the heat. The sun became a physical presence, a punishing hand. People walked as if beaten, heads bowed on wilting stems of necks. At the Rainbow, diners paradoxically ordered spicy soups bubbling in their own black cauldrons. They would slurp and sigh until they took a shower in their own sweat. I preferred *neng myun,* a mound of cold buckwheat noodles in iced broth, topped with a slice of fatty beef and a hard-boiled egg balanced on top like a maraschino cherry. When the *ajuhma* carried it, it looked like strange, precarious island rising out of a sea of cloudy broth.

"I heard *chang-ma*'s going to be bad this year," said Bernie in class.

Not *chang-ma* again. The little animals that fall from the sky and pulled out your hair.

"What *is* that?" I asked Doug. "*Chang-ma.*"

Bernie grinned at me, as if he had a delicious prank with my name on it waiting. "The monsoon season. It rains every day, buckets and buckets of rain, but it doesn't cool things down. It just makes it really humid. You'll feel like you're wearing a suit of moisture, bathed in sweat. Your laundry will always be damp. You'll grow mold."

Doug nodded. "I remember one summer the rains were so bad that people living near river banks got washed away or killed in mudslides. The Han River rose so much it took out the bridge to Seoul."

"It's coming later this year," Bernie said. "That's a sign it's going to be bad." His tone was now merely informative. Friendly, even.

After class, it began to rain a cold, spattery rain.

"Is this *chang-ma*?" I asked Doug.

"No," he said. "Don't worry, you'll know it when it happens."

After lunch, we made our way down the alley toward a *yuhgwon,* one of those tiny boarding houses marked with an electric sign that looked like a cup of tea with waves of red steam rising off it. That meant it had hot water. *Yuhgwons,* a.k.a. "love hotels," were plentiful in our neighborhood, for horny students as well as itinerant travelers, of which Doug and I were both.

The stout *yuhgwon ajuhma* with warts dotting her fingers didn't give us another look as she took Doug's money and placed a key on the low table in front of her. The key opened up a vaultlike room that had a clean yellow floor, a single window, and little else except for some bedding stacked in a corner and a calendar on the wall that had a generic Korean country scene on it. I'm sure in Korean it said something like, COMPLIMENTS OF EDWARD DIEHL, YOUR STATE FARM AGENT, LIKE A GOOD NEIGHBOR.

It had come to this: Doug was going to be the one to receive my slightly outmoded virginity.

Two nights ago, pursued by whiskey-slurred voices and heavy footsteps, life's thread grew unbearably thin and taut. We had hidden among the trees by the side of the road, struggling to muffle our ragged breaths as shafts of light from flashlights poked all around us.

"I thought that motherfucker was weird, right off, he was in his cami's—who wears their uniform out for a night on the town?"

"Some do, you know. Maybe he just got off war games."

"Well, the girl, she was a gook chick, but there was something funny about her, too—I told you she didn't have her badge. And they ran out like bats out of hell when I called you guys. This ain't no pink goddam elephants we're talking about."

"Well, I don't see anything out here now, soldier. Go home and sleep it off, would you?"

When the realization came that yes, we came, we saw, we outsmarted the U.S. Army, exhilaration welled up inside me, so crystalline and powerful that I wanted to shout. When I looked at Doug, I could see his eyes shining in the dark.

We walked all the way back to the bus station, where we waited for the next bus, which delivered us back to the Residence just as dawn was breaking, just as the dorm's night watchman, twig broom in hand, was opening the doors to a new day.

"I want to sleep with you," I had whispered into Doug's ear on the bus ride back. He had appeared to be sleeping, but obviously, he had heard.

"By the way, I'm a virgin."

"I didn't know."

"Guess you had me pegged differently, huh?"

"I didn't really think about it at all."

I wasn't the Virgin Mary, I told him. If I had to describe myself using associative words, as I had in those endless psychological tests of my childhood, virginal, chaste, untouched, were not words that would appear on the list.

I was a virgin, I explained, because I was. No action verbs involved. In high school, when life begins to revolve around that pulsating star of sex, that's when I discovered that I hated absolutely everybody. So I did things like dye my hair unnatural colors, hang around with the most despised geeks and druggies, and I didn't find myself in those situations —prom, overnight ski trips—where sex usually occurs. True, once I was invited to a party being held at an Eden's Prairie three-car-garage-and-indoor-pool home while the parents were away. I'm not sure why my presence had been requested. The jocks and jockettes who called me "chink" or "jap" by day ignored me at night, which was worse.

I stood clutching a beer in a flimsy plastic cup while everyone else around me danced, necked, smoked pot, or guzzled beer from plastic funnel "beer bongs." I was relieved when Spleef Murphy, the redheaded boy who'd later end up as my AP chemistry partner, pointed to a dark bedroom and raised his eyebrows. Though he would always screw up the molarity of our reagenting solutions, that night, the touch of his hand as he groped my breasts, the enthusiastic way he sucked at my crotch as if he were gulping down draughts of punch, the lucid gaze of his pea-green eyes—all this comforted me. I was being felt and seen and tasted in a cavernous bedroom among posters of a blond vixen bent in a racing crouch, naked except for her Nordica ski boots, an ancient poster of Farrah sitting on a Mexican blanket, her famous toothy smile-scream, her nipple winking at us through her swimsuit's flimsy fabric.

I was aware of Doug patting my back, the way one might do when trying to burp a baby.

"I don't think of it as losing," I said, looking into his eyes. "It's gaining. With you, it would be."

He reached into his pocket and pulled out a foil package, flat yet with bones in it, like a kite.

❀ ❀ ❀

On TV and in the movies, post-sex rituals differ, but they seem to always include cigarettes. Doug, perhaps to not disappoint, also lit one up and leaned back languidly onto the *yuhgwon*'s lozenge-shaped pillows.

I found a strange reassurance in the small spots of blood spattering my thigh. I had crossed the line. And with Doug. No emotional aftermath, my secrets tucked safe inside his boarded-up house. The smell of the smoke was an incense, like being together in the tender anonymity of a hazy opium den. Doug put his free hand on my hipbone, his fingers spread wide, as if claiming territory. My tongue loosened. I found myself telling him about my trip to the orphanage. An even more intimate detail than contained in all the folds and crevices in my body that he had explored.

"Shit," he said, softly. "I had no idea." He removed his cigarette from his mouth, began spinning it around the bridge of his thumb, something bored Korean students did with their pens.

"Can you believe the people who call themselves my parents have lied to me, basically my entire life?"

"Well, to play devil's advocate, it's possible the car-accident story originated with the orphanage. Koreans like to fudge, make nice. People with terminal cancer are told they have an ulcer. The doctors don't want to *upset* them."

I had always asked about my biological parents as soon as I was old enough to understand. And they had that story pat and waiting. Often, Christine would change the subject, tickling me or doing something else to get me animated.

"And whose sweetie pie are you?" she might ask, gaily sticking her fingers in all my tickly places. "Whose little pumpkin face?"

"I'm yours," I would answer.

"And who am I?" Fingers, everywhere.

"You're my mommy!" By this time I would be screaming with involuntary laughter.

"I always felt like Christine was hiding something, she had that guilty dog-who-peed-in-the-corner look. When I told them I was going to Korea, Ken was reluctant, but okay. Christine went batshit."

"Batshit, like how?"

"She actually ripped up the brochure and chucked it in the garbage, saying the Motherland Program was *only* for true Koreans, people with Korean last names."

"That's seriously psycho."

I remembered looking around the table: Amanda emotionally detaching by pretending to check her hair for split ends. Ken's comb-shaped mustache quivering. Christine, bottle-blond hair, the thinning patch on top exposed in the harsh overhead light of the kitchen table. Her scalp blazed red, like her face. I remembered thinking, joltingly: *these people are not my family. They're just some random people.*

Doug continued spinning the cigarette, now a dangerous, glowing stub. Each time it stopped, the live end pointed at me.

"She was obviously worried you were going to go back to Korea and stay there," Doug said. "Leaving her."

"But don't you see? That means she *knew*." My voice rose. "She was scared I was going to find my birth mother, and, and—"

I didn't know what lay beyond that "and."

"Which is what you *are* trying to do."

"Yes, I am," I said. "But doing this search would have never occurred to me, had I not gone out on my own and found out the real story. I mean, they fucking told me my birth mother was *dead.*"

"So you seriously want to search for your Korean parents, like an all-out search?"

I sank back into the bedding, nodded. "Why?"

"There's this show. It's called something like *Missing Persons.* People go on there and try to find their lost relatives and friends."

"Really?"

"It's a popular show, mostly these old *ajuhmas* and *harlmonis* who'd had some fight with their sister or something and want to get back in touch. And the missing person often does call in. Maybe you could try to get on it."

My heart leapt at the thought of the studio's phones ringing. Of a woman's voice. Someone who will say, *I'm sorry, I'm sorry,* over and over again. *Let me tell you what happened.* And: *I want you to come home.*

"But you know," Doug went on. "It's possible your birth mother's married, with a whole family who doesn't know about her past, so it could get messy. Do you think you could handle the consequences?"

I didn't tell Doug how I'd been walking all over Seoul, looking. I couldn't help myself. Yesterday I'd gone to the Lotte Department Store. Twelve floors, plenty of Korean women. I almost got lost in a haze of silk scarves, jewelry, and perfume before I realized she wouldn't be there. She wouldn't be among those beringed ladies in French designer suits, scarves cleverly knotted about their shoulders, big jade rings on their fingers, Burberry raincoats draped on their arms.

Rich people had abortions, easy as one-two-three. Doug said that the first question the base doctor had asked his mother about her pregnancy with him was, *Do you want to keep it?*

So I had fled the opulence of the Lotte and her brethren—the Hyatt, the Swissôtel, the Intercontinental—for a place only a few blocks behind these behemoths, a neighborhood of shacks huddling in the shadow of the sleek skyscrapers like fungi at the base of a tree. I kept going until I got to

Hoei Dong, where I was supposedly found. I found a fire station—was it the one? Miss Park at the orphanage had told me that my mother probably set me outside the door and watched from some hidden place until someone took me in. My mother cared about me, she insisted. She did what she did out of the purest form of mother love: sacrifice.

As if Miss Park or anyone could know. Why was everyone so quick to offer me cheap words, when all I wanted was the truth?

I placed myself on a little bench across the street. For the hour I sat, I never saw a single baby laid on the neat stone steps of that building.

"Let's do it," I told Doug. "Let's do this show, let's try."

Doug nodded. "There's a Korean saying, 'Don't let the fear of maggots scare you away from making soy sauce.'"

KYUNG-SOOK
Seoul
1972

Kyung-sook found herself wondering if the visit from the Westerner had all been a peculiar dream. Sunhee didn't mention it. The cook-owner only complained about finding new holes in the rice bags made by mice, which Kyung-sook could feel running across her feet at night.

Later that day, the cook-owner returned from the market with a good-sized cat. It had rich brown fur the color of tortoiseshell, a nose that was half pink, half black like a Korean mask.

The cook-owner didn't bother giving the cat a name other than Mr. Kitty, and she was pleased when it immediately went into the storeroom and came out with a mouse, its neck neatly broken.

Two days later, though, the cat looked sick, and it lay down right in the front entrance of the restaurant. That was the day the Westerner showed up again. He entered carrying a black hourglass-shaped case, which he placed in the seat opposite him, as lovingly as if he were seating a venerated relative. He made his barking noises and pointed at Old Bachelor Choi's cheap noodle dish.

Then he took off his soft hat, which he had not done before. Black hair tumbled out past his ears, almost touching his shoulders.

"Aigu!" exclaimed the cook-owner. "Is he a man or a woman? These fuckin' Westerners are so perverse."

Kyung-sook had never seen a man with long hair, except in Imo's pictures of Christo, but he was a god from olden times. However, she thought the foreigner actually looked better with the curtain of coal-black hair framing the sharp angles of his face. In fact, there was something in the man's face that kept drawing her eyes back to it. The cook-owner, so fond of old proverbs, might have said, "In time, it is possible to develop a taste even for sour dog-apricots."

What place did this man come from, where he could grow his hair out like a woman's with no shame? she wondered.

"Where you come from?" she asked, as she set his noodles in front of him.

The man stared at her, frankly, brazenly, with his amber-colored eyes.

"America," he said, pointing at his chest. "I'm American."

Mi-guk. "The beautiful country," America's name in Chinese characters. She was thinking of something to say about that when there was a shout from one of the customers—"Look what that dirty cat has done!"— which sent the cook-owner running from the kitchen to see what was the matter.

In a dark corner of the restaurant, the cat had had kittens, six of them in all sorts of different colors: ginger, tortoiseshell, white with spots, black. She was proudly licking them clean as the cook-owner came upon her. Bloody afterbirth was smeared on the floor.

"That damned crook!" she yelled. "That man at the market, I gave him a whole bottle of good sesame oil—not perilla oil—for that cat that he assured me was a male. She's a good mouser, but I'll be damned if I'm going to raise her saekkis."

The American, amidst all the hubbub, ate quickly. But he gave Kyung-sook another frank look that made Old Bachelor Choi choke on his soup and scandalized Sunhee before he left. Kyung-sook threw salt on his path to express her outrage at what he had done. But for some strange reason, she was also just a little bit thrilled, as if her drab life had suddenly taken on a few new, unexpected colors. She was even more thrilled to find that the man had left a few coins behind at his table. These she scooped up before anyone saw.

"Kyung-sook-ah! Pick up these goddam dumpling soups before they grow icicles!" the cook-owner bellowed. Kyung-sook hurried back into the kitchen. The cat was lying on an old rice sack on the floor, next to her was a bowl of miyuk-guk, the blood-replenishing seaweed soup that was traditionally given to new mothers—not animals. How strange the cook-owner was, Kyung-sook thought.

When Kyung-sook returned for the next order, she found the cook-owner gently crooning to the drowsing cat as if it were a child. She must really love that stupid, dirty thing, Kyung-sook thought, until she stopped, startled, hearing what the cook-owner was singing:

Kitty fucked a rat, fucked a rat. Out came six little saekkis, six pink rat bastards, naked rat bastards. Oh oh Kitty get rid of those disgusting pink rat bastards.

The next day, the cat was prowling the storeroom as usual, pink teats poking out of her belly-fur like soft squash candy. The kittens and the rice sack were gone. Sunhee asked where the babies had gone. The cook-owner, for some reason, looked at Kyung-sook, not Sunhee, when she replied, smiling a strange smile: "I think Kitty ate them for dinner. Yum. Yum."

Sunhee sighed. "Is that the kind of gross humor you northerners are so proud of?" She grabbed her tray, mumbling how at least at the sieve factory, she didn't have to talk to people while she worked.

Kyung-sook bent to look more closely at the cat as it slunk around the bags of rice. At the corner of its mouth, it indeed had a smudge of blood.

SARAH
Seoul
1993

Doug flipped on the TV.

The dusty console sparked to life in the dorm's TV room. Bouncing breasts and buttocks. Women and men running on a beach. It was *Baywatch*—the last person had left the TV on AFKN, the Armed Forces Korea Network, which made sure that the American servicemen and women didn't have to miss a single episode due to their military duty. Doug turned to Channel 12, SBC, Sejong Broadcasting. A mélange of tearful faces embracing. A smiling cartoon phone ringing. Game-show music. People talking in Korean.

Cut to a commercial. "Lotte custard-filled cakes—so good they'll make your ancestors come back from the dead!"

A bang of cymbals, cheery game-show music resuming.

"Anyonghashimnikka yorubun, anyonghashimnikka!"

A middle-aged man with thick square glasses and an Elvis pompadour emerged with a willowy young woman. They waved to the audience as confetti rained down.

An *ajuhma* and a woman in her twenties waited at side-by-side podiums. Both of them looked grim, despite the bouncy music, smiling hosts, cheering audience.

The young woman was looking for her childhood piano teacher. She had hated taking lessons, she said, as the hosts listened and murmured well-timed, sympathetic *neh neh*s, but she had loved her teacher for continuing to teach her for free after her father had deserted the family in favor of a "small wife," a mistress. She and her mother had fallen into destitution, but the fact that she was still taking piano lessons, a vestige of their former middle-class life, had kept her despairing mother from committing suicide. Her mother had rallied, begun selling nylon stockings at the pedestrian overpass near a famous women's university. By being a fixture there—rain or shine—she had been able to amass enough money to send her daughter to that very college on scholarship. In the rush of college life, however, the young woman had lost touch with the teacher.

"Please, if you're out there, Seo Yoon-Ju Sunsengnim, let me hear from you. I so wish to thank you for all you've done for me and my mother."

Instead of cutting to the phones, though, the hosts turned, smiling, to the *ajuhma*, leaving the young woman crying into a hankie.

The *ajuhma* wanted to find her sister, who had eloped against their parents' wishes years ago.

Sis, I miss you. All is forgiven. She started to cry.

The cameras cut to a phone. Nothing moved except a small ticker at the bottom that broadcasted the phone number.

Ring!

The first call was for the young woman! A disembodied voice said *yo-bosayo?* then broke the news that the piano teacher had been killed with her husband and son in an auto accident. The studio filled with the sound of the woman's wails as two pastel-suited women materialized out of nowhere and discreetly led her off the stage.

Our Madam Auntie, she's received several callers as well, the host said, a bit too cheerily.

One caller asked, *"Does your sister have a crimson butterfly-shaped birthmark on her arm that also grows a small patch of hair?"*

The woman blinked, disoriented, as if she was coming out of a coma.

" 'Yes,' she's saying," said Doug. "Her sister has such a birthmark—her childhood nickname was *nabi*, butterfly. The lady is telling her she thinks her sister lives in her apartment building in Taegu. The lady says she's going to give her sister's number to her."

The audience clapped wildly. The *ajuhma*, howling into her hankie, mumbling *"Nabi-yah, nabi-yah,"* was also led off the stage.

"There's more," Doug said. "The grande finale."

Two little boys in identical bowl haircuts were ushered onto the stage. They looked to be about ten and four. The older one put a hand on his brother's thin shoulder when the hosts drew close. The smaller boy shrank, like a smaller fish hoping not to be noticed by a larger, hungry one.

The stiletto-heeled hostess looked into the camera.

"Aren't they cute?" she said, as if she were selling them. "Whose heart wouldn't be crying for two such lovely little boys?"

"This is a weird one," said Doug. "They're from Kyong San Province —their accents are so thick I can barely understand. Their uncle brought them to Seoul to visit a distant relative but he never showed up to bring them back."

Doug craned his neck forward, frowning in concentration.

"I guess when the relative called the parents, she was told they'd moved—"

"Let me guess, no forwarding address?"

"No forwarding address," Doug spat back at me, almost snarling. I looked at him, surprised.

"What's the matter?" I said. "That's what happened, wasn't it? They moved—poof!—without a trace."

He nodded, mute with anger. What I had done, I couldn't guess. Was I too flip and hurt some hidden, vulnerable part of him? Did I interrupt him? Something else? He was still so much a puzzle to me, a Rubik's cube of endless facets, that to manage one side's solid comfortable color would leave the others hopelessly parti-colored and obscured. Irritation, petulance papered over darker mysteries. Only when we were having sex were things simple and defined.

"So what's going on?" I prodded, as distraction. "On the show."

We waited, along with the two little boys, to see if the phones would ring. The cameras closed in on the boys' humiliated, miserable faces, revealing the incompetent asymmetricality of their haircuts, the ill-fitting clothes that were obviously not theirs. Then, mercifully, the cameras pulled away to show the audience, mostly grannies with tight, kinky perms and cardigans that bagged at the wrists.

"They have a caller."

A woman's voice, tears almost visible.

"*Um-ma yah,*" she said, shrieking as if she'd been poked with an electric cattle prod.

As if simultaneously prodded, the boys started to cry, "*Um-ma! Um-ma!*" The audience cheered.

"It's their mother, isn't it? *Um-ma* sounds like the way a cow would say 'mommy.'"

"She said she's their mother."

The disembodied voice heaved, sobs keening like a whale.

"What else is she saying?"

"She said they had to leave the boys because they were in financial trouble. Their turn came up in the local rotating credit pool, and they lost all the money in some real estate swindle—some ten million won. They couldn't pay it back, so they ran away."

"Bet there are some other people who'd also love to get back in touch with them. Ring-ring."

Doug laughed.

"She says she's going to find a way for them to meet. As you can probably hear, she feels terrible. The kids are all saying, 'Mommy, come get us. Cousin's wife isn't feeding us.'"

I sat up. "It's a sign," I said. "Those kids found their *mother*. Let's do it."

"You want to?"

"Yes."

"Okay, it's worth a try. The fact that you were covered in *ddong* would be hard for someone to forget, I think."

"Do we have to bring that up?" I said. "I mean, what if Choi *Sunsengnim* watches that show? Or Bernie—I'll die."

"Sarah, why the hell do you care so much what other people think? Bernie Lee is dirt. Choi *Sunsengnim* is your teacher. This is *your* life. If they don't like it, tell them to go fuck themselves."

"Okay, okay. Let's concentrate on getting me on that show."

"Well, it's over."

Indeed, the opening scenes of some soap opera were on the screen.

"Next week, I'll watch the show again and jot down the number."

Next week! Impatience rose up like a wave, then subsided. Doug moved closer to kiss me. His thin lips felt surprising full on my mouth.

The door to the TV room swung open, knocking aside the flimsy metal chairs we'd set against it. Bernie Lee walked in, eating sloppily from a box of Captain Crunch that must have been sent from home. He observed the two of us and eyed me smugly. He was probably thinking that now that Jun-Ho was gone, I had a new lover already, slut that I was.

He headed back out the door, spilling tiny, hard nuggets of the cereal.

"*Twiggi*," he said to Doug, not me, before he left.

"What's 'twiggy'?" I asked Doug. "Korean for 'you-are-sleeping-with-a-ho'?"

Doug shook his head. He was biting his lip.

"Mongrel," he said, letting go of my hand.

KYUNG-SOOK
Seoul
1972

No matter how much the foreigner ate, he stayed thin. The rims around his eyes were pinkish, like a rabbit's, the rest of his skin transparent like skimmed milk.

"The sun could shine right through that big-nose," the cook-owner muttered. "Those foreign bastards sure have a nice life. But with that life comes softness. He can't even eat a chili pepper without screaming—what does that mean about *his* pepper, hm?"

The man had come to their dumpy little restaurant again and again. He grew tired of the water-dumplings and noodles and then gamely agreed to try whatever food the cook-owner would make him, even though it would often make him gasp and sweat with the heat or pucker with the salt.

He also had extremely strange eating habits. He never drank his soup, even when the cook-owner subjected him to two-day-old dumplings, dried-out pasty things that would surely clog in his throat like cotton balls.

"I want water, wa-ter, w-a-t-e-r!" he howled to Kyung-sook after eating some hot radish kimchi.

"Mul," she said back to him. "Korean word for water."

"Mooly, whatever!" he said, clutching his throat.

Kyung-sook brought him his water, flavored with burnt barley so he would know it had been recently boiled.

"I want water, not scalding hot tea," he groaned, but he gulped two, three, four cups of the liquid and asked for more. Korean people would never waste so much stomach-space on fluid at a meal. Sunhee giggled and called him mul-gogi, "Fish," or mul-gogi-ssi, "Mr. Fish."

Today, Mr. Fish had managed to communicate to them that it was his birthday. At the market that day, one of the cook-owner's anchovy suppliers had added a nice bag of pundaegi, silkworm larvae, as a reward for her loyalty and also because it was silk-making season, and so the brownish wads, shaken from their precious cocoons, were quite abundant. To celebrate Mr. Fish's birthday, the cook-owner prepared a gigantic plate of them doused in sweet sauce. As Kyung-sook served him, a few of the fat pundaegi levitated off the plate like bees before a flowering bush, but no one seemed to notice. The man, perhaps knowing that they expected him to find the food strange, bent his head toward the overflowing plate and quickly ate it all, the sight of his pink tongue lapping like a dog's astonishing and disgusting them, making Old Bachelor Choi's dentures flop into his soup once more.

"Cook-owner says he make you real birth-day food next time," Kyung-Sook told him. She couldn't help being a little pleased at how her high school English was coming back to her. "He make miyuk-guk, seaweed soups."

"Me-YUCK-GOOK. Oh, goody," the man said in a sarcastic voice. Kyung-Sook didn't understand sarcasm.

"What is it?" she asked, instead, pointing to the black hourglass case.

"I'll show you," the man said. He opened it and took out a Western guitar. It was made of a beautiful, whorled wood that reminded her of her taegum—which she had not played in ages, her fingers bent with fatigue after a day's worth of serving.

The man sat back casually, extending his legs as if he were in the comfort of his own house's living room. He plucked the strings of the beautifully curved instrument. The notes came out soft, much more liquid and melodious than the tones of a Korean harp.

"You like?" he asked. Kyung-sook nodded.

"Then let me take *you* out to a restaurant for a change. And you can hear some more."

Kyung-sook wasn't fully sure she understood the man's words, but she did want to hear more music.

"Tomorrow," Mr. Fish said, giving her that same frank look as he left.

SARAH
Seoul
1993

"Your hands seem to be made for playing the *taegum*," Tae *Sunsengnim* remarked. "I have no idea why you can't play it, then."

Instead of glissandos and silvery notes, the flute hissed at me when I picked it up, or even looked at it. It also required reading music, adding another set of foreign sticks and signs to my already bursting brain even though Jeannie from Korean class had kindly shown me a mnemonic to help me remember the notes: E/very G/ood B/oy D/eserves F/udge.

"Your turn," said the Other Jeannie, the Julliard know-it-all I'd dubbed "Evil Genie." Our group was trying the last instrument, the *changgo* hourglass drum. So far, no one had been able to play that drum well enough to be considered for the upcoming talent show.

Tae *Sunsengnim* sighed in despair, seeing that it was my turn. She picked up the *kaenguri* and started bashing out the beat on its polished brass surface.

Chang-chang-ch-ch-ch-CHANG!

I had the drum strapped on by a cotton sling, not unlike the ones New-Agey people carried babies in. The drum was balanced on the point of my right hip, I had the two different drumsticks—one like a chopstick, the other with a ball at the end. You were supposed to sway the top half of your body back and forth while you hit both sides of the *changgo*, sometimes hitting as if you were playing a snare, and sometimes hitting the two sides separately, sometimes switching lightning-fast between the two. While all this was going on, your feet were supposed to move at a slower beat.

I decided the best chance I had was to just play, not think. *Bang! Bang! Thump! Whump! Tok!* I let my arms fly away like birds.

"Hm," Tae *Sunsengnim* said, lowering the gong to watch me bang away. "Not bad."

KYUNG-SOOK
Seoul
1972

Before that day, she had never eaten going-out food in her life, unless you counted the time she and her friends had spent all day plucking chickens for Widower Rhee, and then had gone to the market and gorged themselves on bowls of steaming fish-cake soup and sweet-bean-filled goldfish bread.

But to go someplace to eat when you had perfectly good food at home seemed unthinkable—an option only for the rich, the fat people who weren't satisfied with nourishing Korean food but who also had to acquaint their lips with the foods of France or China. The food in their restaurant was not so much going-out food as it was sustenance for old bachelors who had no one to cook for them, the occasional student, the hurried businessman looking to put something in his stomach before a night of drinking. Dumplings and noodles, rice, and only two or three side dishes. It was never anything special.

But the foreigner had come to take Kyung-Sook away from the restaurant.

"Go, go," the cook-owner had urged her. "I'll do the serving for a few hours, no sweat. Go stuff your belly till it explodes."

Kyung-Sook had felt shy, and slightly absurd, but the two of them made their way through the alleys to the main street. Kyung-Sook rarely ventured this far from the restaurant: only if she had to run to the market when they were low on this or that vegetable or if they needed more roasted barley. But each time she had been in such a hurry, she had never really looked at what was going on in the street.

Today she saw the street through a foreigner's eyes. The gorgeous colors of a silk store. The legless man wheeling himself belly-first on a rusty-wheeled plank as he held a cup out for coins (and the foreigner even dug out some ten-won pieces and gently placed them in the man's cup; she had never known someone who would treat a stranger—a beggar, no less—with such respect). She noted the dinginess and promise of the closed door of a teahouse, felt the regretful han of a man sitting next to his bucket of squirming eels as he sang.

> I loved her so much
> that when she left me
> I spread azalea petals
> on her leaving path

"Do you like Chinese food?"

They were standing in front of a Chinese restaurant. Its façade was painted a gaudy red and gold, various Chinese signs for health, happiness, and prosperity circling the door. Kyung-sook had heard the word "food" and guessed he was asking for approval, so she nodded.

It seemed strange that a foreigner could teach her so much about her own country, but he did. For one, who would have known that going outside to eat could be so pleasant? Or that Chinese food prepared by Korean hands could be so delicious? The foreigner knew just the things to order, saying the dishes' names to the waitress in a way that Kyung-Sook knew he had sampled them before and found them to his liking.

Chinese food, she found, had a subtle, slightly sweet flavor so unlike the garlic-red-pepper-ginger heat of Korean cooking. He had ordered some black noodles called jia-jia-myun, a dish called Seven Tastes: rice mixed with bits of vegetables and seafood, glowing like treasures. The man even spooned tiny shrimp, pink and curled like a baby's finger, right into Kyung-sook's mouth. She was shocked by his audacity, but still, she obediently opened her mouth for a sliver of meat which he said was Peking *dalk,* but its meltingly silken taste told her it wasn't chicken, but some other kind of marvelous meat.

"Next time, we'll have pork chops," he said, as they finished with tea, fragrant and slightly bitter, the same amber color of his eyes. The man seemed so worldly, although Kyung-sook was a little taken aback when he left his chopsticks sticking up in his half-eaten bowl of rice—didn't he know that would attract the dead?

The man took out a thick wad of won to pay. His dress and bearing was that of a poor student, yet he had paid for a meal she hadn't even had the capacity to dream about. So perhaps it was true that everyone in America was fabulously rich. That money practically grew on trees and all one had to do was pluck it where it hung on low branches, not even having to strain, the way one did for persimmons, which stayed coyly out of reach.

"We're not done yet with our date," he said to her. She didn't understand what he said, so she just smiled, remembering to cover her mouth.

He took her to a teahouse, the Moon River. He must have been a regular customer there because the teahouse auntie barely gave him a glance, and the old men at a table did not break their concentration from the grid of their paduk game when the foreigner walked in.

"Shall I play you a real song this time?" he asked, as he unsnapped the latches on the hourglass case.

He didn't wait for her reply, just cradled the instrument in his lap and began to play, a melody that unspooled, fluid and supple, like a bolt of fine silk dropped to the ground.

Kyung-sook's heart seized. How could she have foreseen such beautiful music entering her life?

SARAH
Seoul
1993

"You know, Sarah, with practice, you have the potential to excel at playing the *changgo*," Tae *Sunsengnim* told me after the next class.

With practice, I could do the same with sex, Doug told me, the next time we went to a *yuhgwon* together.

So Mondays, Wednesdays, and Fridays, I took an extra hour to play the *changgo* under Tae *Sunsengnim*'s instructions. The other days, under Doug's, I practiced making love.

I practiced so much, my fingers blistered from holding the drumsticks in my sweaty fingers, the drum wore a hole in the skin of my hip.

Doug's supply of rubbers ran out and he had to buy some Korean ones. He went to a pharmacy, a *yak-guk,* and came back with a handful, which he spilled onto the *yuhgwon*'s bedding like coins.

When he was a little kid, he and his friends would find used rubbers crushed in the dirt street, and they would blow them up to make funny, cucumber-shaped balloons. That is, until some old *ajuhshi* informed them as to a condom's real function.

Once, when we had been making love for a long time, something funny started up within me. At first it felt like I had to pee. Then it grew to something more. I grabbed Doug's backside and ground myself into him, and I started yowling, a long screech. In its own terrible way it felt good to just let myself scream.

But I couldn't help thinking of Bernie Lee's words, how my birth mother must have been a whore to have had me. Or Christine's words, about the future awaiting me, had I stayed Korean-Korean. Prostitute. Juicy Girl.

"Do you think I'm a slut?" I asked Doug, after a session that had been so energetic and noisy that the *yuhgwon ajuhma* had banged on the door and told us we were disturbing the other patrons. "Bernie Lee said only whores give their kids up for adoption."

Doug looked pained.

"I hope you don't ever take seriously anything Bernie Lee has to say—didn't we have this discussion already?"

"I know. But the one time my adoptive mother got really mad at me, she said that if they hadn't adopted me, I would probably have become a prostitute, because people without family in Korea are rejected by society, it's that whole bloodline thing. I guess boys become street cleaners and girls become streetwalkers."

Doug snorted. "No one should say that to a child."

"But maybe my birth mother *was* a prostitute—maybe that's why they made up the story about the car accident."

"It doesn't matter who your mother was—or is," Doug said. "What matters is who you are."

"That's the trouble," I said. "I don't know who I am. I don't know who I should be."

"Well, you're making it worse by letting other people tell you, especially when they don't know shit."

I felt suddenly empty, scooped out, as if I were hungry, but I knew that wasn't it. I'd gone from the mind-exploding heights of orgasm to being depressed at the sight of our drab rented room, slightly nauseated by the earthy, fishy after-aroma of our lovemaking. And for some reason, I was depressed by Doug's face, his round brown eyes, his sharp nose. I squinted hard to try to construct a face for him that was holistically Korean—slanted eyes, high cheekbones, black straight hair—but I failed.

Doug caressed my hair, leaned in to kiss my ear. His breath stank faintly of kimchi.

I don't know why I felt like crying. Maybe it was because I had a premonition that our *Missing Persons* project was a pipe dream, that I was never going to find out anything more about me or my mother. I was running in circles again, and eventually I'd just go home to Minnesota, to Christine and Ken and all the malarkey of my life there.

"Did you call *Missing Persons?*" I asked. Doug looked like he was about to fall asleep, an "88" cigarette still burning between his fingers.

"Yeah. They don't handle requests during the live show. I'm supposed to talk to someone in their office this week, or next."

I sighed.

The air was dense with humidity, like a synthetic fiber blanket pressing over us. This room didn't have a window, so I couldn't tell if outside it was rainy or clear. The smell of cheap fillers in Doug's cigarette burned in my nose.

What was going to happen, tomorrow and the next day? I wondered. And would I be able to stand it?

KYUNG-SOOK
Seoul
1972

So many sad Korean ballads were about chut sarang, "first love." Kyung-sook wondered if she would recognize such a thing.

A number of unmarried young men, mostly day laborers and low-level clerks, frequented the restaurant. In between bursts of bitter complaining about a government and a society that made no place for hard-working men as themselves, they called her and Sunhee all sorts of vile names like nymphomaniac and bitch, saying that any woman who worked in a place where they had contact with men obviously had questionable morals.

The next morning, however, these same men would slink back, inquiring meekly if the cook-owner might be able to make them a little bit of hangover soup, to take the edge off.

Men like that were pathetic. They inflated themselves with rage and drink, but the next morning would whine that the tails on the soybean sprouts had been pinched off, so that it wouldn't make a proper post-drunk soup.

Maybe her first love had already passed, she thought.

How about her friend Min-Ki? She and he used to play together at the edges of the rice fields until they were seven, when Confucian custom made them separate into their spheres of male and female. From time to time they managed to steal away and meet at a secluded spot on the banks of the Glass River.

One time they had rendezvoused after Min-Ki had returned from a trip with his uncle to Seoul. As they idly sucked on wild cherries and shared a pine-needle cake Min-Ki had stolen from his house, he had excitedly told her about the Western movies he had seen.

"There is a place they call a kuk-jang, a dark place where you actually sit on Western chairs, and you watch these moving pictures of people who walk and talk—a movie, it's called," he said, going on to explain that you could eat snacks while you watched, and a man, a pyon-sa storyteller, stood in front of the screen and explained what was going on. Sometimes, he told jokes, too.

"In the movie, the American man and woman, they went like this." Min-Ki added, grabbing Kyung-sook by the ears and pulling their heads together. He sucked on her lips like a calf at its mother's teat. Kyung-sook remembered that his mouth had been warm and slippery and tasted spicy and bitter like herbs.

"They call it a kiss-u." He let go of her ears.

"Kiss-u?"

"Yeah, kiss-u. Doesn't it feel weird? The Western man and woman in the movies did this forever!"

"Really? Westerners do that?" She had never seen her mother and father—or any man or woman—do this. It was both horrid and exciting at the same time.

Min-Ki, in any event, had married early, for he was a first son and had a duty to produce an heir as quickly as possible. Kyung-sook wondered if he did the kiss-u with his wife.

Now, this foreigner-man was inflicting a kiss-u on her. It tasted of rust, of the time when she had swallowed a one-won coin as a toddler.

Today, she had actually gone back to his flat, a small room in a boarding house. Kyung-sook had wilted a little under the stare from the landlady, who was out in the courtyard hanging up laundry, but then Kyung-sook thought to herself, why did she care? It wasn't Enduring Pine Village, where news of her behavior would be sure to reach her parents, to the village elders. She stared back a little rudely at the woman, giddy with her newfound freedom.

"Come in, come in," the man said, sliding open his door. She and Sun-hee now called him Yun-tan as well as Mr. Fish, because his black hair reminded them of the yun-tan cooking coal. Kyung-sook waited for him to take his shoes off and leave them on the concrete steps, but he didn't. He went right into the room without taking off his dirty shoes! She kicked hers off and followed him.

Yun-tan asked her to play her taegum. She sat cross-legged on the floor (even though it must have been dirty with him wearing his shoes inside!) and she played a short san-jo for him. He watched her as she played, his eyes all moony.

"That's so beautiful," he said, and he took out his guitar. As Kyung-sook continued to play, he strummed along with her.

Then he put his guitar down and gave her that kiss-u. He also pawed at her body in a way that didn't seem too decent, but she didn't know what to do—maybe it was normal and customary in his culture. She wanted to show the man that she was a sophisticated woman, not some silly serving girl, so she pretended she had done all these things before.

"I told you to go stuff yourself with the foreigner's money," the cook-owner scolded, when she returned. "But don't be such a brazen hussy. Remember the old saying: You let your tail get too long, it's gonna get stepped on."

"I didn't do anything wrong," Kyung-sook said, noting that her elongated countrified vowels were now bending into the sharper corners of Seoul dialect, and this pleased her.

SARAH
Seoul
1993

The note in my box contained only a beeper number. I'd never used a beeper before; they were supposed to be for doctors and drug dealers, but here in Korea, they were as common as rice.

I dialed the ten-digit number. Someone's mechanized voice speaking in Korean. I was about to hang up when a different voice said, "Hallo Sarah, this is your friend Jun-Ho Kim. Jim Kim. I am hoping we can meet while I am here in Seoul."

We ended up spending a Sunday together at the Great East Gate Stadium watching a pro baseball game, Hyundai vs. Lucky-Goldstar. Unlike the pro basketball teams, which consisted almost exclusively of white and black players recruited from the States, the baseball teams were all Korean.

I had to laugh: in Korean baseball, a lot of bowing went on—greeting bows from the players to the fans, contrite bows after a strikeout, players bowing to the coach, coach bowing to the fans, and the pitcher actually bowed in apology when he beaned the batter. In the background, flat-chested cheerleaders in short skirts attempted to shake their booties, accompanied by a people on the sidelines beating *changgo* drums.

Soon the fans, bored by a no-hit game, started throwing empty Pocari Sweat cans and pieces of dried squid, all of which landed harmlessly on the field. They hadn't yet learned the American custom of throwing full beer bottles.

The game ended with no runs scored. The teams lined up and bowed to each other, bowed to each other's coaches, bowed to the fans.

Afterward, Jun-Ho and I strolled around the food carts on the street and stopped for some Korean sushi and shrimp chips.

"So how do you like being a KATUSA, meeting Americans?" I asked.

Jun-Ho grinned, a sardonic twist I hadn't seen before.

"Americans, they are funny. They are always yelling and shouting and laughing, so happy."

"Americans are a happy bunch," I agreed. "Yee-hah."

"We Koreans look at them and think, how can America have such a great army? There is no discipline!"

Jun-Ho frowned.

"These guys, they talk to me so fast in their fucking English and then they curse and call me fucking stupid when I not understand. Of course none of them know any motherfucking Korean, not one word, and we are here, in Korea, no?"

"Jun-Ho," I said. "I haven't heard that kind of language since I left the navy."

"Excuse?"

"Oh, I make joke. I'm sorry—I didn't know you were having such a hard time."

"Those soldiers, they are not trying any Korean foods, not even plain noodles. At messy hall, there is only fucks, so I'm always getting stuffs on my shit."

Those long lists of arcane words—*curator, crepuscular, urinary sphincter*. I longed to hear them.

"See, I never use fuck before," Jun-Ho said, holding his fist as if he's grasping a garden trowel. "So the food drops down onto my shit." He tented his shirt out.

I laughed.

He joined me. He went on to tell me he was going on a Meg Ryan boycott because she had been caught on Letterman saying derogatory things about Korea.

"She said to that man, 'Well, if Chinese or Japanese or whatever are so dumb they buy things just because my picture is on them, then that's their problem not mine.' And she make complaints that our country—she don't even know which one she is in!—smells bad. That *i-nyun* so stupid she don't realize we can see American TV over here!"

"So what happened, did the Koreans cancel her SEXY-MILD contract?"

"Of course Koreans angry—Koreans make an idol of Meg Ryan. She realize this, realize she is going to lose bunches of monies, so she sent a very apologetic video, saying she was just kidding, what she said, that she knew all the time she was in Korea."

I sighed, wondering how many things I bought just because some celebrity told me to.

"And thank you for telling me about 'fag,'" Jun-Ho went on. "I looked in another dictionary, and this one says 'cigarette.' I was so confused. Now, why are American soldiers so stupid to be calling me that? Everyone knows there are no homosexuals in Korea."

"Don't ever say 'fag' out loud," I said. "Someone is *definitely* going to take it the wrong way. And that other expression you asked me about, it's 'nip it in the *bud*,' not 'nip it in the butt'—maybe you should just skip saying it altogether, it's kind of old-fashioned."

He sighed. "I know my family is going to be angry, but I quit KATUSA program."

"Quit?"

"I thought being with Americans, it would be like being with you, but that was not so. Anyway, the Americans and Koreans, we kind of keep to ourselves, *uri kiri,* our own two groups, so I'm not learning that much Englishes anyway. I applied for transfer and was granted. I am coming back to Seoul to be in the riot police."

"Riot police?"

"Yes, we keep order when there is, say, a demo."

"Demo?" Demo records?

"Demo. Students with signs, making noise?"

"Oh, a demonstration." I remembered seeing a bunch of men in Darth-Vaderish helmets carrying shields and clubs massed along the main gate of Chosun University one day—apparently Chosun Daehakyo was famous for having political firebrands for students, government officials were always urging the professors to give out more homework to keep them busy. But that time I had seen the demo, the police had just stood there, and I hadn't seen them on campus since.

Jun-Ho ate even that last little end-piece of Korean sushi with a toothpick, his little finger delicately raised as if we were at high tea at the Waldorf.

He checked his watch and said he needed to get back to see his parents around dinnertime. It was three o'clock.

"Will I be able to see you again before I leave?" I asked.

He shook his head. "I will be in my military duty for the next six months, no exits."

"So this is our last meeting, this one day?"

He nodded. "My furlough is only three days, and my parents, I have a lot to do for respects for them."

I was suddenly touched to know that he was spending his limited time with me.

"What would you like to do now?" he asked.

"I don't know." I couldn't think, it was so crowded—people from the baseball game, shoppers, vendors. The sidewalk was narrow and people were shoving us aside like rag dolls, the bent-over senior citizens the most insistent.

Maybe I've finally become part of the many-legged Seoul organism, I was thinking, with equal parts resignation and amusement. Before, I used to shudder when a stranger in a crowd would touch me, as if my body was merely an extension of their own. Now I just took it in stride, being tossed about like anyone else, occasionally pushing back and being amazed that no one even glanced back, much less stopped and yelled, "You want a piece of me!?"

With Jun-Ho, in his green-speckled army uniform—a very common sight in Seoul—no one even seemed to notice we were speaking English.

"Is there a *yuhgwon* around here?" I asked him, suddenly.

His eyes opened wide.

"Excuse?"

I repeated myself.

"There is always *yuhgwon* around," he said. He was staring at me, as if I were changing shape before his eyes.

"Let's find one then." Old buddy, old pal. There was something about the thought of being with someone who was of my race, a mirror image of me, that had gripped me just then—and it was rapidly being translated into sexual desire.

In an ironic coincidence, the *yuhgwon* Jun-Ho chose was the Edelweiss, straight out of *The Sound of Music,* dark strips of wood hammered over the pollution-stained stucco in an admirable attempt to create an alpine chalet. Inside, it was the usual place, yellow linoleum floors, a pile of bedding with fraying covers in the corner, the free calendar.

We were out of our clothes in a few minutes flat. I had on a new bra, a Korean one I'd purchased at a department store. A regular nylon-and-lace jobbie, but it had a picture of a teddy bear in the middle. Everything in Korea, from drugs to gasoline, had to come with a cute mascot. I had been planning to wear it as a joke, for Doug. I hurled it to the floor.

Jun-Ho didn't seem surprised to see my body, but I was in awe of his—his torso was completely smooth, like a statue. He had a dusting of hair on his legs, even on his toes. But his chest was some kind of soapstone, lacking pores or follicles. When I leaned in, I smelled nothing, not a whiff of that rank animal odor I always smelled on men back in Minnesota. Smelling Jun-Ho was like smelling a rock.

Jun-Ho kissed me on the forehead, but didn't attempt to kiss me on the mouth. He even ignored my breasts and went straight to the sexual act, performing it as dutifully as he used to switch from English to Korean during our language exchanges.

I knew I should feel guilt or shame, knowing that I was also sleeping with Doug, who told me he loved me every time he reached orgasm.

When we were done, five minutes later, Jun-Ho put his uniform back on, including his hat, lacing and double-knotting his boots. I lay naked on the bedding, feeling a drop or two of his semen make its way to my thigh.

Am I fertile right now? I thought suddenly, counting back to the day of my last period. Shit.

"I will have to return to my parents' house soon," he said. Outside, the shadows had shifted.

My clothes had been discarded in a heap, petals from a daisy. I gathered them up.

"You go, then," I said, covering myself with the jumble: pants, shirt, bra, underwear. "I don't want you to be late. I'll just sit here for a while."

He smiled his mischievous Jun-Ho grin.

"I cannot leave you, Sarah," he said. "I must at least accompany you to the subway station, that is the Korean way. When I leave to the army, my mother says she accompany me as far as the front door, only, but then she was going out all the way to the front gate. And then she was going down the alley. I tell her to go back into the house, again and again, but she keeps coming out, farther and farther, until I think she will walk all the way to the base with me."

We walked back out into the street.

"Now, you know your way around Seoul a little bit, Sarah?" Jun-Ho asked, as we wound our way around the vendors and their wares massed at the mouth of the station: pantyhose tied in bundles, penknives, a tiny toy that did somersaults. We stopped in front of the turnstiles. "*Chal ka*," he said. Go in safety. There was a change in the tone and timbre of Jun-Ho's voice. Then I realized that during our weeks of language exchange, he had always used the formal-polite level of speaking. Now he was speaking in the intimate style, which had its own vocabulary, also dropped the formal sentence endings. *Chal ka yo* became *chal ka*. As if it were now understood that we could finish each other's thoughts.

From far away, the whine of an incoming train.

"Well," Jun-Ho said. He looked at me, then he bowed. A gentle incline, not the P. T. Barnumesque flourish he had greeted me with that first day at the Balzac. I hesitated, then bowed back, mimicking his posture, the way his head bent first, followed by a slight rounding of the shoulders. Somehow, the gesture of bending toward each other, of exposing the tops of our heads seemed even more intimate than if we'd shared a tongue-smashing soul kiss as a goodbye.

Every time I turned back, he was still there standing, a rock in the river, as other commuters flowed around him. Even as I walked up the stairs, which would cut me off from his view, he remained. I was tempted to scoot back down and see if he was still there, but instead, I let the tide of people carry me up the stairs to the platform.

Five stations into my trip, I noticed that the station-numbers were decreasing. They were supposed to be going up. I was going in the wrong direction.

My first reaction was to panic. But then I remembered that the green line was one sinuous circle. If I stayed on long enough, I would get to where I was going.

At the next station, a man who looked to be about two hundred years old and partially mummified, entered. He was clad in a traditional vest, lavender pants tied at the ankle, and he held a cane as he tottered aboard.

I offered my seat, as Koreans always seemed to do for the elderly. He grunted and settled into the sea-green velveteen seat, rested his gnarled hands atop the burled wood of his cane. An anachronism next to men in sharp-cut Western suits, women carrying designer handbags, the kind that would be too fancy even for Dayton's. But no one gave him a second look.

I held onto the pole and looked out the window—this part of the green line was above ground. I watched the tall buildings with twinkling lights, the red neon crosses atop church steeples just starting to glow in the dark, bowling alleys with gigantic bowling pins mounted on their roofs. Then the train rushed into the blackness of a tunnel.

Back in our subway car, no one was staring at me. I was a part of this scene, this Korean tableau. For the first time, I felt, even if fleetingly, like I belonged somewhere.

KYUNG-SOOK
Seoul
1972

The foreigner's name was "David." He was in Korea through an American group he called the "Peace Core" that was somehow supposed to help Koreans. This Peace Core had sent him to the countryside on the mountain seacoast to live for two years, but he hadn't liked it, so he had quit and come to Seoul to take an English-tutoring job with a wealthy family.

"I was planning on going back to America right away, but I'm glad stayed," he said. "Otherwise I wouldn't have met you. Eventually I need to get back to America to go to graduate school—I deferred into an ethnomusicology program."

"Ed-no—"

"Professor school," he said. "In music."

Then he said, "Why don't you come to America with me?"

Kyung-sook could only laugh at this man's audacity.

"Why not?"

"You stop kidding me, you honey," Kyung-sook said.

"No, I'm serious," he said. "In America, you could make a living playing your wonderful flute. If you would just wear your Korean kimono, put your hair up, people would eat you up. You could become famous. There was a group called the Kim Sisters who dressed up in their Korean kimonos and sang 'Arirang' on the Ed Sullivan Show—apparently they were a riot."

Kyung-sook had absolutely no idea what he was talking about.

"Americans like all kinds of music," he said. His voice became fast and excited. "Like the blues, which is a kind of music that has its roots in tribal Africa. It's secular music, derived from folk traditions—you know, it's like your Korean opera, where the woman sings and the man plays the drum."

He was talking about p'ansori—long, lugubrious ballads sung by a lone singer with nothing to accompany her except the faraway sound of the changgo or the puk. Kyung-sook couldn't believe a foreigner could be so interested in her country's music.

"Is it true that in order to do that kind of opera, the singer has to sing until her throat bleeds?"

Kyung-sook knew very little about p'ansori, so she only nodded, to acknowledge that she had heard his question.

"That's fascinating—to be so dedicated to your art that you destroy your body. Now, let me play you a song of the people."

> Yo soy un hombre sincero,
> de donde crece la palma.
> Y antes de morirme quiero
> echar mis versos del alma.

He sang it in a different, mellifluous voice, in words of an English dialect he called "Spanish": *I am a truthful man from the land where palms grow/I want to share these poems of my soul before I die./With the poor people of the earth I want to cast my lot . . .*

How beautiful!

There was much she could learn from this man, Kyung-sook thought. How she wished that she could stop the hurtling movement of her life. But eventually, her parents would expect a return visit to the village when the school year ended in July. It was possible they might even have a match for her by then.

Marie Myung-Ok Lee

Her bright dreams—what had happened to them? She hadn't anticipated Seoulites' attitude toward traditional music: that it was unsophisticated and sentimental. To find other folk musicians, she had had to search out ratty bars, where men would raise their eyebrows at her, thinking she was a kisaeng girl. The musicians she found guffawed when she mentioned her dreams of playing solo improvisational pieces of hyang-ak, native music, in front of an audience.

They scoffed, "This isn't the Chosun Dynasty any more. Koreans want the operas of Verdi and Mozart played on their new electric gadgets. Even the teahouses play only Debussy waltzes these days."

Just as the stone walls of the Western churches were beginning to edge out the wooden Red Arrow gates of Buddhist temples, Western music was beginning to take over the Korean consciousness. When Kyung-sook saw a place that advertised itself as a "music school," she would see well-dressed children making their way up the stairs carrying sheets of music and Western violin cases.

Sometimes, the traditional musicians invited Kyung-sook to their flats, where they lived four, five to a room. They ate only cheap fried noodles because that was all they could afford.

"And you have to learn popular tunes, so you can play at the rich people's parties—to survive," they told her morosely.

That Kyung-sook could not do. She couldn't trap her music amidst the lines and stiff wires of this Western scale, submit them to the nasty-sounding conventions, "sharps" and "flats." When she played a san-jo, she improvised what her spirit moved her to play, which was the very purpose of this kind of music—what in nature was scripted and bound by wires, broken down into a calculus of notes and measures?

"There's nothing for you here," the David man said, tugging her down toward his bedding, which he let sit on the floor all day. "Let me take you away from all this."

Kyung-sook recalled the day she had defiantly sat herself down in front of Seoul Station with her taegum and begun to play. If people would just hear, she believed, they would be reminded of this ancient instrument's power: how its music was so beautiful it had been said to stop wars and heal disease in the ancient dynasties.

150

A small, curious crowd had immediately gathered. The younger people stepped over her, huffing about her being in their way. The people who stayed exclaimed how they hadn't heard that kind of music in a very long time. A granny even wiped her eyes and gave her a whole bag of just-roasted yams to take home. A bent-over old man donated all the coins his daughter-in-law had sent him off with that morning.

As the shadows grew long, people drifted away, and a police officer came up to her and told her there were laws against panhandling. The number of coins she'd received were barely enough for a trolley ride home.

"Better watch out, little sister," he warned. "Bad things happen to people who are out at night, after the curfew."

The man looked like he wanted a kiss-u, again.

Kyung-sook wanted to hear the song about the man from the land of green palm trees again. She lifted her flute to her lips and began to play. The man strummed his guitar, their notes weaving together as easily as two small rivers become a larger one. Kyung-sook at last began to relax, letting her mind become tangled in its own melodies, going to a place where there were no worries.

SARAH
Seoul
1993

"Why don't we do something different?" I said to Doug. "Why don't we try to find the *Doksuri* teahouse, the one they keep talking about in our textbook? It's supposed to be the official teahouse of Chosun University."

"*Pabo-yah*," Bernie leaned in before Doug could answer. "Our textbook is obviously about a hundred years old—it has stuff like 'don't take me on a five-won plane ride.' You couldn't find a teahouse in this neighborhood if you looked for days. Everything is *ka-peh*, like the Balzac *ka-peh* where you go with your army guy."

I sucked in my breath.

"I didn't ask you," I said, and added, knowing he hated his American name, "Ber-nard."

At the Rainbow, I choked on guilt as well as noodles, so when Doug suggested going "somewhere," I readily agreed, even though I had music class. To further assuage my guilt, I handed him a key to my room that I'd just had made by an *ajuhshi* who had a little tent-stand full of keys on the street. I thought he'd have a noisy vibrating machine, like the one at Ace Hardware, but instead, he glanced at my key, sat down, cross-legged and barefoot, took out a blank and began shaping it with a simple metal file, smoking a cigarette, looking as inattentive as if he were trimming his nails on a boring afternoon. But in short order, the key was done, and I went back to the room and tried it—it worked.

"*Mi casa es tu casa,*" I told Doug. "By the way, what does *pabo-yah* mean?"

" 'You fool.' "

I sighed. "Why does Bernie hate me so much?"

"He doesn't hate you, he's like the fifth grader who throws rocks at the girls he likes. He's obviously attracted to you, your nice face, your double eyelids—"

"Double eyelids? I'm some kind of lizard?"

"The fold," he explained. "Only a few Koreans naturally have that. Most people have to get surgery."

Korean women—and some men—apparently had surgery to make their eyes look more "Western." In the *Korea Herald,* I'd read an article about a famous young movie actress who had refused to get the surgery before playing Ch'un Hyang, a Korean folk heroine known for her beauty and steadfastness. The surgery had been mandated by her contract— "Whoever plays Ch'un Hyang has to have beautiful eyes," a studio executive had been quoted as saying. The actress wasn't working anymore.

"And your hair," Doug went on. "I've never seen anyone with such thick hair."

"My hair," I snorted. "When I was in sixth grade, I wanted a Dorothy Hamill wedge like everyone had. It looked like the bottom of a broom after it was cut."

Doug laughed.

"Why should you want to look like Dorothy Hamill? She's not Korean."

I smiled. The Fabulous Sarah Thorson thought she looked great in a wedge, the gold colors of her hair flowing in creamy waves. In reality, my hair would do only one thing: point to the ground. Even when soaking wet, each strand stayed true to itself, separate as sand. I found myself wishing for a snarl, a comb-stopper that would make me smirk and grimace as I tried to jerk it out, something that would give me a reason to use No More Tangles, like Amanda.

"You're so strange," he said. "It's as if you can't see yourself."

Who can truly see themselves? Mirrors, film, only project in two dimensions. We live in a world with three. Maybe the closest was having someone else see you. I was thinking of the time I was caught digging in the cat box.

Christine had asked me to fetch something from the basement, and underneath the pegboard that held the fishing rods, cross-country skis, tennis rackets, I came upon a sand-filled tray. My fear of the dark had kept me out of the basement (four-year-old Amanda somehow used to be able to shut off the light and slam the door, trapping me in eternal darkness with spiders), but now the sand caught my eye with its minty color, how it was level, almost groomed, inviting as a pan of cool water. I stopped, plunged my hand in, liking the way the sand felt dry and granular, not gritty and creepily damp like sandbox sand.

First, I saw her feet. Slim, tanned ankles in white canvas Tretorn tennics, white cotton bootie socks with pom-poms sticking out over the edges.

Her hand pulled my collar as if it were a scruff.

"Dirty!" Christine's chest reddened over the V-neck of her tennis whites. "Are you crazy? Did you learn that awful habit over there?"

The blue in her eyes, the white of the pearls circling the base of her neck. She looked improbably beautiful, even as she was screaming at me. How was I to know that the Persians peed and crapped into this *box*? I thought they were creatures that didn't *go* at all; I saw no evidence of them going outside, like our neighbor's black lab, Captain Midnight, who was always crouching around, tail in a question-mark, leaving cigar-shaped sticks all over our yard.

"Look at me," she said, pulling us nose-to-nose. "You. Do. Not. Dig. In. The. Cat. Box."

Her irises expanded and contracted, a camera's shutter clicking. Flash-frozen in her gaze, I saw her seeing me: a dark, foreign object, denizen of the basement, defiler of the cat toilet.

"You hate me!" I wanted to scream.

Then she swept a strand of blond hair from her eyes. Her eyes their normal cerulean blue. Her lips curved up in a smile.

"Let's go wash our hands, honey. Why, it's almost time for lunch, isn't it?" She paused to carefully enclose the round head of her tennis racket into a square, wooden press, even let me, slowly, fumblingly tighten the screws.

Doug unrolled the cotton *yo* piled in the corner and pulled me down on it as if it were a blanket on the beach.

"I called the TV station, Sejong Broadcasting, by the way," he said, into my hair.

"You mean *Missing Persons*?" I yelped, sitting up.

"Yup. The show's actually called *The Search for Missing Persons*— dramatic, eh?"

"What happened?"

"They're very busy. So many people have someone missing in their lives."

"Oh."

"So I told them you're American, only here until the end of the summer. I called and asked them again and again. Oh, maybe fifteen times in the last two days."

I sat, watching him.

"You've got a slot, two weeks from Tuesday. Sejong Broadcasting is in Yoido, which is this little island on the Han River where all the TV stations are."

I sat in shock.

I've been to Yoido already, I almost said.

"It might take an hour to get there by cab if there's traffic. So get ready to take a little trip after lunch two weeks from Thursday. I'll go with you— if you want me to."

"Of course I want you to. Thank you so much," I said.

Then I started crying. I could feel his hand, warm and reassuring, on my back.

KYUNG-SOOK
Seoul
1972

Yun-tan, he never stopped talking about America. Soon the word itself, A-me-ri-ca, played like a song inside Kyung-sook's head.

The other day, when Kyung-sook had gone to his flat, he had had a present waiting.

Bananas!

Kyung-sook didn't think she could accept such a costly gift. Just the other day, he had taken her to a Western restaurant where she had eaten breaded pork cutlets and corn salad for the first time—she had never had anything so delicious before. The man told her the bananas were for her. After she recovered from her shock and disbelief, she carefully wrapped the golden curves in her wrapping cloth to take back to share with the cook-owner and Sunhee. The man David, he just laughed at her, saying that in America one could eat bananas all day if you wanted, like a monkey.

"Wah!" said the cook-owner, back at the restaurant. "I've never even *seen* a banana before."

The three of them stared at the fruit as if it were made of pure gold. When they finally ventured to try it, they carefully shaved tiny, sweet bits off one banana, left the rest on top of the little table by the counter as a luxurious decoration. After a few days, however, they turned brown and rotted, spreading a sickly-sweet smell through the restaurant.

"You need to consider your happiness for a change," the foreigner–man said. "I know that in Korea, women sacrifice as daughters, then as wives, then as mothers. They never have anything to call their own."

Kyung-sook was irritated with the man's tone—he seemed to say that he understood her country the best, and that she needed *him* to explain it to her. Still, she couldn't help recalling Bong-soon, the girl named after the pink balsam-flower, who was the prettiest, most sought-after girl in the village. Even after bearing her husband Hyung three sons and taking meticulous care of his elderly parents, Hyung had gotten the wind in his blood and had taken a mistress—one that he married shortly after Bong-soon killed herself by filling her apron with stones and wading into the Glass River. She had barely reached thirty.

Kyung-sook spit out the sticky squash candy she had been chewing. Stuck inside it was one of the lead fillings from her teeth. The man looked into her mouth with alarm.

"I'll take you to the clinic at HanYong University."

The famous HanYong University had been founded by an American missionary family, the Overtons, so the school was particularly prized by Koreans. It was one of the most difficult ones to gain entrance to, second only to Seoul National University.

Kyung-sook found herself among the stately stone buildings, square courtyards, groomed topiaries, the dignified statues of various Overtons that stood erect as if overseeing the flowering rose gardens.

"The architecture is modeled after Harvard, a famous university in America—they even imported this ivy that's growing on the walls," the man said, then added, "Harvard, that is where I'll be going to graduate school."

Of course all Koreans knew about Harvard, the school that was famous even in A-me-ri-ca, land of famous schools.

"How you know so much about this HanYong University?" Kyung-sook asked.

"The descendants of the first Overtons still live in Korea. Hargrave Overton had a party for all the Peace Corps workers before we were sent to our various postings," he said. "He had his family there—he has a beautiful Korean wife and three children, one of them an adopted orphan. And you know what's funny? None of the kids—not even the Korean orphan—speaks a word of Korean!"

"Not a one word?" asked Kyung-sook.

"You're always teasing me about not learning much Korean," he said, pinching Kyung-sook's arm playfully. "Okay, I still haven't picked up han-gul, your Korean alphabet, which you *claim* your wonderful King Sejong devised so that it can be learned in an hour. But you know, Overton said that old-time missionaries used to call Korean 'the devil's language.' "

"Why?"

"Because the devil purposely made the language so hard to learn in order to keep the missionaries from Christianizing people. Overton himself comes from a family that's been in Korea for three generations, but he doesn't speak any Korean himself, either. He sends his kids to the Seoul Foreign School, where they only speak English."

"But what about mother, you said he Korean lady?"

"Yeah, *she*."

"But—" Kyung-sook said. "To children? How she speak to children?"

"Well, she speaks a little English, although it's not as good as yours. She'll just have to learn it better if she wants to communicate with her children and husband."

David led Kyung-sook to a large white building. The university's hospital—fully Western, he said. "If you want to get that stuff with the needles or the burning herbs treatment, you have to go somewhere else."

Inside the building was a place called the Foreigner's Clinic. It was spacious and orderly, not at all like a Korean clinic, which was usually as noisy and raucous as an open-air market. Here, Westerners sat quietly, neatly lined up in chairs, while Western doctors strode the halls looking extraordinarily tall.

At the dental hall, a Korean nurse in a white uniform and a stiff, starched hat curved like a paper lantern greeted Kyung-sook so politely, she was taken aback; as a waitress, she was used to people using familiar language with her. David showed the nurse a blue book with a gold eagle stamped on the cover. She nodded and asked them to wait.

Kyung-sook needed to use the bathroom, and she was impressed that there was actually one right inside the building. However, she was dismayed to see the Western toilet.

It was built like those chairs that Westerners were so fond of. Westerners seemed to like to inhabit that strange middle space between sitting and standing—but what a waste of the ondol-heat from the floor! And now, this pyonso, she couldn't think of a more repulsive contraption. She made sure to keep her ongdongi from touching it, but because the seat was too high to let her squat, her urine sprayed everywhere.

So strange! she thought to herself. At least there was paper for wiping, right there. She gathered up an extra wad of it and stuck it in her pocket, for later.

She and the man were ushered into a stark, white room. She was told to sit in a chair that looked like it was made to hold a giant. A man with gold-red hair covering his exposed forearms like fur looked into Kyung-sook's mouth. She was scared when he started up a machine that gave off an awful whine, but the Korean nurse told her not to worry. Before she knew it, the hole was filled. Not like last time when the tooth-doctor spent almost an hour clumsily chipping at the tooth, spilling bits of metal in her mouth. The Western doctor handed her a mirror. She was surprised to see that she had a gold—not lead—filling. Kyung-sook smiled at David the foreigner, wishing she could smile wider, so that everyone could see the glitter.

All this fuss the foreigner-man, Yun-tan, had done—all for her.

A-me-ri-ca, the song played, over and over.

SARAH
Seoul
1993

Later in the week, it began to rain. And rain. Every morning the Seoul sky groaned gray and swollen, seeming to release its liquid burden in exhaustion. Six-inch-long earthworms slithered out, then drowned, bloated and pale, on the sidewalk. Rivers of dirty water slid down the hill by the Residence, carrying twigs and garbage and once, a child's plastic shoe. The mornings were damp and clammy, the small respite of noon sun was followed by an afternoon downpour. Garish orange squash blossoms appeared everywhere, the thick, trumpet-like blooms drooping heavy with collected rainwater.

Doug was right. I didn't have to ask when the *chang-ma,* the monsoon season, started.

One week, rain poured straight from the sky without rest. We were wet all the time, the Residence's halls became cluttered with umbrellas, damp pairs of shoes. Sopping socks draped like Dali watches over every available piece of furniture. The girls went to the HYUNDAI Department Store and bought colorful rubber boots.

"It's like living at the bottom of a fucking toilet," Bernie Lee grumbled, as the very existence of the sun became an unsubstantiated rumor. "The sky is vomiting water."

I enjoyed the steady patter of fat drops, the dust-colored light that made two o' clock in the afternoon seem like evening. The *chang-ma* drove me inside, the perfect place for me to wait. For her. I used that time to dream about meeting my mother. How she would have blacker-than-black hair like mine. And she would wear it youthfully long, so when she bent over to kiss me, it would brush my face.

Her hands, elegant and agile. Every morning of her pregnancy she would have tapped out a little welcoming tattoo, a reveille to me, her pressing fingers a kind of embrace.

I would have kicked back. Perhaps she laughed when I did this.

She would have a soft voice. Not like Christine's, which tended to get tense and shrill as if she didn't believe people were listening to her. No, my real mother's voice would be soft, so soft that people would pause, incline their heads toward her, because they wanted to hear what she had to say.

I had begun seeing flashes of her, her face this time. Sometimes in that precarious space between sleep and waking. Or her profile might materialize in the steam floating off my rice, sketched in a bowl of noodles. Once, when I was playing the *changgo* drums, her whole self appeared, floating. But she only appeared on the edges of things, like those floaters that exist in the vitreous fluid of your eyeballs; when I tried to look at her dead-on, she'd vanish.

"Who do you think my mother was?" I asked Doug after we made love in my room, his hand clamped tightly over my mouth to keep me quiet. "You know. When she had me."

He thought for a moment.

"You can't take too much stock in these things, but you don't have the face or the coloring of a peasant," he said. "My guess is that your mother could have been a college student who'd had a fling, or a high-class hooker who chews flower-gum."

"Very funny."

"How about your birth *father*? It could have been he who abandoned you. In Korea, the fathers get custody. Maybe he was divorced and wanted to get remarried. It also could have been a case of a poor couple with too many mouths to feed."

I knew this was just a game, a create-your-own-identity game. But lately I'd been playing it solitaire for hours, meandering on journeys all over the known universe, but ultimately going nowhere, caught on the endless surface of a Möbius loop.

"Have you ever thought about your birth father?" he repeated.

"No." He seemed shocked, so I explained: "With my mother, well, I started dreaming about her when I was thirteen. If I shut my eyes quickly I can just catch a glimpse of her inside my eyelids, or sometimes I see this shadow just as I'm falling asleep. Even though I've never gotten a good look at her face, she has a presence. Not so with my birth father."

Maybe that was just the way of fathers: one's language was the mother tongue, one's country the motherland. Take Ken. In the realm of our family, he was the marginal figure forever in the penumbral shadow of Christine. Christine was the one who decided what we had for supper, where we went on vacation, and generally any and all decisions regarding The House and The Children.

So to Amanda and me, Ken remained two-dimensional: law-school diploma, meal ticket, a portrait on the wall. He didn't protest his secondary status, on the contrary he accepted it, maybe even enjoyed being free of those messy emotional encumbrances that sometimes caused dishes to be broken, doors slammed, children to be told they might have become prostitutes in an alternative life. And, like the portrait on the wall—the one that had eyes that moved only when certain people were looking at it—Ken had his own ways of getting things across, of letting his daughters know he loved and cared for them.

"A week to go, until the show," I reminded him.

"The Search for Missing Persons will begin," he agreed.

KYUNG-SOOK
Seoul
1972

"How do you like it, Karen?" David the foreigner asked eagerly. He called her "Karen" because, he complained, "Kyung-sook" was too hard to remember.

She nodded vigorously, politely. "Is very good."

"In America, you could have pizza every day if you wanted," he told her. "There's a pizza place on practically every block."

This *pi-ja* might be more palatable, she thought, if she could add a pinch of sugar and a goodly amount of sweet-hot red pepper paste, maybe some fish or kimchi. And if she could scrape off the *cheez-u*.

It was amazing to her that Koreans paid handsome sums of money to eat this kind of food. Some Western foods, like the fried pork cutlets, were perhaps more delicious than Korean foods. But Westerners seemed to assume their things would always be better, more civilized, and Koreans seemed to silently agree by slavishly copying their ways. Take this *pi-ja* for instance. That stuff they called *cheez-u* that they were so proud of smelled like human shit—no other way to describe it. And then, you ate the *pi-ja* with your *hands*. Sunhee had whispered to her that she heard that Westerners indulged in a puzzling practice of sitting in their own dirty bathwater.

Was that why the foreigner-man always smelled a bit rancid, as if he'd washed with water only and not soap? Not scrubbed the old layers of skin off with a pumice? When Kyung-sook was a child, her mother considered her clean only once pea-sized balls of flesh rolled off her arms and legs in profusion.

Kyung-sook put those thoughts out of her mind as she forced herself to eat the rest of the *pi-ja*. She wondered if she was going to be in Seoul or back in the village by the next Harvest Moon Festival. Or, was it even possible, she might even be in A-me-ri-ca?

She thought about autumn, the season that traditionally made Koreans melancholy—the leaves dying, the cold winter coming. But autumn was one of Kyung-sook's favorite seasons. To her, it was the time for the leaves to hold nothing back and bask in their blazing glory, for the moon to grow so fat and bright the sky could barely contain it. The drummers in their flowing white, red, and blue clothes would dance up and down the dirt paths, pounding out the familiar rhythms that would set blood jumping, giving strength to the farmers to cut, bundle, and thresh their harvest.

The autumn was still far off.

The next day Kyung-sook complained about her stomach. The *pi-ja* seemed to be liquefying and flowing out of her. She collapsed at the restaurant, sending trays and dishes flying. Sunhee helped her up, dragged her to the kitchen, where the cook-owner waited with a sharp sewing needle in hand.

"They say that if one of the body's heavenly gates gets jammed up, you have to break it open," she said. She grabbed Kyung-sook's thumb in a viselike grip, wrapped the knuckle tight with a string, and then plunged the needle deep into the bulging spot right above the moon of the nail. Kyung-sook screamed as blood spurted everywhere.

"See, the blood is dark, corrupted," said the cook-owner with satisfaction. "Once it flows out, it'll clear up the congestion in your innards."

Now Kyung-sook's thumb throbbed, as well as her stomach.

At around dinnertime, David the foreigner came to the restaurant. He looked at Kyung-sook's wan face and said she should stay with him because she was sick. Kyung-sook agreed; she couldn't imagine laying her aching bones on the cold cement floor of the storeroom, even though the cook-owner *tsk*ed loudly when she saw the two of them leaving together, and Sunhee said incredulously, "Oh-moh—you're going to go stay the night with Mr. Fish?"

Kyung-sook was too weak to reply.

At his flat, David had her lie on his yo in the warmest part of the room. He told her he was going to make juk, the rice gruel Koreans eat for upset stomachs. He said he had watched his "country mother" make it many times.

Kyung-sook, despite her queasiness, was amused. No one besides her mother and Imo had ever prepared food for her before. So even though he forgot to wash the rice, resulting in lumpy yet watery mush—"not quite rice, not quite gruel" as the saying went—she ate it as enthusiastically as her upset stomach would allow.

When Kyung-sook felt better, he entertained her with photos of his family. Mixed in with these photos was one of a woman with hair the color of barley straw, her eyes the strange, immovable gray of slate. This photo he did not explain, sliding it quickly back into the pile.

"Who is that lady?" Kyung-sook asked.

"No one important."

"But her picture with picture of family."

He sighed melodramatically.

"If you must know, she was my first love."

First love!

Kyung-sook did not feel jil-tu, jealousy. Instead she felt charmed that someone else had loved this David man before her. When he left to use the outhouse, she flipped the picture over.

> *To David,*
> *Friends always,*
> *Annie Borchard, Wilton High Class of '68*

What a strong sentiment, Kyung-sook thought. Friends. Always!

He showed her the rest of the pictures: his family posed against a background of a blue ocean with white sailboats—it looked like a painting. He said the place was called "Cape Cod." Kyung-sook replied that she thought it was strange to name such a beautiful place after a fish.

He laughed.

"It's so wonderful to see things fresh through your eyes," he said.

Kyung-sook sat up. Her stomach lurched, although she didn't know if it was from being sick or from being anxious. Thoughts of her future increasingly filled her with dread. When the man left Korea, could she try to return to college? Should she go back to the village? Keep working at the dumpling house? This foreigner had brought so many strange colors and sounds and sensations into her life, she feared that when he left, everything would become unbearably dreary.

"You wanna me to go to A-me-ri-ca?" she said experimentally.

"I love you, Karen," he said. "You must see that Korea isn't big enough for your dreams—your music."

"My music?"

"Yes, your music, your country's music. Your people have let themselves be swept up by Western capitalist values, letting valuable traditions languish and die. I see it everywhere: people would rather listen to some third-hand recording of Beethoven instead of merely stepping outside and experiencing true Korean music, the kind that has sustained your people through the ages."

He leaned over to Kyung-sook and took her hand.

"I want to give you everything America has to offer, Karen," he said. "I know what your life was like, I lived out in the country. I could hardly believe the primitive conditions."

He laughed a rough laugh.

"The shit and piss from the outhouse went right into the pig's trough," he said, with evident disbelief. "And one morning when I'd gotten up early, I saw the country mother collect the chamber pots and then pour their contents into the ash-house—and then use the ashes for fertilizer in the vegetable garden! Can you believe it, Karen?

Kyung-sook was puzzled.

"We Korean, we dunna waste," she said. Anyone fortunate enough to own a pig let it eat waste, everyone else used the night soil for fertilizer—some enterprising farmers even put lean-to privies right in their fields to beg for more from the passersby.

She said to the man, "How else you gonna get plant and piggie to grow big?"

He shook his head and muttered something about how whenever he—and no one else—used the outhouse, the pig would get excited and run over, grunting and squealing, and the villagers would gather and laugh at the spectacle.

"In America, it'll be so different. You'll have sanitary flush toilets, you'll be able to take a bath every day, not just once a week at the bathhouse. You'll have TV, telephones, vaccines, you'll be able to drive a car, even."

A car? She didn't know anyone who'd even ridden in, much less driven, one. But the man had brought her bananas, gold for her teeth, delicious, rubbery chewing gum that he called Wiggly.

"Most importantly, in America, it's a democracy, not a military dictatorship. The president doesn't order the police to shoot people on the streets. We have honest elections, women have equal rights. We call it 'women's lib.'"

"Womens-u rib," she repeated, hardly understanding his excited chatter.

"We're going to have to work on your pronunciation," he said. "Women's l-l-lib."

Kyung-sook sighed. This man, in all his time here, knew little Korean other than *give me this* and *I know*. Sometimes, he called her his "yobo," as if they were married, or his "saek-ssi lady," obviously not knowing he was just redundantly calling her "lady-lady."

"And my name isn't Da-bid, it's Da-*v*-*v*id." He crunched down on his lower lip with his teeth and instructed Kyung-sook to do the same.

"Vee," he said.

"Bee," she repeated.

"I want you to be able to say the name of your future husband," he said. He took Kyung-sook into his arms and kissed her, pushing his tongue into her mouth, crushing her onto the yo. In the back of her throat, Kyung-sook tasted the man's peculiar smell that rose off him like vapor—it reminded her of stagnant water, that kind lotuses and the giant red carp grew well in.

"Da-bid, Da-bid," she whispered.

The next day Kyung-sook told the foreigner she would go back to America with him.

"Groovy," he said. He told her to wait while he went out. He returned smiling, his hands hidden behind his back. He teased her, making her guess which hand held the surprise. She tapped his left arm, then his right arm. Both wrong, it seemed.

Finally, he presented her with a closed fist, which he opened with excruciating slowness. Resting on his dry palm was a jade ring, moss green and dark all the way through. It wasn't the translucent almost-white of their country's fine jade, but she smiled and let him put it on her finger. It was a sign of his promise.

The next time she looked through his pictures, she found, with much satisfaction, that the photo of the woman with the slate eyes was gone.

SARAH
Seoul
1993

The day had finally come. Onward, to the Gilded Lego City of Yoido.

I felt jittery, my eyelids scratchy as if I hadn't slept—I hadn't. Yesterday, I'd actually gone out and bought makeup, hair spray. My hair turning out "right" suddenly became one of the most important things in my life. But how could it be otherwise when there was a chance that my Korean mother might see me for the first time?

I chose to wear, with no lost irony, the purple sundress Christine had forced me to buy for this trip. The dress was totally her style, very Talbot's, not mine, which ran toward Salvation Army and Ragstock. I had almost thrown it away—no way I was going to let Christine dress me in her image over here—and now here I was, decked out in purple since everything else I had was jeans, too slangy and American. I wished I had a Korean dress.

"You look great," Doug said, taking my hand as we leaned into the street, searching for cabs. We were nervous about traffic. Seoul these days was a maze of concrete barriers and construction signs. All roads eventually led to a clogged artery of cars inching around an Ozymandias-esque ruin of concrete, metal, and raw earth, as the old was razed for new buildings and bridges, or additional subway lines, which, when completed, would do nothing to alleviate traffic because the accelerating prosperity would make drivers out of people who, ten, fifteen years ago, could scarcely have dreamed of owning a car.

On that first Yoido day, Jun-Ho had pointed to a sign on the side of the road, one with movable text and numbers.

"It is the number of traffic deaths on top, the ones who have hurt on the bottom. Today: 25 deaths. 132 hurts—in Seoul, only."

Back then, I had thought of my parents in that group, the scary-sounding word, *sa-mang*. Death. But in a day, everything had changed.

Doug eschewed various hatchback taxis until a silver-and-blue "88" cab—one manufactured for the Olympics, specifically for the larger frames of foreigners—appeared. He opened the door for me, climbed in front with the driver, and told him where we needed to go.

❀ ❀ ❀

I remembered seeing Sejong Broadcasting on my trip with Jun-Ho, but of course I didn't say so. Inside, the building looked unnaturally clean, as if it had been boiled recently, its chrome-paneled elevators sleek and sterile as surgical instruments. The people walking around seemed to shop at the same store: identical navy blue suits and crisp white shirts, men and women. This whole place was a country apart from the grimy, recalcitrant elevators of our school building, the janitor-*ajuhshis* doing the Third-World squat in the halls, smoking their unfiltered cigarettes, spitting oysters of mucus to the floor. The unreality of Yoido's interiors as well as exteriors did not disappoint. From some futuristic antenna on top of the building, my image was going to float in particles through the air to nest into people's TV sets all over Korea.

As we stepped from the elevator, a man in a navy suit greeted us, clipboard in hand. He repeatedly apologized for his "poorly" English as he led us to the room where the other guests were waiting: an elderly man with white dandelion fuzz for hair, a quintessential overpermed *ajuhma* who was kneading some Kleenex into a paste. I was handed a scalding Dixie cup of coffee, which I sipped reflexively, the superheated sugar becoming napalm in my mouth.

The man with the clipboard came back to me.

"Name?" he said, pen poised expectantly as I coughed.

"Sa-rah Thor-son," I finally choked out.

"Korean name?"

"Lee Soon-Min." My throat felt strafed. "But that's not my real name. That's the name they gave me at the orphanage."

He looked at me, puzzled. Doug hesitated a second, then stepped in with Korean.

"Oh. Oh," the man said. "Just minute, moment." He scurried away and was replaced by a young woman with a cookie-round face and tortoiseshell glasses.

The woman extended her hand Western-style.

"My name is Kyunghee Noh. I am a producer here. I will act as a translator for the show."

"Hello," I said, taking her hand. "Have you ever been to America? Your English is very good."

"No, I have never left Korea," she said, bowing slightly in thanks. "But I enjoy studying languages."

Kyunghee Noh proceeded to ask me the rest of the questions. Whom (yes, she said "whom") I was looking for, and why? What could I tell them about the situation to help someone find me? I gave her every detail, which I'd written in advance.

When we were done, she showed me her clipboard, awash in Korean characters, as if I could read it. "When you are on TV, you will speak Sarah's story again, and I'll translate what you say."

"Actually, could my friend translate for me?" I gestured toward Doug. "He knows the whole story already, inside and out."

Kyunghee Noh looked at me as if I'd just slapped her across the face.

"I am sorry," she said, recovering her professional smile. "I am the translator. You see, it is already here, on my paper."

Rules are rules, I supposed, but my story was like a newborn infant, all untried limbs and floppy head. I wanted someone I trusted to take it from me, to release it to millions of strangers. I felt a sudden resentment toward Doug's choice of wardrobe for my Most Important day: battered T-shirt and jeans with a hole in the knee, the strange military star-pin. Maybe they couldn't let him on TV dressed like that.

From the green-papered waiting room, the other guests got up and left. They reappeared, miniaturized, on the TV mounted in the corner, like in a hospital room. I didn't pay any attention—I didn't have any to spare. I was concentrating on stopping the deluge of sweat pouring out of the pores of my face and armpits. I kept all nonessential physical activity to an absolute zero, but still, I could feel the dampness spreading.

The navy-suited man came back to the room and gestured to me with a downward dig of his hand as if he were paddling in water. I was hustled to the entrance of the sound stage. A green light went on, someone gave me a parting push.

"Sal-Ah Dorson!"

They played tinkly calliope music, as if I were a circus elephant. Everyone applauded.

After being in the dim greenroom, the sudden barrage of stage lights blinded me. I groped my way to the podium, gripping it for support, but it was a cheap veneer one, and it almost toppled over. The *ajuhmas* in the audience tittered appreciatively.

"Hallow," said the host, his shellacked Elvis pompadour seeming to rise up like a wave and try to reach me. "Hallow. *Anyonghasayo?*"

"*Anyong-ha-say-yo,*" I replied.

He said something else in Korean, his eyes sparkling behind the windows of his thick rectangular glasses, each a separate TV screen.

He repeated his question—it was likely he was making a joke at my expense, so I just said *I don't know* in Korean.

Peals of laughter, like shattering glass.

Later, Doug told me the host was asking me if I spoke Korean, a phrase I had encountered at least eighteen thousand and twenty times before.

Do you speak Korean? I don't know. I was such an idiot. I would have asked for a do-over, but this was, of course, live TV.

Kyunghee Noh came out and stood next to me.

"Tell your story."

I looked at the paper in my hand and read. A few times I waited, thinking that she was going to translate what I'd said, but she merely nodded, so I went on.

After I finished, she read from her clipboard in a continuous Korean. I could see a few of the ladies in the audience dabbing at their eyes with paisley handkerchiefs.

Then the silence settled over everything, like dust.

KYUNG-SOOK
Seoul
1972

The man David put a hand on her hip.

"You're losing your slender figure to all this American food, aren't you?" he admonished. "We're going to have to put you back on a Korean diet, with all its funny vegetables and seaweed and soybean curd now, aren't we?"

Kyung-sook did all his cooking. The first day, she had brought gulbi fish and hot peppers to make stew, but he told her to use the supplies he had already purchased on the black market: different kinds of *cheez-u,* red-and-white cans filled with some kind of sand-colored goo (he claimed it was soup), MAXWELL HOUSE, and the precious spicy-pink meat, SPAM.

One day, he declared he was sick of rice. He told Kyung-sook to make him some *mac-a-loni.* She boiled it as he took a nap. When she'd finished, she didn't know what to do—the *mac-a-loni* was quite bland, and he was still snoring away.

She tried sprinkling some sugar on it, as she had seen him do on his food in the morning. Quite a bit better. It would be even tastier with a splash of soy sauce and a drop of rich sesame oil, but he didn't seem to like Korean tastes all that much, so instead she poured a can of PET milk into it, until it was nice and soupy.

"What are you doing?" he yelled, making her jump back. His black *yun-tan* hair was all disheveled around his face.

"Make dinner?" she ventured, in a small voice.

"Je-sus," he said. "You don't put sugar on pasta, you put cheese and tomato sauce."

He had been referring to the can with strange red fruit with the hat on—the *toh-mah-toh*—the shit-smelling *cheez-u* from the green cylinder.

"Okay, you didn't know," he said, finally, patting Kyung-sook on the arm, the same way her father patted their long-haired ox.

Kyung-sook took the bowl; she would eat her own creation, then.

"No, don't," he said. "You put so much sugar in it, you're going to get fat."

He made another dish of the pasta, showing Kyung-sook how to put the red fruit and cheez-u on top of it, and she had to admit it was actually sort of tasty that way, if you held your nose when the *cheez-u* smell was too much.

When she began to clean up, he instructed her to throw away the left-over bowl of *mac-a-loni.* Staring into the garbage pail, she remembered the winter when they ran out of food, and how Hye-ja, the one who was scorned by the housewives because she worked at the Yankee army base, had lugged a full bucket of American garbage all the way back to the village. The bucket had been filled with egg-shells, bones, moldy food, some kind of dark, acrid sand that Kyung-sook now knew was coffee grounds, and even an army boot. Hye-ja had boiled the whole thing in the town plaza. Even the housewives had stepped forward, tongues silent, stomachs empty, and had greedily, gratefully drunk up their portion of the "piggie stew."

"Just dump it, Karen."

She hesitated a moment, then did what he asked. The song in her head played again. A-me-ri-ca!

SARAH
Seoul
1993

I could actually see the dark eye of the camera coming closer as it zoomed in for the misery shot. Sweat sprouted from my pores as if I were a saturated sponge being squeezed, I had Nixonesque stains under my arms. My muscles ached. I needed to move, but of course, I couldn't leave the podium. I settled on letting my tongue explore the coffee-scorch blister on my soft palate. It was meaty and soft, like the inside of a grape.

The hosts stood in front of me, all I could see was their backs. They said something to the audience.

"*Aigu!*" someone exclaimed. Kyunghee Noh whispered to me, "No callers. I am sorry."

How could this have happened?

I was glued to the stage in shock, but the two feminine bouncers came to pry me off, while the host chatted jocularly with the audience and got them to laugh again.

Doug took my hand as I numbly entered the greenroom.

"You did great," he said. "You were wonderful."

"Lot of good that did."

"But they didn't mention the *ddong*," Doug said, his free fist balling up. "They omitted that whole thing."

"But why—" I sat down, the full weight of events falling like scales on my shoulders.

The short man came back to usher us out. Doug immediately launched into a tirade. The man stepped back cautiously away from him, mumbling something, and scurried away again.

"He's just a flunky," Doug muttered. "I told them to get whoever's in charge if they don't want their greenroom trashed."

Kyunghee Noh appeared. I stifled the urge to fit my hands around her neck, begin beating her with her own clipboard.

"Mr. Lee says you have some problem?"

"Yes, we have a fucking problem," I said. "How could you leave out the part about how I was found with excrement smeared all over me?"

Kyunghee Noh frowned.

"Of course we can not say such a thing even if you will be telling it like that."

"What?"

"We have a policy for our show, standards. What you said about the *ddong,* there are many people who will be thinking it is disgusting."

My mouth opened in disbelief. I was aware that Korean women were expected to never let their teeth or the inside of their mouths show, and here I was letting myself look like Mr. Ed. Kyunghee Noh seemed to note this, and added, "If you want disgusting, you watch the American Armed Forces channel."

I sputtered. "But it's the truth. This happened to me. ME. Some Korean person did that to me. A Korean, like the people who watch your show. A Korean left me there, covered in shit! Do you think it was easy for me to tell you this?"

Kyunghee Noh bit her lip, her eyes skittering back and forth as if she was reading something in front of her. "I am sorry. I can not explain well in English. How to say it, our show watchers are looking for happy stories, that is why they watch. You do not watch a TV story on animals if you do not have interests in animals, yes?"

This was making no sense.

"Try it in Korean," I said. "My friend understands."

Kyunghee Noh sighed, the same way Choi *Sunsengnim* did when I couldn't say *neh.* I wondered if she was dying to go home, maybe meet her boyfriend for coffee instead of spending her time talking to some psychotic

Americans. Resignedly, she spoke in Korean. Her words sounded elegant and educated. I wanted to hit her more than ever.

Doug said, when she finished: "She says there's too much *han*—sadness and regret—in people's lives already, so they watch this show to escape their *han* for an hour; they look to the happy stories to give hope to their own lives."

"But I'm not here for these people's entertainment!" I was practically screaming. "I'm trying to find my mother."

Kyunghee Noh shook her head. "I am sorry," she said. "Perhaps it was a mistake to have you on the show. We can not guarantee that anyone will receive a call. But I will pray for you that you can find your mother. Maybe someone will call later. You check with the station." She handed me a card.

I took it. We both understood it was a palliative, a piece of candy from the doctor that we were both pretending would take away the sting of a shot. I turned the card over. *Saejong Braodca§§ting,* it read in a quasi-Teutonic font, the rest of the Korean was lost to me.

"Let's go," I said to Doug.

We followed Kyunghee Noh through the labyrinthine corridors.

She gave us a parting bow as we walked out of the building back into Yoido's strange phosphorous light. I imagined she would lock and bolt all the doors when we left, pull up the drawbridge.

What had just happened to me? Somewhere within the gilt and neon and bitter dirt of this country was a woman who held a truth that I was so desperately seeking.

Mother!

KYUNG-SOOK
Seoul
1972

"Ai-gooo," the cook-owner said, noting Kyung-sook's expanding belly. "*Tsk-tsk-tsk.*"

As a girl, Kyung-sook had once asked her father, the smartest person she knew, exactly how a baby came into the world.

Her father had paused in his lunch. His spoon wavered over his rice and soup, as if he couldn't decide which one to start with first. He took a big scoop of the soybean-paste soup followed by a scoop of rice that had barley and purple beans mixed in. It was a flush year, that year.

"Ho, my child is grown enough to bring lunch out to the fields all by herself, and now she wants to know all the ways of the world, doesn't she?"

"Tell me, please, Appa."

"Well, if you want to know. First, a woman and a man get married—"

"Ah, it's the marriage that does it!" she'd cried. "I knew it—when Teacher O's daughter married last fall, she grew a big belly right after."

"Wait, wait. It's not just the marriage that does it," her father had laughed. "That's first, you're right. Then if the husband and wife sleep together, a baby crawls into the mother's stomach. Of course at first, the baby is just a tiny seed, but then it grows and grows, just as the rice sprout eventually becomes a full head groaning with rice."

She contemplated this. Then she said, "Sleep with someone to grow a baby?" She'd suddenly remembered the time she and Min-Ki had fallen asleep together in the shade of a tree by the celadon-green coils of the Glass River.

"I've got to work now." Her father picked the last, tenacious grains of barley sticking to the bowl, sipped the very last spoonful of soup. He set the bowls on Kyung-sook's carrying-cloth, then stretched out his arms as if he were trying to reach the sky. He rubbed his back, sighed, groaned, and spat. Then he yelled for the men to bring the ox over.

"Just remember that the marriage comes first, child," he said, as he began his stiff, tottering walk back to the fields. "You see, it is possible for the baby to accidentally go to an unmarried mother. But that causes so much sadness—no one is happy to see it, even if it's a boy. Horrible things will happen to it, the way Unmarried Shopkeeper Auntie's child was born without a nose."

Kyung-Sook had watched her belly in the days that followed, worriedly checking. Some days it looked like her normal nine-year-old girl's belly. But other days it seemed to be growing, expanding. Her father had said it was possible for a baby to make a mistake and come to a girl who wasn't married, wasn't that right? How would she tell her parents she was pregnant? She thought anxiously about it at night, fingering her belly, trying to feel for a baby-shape under the skin.

After the Month of Pure Brightness passed, her stomach turned definitely bigger. If she turned to the side and looked at her shadow, her stomach curved out like a burial mound. There were no mirrors in the house except for the broken fragment of one that her mother kept. Kyung-sook came back early from the fields one day and struggled to view her stomach in the slender shard.

What kind of deformed baby was growing in there?

"Mother, I think I have a baby."

Her mother did not glance up from the rice she was washing.

"Ai-goooo!" she lamented. "Who has put such idiotic ideas in your head?"

"Mother," she had said tremulously. "Once, I fell asleep with Min-Ki by the river. He fell asleep, too."

"Yah! We need to have an exorcism for you," her mother said. "Some bad spirit is whispering things in your ear. You cannot have a baby until your blood begins to flow every month. Then if your husband sticks his pepper inside you, the blood will stop and you'll want to throw up all the time. Then, and only then, will you have a baby. Or maybe after you've heard all this, you won't want to. Now, quit bothering me, do your schoolwork." She had begun shooing Kyung-Sook away with wet hands that had grains of rice stuck to them.

"But Mother," Kyung-Sook had protested. "Look at my stomach!" She had pulled down her black Japanese-style monpae pants to show her.

"Are you studying or are you spending all your time looking at your stomach?" her mother had yelled at her. But she did take note of her belly and the next day dragged Kyung-Sook to the country doctor, who made her swallow an envelope of the bitterest powder. When Kyung-Sook went to the outhouse later, she saw long, white worms in her ddong. Soon after, her stomach returned to its normal size. How could it be, she wondered, that a girl's stomach could hold both worms *and* a baby?

Kyung-sook looked back at the cook-owner. For the last couple of days, every time she looked at her, she saw not the cook-owner's face, but an opaque black spot. No matter how much she blinked, it would not go away.

"Is that kid going to be three feet tall and talking by the time the barbarian notices?" the black spot said.

"He's going to marry me," Kyung-sook said. "And I'm going to America with him."

"Well, tell him to hurry it up, Blinky. Doesn't he know we can't have you walking around with a big belly and no husband?—you're scandalizing the customers!"

Kyung-sook wanted to laugh out loud, thinking of their restaurant's clients, the men stopping for a cheap dinner before a night out at the kisaeng houses. The married construction worker who was busily trying to seduce Sunhee. Or the cook-owner herself, passing her ongdongi under Old Bachelor Choi's nose every day—who was she kidding, preaching to her?

It was true that the man David didn't come to the restaurant any more, but he said it was because the cook-owner made him nervous. Every time he showed his face, the cook-owner would throw salt at him, as Kyung-sook had done that first day.

"Your silly Korean superstitions," he said, the last time they had left the restaurant, the cook-owner venturing out even into the heavy monsoon rain to fling salt in his wake.

"That's why the East will always be stuck behind the West: Korea's thought is based on ghosts and goblins, not science."

Kyung-sook wasn't exactly sure what was so superior about Western thought. This man wore his shoes in the house, no shoes out (he regularly walked out into the courtyard barefoot like the worst kind of beggar). It was appalling to watch him touch his food with his hands instead of using utensils or wipe his nose with a dirty cloth he used over and over. And of course, there was the matter of those awful toilets. She wasn't exactly sure what was so superior about Western thought.

"I don't want to see you throwing salt or worshipping those dried fish," he said. "You're going to be meeting my professors and lots of other important people, so I want them to see what a sophisticated young lady you are."

Kyung-sook, nodded, even though from time to time, she, too, felt an urge to ward off bad spirits by throwing salt at that man, to scrub the coarse grains into places he had touched her. But then she thought about how she had once slipped a bill from his pile of American money and taken it to the credit-house. She had been amazed at the profusion of won she had received for that single American bill. She went to the silk market and purchased a jauntily olok-dolok-striped hundred-day outfit for the child. It gave her a thrill to think of raising her child in the Beautiful Country— she could probably have servants, even. And eventually, she would convince this man to send for her parents, so they could all live together in the bounty of A-me-ri-ca.

Out on the main street, a line of trucks roared by, so loud it made the ground shake. Army trucks, filled with soldiers, guns at the ready. They sped by once, maybe twice a day lately. Old Bachelor Choi said it was because of the student demonstrations.

"I hope it's not going to be like the riots of '60 and '61," he said. "After the body of that high school student demonstrator washed up on shore in Masan with torture marks all over him, all hell broke loose. Even housewives and maidens took to the street. The police got all panicky and would sometimes just shoot wildly into the crowds. So much bloodshed."

The trucks invaded the foreigner's neighborhood, too. The man David watched the soldiers go by as he and Kyung-sook opened the gate to his flat. He spat on the ground as if he had a bad taste in his mouth.

"See?" he told Kyung-sook. "Those brave protesting students just want fair elections. And the government is killing them—just the way they tried to kill Park's legitimate political rival, that man Kim. This is what's happening right now. Your Korea is being ruled by dictators who are planning to run your poor country into the ground."

Kyung-sook didn't know what to say. She didn't want David to know how ignorant she was of her country's politics. In the village, it had made little difference if this president or that one was elected; you were just not to say anything critical about the sitting one, that was all she knew.

In the restaurant, they could all hear the army trucks roar by again, the noise seeming closer this time, almost as if the trucks were in the alley itself. The cook-owner swore as the dishes rattled, as the usual noontime din was drowned out by the noise of powerful engines.

"Sis," said Sunhee to Kyung-sook, after the trucks had passed. "Cook-owner said you're going to get married and go back to America with Mr. Fish. You lucky thing! Oh, I should start studying English so *I* could meet a Westerner. I'm almost an old maid, working in this dump with no prospects."

"What are you calling a dump?" the cook-owner sniped, still a black spot in Kyung-sook's eyes. "It is said, 'Kick a stone in anger and you hurt your own foot.' Feel free to go elsewhere for your fucking employment!"

"I was just kidding," Sunhee said, hanging her proud head a little. She had obviously once been a beauty, which was what had gotten her in trouble in the first place at the sieve factory, between the enmity from the other female workers and the extra attention she received from the married male boss. "Where else do I have to go?"

She looked at Kyung-sook enviously.

KYUNG-SOOK
Seoul
1972

Kyung-sook woke to find that the baby had moved between the winged bones of her hips. Now less weight on her ribs, but down beneath, everything pressed, so heavy. The man David snored beside her, his mouth flung open.

Kyung-sook rose and began rummaging in the box of food. There was a banana and a few sweet biscuits. Some rice was needed, also. She put the banana and biscuits in the windowsill first.

Please, merciful Birth Goddess, please make the baby wait to come out until we are safely in America.

David walked over to the window, wiping his eyes, just as Kyung-sook took up a handful of rice.

"What the hell is this?" he said.

Kyung-sook leaped toward the offerings as he swept them from the windowsill. She still had the rice in her hands, and the hard grains slipped through her fingers as the banana and biscuits tumbled ignominiously to the floor. She wanted to weep.

"Karen, it's unclean to leave food out like this! Do you want us to have flies and roaches in here?"

The fruit and shattered biscuits lay scattered on the floor. Between them, the rice grains stood up on their tips, every one of them pointing up at the sky. A sure sign the Goddess was displeased.

"Oh, if that doesn't take the cake," David muttered. "A goddam mess all over the floor, and I haven't even been awake for five minutes."

Kyung-sook looked back at him. She didn't understand him any-more—he wasn't pleased with anything she did. Just last week she had gone to the beauty parlor and gotten a modern bobbed haircut and a perm. But when he saw it, he just looked at her and barked, "What did you do to your hair?"

He was staring at her with hard eyes, the colored part going up into the lid—what Koreans called snake-eyes.

The snake-eyes frightened her.

"You are just an Oriental peasant at heart, aren't you?"

Again, she did not understand. Instead, she grasped her stomach and showed him.

"What about baby?" she demanded of him. "Why you never say no thing about baby?"

He shook his head.

"You can't come back to America with a baby," he said, calmly. "I thought it was obvious."

What did he mean?

"I don't want children. I'm going to graduate school. The fact that you're still pregnant makes me think you don't want to come to America with me."

"I wanna go A-me-ri-ca."

"Then you have to get rid of the baby—it's getting to be almost too late. Do you understand what I'm saying?"

Sometimes, when the man spoke too fast, the meaning of his words was a fluttering thread that slipped out of Kyung-sook's hands. But now, his meaning was becoming all too clear.

He was talking about nak-tae. Abortion.

Kyung-sook began to cry. Was this man a human being?

"That's the only way," he said. "Did you think it was going to be easy for me, bringing home a foreign bride? There's a war going on in Asia that people aren't too happy about. This is going to be very hard on me. Do you understand what I'm saying?"

"Baby," she said.

"I know it's hard subverting the maternal instinct," he said. "But it's only a fetus, fe-tus, it's not a baby yet. The unpleasant part will be over before you know it, and we can go on to America. Can't you see your country is collapsing? Your president is a murderer of his own people, Karen. The army went and shot all those protesters in the middle of the day, some of them were mere children. There's no chance for democracy here. My government wants me to get out, too."

Kyung-sook was so tense, her teeth began chattering.

"Go to this clinic tomorrow and have it done. I know the doctor—he'll take care of you, let you stay overnight. The day after, I'll pick you up and we can go to the Bando Hotel together and get our plane tickets."

He handed her a piece of paper, with the name of a Dr. Rhee and an address scrawled in transliterated Korean. And, as if he were making a huge sacrifice, the man David handed her a ten-thousand-won bill.

"This is all I can spare because I need to prepare for our trip," he said. "Go get your savings and bring it with you. Forty, fifty thousand at the very least."

Kyung-sook found herself in the section of the city right behind Chong-no, Bell Street, in the Chinese medicine neighborhood. The smell of herbs and roots and dried animal parts made her feel even more nauseous. She walked by several stores that said, WE SELL DEER ANTLER and TIGER PENIS, GENUINE RED GINSENG.

The office was on the second floor of an acupuncture clinic.

She staggered up the steep stairs to the door that proclaimed "Dr. Rhee." Inside, it was dark and hot and smelt of rotting wood, so different from the shiny foreigner's clinic at HanYong University. The walls bore ghostly stains of cigarette smoke and grease from a hot plate sitting on a table. There were no nurses in white uniforms, just Dr. Rhee, an old man with a mole that looked like a giant leech eating up almost half his face.

He didn't look like a doctor, Kyung-sook thought. Maybe a tol p'ari doctor, a quack doctor. There were no certificates on the walls, only a table with a fraying curtain that went around it and a bucket that had some metal tools soaking in cloudy water.

Dr. Rhee glanced at her stomach and cackled. His fingers were stained with tobacco, a pack of cheap Peacock cigarettes sat on his desk.

"You are very big, very close to delivering, I'd say. This is not going to be an easy operation. How much do you have?"

Kyung-sook reluctantly showed him the pile of bills she had pulled together, all the wages she had scrimped and saved.

"That's not enough," he said, scowling. "That's not hardly enough. I'm breaking the law, you know, risking my own neck."

Then he turned away and hawked, as if he was going to spit.

Kyung-sook's head was spinning.

"Please," she said. "How much more do you need?"

"One hundred thousand won."

One hundred thousand! Kyung-sook looked around wildly, as if there was money to be found for the picking in the office. She found herself looking at the curtain around the table. There were stains of dark blood, like pinpricks, sprayed on the fabric.

Kyung-sook ran headlong down the steep stairs into the street, where she retched into the gutter. When she looked up, saliva dripping from her chin, she saw Dr. Rhee in his second-floor window looking down at her.

"You stupid poji-cunt, Yankee shit-whore." He shook his head, then slammed the window shut.

Kyung-sook went back to the restaurant. For some reason, the door was unlocked, but no one was there. No cook-owner, no Sunhee.

She had to think. Maybe the cook-owner could loan her the money. And maybe David could bring her to the foreigner's clinic, so she wouldn't have to face that terrible Dr. Rhee. She had to do it all soon, while she could still convince herself that the bulge in her belly was really not a baby, but an obstacle, the one obstacle lying between her and a new life in A-me-ri-ca.

She was so weary, she sat down and fell into a deep sleep in the back of the restaurant, and before she knew it, it was morning.

As soon as she awoke, she ran to David's boarding house. Impatient, she slid open the rice-paper panel. The room was bare, except for a bucket and a rag sitting in the middle of the floor, a crumpled English-language *Korea Herald* in the corner.

Kyung-sook ran into the courtyard. There, the bent-over landlady was sweeping.

"Ajuhma," she said to her.

"Don't tell me you're looking for your big-nose boyfriend," she snorted, beginning to sweep more vigorously.

"I am."

"Well, he flew the coop, Missy. Been gone since day before yesterday."

Kyung-sook heard a noise, like a rushing wind. The sound of her past, present, and future flying away.

When she woke, she was under the covers in an unfamiliar room. The landlady came in with some cold barley tea and helped her to sit up while she drank it.

"That big-nose ran out on you, too?" she asked, then clicked her tongue in reproach. "That bastard nom owes me two months' rent, which is nothing compared to what you—"

She stopped herself.

The landlady let Kyung-sook stay in the warm covers for another hour. Then her husband came home, and she said Kyung-sook had to leave.

Kyung-sook walked away, dazed, cupping her abdomen. The baby kicked right under her hand. Without thinking, she felt herself squeezing back with her palm.

Maybe it'll be a boy, she mumbled to herself. A boy is still a boy, someone who could help her support her parents, then herself, in old age . . .

"Where have you been?" shrieked Sunhee.

"What do you mean?"

"The cook-owner is dead!"

Dead!

"Oh, it was horrible! They said she was returning from the market, and as she was crossing the street she was run over by one of the army trucks!"

"What?" said Kyung-sook.

"The soldiers, they just drove away. I stayed with her all night until I could finally get someone to help me bring her body back here to the restaurant. I was so upset I just drove all the customers away. I didn't know what else to do."

Kyung-sook thought she was going to retch again when she saw the cook-owner's body laid out on the concrete floor of the storeroom where she used to sleep. Blood and dirt were matted into her hair. Sunhee had tried to nudge the body onto a mat, but the cook-owner, in death, had become like a rock and was impossible to move.

Kyung-sook sat, numbly.

"One of the customers said there's some kind of rioting going on down south," Sunhee babbled. "So the President declared a national emergency and sent the army into Seoul to keep order here. The streets are just crawling with soldiers and police."

Kyung-sook just rocked back and forth, holding the bulge in her stomach in between her hands.

Sunhee hurriedly scrawled a sign saying "Closed because of death" and bolted the door.

"Are you just going to sit there?" she said to Kyung-sook. "When are you going away with the Westerner?" Kyung-sook didn't answer her. The two of them sat in the restaurant all night, listening to the occasional roar of army trucks.

Early the next day, a young, well-dressed couple knocked on the door of the restaurant. They said they were the cook-owner's niece and nephew-in-law. They viewed the body without emotion, looking around at the restaurant's furnishings with more interest. Some workmen came to take the body away.

"Thank you for your services to our esteemed aunt," the man said. "Now, we can take over from here, so your services are no longer required."

"Wait," said Sunhee. "How do we know you are who you say you are? I have been working here for five years and I never saw you come into this restaurant once to pay a respect-visit to your elderly aunt!"

"How dare you speak to me like that!" Light flashed from the fancy gold cufflinks on the man's sleeve. "If we catch you here tomorrow morning, we'll have you thrown in jail for trespassing. The police chief in this district is a personal friend."

That afternoon, Sunhee fled, taking with her some of the steel bowls and a bag of rice. Kyung-sook sat in the back, packing and repacking her meager belongings, fingering her flute.

She cooked herself some rice, but then wasn't able to eat. The smell of death pervaded the place.

She couldn't stay.

Could she face her imo? she wondered. She knew no one else in Seoul.

Kyung-sook's mother had once told her that when she and Imo were young, Buddhist monks used to come to their house, begging. In their filthy robes and their shaved heads, they looked so frightening that their mother could discipline her by threatening, "If you don't behave, I'll give you away to the next monks who come to the door!" Imo, however, always reached through her fear to sneak them a bowl of barley.

Christo-religion is such, she said, that one is supposed to help another person, no matter if they are your enemy, if they follow Buddha, no matter who they are, you must help if you are asked.

Kyung-sook made her way back to Imo's, traveling as fast as she could with just her light bundle.

The store was closed and locked. She banged on the door for many minutes, until her hands were sore.

She went into the sealmaker's shop next door.

"Is that you making such a racket?" the sealmaker said. "Arirang Ajuhma's gone with her church someplace in the mountains to pray about all this goddam violence."

Gone!

Kyung-sook made her way to Seoul Station. There were more army trucks downtown, soldiers patrolling the streets.

At the ticket counter, the man said something she couldn't hear, so she leaned in closer.

"There are no more trains," was what he said. "Until further notice."

Kyung-sook didn't know where else to go, so she went to a nearby park and sat. When she became hungry, she went to one of the red-tented pojangmach'a carriages and used a few spare won to buy a bowl of noodles. Most people went to the pojangmach'as to drink, not eat. When Kyung-sook spooned some crusted-over red pepper condiment into her soup, the clump turned into wiggling worms when it hit the tepid broth. The stone-faced ajuhma, stirring a pile of roasting sparrows, glared at Kyung-sook, daring her to say something. Kyung-sook bowed her head. She was very hungry, so she scooped out the bugs and silently ate the soup. The ajuhma spooned something into her empty bowl. It was a runty sparrow, burned black as a piece of coal. Kyung-sook thanked her.

It had become darker. Her hunger abated, Kyung-sook realized she hadn't thought about what to do for the rest of the night. She sat on a bench and watched the light fade, watched the people leave the streets, one by one.

The pojangmach'a ajuhma packed up shortly before midnight.

"The curfew," she reminded Kyung-sook. "They're enforcing it pretty heavily with all the to-do, you know."

The curfew!

As if from the sky itself, a high-pitched siren screamed.

In a few minutes, large vehicles rolled down the streets waving eerie blue lights.

"Attention citizens!" boomed from a loudspeaker attached to the roof of the vehicle. "All citizens should be off the streets for the midnight curfew. Anyone found in the streets is in violation of the law and will be arrested as a subversive. Attention citizens!"

Kyung-sook bolted, running into an alley to escape the searchlights. She backed up further and further until she was hiding behind a pile of rotting garbage. The baby kicked and kicked.

Sometime later, she was awakened by voices. She forced herself not to gasp or scream.

It was the voice of a young man.

"Mother," he said. "We are almost to the hospital. Just hold on a little longer." There was a quiet groan in reply.

The bright lights swept into the alley again, and Kyung-sook saw a figure of the man with his mother slumped on his back. In silhouette, the man-and-mother looked like a single animal.

"Halt!" Another voice, heavy footsteps.

"But, but I'm just taking my mother to the hospital. She's very sick."

"I said halt!"

"But my mother! She collapsed on the floor of the house a little after midnight—I think she might be hemorrhaging."

"Hah! How do we know you're not a Red infiltrator? An antigovernment terrorist pulling off a neat trick? No more words, come this way."

"No, I mustn't—"

Kyung-sook heard blows, a muffled cry of pain. When the light came sweeping that way again, the man and his mother were gone.

Awake again, the baby kicked on Kyung-sook's left side. She put her hand on that place. She felt the outline of the folded-up body and suddenly had the overpowering belief that the baby was a girl. She didn't know why, but she was as sure of the baby's sex as she was of the nose on her own face.

How had her life gone spinning out of control like this?

I'm sorry, I'm sorry, she said to the wretched baby, over and over.

SARAH
Seoul
1993

On the way back to the Residence, Doug and I stopped at the Baskin-Robbins. I chose a green honeydew-melon ice cream, he got a "General Yi's Turtle Boat Ship," a treat that tasted just like a Dove bar.

We licked our treats contentedly as we approached the main gate of Chosun University.

Something was different.

Lined up in rows just outside the stone arches were hundreds of riot policemen in helmets with opaque visors, carrying shields. Mixed in with them were some extremely tall men in denim jumpsuits and sunglasses—

they looked like some strange Korean traveling basketball team. Parked all the way up and down the street were dozens of buses with steel mesh covering the windows. None of this had been here a half-hour earlier.

"I wonder what's up," Doug said. As we walked through the gate, planning to cut through campus to get back to the Residence, we could hear faint chanting from the inner campus. A few students were already massed about the entrance, holding picket signs and wearing headbands with Korean characters written on them.

"What're they saying?"

"Something about wanting to send a delegation of students to a peace festival in North Korea, to discuss *tong-il,* reunification."

The chanting suddenly grew louder and nearer, a parade of students crested the hill and began to head down the street toward the gate, toward us. A vibration seemed to pass through the rows of riot police, the high-tension-wire feeling was palpable.

"I don't like the look of this, Sarah. I think it's best if we don't stick around."

We turned back to take the long way, but the crowd of police behind us cut us off from the exit. As the shouting and chanting became even louder, the police began to ooze into the campus, a slowly spreading ominous pool of black.

I don't really know what happened next. Doug said he thought someone might have thrown a bottle. There was a crash, a shout. Then the police unhooked their clubs, hunkered behind their shields, and started running into the campus, hitting everything in sight.

It was like being in a school of minnows. There was only one way to go—away from the gate. People were clawing and trampling. Someone stepped on the back of my sneaker, pulling it off. I stopped to grab it, but Doug pulled me along.

The denim-clad men caught up to our section of the crowd. They rushed in, martial arts moves felling people like trees. One of them executed a jumping kick to the head of one of the students, sending his glasses propellering away into the air. Another pulled a woman by her hair and started dragging her back in the direction of the gate.

"What's happening?" I screamed to Doug. Suddenly there were so many of them, the denim men, the police. I thought suddenly: was Jun-Ho here? Would I recognize him?

Doug was fumbling in his pants pocket. I thought he might have some kind of secret weapon. He pulled out a small blue book. His passport.

"We're Americans!" he screamed in English, waving it around like a can of mace. "Leave us alone!"

A denim thug punched Doug in the face. I saw it happen in slow motion. Doug dropped the passport. I ran toward them as the man grabbed a bunch of Doug's T-shirt and pulled. It ripped across his back.

"We're American citizens!" Doug yelled again, blood trickling out of his nose.

I grabbed the passport and shoved it in the man's face. I wanted to shout, but no sound came out.

Then, as quickly as he came, he disappeared. In fact, most of the police seemed to have melted away. Students were still lying on the ground, weeping, bleeding from cuts and head wounds. The ones still standing started putting on surgical masks and began running back toward the gate, fists raised, shouting.

From the direction of the gate there was a sound, like *WHOOM!*, and something that looked like a bomb came hurtling toward us. It landed about a hundred feet short of us, spewing plumes of smoke.

"Oh shit, tear gas," Doug said, dragging me up the hill by my elbow. I didn't feel anything for a few seconds, but suddenly, I couldn't breathe, my nose and mouth seemed to have swollen shut.

"Come on," Doug croaked, coughing. "They might shoot some more."

We heard a few more *WHOOM*s, but they landed behind us. Doug pulled me to the top of the hill, which was, luckily, upwind, and we collapsed on the curb. My eyes were still burning, tears and snot were pouring out of my nose. I used my shirt to wipe my face. My ice cream was gone.

In a few minutes, the pain subsided, and I started crying regular tears. What had just happened? Why had the police started beating up on the students like that?

"You okay?"

I had a small scrape on my knee, my foot was cut where I'd stepped on something, but otherwise I was unhurt.

"Why?" I gurgled. "Did you see them kick that guy lying in the street? They kicked him in the *head*."

Doug's right eye was red, where vessels had burst. Blood crusted around his nose. His diagonally torn shirt made him look like a playing card.

"I have no idea what's going on. Let's just get back to the Residence."

As we got up, a few students carrying signs walked by us, wiping at their noses with brightly colored handkerchiefs. They did it nonchalantly, as if today were merely a high pollen-count day, not a day when their own government was trying to hurt them. Some of them were laughing, a care-free college student's laugh. I didn't understand it at all.

Back at the Residence, on the bulletin board in the lounge, there was a notice from the police warning in garbled English of a possible "action" at the *dae-mun,* the main gate, today, and they advised us to use the *chung-mun,* the back gate. I never paid attention to stuff on the bulletin board because it was usually advertising culture shows, cookouts, things that I avoided like the plague, as did Doug. From now on, I'd pay attention.

The next week, they posted warnings about the civil defense air raid drill, which they have at regular intervals. My sense of Korea's geography was so off, I hadn't even realized Seoul was only a few miles from the 38th parallel, the pie-slicing line the Russians and Americans had devised to separate North and South Korea after the Second World War. Because of pride or boneheadedness, the South Koreans had refused to move their ancient capital further south, so here we sat, within shelling distance of the North. No wonder Seoul had been bombed to the ground several times over during the Korean War.

This time, Doug and I made sure to stay inside the Residence at two o'clock when the sirens began wailing and people ran like roaches into underground tunnels. Into the eerily deserted streets, the soldiers and the medics ran, pretending Seoul was being bombed and poison-gassed by North Korea.

KYUNG-SOOK
Seoul
1972

Army trucks were still roaring up and down the streets the next day when Kyung-sook painfully unfolded herself from her squatting position. No one took any note of her when she emerged from the alley.

At the train station, there were notices posted that travel was being restricted. Her train was running, at least. She used the last of her money for the ticket.

"Going home to your mother's house to have the baby, yeh?" said the woman sitting next to her. She opened her bag and offered Kyung-sook some of her rice balls dipped in sesame seeds and salt, and Kyung-sook gratefully accepted. She was hungry, and she found herself thinking that the baby must be hungry as well.

"Oh, I remember," the woman said, her eyes twinkling. "I remember when I returned to my mother's house for my first labor. It was so horrible, I thought I was going to split in two! So much blood, so much pain. The midwife said she'd never heard someone yell as much as I did—she was afraid I was going to wake my ancestors. I passed out after that final push, but when I came to, there he was, all swaddled up, a nice swatch of hair, those eyes, the dear little fingers. Oh, it was heavenly that month. My mother made me seaweed soup three times a day and I just nursed and slept and gazed at my precious jewel. I felt like I was a princess, or a noblewoman being waited on night and day. Heh-heh, if I could have, I'd've had a hundred children, just for the resting time, just for the time to be spent with my gone-to-heaven mother!"

The woman left the rest of the rice balls when she departed, saying Kyung-sook needed to eat well.

As the train began moving again, Kyung-sook looked out the window at the familiar sight of the mountains. She had let the woman think that indeed she was traveling to her mother's home to have her baby and once that was done, she would return to her husband in Seoul.

If that could only be true! Not even going across the sea to America, but to have a husband and a life to return to. Except for the Shopkeeper

Auntie of her youth, Kyung-sook had never known any woman who'd had a child without a husband. Not even Hye-ja, the one people said had once been a prostitute for Americans in North River County; in the bathhouse she took great pride in her upright, cup-shaped breasts that had never nursed.

Kyung-sook drummed her finger on the train's window. The jade ring knocked against it with a cheap ticking sound. Kyung-sook yanked the ring off—it was difficult because her fingers were swollen—and she hurled it to the floor, where it broke into several pieces.

Real, pure jade sang when you struck it.

She looked out the window when the train pulled into the station, almost as if she believed someone would meet her.

Of course, there was no one. She had a long way to walk to return home.

Kyung-sook noted the water stains on their gate.

That summer had been one of the worst monsoon seasons ever. Because so much of the land in Enduring Pine Village had been cleared as fire-fields, there were no more trees to stop the water rushing off the mountain. At some points, stains reached several meters high.

Did that mean the rice harvest had been ruined? she wondered. Were her parents all right? Sudden concern for them caused her to bang on the gate's door.

Her mother came out first. When she saw Kyung-sook standing forlornly outside the gate, wretched bundle and flute in hand, she put her hand to her mouth. Then she saw Kyung-sook's pregnant stomach, and she screamed.

Was this a malevolent mirage? This was not the same daughter she had sent off to the Seoul Women's College of Education many seasons ago.

Kyung-sook's impulse was to bow, low, until her forehead touched the ground. But in her condition, she could not.

Her mother ran out, screaming like a madwoman, but Kyung-sook's father followed her quickly and intervened, murmuring that everyone needed to come inside the gate before anyone saw what was happening.

"Na-ga! Leave!" her mother shrieked, when Kyung-sook was brought into the yard. "Get out!"

Her father kept shaking his head.

Kyung-sook wanted to die.

But the baby inside her kicked. It was alive.

Kyung-sook's mother and father argued, then her father merely said to Kyung-sook, "Go in there." He pushed her toward the old pigshed.

At mountain-chilly nightfall, her father left a burlap seed sack and a bowl of millet cereal outside the shed.

He hadn't left a spoon, so Kyung-sook ate the cereal with her hands, using her tongue to lap up the last, bitter grains. This was barely human food, she thought. In flush times, it would be a mash they'd feed the pig. She put a hand up to her face and felt bits of millet stuck there. She had no choice in her life anymore, did she? She spread the burlap onto a pile of musty barley-straw, hugged herself for warmth, and fell heavily into sleep.

In the middle of the night, she stirred. Something hurt. In her present condition, too many pains and discomforts vied for her attention. So she merely waited for the pull of fatigue to drag her back down into the dark hands of sleep. Then she slept as if dead—for minutes? hours? days?— but eventually found herself unwillingly bobbing back to the surface of consciousness.

Her bowels needed to be moved.

She couldn't imagine moving her bulk up from where it had sunk into the moldering straw like quicksand, so she forced herself to sleep on, hoping that urge would go away, but eventually she felt painful, unignorable cramps beginning to stitch into her bowels.

She couldn't soil her sleeping place. Even the pig wouldn't have done that. She finally managed to drag herself the few meters to the outhouse, and returned.

Just before sunrise, a different kind of pain jabbed into the blackness. First, a few pinpricks, then more and more until there were so many holes, the whole fabric of sleep gave way in one blinding burst of agony.

She gasped awake, instinctively clutching her stomach as if it were a precious package someone was trying to take away from her. The baby, caught in the tightening vise of her womb, frantically thrust its legs, banging into her spine, agony radiating down the backs of Kyung-sook's legs all the way to her toes. How could she ever feel worse than she did at this moment? She was cold, she needed to throw up and release her bowels at the same time—but the pain in her back was so terrible she could only roll like a weevil on the dirt floor, hoping to find a position that would make it stop.

Then she vomited, warm and wet on her protruding stomach.

The pain seared her in waves. During a small, electric interval between its peaks, she managed to drag herself, wild with fear, to the outhouse once more, managed to position herself over the hole. The smell of vomit and excrement made her want to throw up again, she prayed she would finish her nasty business here before her whole body seized up again.

She felt something strange. She put a hand in between her legs, feeling in the silvery darkness. Her fingers brushed up against slime. And hair. Not her own pubic hair, but slippery seaweed hair. The baby's head was crowning in the jungle of her fur.

She screamed.

KYUNG-SOOK
Enduring Pine Village
1972

Her mother's eyes. Soft, unguarded, the way they looked whenever Kyung-sook had been sick as a child.

"No one can describe the pain of labor." Her mother's voice, through the fog. "My mother didn't tell me, either."

Kyung-sook's mouth was so dry and chapped, she couldn't answer. She was in the house, lying on the warmest spot on the ondol floor, normally reserved for her father. What had happened?

"The baby has a lot of hair, like you did when you were born."

The baby!

"Where?" she managed to whisper.

"Here." She showed Kyung-sook a grayish mass swaddled in a pojagi.

Kyung-sook opened the pojagi. Just as she had sensed: a cleft between the legs, tiny like the slit in barley. Bits of white slime, blood, and something black and smelly covered the curled-up body.

"The baby is healthy," her mother said, rewrapping the pojagi. She paused, then added, "So there's no need to call the midwife."

Her mother hadn't noticed yet that the baby was not all Korean. When the baby grew a bit, the secret would most certainly emerge. Then what? Her proper parents would have no choice but to expel her and the child, for it would be necessary to distance themselves from a hon-hyul, a mixed-blood child. Even more importantly, lacking a father, the child could not be entered into the family registry. Such a child could not enroll in school or have an official marriage—and as a mixed-blood, there was no chance in the world a respectable family would accept her, anyway. She would be destined to life as a ghost, spoken about only in whispers.

The only solution was to get to America, try to find David, she thought. Oh yes, as if she could just walk across the sea . . .

The baby began to whimper softly. Kyung-sook wanted to hold her, to lick her clean like a mare does to her foal.

"There is no need to call the midwife," her mother repeated, turning her back so that the baby was out of Kyung-sook's sight. "Everyone has been busy and distracted since the flood."

Kyung-sook lay back on the bedding.

"What shall I do?"

Her mother didn't look at her. "I can go to Seoul. There are places that will care for her . . . But I will have to go now. Secrets cannot remain so for long in this village"

Nothing was real to Kyung-sook any more. Not this baby. Not her pregnancy. The foreigner least of all.

As if through a fog, Kyung-sook heard her own voice say, surprisingly calmly, "Mother, go, then." Kyung-sook had heard about these orphanages, started by a kindly American man who had felt so bad seeing pictures of all the orphans wandering the streets after the 6.25 War. These places took in babies and tried to find them homes—in A-me-ri-ca. Kyung-sook was struck: perhaps this child could now go to the Beautiful Country, on her own.

Don't even hold the child, a voice said. Or else it will be too difficult to let her go.

Kyung-sook shut her eyes.

"Yes, please go," she whispered, and waited. When she opened her eyes, her mother was gone.

Kyung-sook panicked.

No, I want her back. I'll raise her, even if you banish me from the house. I'll find a way.

Kyung-sook rose, felt blood pouring out of her womb like a tipped water crock as she ran toward the door of the house, arms outstretched.

"Baby!" she cried. "I'll find a way!"

What way? said the voice. Playing your flute at Seoul Station for pennies and bags of yams? Going to the American army base by North River County and selling your body to soldiers? You, a descendant of one of the oldest families in Enduring Pine Village?

Her grasping hands fell away. Her sobs folded her sore and battered body in two.

Beyond the rice-paper door, beyond the stained gate with her family's ancient seal, her mother was walking away, with her baby.

Kyung-sook slept as if dead. When she awoke, her mother was coming in to see her, bringing in a rice table. Kyung-sook recognized her bowls, one filled with rice, one with broth and feathery pieces of mi-yuk seaweed. Her old chopsticks, her spoon. Kyung-sook fingered those worn, familiar objects.

Her mother spooned the soup into Kyung-sook's mouth, as if Kyung-sook were her tiny child again. The broth was warm and salty, and Kyung-sook's very bones cried out for it.

"Eat slowly," her mother said. "Eat a lot. Then rest."

Kyung-sook sighed. Her very first taste of food had been rice eaten off her mother's fingers. Her own baby would never know the taste of her hand.

Where is she, she wanted to say. Where is my baby? Milk had already begun leaking, drop by drop, out of her swollen breasts. But her womb trembled and contracted. Her body was already preparing to forget that it had ever had a child.

Kyung-sook's mother came with some clean white bandages that she wrapped tight around Kyung-sook's chest. She helped Kyung-sook lie down into the familiar, warm bedding.

Marie Myung-Ok Lee

"Have a deep rest," she said, again. "Then eat some more soup. I'll go out to see if perhaps a pumpkin is ready, so I can make you some juice-tonic."

Kyung-sook also dearly wanted to know where her flute had gone, but of course, she didn't dare ask.

"I'm sorry, I'm sorry, please forgive me," she moaned, over and over again, not even knowing who she was saying it to.

196

PART III

KYUNG-SOOK
Enduring Pine Village
1993

Cooking Oil Auntie moaned, swinging her considerable ongdongi around on the bench.

"Aigu, what's going to happen to poor Okja?" she said, wringing her hands. At the bottom of the TV screen: LOYAL VIEWERS, PLEASE TUNE IN NEXT WEEK AT THIS TIME.

"Damn!" Cooking Oil Auntie pounded her fist on the bench. "Why do they always do this—how can I wait until next week to find out what happens?"

Kyung-sook didn't know why Cooking Oil Auntie let herself become so sucked in by cheap, sentimental soap operas like this one, *The Date Tree*. Cooking Oil Auntie, the most tight-fisted businesswoman in the market, wept and exulted over these paper characters as if they were members of her own family.

In the late afternoons, when customers were scarce as frogs in winter, Kyung-sook occasionally accepted Cooking Oil Auntie's invitation to watch the soap operas because watching TV was such a novelty for her. And the previous soap opera, *The Dark Yushin Era and Beyond,* had been based on the true history of President Pak Chung-Hee's so-called *Yushin,* "Revitalizing Reforms."

The drama had been beguiling, following the story of two friends who make their way from a small, dirt-poor village to Seoul. One man becomes a hired thug for the strongman government, the other—embittered because his teacher father was executed as a suspected Communist sympathizer—gains entrance to the famous Seoul National University and becomes a prosecutor, fighting the corruption of the government. The plot twist was that both friends fall in love with the same Seoul girl who joins the underground student democratic movement. But when she is killed in a police raid, the former rivals-to-the-death join forces to exact revenge.

Watching the show brought Kyung-sook back to that time of the roaring army trucks, the soldiers and policemen running on the streets.

On the TV, another ticker moved across the bottom of the screen:

... GIRL LOOKING FOR KOREAN BIRTH-GIVING MOTHER NEXT
ON *THE SEARCH FOR MISSING PERSONS*!!...

Kyung-sook's heart contracted.

"Hm, finally, something new and different on that show," Cooking Oil Auntie remarked. "Usually it's just wailing harlmonis."

"Are you going to watch?"

"Uhn, why not. It'll take my mind off Okja."

"Well, maybe if you're going to keep the TV-machine on, I'll stay, too—if that's okay."

"Suit yourself. Do you have any snacks in that pojagi, by any chance?"

Kyung-sook did have some baby-finger shrimp as well as some spiced squid and boiled peanuts that she had purchased for Il-sik, her husband, who liked eating light snacks and drinking beer at night, sometimes relieving Kyung-sook from the duty of making him dinner.

"I've got the shrimp you like so much," she said, taking it out of her wrapping cloth and handing it over.

"This show is all stories about the human condition," Cooking Oil Auntie explained, as if she were a schoolteacher and Kyung-sook her student. "First loves, people with crushes on their elementary school teachers, things we've seen a million times before right in the village, unh? But they've never had a foreigner on the show before—that should be really interesting."

"A foreigner?"

"The girl's from America."

The hosts, an older, squat man and a young woman much taller than he was, came out smiling and joking with the audience. They greeted a middle-aged woman and a shrunken-looking ajuhshi.

Where was the girl?

"Shucks. Figures they save the interesting one for last. Say, d'you have any more snacks?"

Kyung-sook handed over the spicy squid.

"Holding out the best stuff, huh?" Cooking Oil Auntie ripped off a huge leathery piece and stuffed it into her mouth. Then she made a face and gagged.

"Pwah! There's an ocean's worth of salt in this stuff—I told you not to buy at Oakla's snack stall. Urrr! Now my throat's a desert."

Kyung-sook sighed and took out a can of POCARI SWEAT, one she had bought as a treat for herself, to drink while keeping Il-sik company.

"—Wasn't that wonderful, seeing all the people who called for our honored guests, Dr. Shin and Mrs. Choi?" The female hostess's voice flowed like honey, so refined and smoothed by a perfect Seoul accent, quite discordant with the shock of her low-cut top and short skirt.

"It sounds like we have another heartwarming reunion in the works, thanks again to *The Search for Missing Persons!*"

The squat male announcer moved in front. His hair, Kyung-sook thought, was too black. A man his age should have at least a touch of gray, or white, like Il-sik had.

"For our next honored guest, we have someone who came a-a-a-all the way from America," he intoned.

"This girl was abandoned here in Korea as a baby," the woman announcer added, from behind him.

Kyung-sook's throat tightened. The woman had used the same word for "throw away the garbage."

". . . She was sent away from Korea and adopted by a white family in America. But now she has returned to seek her lost truemother. Ladies and gentlemen, let's listen to her touching story and see if we can help her."

The hostess waved her arms at a closed door as if she were a shaman imploring a spirit to come out. The door opened, and a girl of maybe twenty or so walked out. She was wearing a pretty purple dress and she stood very tall and confident as she walked out.

Kyung-sook squinted at the screen.

"Hmph, look at that, she's grown up on American food and see how tall she is—if she were a Korean man they would send her straight up to the DMZ for her military duty, show those North Koreans what giants we've become," Cooking Oil Auntie commented. "And look at that hair."

The girl's hair was so black and shiny that in the camera's lights it looked alive, the way animal fur looked alive. Kyung-sook's own hair had grown thinner over the years, with age and too many troubles, but when she was young, she, too, had such an abundance that no matter which way you pulled a clump of it, you couldn't see even a sliver of white from her scalp.

The male announcer asked the girl how she was doing, was she happy and at peace to be there? Now the girl looked scared. She stared back, frozen.

"Do you understand Korean?" he asked her. The girl coughed, screwed up her face.

"I-dunna-know."

The audience roared.

"What a riot," said Cooking Oil Auntie. "That girl looks Korean, but out of that mouth comes the exact yabba-yabba of those missionaries who could never learn to speak Korean properly. So strange, like watching a puppet or a retard, isn't it?"

The girl started to speak English, reading from a piece of paper. Kyung-sook wasn't surprised to find that she didn't understand a word anymore.

"I'll tell you the story, dear audience," said the translator. "This girl, Sal-Ah, doesn't know anything about her Korean truemother or true-father. Her white American parents adopted her even though of course there was no blood connection—isn't that a nice Western custom? She has come to Korea and is studying in the Kyopos-come-back-to-Korea program at Chosun University. Her adoption records say she was abandoned on—"

"Welcome, please enter!" boomed Cooking Oil Auntie. Kim Grand-mother, one of the maids at the wealthy Merchant Pak's house poked her head into the stall like an inquisitive turtle.

"... She was raised in the care of the Little Angels orphanage until she was adopted. Truemother, if you are out there and want to atone for your deed, or if there are any other family members, or anyone knows anything about this girl, please be so kind as to call us now at the station. 02-332-8175."

Cooking Oil Auntie inserted a cork in the bottle of rich, brown sesame oil and sent Kim Grandmother on her way.

"Did you catch when that girl was, um, left behind?" Kyung-sook asked.

"Unh? No. But she looks like she's in her early-adult season, doesn't she? That would make it sixties? seventies when she was dumped? Sounds about right: that was the time when women were starting to work in the factories with men—and of course, getting in trouble. Remember how that police box in North River Village added that window you could push a baby through if you wanted to throw it away?"

"Well, I'm not sure all the babies were 'thrown away,'" Kyung-sook said, that horrid word sharp on her lips. "I'm sure there were reasons."

"Reasons, sure. These mothers *all* have their reasons. Like the mothers who abandoned their kids right after the 6.25 War. Some of those kids wandering the streets were true orphans, of course. But the biggest bunch of them were mixed-blood U.N.-soldier spawn—I saw that on the *Evening Garden* news program. I guess their mothers found it pretty convenient to just ditch 'em and start fresh, huh?"

Kyung-sook thought of the proverb, "If you keep your mouth closed, you cannot bite yourself," and she did just that. She kept her eyes on the TV screen.

In the TV studio in Seoul, there was silence. A silence that filtered all the way to Enduring Pine Village, to Cooking Oil Auntie's stall. Kyung-sook couldn't even hear a cock crow in the market.

Who could break such a silence?

"Aigu, nobody's calling for that sorry child." Cooking Oil Auntie began to polish her blue-green oil bottles, the same beautiful color as the flies that buzzed around the dungheap. Kyung-sook felt the heat from the roasting sesame seeds searing her face.

The camera didn't move from the girl's face.

The male announcer walked in front of the camera.

"We're sorry, folks, but no one called for this lost American girl. Maybe the caller is just too shy. At the bottom of our screen we're going to run our studio number again. This girl is going to stay in Korea for the rest of the summer, so if you know anything, be sure to give us a call. Once again, it's 02-332-8175. And keep watching *The Search for Missing Persons* especially to see if the woman from Mokp'o who called today is really Mrs. Choi's sister! If so, that means we have two sisters from the North separated by two wars finally reunited here in the South—it promises to be a very touching reunion. So stay tuned and kamsamnida ladies and gentlemen till next week!"

"That poor kid," Cooking Oil Auntie muttered as she flipped off the set. "Talk about children who suffer for the sins of their parents. How could a human mother fling her child to the four winds like that? A half-nigger GI baby I could see, maybe. But a beautiful Korean girl like that? I don't care *what* the circumstances might have been—if she were my child, I would have become a beggar, done anything to raise her. You *do* that for your own child."

She looked at Kyung-sook for confirmation. Kyung-sook was looking the other way. The girl on the screen, she looked to be of pure Korean blood. But was it possible? The foreigner-man, after all, had been tall and he'd had his yun-tan coal-black hair.

"Those women, especially those so-called 'modern women'—their attitudes threaten our whole society!" Cooking Oil Auntie went on. "They should have abortions instead of heaping so much shame on us as a nation—it makes us look so backward, having Korean kids raised by foreigners. Part of the fault is that it's too easy—they can just pretend to forget the kid on a park bench, as if a child were a package of green onions—"

"That girl probably would have had a terrible life growing up in Korea!" Kyung-sook suddenly exclaimed. All the blood in her body seemed to have found its way into her face, which threatened to burst like a child's cheap rubber ball. "You shouldn't make judgments on situations you know nothing about!"

"The same could be said for you," Cooking Oil Auntie said, slowly scanning Kyung-sook's face. "I at least know what it's like to have a child, don't I?"

Kyung-sook rose quickly from where she'd been sitting. She bit the inside of her cheek to keep the tears inside. Her mouth filled with a warm taste of iron.

Cooking Oil Auntie paused.

"Look here, Sister, it took me many years to have my son, I know too well the pain of being barren—it was even worse than having my husband die on me."

Kyung-sook still didn't say anything.

"If it helps, I've heard that wanton women get pregnant much more easily than dutiful wives like you, or me with my one son. Maybe there's something to that—the merciful Lord Buddha will reward us with a hundred male children and fifty daughters in our next lives."

Kyung-sook spun on her heel, grinding a small hole in the dirt floor. Cooking Oil Auntie didn't call after her.

SARAH
Seoul
1993

The phone call was for me.

"Miss Sarah Thorson? This is Noh Kyunghee."

A rustling of paper.

No Kyung Hee? Korean names, endless combinations of strange syllables. Kyung/Mi/Jae/Ho/Jun/Ok. Did I know her?

"Uh, hi."

"How are you?"

"Fine. Uh, do I know you?"

"Sejong Broadcasting."

The Search for Missing Persons. Kyunghee Noh.

"We had a call for you arrive this afternoon."

"For me?" Was I hearing right? "From who, whom?"

"From a lady who says she's your mother."

SARAH
Seoul
1993

The woman's name was Mrs. *Lee.* Lee Ok-Bong. My mother. She lived here, in Seoul. All this time. And now I had her number.

When I informed Doug of the news, he shouted, lifted me off my feet and spun me around like the Tilt-a-Whirl at the State Fair.

"She finally called the station," I gasped, giddy, a whole new world of possibility spiraling out before me.

But then I didn't call her. I woke up the next morning, a leaden lump in my stomach.

What if I'm not ready? How will my knowing her change me forever?

Doug seemed almost irked by my sudden recalcitrance. He practically tore the number out of my hands, spoke tersely to whoever answered, and set up a meeting. We were going to meet at the Little Angels Orphanage, Doug's idea. Kyunghee Noh had been pushing for an on-air meeting at the station—she was sorely disappointed with me, she said.

KYUNG-SOOK
Enduring Pine Village
1993

"What is this number?" Il-sik said to his wife. Kyung-sook looked to see a tiny scrap of paper held in his good hand. Had it fallen out of her skirt pocket when she was bending over the wash?

"Oh, it is nothing." She took it back from him. "Cooking Oil Auntie told me about a supplier in Seoul who could get me the storage tins for the shrimp paste more cheaply—no one on this earth knows more about saving money than she."

"Are you all right?" he asked. "It seems like you've been very tired lately."

Kyung-sook looked at her husband. His right hand, less like a hand than a crabbed piece of old gingerroot.

"I tire in the dog days of summer, that's all," Kyung-sook told her husband. "All day in the market listening to those squawking customers and then coming home to take care of Father, changing his diaper like he's a baby."

"You are a filial daughter, your father is very fortunate," he said.

"I am fortunate in marrying you—I have no in-laws who would forbid me to do this," she said.

"You know, you have some white hairs now," her husband said.

Kyung-sook patted her hair. She never looked in the mirror anymore, she could tie the strands into a married-woman's bun without one.

No one wants to grow old, Kyung-sook thought. When she was a child, her maternal grandmother and grandfather had seemed of a completely different, if friendly, species. They had skin like rice paper that had gotten wet and dried again. Their voices were tentative and quavery, like someone who had once been sure of himself but had now grown to doubting.

She was beginning to see the same lines on her face, hear her own voice sounding strange to her ears. But was that so bad?

She gave her husband a caress in the privacy of their inner room. She thought with affection how they had eschewed both a folk wedding and a Western-style one at the wedding hall, instead opting for a simple ceremony under the watchful eyes of Christo and the rough-hewn beams of the church. That is what Il-sik had suggested, and Kyung-sook was so grateful to him. When he reached for her in the dark, she did not see his disfigured hand, nor did she see his wrinkles. In fact, their bodies fit together as nicely as the yin-yang symbol on their country's flag. She was disappointed on the nights he didn't touch her.

"That's the way we will be, then, two old mandarin ducks," she said quietly. "Hae-ro, swimming in slow circles, old together."

In her pocket, she could feel the number, the weightless scrip of it. She wondered if anyone else had called for the girl. She didn't know why she hadn't just done so right away to find that most likely she was wrong, and could put her mind at ease. But Cooking Oil Auntie had made her so upset, she couldn't think. And then she had returned home to Il-sik and realized she had more to consider than just her ease of mind—there was also her husband and the entire life she had built up for herself, hanging on that slimmest thread of possibility. What was the right thing to do?

SARAH
Seoul
1993

What a sense of déjà vu, the Little Angels hot inner office.

"Hello, it is nice to see you," Miss Park greeted.

"You have a lot of babies here." Doug peered through the office's window at the rows of cribs, lined up like shoeboxes. "Do you get a new delivery every day?"

"I am fine, and you?"

"Great, thanks." He turned to me.

"You amaze me, Sarah, how you managed to find this place and get your file without help, without anyone translating for you. I guess if you set your mind to something, nothing can stop you."

"Well, I—"

The door to the office opened. An *ajuhshi* in a chartreuse polo shirt walked in, leading a doughy woman with short, permed hair that was a matte, shoe-polish black.

I couldn't speak, something welled up inside me.

"Agi-yah?" she said, looking at me.

I was frozen. The *ajuhshi* pointed at me and muttered. I stared at the freckles on this woman's face, the color of bruise spots on apples. I had moles, brown moles, soft as gumdrops—but no freckles. What did this mean?

Miss Park said something to them in Korean, and they sat down. The woman kept staring at me.

A slim teenage girl walked into the room. She put her Louis Vuitton bag down on the table.

"Sorry," she said to us. "I got hung up in traffic and the battery in my cell phone died."

"Who are you?" I asked.

"Julie Koh. My mom's HeeJung Koh, the director of Little Angels. I'm here to translate."

I was about to say that I had brought Doug to translate, but then I decided that would be rude, she'd come all this way. Doug hadn't said a word in Korean yet, anyway.

"Your English—" I began. I didn't know how to put it—I hated it when ignoramuses in Eden's Prairie praised me for speaking English so well.

"It sounds so perfectly American, your accent," I said.

"Oh, I go to the Seoul Foreign High School where it's all expat kids, and only a few Koreans, like me and my sister." She checked her watch, a

Swatch. "And we watch Armed Forces TV all the time. I love *All My Children*."

Miss Park said, "We, *chuhh*, start?"

The woman was indeed "Mrs. Lee." The *ajuhshi* was Mr. Lee, her brother—my uncle. They both lived in Seoul. Mrs. Lee asked me again, *"Agi-yah?"* which Julie translated as *Are you my baby?*

I said I was the girl she saw on TV.

She came over to me, began thumping my back and wailing.

I hugged her. Something about her felt right; Christine was all corners and angles, honed by hours and hours of tennis and feel-the-burn Jane Fonda leg lifts. But this woman was all loose, warm flesh that seemed to envelop me. I started to cry, too.

Someone tugged on my arm. Miss Park. She handed us both some Kleenex she whisked from a shiny, satin-quilted box. She took one for herself and turned away and discreetly dabbed at her eyes.

"Okay," Julie said to me. "I'm sure you have some questions for her."

"I want to know why," I said. "Julie, could you ask her why she gave me up?"

Mrs. Lee, still sniffling, babbled back.

"She says she had to give you up when her husband died suddenly, just after you were born," Julie said.

Mrs. Lee looked at me searchingly—I didn't know what kind of expression I had on my face—and added more words. *Dae-hak, you-hak,* words that had to do with school.

"She didn't think she could give you any kind of life, being poor and without a husband. She wanted you to go to college, study abroad."

She couldn't keep me, just because she was poor and single?

"More questions?" Julie said, eyebrows raised.

I blinked.

"I was covered with *ddong*," I said to Julie. "Ask her about that, ask her why she did that."

Julie stopped, shocked.

"It's in my orphanage records."

Mrs. Lee sucked at her teeth. When Julie translated my question, she seemed taken aback. It took her a few seconds to answer.

"It was such a long time ago, she doesn't remember, she said she's blocking a lot out. She must not have had time to clean you up properly. She says she's sorry."

My big, burning question gone, just like that.

I didn't know what to do now. I was with the woman who gave birth to me, but the urge to cry out *"Um-ma!"* didn't happen. She was a woman with a bad dye job, a thick waist, polyester pants. Her brother had shifty, nervous eyes and slicked-down hair, which made him look like a weasel. I wanted to automatically feel love for these people, my blood family, but I didn't feel anything except numb.

Miss Park spoke up in Korean.

"Don't be too hard on your mother, is what Miss Park said. I know it might be difficult to understand as Americans—" Julie looked significantly first at Doug, then me. "But bringing a child you can't care for to a police station, or to Little Angels is a caring act. It's not abandonment. These mothers do it so the baby can have a better life."

I was thinking of a story I'd read in the paper last summer, of a girl on Long Island who had given birth in a public restroom at her prom, cut the umbilical cord on a metal toilet paper dispenser, thrown the kid in the trash to die—then went back out onto the dance floor. Or the Hmong girl in Minneapolis, only nineteen and already a mother of five, who somehow left three of the children out in the car on a subzero night. Two froze to death, the third lost all the fingers on her left hand. Suddenly, the Korean way seemed more humane, enlightened, civilized.

Korea is a Third-World country.

"This is a lot for me," I murmured. "Maybe we should meet again, alone."

Mrs. Lee liked this suggestion. She smiled at me enthusiastically, crescents of gold in her teeth smiling along with her.

"She says she'd like to spend some time with you, also. She wants to invite you to her house."

I nodded, getting up. Doug followed.

I wasn't sure how to say goodbye to her, so I sort of half-bowed and mumbled *an-yong-ha-say-yo,* which I realized, too late, was "hello" and not "goodbye." Mrs. Lee waved at me.

"Bye-bye!" she said.

SARAH
Seoul
1993

When I had received the materials for the Motherland Program, I had eagerly flipped through the pages explaining the language and cultural programs, the instructions on what to bring. Then I got to the last page, which said:

A physical examination proving good health is mandatory for all Motherland Program applicants. Please have your doctor fill out and sign the attached form.

I didn't want to have to see our family doctor, Dr. Solvaag, the creepy guy with too-warm fingers, the one Ken and Christine always chatted up at the Eden's Prairie Country Club parties. Then I realized, I'm almost twenty years old. I can have my own doctor. I searched in the phone book, called the first GP listed. Dr. Susan Aas.

When I got to the office, a receptionist had handed me the forms on a clipboard that said PROZAC on it, a pen thoughtfully velcroed to the top.

Name. Address. Social Security. Insurance. Whom to contact in an emergency. Occupation.

Do you exercise regularly? Have you ever had the following (Please check yes or no):

Alcoholism. Cancer (check type). Cataracts. Heart Disease. High Blood Pressure. Kidney Disease. Surgery Requiring Hospitalization. Urinary Tract Problems.

No and no and no and no. I had felt like a conscientious student who has prepared well for a test.

Have you ever been pregnant? (list children's ages and delivery type, code V-vaginal, C-caesarean). Miscarriages? (list date and gestational age). Abortion? No, no, no, no.

Page three. FAMILY HISTORY.

Is there any family history of the following: Alcoholism. Cancer (list type). Heart Disease. Thyroid Disease (Graves', Hashimoto's). Multiple Sclerosis. Hemophilia. Depression.

Is mother or father known to be a carrier of the Tay-Sachs gene? Are either of your parents Ashkenazi Jews? Is there a history of diabetes in your family? (list type: juvenile onset, adult onset, gestational onset).

Allergies? Sickle cell anemia? Do you know if your mother took DES when she was pregnant with you?

My hand began to shake, ever so slightly. Ken had had a mild heart attack two years ago. Christine was allergic to penicillin. Nana had died of a combination of breast cancer and old age.

Are any parents or siblings deceased? Please list date, age, and cause of death.

I went back to the white spaces that stared at me, forever blank, and I scrawled NOT APPLICABLE in huge letters, so hard that the ballpoint ripped through the pages. I handed the mutilated forms in, pen neatly reattached to the velcro.

Dr. Aas asked me in a clipped tone if I had "issues" about disclosing my family's medical history. I shook my head, too angry to speak.

But now, from the sky, my genetic history had fallen into place.

Mrs. Lee, when writing out her address, had done so with her left hand.

No one in the Thorson family is left-handed.

I am.

"Does 'Anyang-dong' mean 'car neighborhood'?" I asked Doug. This neighborhood where Mrs. Lee lived was rows and rows of storefronts with metal car parts spilling out: hubcaps, bumpers—various amputated metal pieces lying helpless and dying on the sidewalks. The air was filled with the whizzing noises of welding torches, bright showers of sparks, the petroleum smell of burning metal and rubber.

Doug and I went around and around. At one point, we found ourselves back at the subway station (had they moved it in the last hour?), and had to start again.

A legacy of the Japanese imposing their queer addressing system on Korea during the colonial period, Seoul was laid out by vague neighborhood names but no numbered addresses or street names. Adding to the confusion was the laissez-faire way the alleys and walkways were constructed, meandering first up then down the hill or merely ending for no discernible reason.

We were faced with dozens of narrow alleys that broke off, capillary-like, into more alleys. The houses were hidden behind tall gates and smudged walls, the only proof of their existence crooked TV antennae breaking up the dull color of the skyline.

Julie had written out Mrs. Lee's instructions in English. We located the neon green cross of the pharmacy (the correct one, this time) and entered an alley that led us up a hill. *Sharp left at* DIE SCHÖNE *dry cleaner's. Take right fork at video store. Straight up the hill past the* HYUNDAI *apartment building.*

Another residential neighborhood. A combination of pollution-stained stucco shacks and high-rise apartment buildings with futuristic translucent tubes enclosing their stairwells. The alley was clogged with both rusty handcarts as well as compact cars parked head-to-tail like the colorful segments of a tapeworm. As we stood, taking this all in, several little kids in billowing karate uniforms whizzed by us on clattery bikes. When they saw Doug, they yelled, "Hello! A-me-ri-ca! Hello!" and waved, grinning with sharp, pointed teeth. Doug waved back.

Mrs. Lee waited outside the small, unmarked gate of her house. Her head was haloed in a pastel, shimmery light.

She came up to me, stroked my arm and said something in Korean.

"She's asking if you have a cold," Doug said. I constricted my throat, searching for a tickle.

"Why, do I look sick?"

"No, it's just a motherly thing to say."

"Now what'd she say?"

"She wants to know if I, the 'American,' understand what she's saying. Do you want me to be translating?"

I shook my head. My mother. I would need to learn to communicate with her myself.

Mrs. Lee opened the gate and made a motion, hands down, fingers wiggling like squid tentacles, inviting us in. Doug had told me that the American overhand sweep of the fingers was a disrespectful gesture, one you'd only use with a dog.

At the top of the gate, light refracted through shards of colored glass embedded in the cement. The effect was artful, almost beautiful.

"*Doduk-i*," Mrs. Lee said, when she saw me looking. I opened my Korean-English dictionary: Thieves. The glass, from broken *soju* bottles, was low-rent razor wire.

We entered a cluttered courtyard. Around a single spigot in the middle orbited the detritus of daily Korean living: plastic tubs, laundry stiffening to cardboard on wire racks, leggy plants leaning out of plastic tofu containers, a weightlifting bench—and two child-sized bicycles lying on their sides.

My first thought: Mrs. Lee, at her age, had had more kids?

Then I realized this courtyard was shared by three families; each entryway had a raised concrete platform where battered leather shoes and flip-flops were lined up like the clearance shoe rack at Dayton's.

Mrs. Lee led us to the middle dwelling. Doug slipped off his sneakers in a smooth motion and walked right in, but I had to sit down and untie my shoes. Mrs. Lee gazed fondly at me and helped me pull them off. She was wearing white canvas tennie shoes, Keds knockoffs with the backs smashed flat by her fat heels so they had become, in essence, sneaker-clogs. She carefully arranged our shoes in a row, toes pointing out.

Inside was that same yellow linoleum floor from the *yuhgwons*. It curled upward at the corners slightly, and I saw that it wasn't linoleum at all, but layers of some kind of oilpaper pressed together.

Her "house" was a single room with a phone-booth-sized kitchen that was lower than the rest of it and half outdoors, the stove powered with cannisters of propane. Mrs. Lee gave us some oblong pillows that looked like giant fluorescent-green-and-pink after-dinner mints, and then she disappeared.

Doug and I sat on the floor, our elbows propped on the pillows. On the windowsill sat some green bottled lotion called ALOE ESSENSE 54 and a plastic squeeze bottle of some cream-colored stuff that bore a picture of a big-eyed doll and read KEWPIE in English. A skeletal wire rack held clashing peacock-hued *ajuhma* blouses and trousers.

Mrs. Lee returned lugging a small table chopped off at the knees. It contained a metal teakettle, two plastic cups (the kind little girls play tea-party with), an apple the size of a softball, tangerines, a roll of toilet paper. Inside the cups was what looked like brown sugar, but when she poured the hot water, I smelled the familiar pang of ginseng. She sat herself down and peeled the apple with her left hand, shaving the freckled brown-gold skin into a coil that eventually dropped to the table. She cut the apple into boomerang-shaped wedges.

I glanced over at Doug. He was looking a little bored, a stark contrast to my tense, braced student-driver posture. What was I supposed to do, how was I supposed to act? Like a guest? Like a daughter? Like a stranger?

That weekend, when Doug and I had been having sex, afterward, he rolled up and said to me, *"Sarang-hae."*

"What does that mean?"

"I love you."

My breath quickened, not because of him, but because I was suddenly thinking of Mrs. Lee, my mother. I was thinking that maybe the next time I saw her, I could use those words. I was crazy with wanting to use those words I'd saved for so long, just for her.

Sarong hey, I'd written into my notebook, the minute I was alone.

I watched the woman arranging the fruit on a cheap plastic plate. She impaled a piece of apple on a toothpick and held it up to my mouth, a hand solicitously cupping underneath.

The apple was sweet, with the cold, grainy texture of a pear. Mrs. Lee retrieved the KEWPIE bottle, uncapped it, and liberally squirted the creamy goo—which, I had to say, looked uncomfortably like semen—all over the fruit. After surveying her work, she gave it another fart-sounding squirt for good measure, then set the bottle on the low table as if she were contemplating a third pass.

Idly, I glanced at the squeeze bottle. The way the Korean letters under KEWPIE were situated, in a long, strange sequence, I knew the word was a *rae lae oh*, some kind of transliterated foreign word: ra-di-o, el-e-ba-tor, stu-ress-u.

She speared a piece of tangerine through the goo, and held it out to me again. To be polite, I ate. The white stuff was sticky and warm and didn't have much taste—it was more like a lubricant, the ALOE ESSENSE lotion, maybe.

Then I realized.

Ma-yuh-nae-ee-su, was what the letters had spelled.

Mayonnaise.

That bottle, sitting unrefrigerated, in the warmth of the sill. Gag reflex. I took a huge gulp of the tea, grown lukewarm, not hot enough to sterilize my mouth.

"Doug, that's mayonnaise," I croaked.

"I'm aware," he said.

"Thanks a lot for telling me!"

Mrs. Lee offered me another piece, apple this time. I shook my head. I asked her where the bathroom was.

She sent me to a corner of the courtyard. It wasn't an outhouse, exactly, but more like a freestanding shack. The standard porcelain trough of a Korean squat toilet (thank God they had Western toilets at school) with a pull-chain flush, the dingy water in the plastic tank looming dangerously overhead. The wastebasket in front of me overflowed with used, brown-smeared TP even though there was nary a square in the holder. The bad smells and the warm, queasy feeling of mayonnaise suddenly overcame me and I vomited.

When I returned, we sat around the table again. Mrs. Lee had brought out a box of chocolate-and-marshmallow-covered mini-pies called OH YES!, each wrapped individually in plastic. Again, to be polite, I ate one. Sugar and chemicals, completely boneless, like biting into foam.

When we left, she gave me a bag of tangerines and the OH YES! pies, then stood outside the gate, waving until we were out of sight.

In my horrible Korean, I had made plans to see her again, next week.

SARAH
Seoul
1993

I visited Mrs. Lee again, with Doug, then every free afternoon. I even missed music class once, but Tae *Sunsengnim* yelled at me, and I had to promise I wouldn't do that again.

But that left three, maybe four visits a week. I left Doug behind to force myself to speak only Korean. But my Korean words didn't come rushing back. Whenever Mrs. Lee said anything to me besides *Did you eat rice today?* (another motherly greeting, Doug told me), I didn't understand her.

By my fourth, fifth visit, our communication was still facial expressions and hand-patting, but I had decided I didn't need words to communicate with her.

Each time I arrived, her face broke out in a smile, so wide it turned her eyes into black tildes that might grace a word like *mañana*. She helped me with my shoes (even if I was wearing slip-ons), waved me into the house, where she would have the low table set, some kind of treat waiting. The first time, a sandwich: two perfectly square, perfectly white pieces of flimsy bread hugging some kind of roasted meat, grated carrots, green onions, plus a layer of sliced bananas swiped with strawberry jam.

San-du-weech-u.

Her face looked so expectant, I had to eat it. But after, I said to her in Korean something like *Me Korean. Eat Korean food.*

She was delighted to discover that I liked *ddok* rice cakes. She bought me *ddok* in the colors of the Italian flag, *ddok* with a crusty layer of sesame seeds, *ddok* that tasted like cinnamon toast. She began insisting I stay for dinner, and she made dumpling soup with pillows of chewy rice cake floating in it, tofu stew, fish fried in eggy batter, always anxiously watching my face as I ate.

The last time, she had purchased her own Korean-English dictionary. After dinner, she opened it and pointed to a word, *sleep*.

I nodded back eagerly. She set out some bedding, a pillow stuffed with some kind of rustling husks. She covered us with a thin quilt made of linen. The piquant smell of mothballs rose from her shoulders. She lay half on the floor to give me more room. In minutes, she was snoring. At one point, she threw a leg over me possessively, something Doug did when we spent the night together.

In the morning, she came in with a stew and some vegetable side dishes on that low table. She also produced a bottle of psychedelically colored FAIRY orange pop.

She handed me chopsticks, left hand to left hand. The knot I always had inside me seemed to loosen. Her other-handedness, my true inheritance. Back in Eden's Prairie, it had been an abnormality, an asymmetricality, like a chiral molecule, one that has the same basic structure as others, but doesn't fit in anywhere. Christine wrote SARAH in indelible marker onto all my scissors.

I took sips of the soup, which had a pungent, old-sock smell. I ate heaping spoonfuls of clean, white rice that remained in a homogeneous clump, didn't fall apart and scatter like Minute Rice or Uncle Ben's. I even ate a few pieces of the kimchi, stippled with semicolons of hot red pepper that burned and radiated to all parts of my body as it filled my stomach. The orange pop was the only thing I didn't finish.

At school, I announced to Choi *Sunsengnim* that she should call me by my *Korean* name Lee Soon-Min.

"...Nobody doesn't like Sara Lee..." Bernie hummed at me as we left class. "You know, your name has the word 'Soon' in it. Koreans like to give abandoned girls the name 'Soon'-something as a joke—it means 'Jane Doe.'"

"Bullshit," I said.

He countered, "How about the Woody Allen and *Soon*-Yi scandal? She's an adoptee."

Even these small, tattered Korean things I had won for myself, Bernie had to take them away, like a bigger kid taking candy from a smaller one.

"Bernie, why don't you leave her alone?" Doug was suddenly behind me. "Why do you have to be like that? She's never done anything to you. Why be such an asshole?"

Bernie's eyes narrowed.

"You know, I used to spend summers as a little kid with my cousins who live in Songt'an, right outside Osan Air Force base," he said. "Our thing to do for fun was to go to the gate by the PX when the shift was letting out and sing to the shop-girls as they left:

> *Yankee whore, yankee whore,*
> *Where are you going?*
> *Shaking your ass, where are you going?*
> *Off to sell your stinky poji-cunt, that's where.*

He sang it to the tune of San Toki, the mountain rabbit song. Doug's expression didn't change, but his nostrils flared and turned white. His body began to lean, almost imperceptibly at first, in the direction of Bernie.

"Heard that song before? All the little kids know it, *kkang-chung*."

Doug continued to lean. Bernie took a step back, assumed a martial arts stance. He had been taking tae kwon do as his elective class.

I yelled at Doug to stop, but he was like a tipped-over boulder, gaining momentum, hurtling, lunging at Bernie.

Bernie cocked his leg. Doug barreled past and landed a plain old barroom-brawl punch right into the round PRINCETON seal of Bernie's T-shirt. We could all hear Bernie's wind leave his body in a sharp sound like a kite flapping in a stiff breeze.

"The stomach doesn't leave marks," Doug said, to no one in particular. "That's one thing the old man taught me, at least."

Bernie was lying on the dusty ground, writhing like a worm.

"Don't . . . hit . . . me . . . again," he gasped.

"Then leave her alone," Doug said. "It's that simple."

SARAH
Seoul
1993

Mrs. Lee set a plate in front of me. An overlapping stack of pancakes. Instead of Mrs. Butterworth's, there was a dish of soy sauce. She showed me how to cut the pancakes by crossing my chopsticks in the middle and levering them in opposite directions, like scissors. I dipped a piece in the sauce and lapped up that dark, saline taste. The pancakes were filled with something that looked like grass that would later make my shit bright green. She smiled approvingly.

I thought about calling her *Omoni,* Mother, today, but I didn't. That time would come. She called me "Soon-Min-ah." I had thought, weirdly, that she was calling me "Minna," which was Nana's name, Norwegian, of course. But later I caught on that *ah* was a sort of diminutive, sort of the opposite of the formal *ssi* we added to our names in class, to signify "Mr." or "Miss." Mr. Bernic Asshole Lee.

To Jun-Ho, I had written, *I found her—can you believe it? And her name is Lee. Do you think perhaps that means I might be a Chunju Lee, descendant of the great King Sejong?*

I moved to help Mrs. Lee clean up after dinner, but she playfully pushed me away. She flipped on the tiny TV set and motioned for me to watch as she took the remnants of our dinner back into the indoor/outdoor kitchen.

Outside the sliding rice-paper door, my sandals and her tennie-shoe-clogs sat side-by-side on the cement steps, announcing to the world that she and her daughter were spending time together

I was excited to think I was slowly becoming *Korean*. I had come to regard her house as my own. When nature called, I made my way through the cluttered courtyard to the toilet, squatting over the porcelain trough as if I'd done this all my life. Sometimes, I imagined oh-so-proper Christine balancing the alabaster globes of her ass over the bowl, and it set me to evil giggling.

Besides that, I didn't even think about Christine and Ken much any more. Not even about calling them up and confronting them. Some kind of hole in me had been filled, and I felt newly radiant, my blood thrumming and singing, like driving on new asphalt, a sensation that flowed over everything, even the small, green need for revenge.

Lee Ok-Bong came back with the low table and peeled us some yellow fruit with a hard rind and soft, slippery insides lined with tiny oval seeds. She said it was called a *cham-weh*. We ate the pieces, un-mayonnaised, with tiny silver doll forks.

When it was time to leave, I slid open the door and sat on the steps, putting on my shoes. She disappeared back into the house, then pushed a bag toward me. You weren't supposed to open a gift in front of the giver, so I carefully folded down the neck of the paper bag.

"*Komapsumnida, Omoni,*" I said. Thank you, Mother. There, I'd said it. Her tilde-eyes turned moist.

She shuffled behind me in her tennie-clogs up to the gate, held my hand, and wished me *"Chal mok-oh"*—eat well. She didn't let go of my hand when I walked away, instead, she extended her arm until our physical connection broke, and then she kept her arm outstretched, as if preserving some kind of invisible force that connected us.

Half-way down the lane I peeked into the bag. A six-pack of tiny yogurt drinks, each of the plastic bottles hardly bigger than a spool of thread. I didn't know if I should tell her that Julie Koh from Little Angels had called suggesting that we get a DNA test to confirm everything.

Under the yogurt drinks were some rice crackers, baked so crisp that later, in my room, they would crackle in my mouth like shattering pottery.

KYUNG-SOOK
Enduring Pine Village
1993

Kyung-sook had decided that life itself was an unfathomable, unreliable puzzle. You looked at it from a certain angle and you felt one way, looked at it from another and you would feel differently.

Of course, anyone who knew of her past would be astounded to learn that she had married at all.

Hyun Il-sik was fifteen years older than Kyung-sook, and everyone regarded him as the village cripple. His father had deserted the family after he saw Il-sik's deformed hand, but his mother raised him just the same as if he'd been whole. Indeed, Il-sik learned to do skilled woodwork, his father's trade, with just one hand.

Il-sik's mother died when he was twenty-five. Since their family wasn't originally from Enduring Pine Village, Il-sik had no kin. He left the village, and by the time he came back, Kyung-sook was working at her job in the market, her own mother had died, and she was taking care of her father.

Kyung-sook didn't take much notice of Il-sik except that he had bought a small patch of worn-out land, and he busily refurbished the old granary, relic of the times of rice and barley, that stood upon it. Somewhere along the line, he, like Imo, had become a Christo-follower.

Christo himself, he announced to the villagers, had told him to return to the village and start a church.

A few people began attending. Kyung-sook saw them making their way to the old granary in their best clothes, carrying their books of the Christo-word as well as books of Christo *music*. Kyung-sook found herself intrigued. When she peeked into the building during the week, she saw nothing special: a raised platform, a few simple wooden benches.

At the front of the church sat the two joined sticks.

Kyung-sook had always been struck by the way the Christo religion could be represented so simply. Looking at this spare but unmistakable symbol of Christo gave her an odd but natural feeling of calm, the way coming upon song-hwadang, the piled rock pagodas, deep in the mountains first startled her—the hand of man, here in the mountains!—then made her feel reassured. Each passing traveler had added a stone, carefully selected to fit with the others, placed atop the delicate balance of the column with a prayer, his personal entreaty adding to the countless prayers for safety and well-being that had come before.

When no one was looking, Kyung-sook slipped into the church again, and again. Day of Water, Day of Fire, Day of Gold. Every day except the Day of Sun. The stillness encompassed in that old granary reminded her of the chapel at the missionary school. She used to sneak into that space, reveling in that clear, silky silence for as long as she could. If someone came upon her, she'd duck her head and pretend to be praying to Christo. But she hadn't been there for Christo, or any other deity. She loved being able to sit in one place, and just *be*. Other than her favorite places by the Three Peaks Lake or the Glass River, nothing else offered her this solace.

"Praise the Lord!"

Il-sik had come up behind her one day when Kyung-sook was peeking into the open door of the sanctuary. He invited her to the Sunday's service and Kyung-sook, embarrassed, could find no way to gracefully refuse.

"There is something wrong, dear wife," Il-sik said. Worry had carved a new wrinkle deep into his brow.

You cannot vanquish your past, Kyung-sook thought. Even though her belly was the soft, useless one of a middle-aged lady, it still had the memory of being stretched tight as a drum, the baby inside rolling and tapping to her own rhythm. She remembered how she used to tickle her navel—that place where she had first been connected to her own mother—and how the baby would kick.

And now, the more she tried to forget, the more the memories pushed inside.

Il-sik began asking her again what was wrong, really, was she sick? She said no, but some days she could barely get up, she would have such shooting pains in her stomach. At night, she shivered under the covers as a fever raged. Il-sik urged her to see the doctor. Finally, he carried her on his weakening back all the way to the hospital. The doctor listened to Kyung-sook's pulse for many minutes and then proclaimed that she had hwa-byung, the fire sickness.

There is no medicine, the doctor said. You have to find the source of the fire and let it burn—until it is finished. If you insist on containing it inside, it will continue to destroy you.

"Please," Il-sik said to his wife, as he gazed upon her laying on their yo. "You must tell me the source of your torment. I will wait here, forever if I must, until you tell me."

Kyung-sook struggled to remain calm, cool as summer fruit. But the fire, which had been raging for almost twenty years, jumped within her. Sweat boiled out of her pores. Kyung-sook felt so very weary. She was no firekeeper, not anymore. She needed to let it out, endure the scorches from the outside instead of the slow incineration from within. She told Il-sik everything of her past. Everything.

"Divorce me," she said, when she was finished.

"I cannot judge," Il-sik said. "Only Our Father can do that. For us on earth, we need to forgive, the way Christo forgave even his betrayers and doubters, that is His grace." But Il-sik did not speak in his confident church voice; it was more in the manner of one who, by repeating something over and over, hopes to convince himself that something impossibly foolish may yet be true.

"Yobo, I don't know what to do—about the child. If that is the same child."

"You do what you have to do, Wife," Il-sik said, and he turned his tear-stained face away.

SARAH
Seoul
1993

A spatulate, toothpick-like stick swabbed painlessly on the inside of my cheek, that's all it took. Miss Park had convinced me to go through with the test, Little Angels would pay for everything. I was the first successful "reunion" they'd ever had, and now they were struggling with what kind of protocol they should have in place, if others should follow my same journey.

I didn't mind. In fact I would be reassured to have all this confirmed through the quantifiable conclusions of science, to know that I shared with Mrs. Lee the one-in-five-billion pattern of DNA that marked us, irrevocably, as belonging together.

KYUNG-SOOK
Enduring Pine Village
1993

"September 3, afternoon, that's when the baby was dumped, according to the orphanage records the American girl provided us with," the voice on the phone said. "Do you know anything about this girl?"

"No," Kyung-sook said, clutching the phone's receiver. "She is the wrong girl. Thank you for your effort." And she hung up.

September 3, her daughter's seng-il, the day she had fallen into the world so inauspiciously.

Some years, the date passed without Kyung-sook noticing it, a blessing. But most years, she revisited the smell of excrement, the red curtain of pain, her empty arms and breasts that cried milky tears.

But was that girl the child? How many women that day might have been weeping as a child left their arms?

"I'm going to go to Seoul," she told Il-sik. "I've arranged for Song Grandmother to take care of Father for a few days, to come in and cook for you."

Il-sik's face was tight and anxious, quivering like a bowstring.

"I won't be gone long," she said.

SARAH
Seoul
1993

WHAT HAPPENED TO THE PLEDGE, "WE'LL KEEP THE FLAME ALIVE FOREVER"? The newest scandal, according to the hodgepodge, sometimes ungrammatical *Korea Herald* (put out by American expats), was that despite heartfelt vows to keep the '88 Olympic torch burning into eternity, the flame had fizzled out, and no one had noticed for over a week. As Lotte World added Lotte Swimming, Lotte Folk Museum, and the Lotte Magic Island to its vast complex, the Olympic Stadium, which was next to it, languished. It hadn't seen any action since the Reverend Sun Myung Moon united 35,000 Korean "Moonie" couples in marriage last August. I hadn't even known that the Moonies were Korean.

I put the paper down, glanced at the clock. It was time to head to the school's auditorium for the Talent Show. I had invited Mrs. Lee, and I wondered if she'd be there. I had vacillated about asking her—at the time it seemed so seventh-grade piano recital—but now I wondered whether I'd be disappointed if she didn't come.

A strange thing happened there. Stranger than the sight of Bernie Lee doing tae kwon do moves set to opera music. Stranger than James Park ("Jam-EZ is how I pronounces it," he said), a gangsta-rapper-wannabe who sang an original song from his soon-to-be-released Korean CD, "Yellow Niggah." Maybe even stranger than the girl who took off all her clothes, spit milk on the audience, and rolled around, naked, on a bed of rice. Our own Korean Karen Finley.

I was supposed to play the *changgo,* which in itself wasn't so weird, but at the last minute, the Traditional Drumming Group of Chosun University had commandeered Tae *Sunsengnim*'s *puk* drum and *kaenguri* for some anniversary performance, so instead of playing as part of a group, I was told I was going to perform an impromptu drumming solo.

Tae *Sunsengnim* informed me of this maybe half an hour before the performance. I felt like a trained donkey, and I balked. Tae *Sunsengnim* merely shoved me out on stage with her mighty ham-hands. I couldn't remember a single thing I was supposed to do—usually I just followed the beat mashed out on the gong.

So I just brought the drum and the stick together.

Then, it was as if I'd brought two charges together. My whole body shuddered. The room started spinning. What was that Korean phrase about spinning?

... *bing! bing! tol-myun-so* ... Like the Fourth of July when Amanda handed me a live sparkler and it exploded in my face, all I could see was light. My feet were moving on their own. My arms were moving on their own. I was a puppet jerked by some spastic puppeteer. I was crying. I was laughing. I could hear people speaking Korean, and I was shouting back to them. I could hear other drums pounding out an insistent beat that drowned out my pulse. I couldn't breathe. I was going to collapse right in the middle of the stage.

Pinwheels of pistachio-colored light were still twirling in front of my eyes when my body finally slowed. My arm dropped, I stopped frenetically beating the drum like those toy monkey drummers. The light was replaced by faces in the audience.

Then, for the smallest second, I thought I saw *her*, although it wasn't Mrs. Lee. It was someone with a sad, sad face.

Backstage, Tae *Sunsengnim* unknotted my white headband, soaked with sweat.

"Sarah," she said. "I've never seen such an inspiring solo. You must come back to Korea and perform with our traditional drumming group."

"No shit, man," called Jam-EZ, as he fussed with his American-flag do-rag just before he went onstage. He turned and called over his shoulder, "That spinning split at the end woulda given James Brown a hernia!"

Someone was behind me. I turned quickly, wondering if I might catch another glimpse of that fleeting, sad face.

"Agi-yah." It was the happy voice of Mrs. Lee. She clapped her hands and looked at me, as if particularly moved, and said, *"Chotta!"*

SARAH
Seoul
1993

"I've never seen you eat things like that," Doug said.

I shrugged. The octopus stir-fry had actually been pretty tasty, suckers and all, and I'd even ordered it myself by hollering, *Ajuhma! Nak-ji bokum hana ju sae yo!* I made a big show of slurping up the last rubbery tentacle.

"How about something really different?"

For dinner he took me into the Chosun neighborhood to find a *pudae chigae* restaurant.

Poo day chee-gay.

Wasn't that what Bernie et al. had been clamoring for, that first week of class?

There was a *pudae chigae* restaurant a stone's throw from Chosun's arched stone gates. At six o'clock in the evening, most of the tables were packed, college students poking chopsticks into a communal well, drinking cheap *soju*.

The waiter lit a small butane warmer at the bottom of the giant wok built into the center of the table, and then he returned with a block of ramen, some rice cakes that looked like extruded white Play-Doh, a handful of weedy-looking greens. He put them all into the depression and poured boiling water plus hot pepper paste over the mixture. Then, Benihana-style, he diagonal-sliced some hot dogs and a few good chunks of SPAM and ceremoniously dumped it all into the wok's maw. When the whole mess got to boiling and gurgling, he added a few blaze-orange panes of American cheese.

Doug ordered us a ceramic pot filled with *soju*. He showed me how to drink it Korean-style, the younger person pouring it into the shot glass for the older person, using two hands to show respect. You toasted, shouting *"kom-bae!"* and then you were supposed to knock the incendiary liquid back in one swallow.

We drank as we waited for the *pudae chigae* to cook. At the next table, some drunk male students screeched and gave each other noogies, knocking their purses off the table.

"They're hopeless young romantics talking about azaleas," Doug said. "Azaleas. My mother said when she was young, she used to eat them."

"How fancy-schmancy," I said, feeling pleasantly blurred around the edges. That had also been Christine's thing. For a party, along with smelly mold-encrusted French cheeses, plates of baby vegetables, she always ordered edible flowers. Violets, flamelike nasturtiums, yellow-and-purple brindled pansies in clear plastic containers from Byerly's. She had gotten the idea from Ladies' Home Journal.

"It was that or die waiting for the first barley to ripen," Doug said. "There's a month in spring the lunar calendar calls the 'month of hunger,' when the winter supplies run out but nothing's ripe yet. She said one spring, the mountainside looked like it was still the dead of winter because so many families had gone out and stripped it bare of every green thing."

"Oh," I said. Doug ladled out some of the soup, the texture and color of molten lava. The sweet, spicy, syrupy goo was delicious. It reminded me of back home, how I would make ramen noodles: throw out the spice packet, make my own soup out of crushed garlic, one dash Tabasco, spoonfuls of La Choy soy sauce, squeeze of ketchup, and last, a single drop of honey. Noodles hot and sweet and salty, totally unlike the "Oriental Seasoning packet" but eerily like our *pudae chigae*. Was this craving, then, part of my Korean genetic code, tattooed on that winding helix of DNA?

But Koreans also ate plenty of strange things that I would gladly pass on. Crickets, sightless sea slugs, and something called *pundaegi,* silkworm larvae that looked (and smelled?) like prehistoric trilobites. On campus, girls carried black-and-gold-chain Chanel bags in one hand, greasy paper cones of *pundaegi* in the other.

Once, I was watching Doug eat some kind of seafood stew from which he pulled out nacreous shells like coins. I impulsively reached out with my long-handled spoon (Korean spoons made expressly for this purpose?) and stole a sip of broth. The broth was scalding, and so spicy, it made tears jump into my eyes. The taste was fishy, hot, horrible, and I was glad I hadn't known about the slimy fish-egg sacs, lying like amputated thumbs beneath the opaque broth.

But there was something in the taste that drew me to it—I took another sip, then another.

"You're Korean," Doug said simply. "That soup is too salty and spicy for Westerners to handle—it's called 'spicy soup' in Korean. On the base they used to make the newbies eat it, as a joke."

I wiped my eyes and took a sip of beer.

"Cut open a Korean and that's probably what you'll find: salt and hot red peppers," he said.

Was I really this Korean? I wondered. In Minnesota, cinnamon is too spicy for some folks. And nothing on the Scandinavian menu is pickled in salt—even *lutefisk* is pickled in lye. When the *ajuhmas* made kimchi at the Rainbow, they dragged giant plastic trash barrels outside the restaurant into which they'd mix limp cabbage with hot red peppers, thumbs of ginger—and entire bags of rock salt, the size of the bags Ken used to de-ice the driveway.

But, yes, Ken. When we used to go to Sand Lake in the summers, he would always make sure a bag of spuds—and three different kinds of salt—were on the grocery list. At the cabin he would slice the raw tubers into discs, whose starchy whiteness he'd dip first into onion salt, then double-dip into regular salt. He also stole pinches of raw hamburger before he put them on the grill, rolling them in coarse salt the way Nana rolled cheddar cheese balls in nuts at Christmastime.

Was there anything better than cramming a hard piece of oniony potato into my drooling mouth? It was our Sand Lake tradition, just the two of us. He would always start it by saying, "Madam Sarry-Sar, how about some po-tah-toes?" with a snooty lockjaw accent like Mr. Howell on *Gilligan's Island*. Or, "We're having hamburgers tonight, how about starting with some *hors d'oeuvres*?" which he would pronounce as "horses' doofuses" in that same accent, which always made me giggle.

"You know how *pudae chigae* originated?" Doug said. "During the Korean War, people were starving, so they would bring back garbage from the American army bases and boil it to make soup."

"You always tell me these things *after* I've eaten them," I said, but then I got to thinking. What was my mother's life like during the Korean War? Did she, like hundreds of other people in Seoul, hover around the garbage pile of the Eighth Army base, wishing for a piece of meat-fat or bone that had already been in someone's mouth so she could make some soup?

I cashed some of my travelers' checks and brought them the next time I went to visit Mrs. Lee. I offered it respectfully with two hands, but she didn't make a move to receive them, so I pushed them into her hands twice, three times, explaining that I felt bad about how she was spending a small fortune feeding me. She cried and flung the bills back at me, so when she was in the toilet shack, I slipped them in the mini-root-cellar box she kept in the corner of the kitchen. When she finished with that ten pounds of garlic, probably in a day or two, she would find the money.

I wanted her to accept my help, to have her know that I didn't feel the least shred of anger toward her any more, now that I knew her. I hadn't had a terrible life with Ken and Christine. Materially, it had been a resounding success.

That night after we'd gone to bed, I looked at her pillowy face and wondered what her expression had been right after I was born. Happy? Sad? Dismayed? Did she see bits of herself or her late husband looking back at her?

I recalled going out with Christine and Amanda to the Magic Pan, maybe a year ago. I'd noticed how Amanda and Christine had eaten their crepes in an identical way, wielding forks and knives as precisely as gem cutters, picking out the pieces of meat and leaving the shroudlike crepes behind. Even their similarly shaped mouths pursed the same way, like drawstring bags, lapidary movements, invisible threads connecting bone to bone, flesh to flesh.

I remembered thinking: I'll never have that, someone to compare myself to. But now, of course, I did.

Only the tiniest bit of doubt remained. A dusty dark seed that looked spoiled and old and dead—unlikely to sprout and cause its trouble.

But if it did crack open, extend a tentative root, I would be forced to follow that pale thread to its very end.

Mrs. Lee would be a complete stranger.

SARAH
Seoul
1993

There are things, Doug told me, that only exist for Koreans, that aren't explainable in the English language.

Like *han,* that wrenching, incurable feeling of regret. Or *nun-chi,* the ability to size someone up without even talking to them.

"Like that first day you asked me to eat lunch with you," he said. "My *nun-chi* nudged me, told me you were someone I'd want to get to know—even though after meeting the other Motherland Programmers I doubted there would be a single person on the program I'd want to be friends with."

The DNA test results had come in. Miss Park wanted both me and my *omoni,* my *um-ma,* to meet in the office. I was sure if the DNA didn't match, she would have said so on the phone. Now, I was so excited and relieved that my mother and I were going to be official.

❀ ❀ ❀

Miss Park's face looked tight and drawn.

"I'm so sorry," Julie said. "Mrs. Lee is not your mother."

The wind was rushing in to fill parts of my brain that had suddenly gone blank.

"Excuse me?" was all I could say.

"The DNA tests confirmed it." She showed me the report. The samples had been sent all the way to America. The results were in a language I could read and understand. My name, hers. NO MATCH. I stared at Mrs. Lee. Why? My eyes burned. Had she been pulling some kind of scam?

"Could you ask her why—" I had to pause, then went on, "why she was so sure I was her daughter?"

Mrs. Lee balled up a paisley hanky and spoke in a sobbing Korean.

"She said she just knew when she saw you on TV—you look a lot like her late husband when he was a boy. She also said you two like all the same things: you're both left-handed, she used to love to play the *changgo* drum when she was your age, too."

Mrs. Lee gripped my hand. A warm, familiar feeling. But I gently slipped it out. I felt a sudden, unaccountable loyalty to Christine, of all people. I would never let her hold my hand—or even touch me the tiniest bit—the way I had let this woman, countless times.

Mrs. Lee sniffled, said something.

"She said she was a little troubled hearing you say you'd been found at a fire station, because she had actually brought you to the Little Angels orphanage herself. But she thought that perhaps someone had miswritten in your file, because after she had placed you on the steps, another baby was brought in, not long after, and the two of you were taken in together."

I blinked. The *other* baby was probably me, brought in shit-slimy from the fire station. That meant there was yet another, shadowy woman out there that I needed to find. And there was some other Korean adoptee, perhaps in America, who was Mrs. Lee's daughter.

"*Agi-yah, mi an hae,*" Mrs. Lee said, still crying. Child, I'm sorry. That much, I understood.

"I don't think she's lying," Julie said. "We did once have a woman who came here claiming to be a mother, but you could tell she was wrong, right off the bat. She acted, I don't know, cold. We had doctors examine her and it turned out she'd never had a baby at all, I think she just wanted to get some money or something."

I thought of the bills lying under the papery heads of the garlic. I could feel the weight of the *han.*

"*Mi an hae yo,*" I said to the woman, Mrs. Lee Ok-bong.

"They're saying 'I'm sorry,' " Julie said, looking at Doug, a touch condescendingly.

Doug answered her in Korean.

"Oh," she said, taken aback.

"Things aren't always what you expect them to be," he shrugged.

KYUNG-SOOK
Enduring Pine Village
1993

"Excuse me," Kyung-sook said to a passerby, the third person she had approached. "But is this Han-Mi Dong?"

The young woman's hair was cut so short, it looked like a feathery cap twirling around her head. She scowled at Kyung-sook, who had stepped in front of her to make her stop.

"Is this the Han-Mi neighborhood?" Kyung-sook repeated.

"Yeah, what of it?" she said, walking off in a huff.

Kyung-sook looked around, then around again. She didn't recognize anything. She was sure that the dumpling house had been right in front of her, but instead of the corrugated tin roof she searched for, she was greeted by a modern apartment building rising straight up from the widened street. Colorful quilt-covers airing on balcony railings fluttered like flags from different nations. It hurt Kyung-sook's neck to try to peer to the very top.

"Are you looking for something, Older Sister?"

The country accent was music to Kyung-sook's ears. A woman taking out a bound plastic sack of garbage was looking at Kyung-sook with friendly curiosity.

"I think I used to live in this neighborhood, many years ago," Kyung-sook said. "Do you remember if there used to be a dumpling house right here? The neighborhood folks called it 'King's Dumplings.' There used to be a silk store down the lane, Jade Moon Real Estate on the corner."

"Oh, my, I remember the silk store," the woman said. "But that was an awful long time ago, even before they tore down the neighborhood.

"Tore down?"

"Oh, yes. This neighborhood was designated an 'eyesore' by the government—they used to call it 'Shit Alley' because of the sewage stench from the shanties—so they razed the place to tidy up for the Olympics."

"It was all torn down?"

"Well, those awful mud shanties certainly wouldn't have made Korea look very admirable to the outside world. 'Course, no surprise we didn't have any foreigners visit the neighborhood, being so far away from the Olympic Stadium and all."

"So do you remember the establishment that was right where this apartment building is? A tiny restaurant, it had a sign that said 'noodles and dumplings' out front."

She shook her head. "I don't have the faintest recollection of a noodle house, here. Sure could use one, though."

How could this be? It was as if she'd never been here, nor Sunhee, nor the cook-owner, nor Old Bachelor Choi. Their diner, the teahouse, the Chinese restaurant she'd gone to with *him,* all these things were gone, replaced by sharp-angled buildings, shiny glass enclosures where men and women sat casually together drinking coffee right in view of anyone. A woman even began smoking—in public!

Kyung-sook felt as if she were in a foreign city. Seoul Station was still in the same place, but when she made her way to where her imo had lived, she found a giant building, "One-Hundred-Kinds-of-Things-Store," occupying the *entire* block. Crowds of people were going in and out of it, carrying colorful shopping bags that said "New Generation." No one stopped to ask if she was lost, they only pushed roughly past her, stamped on her feet.

Imo gone, as well as the sealmaker. Along with the houses with the terracotta tile roofs that curved up like wings. Now everything was boxes, all sharp boxes.

There was only one, last place she could go to try to retrieve her past. Chosun University.

SARAH
Seoul
1993

"There's this place I want to take you," Doug said. "My mother told me about it—we always had plans to go there, but somehow never did. She said it's a village that time forgot."

"A Korean 'Land of the Lost'?" I teased. "Will we see dinosaurs, giant ferns?"

"Maybe," he said. "It'll definitely be different than this—" He gestured around the café we were in, the Doctor Zhivago. Inside, it was highway Americana—Route 66 signs, license plates, diner menus. Plastic saguaro cacti on the tables, a Confederate flag hanging over the door. From multiple speakers, Whitney Houston belted the theme song from *The Bodyguard*, which had, in the last week, become a kind of garish aural wallpaper plastering the interiors of all the cafés and stores.

Doug and I took a bus going north, an hour out of Seoul. Then we took a cab ride over an unpaved road that led to a place where the flat plains of rice seemed to meet the jutting mountains. A shallow, grass-green river meandered almost completely around the village, giving you the illusion that it was an island, a floating raft of rice.

River Circle Village.

We rode *hapsung* in the cab with another young couple and their toddler. The driver doubled his money by collecting the full fare from both parties. We were ferried across the water by a sullen *ajuhshi* poling a crude wooden craft.

Was this place was for real? The alleys were lined by long earthen walls covered by morning glories and four-o'clocks, creeping vines with gourds hanging off them like decorative light bulbs. Behind the walls sat old-time houses with thatched roofs, an occasional tiled one with edges curved like wings. The people walked around wearing the baggy farmer clothes that the actors had worn at the Folk Village, a Korean Colonial Williamsburg, that we had visited for a class trip.

The Korean couple had similar expressions of awe on their faces. The village folk ignored us.

"Why is this like this?" I asked Doug.

"The villagers decided they wanted to keep living the old way," he said. "In the seventies the government instituted this 'New Village Program' where they forced modernization of all the country houses, but the government officials probably didn't want to muddy their shoes with ox shit to get out here, so they left them alone."

On our way here, we had passed another isolated mountain hamlet, but it couldn't have looked more different: paved roads, a medieval castle-esque WEDDING TOWN with crenelated towers. In the town square, kids in Nike basketball shirts squatted outside MOTHER'S STORE eating ice cream. A train depot moldered outside of town.

"That's a shame," I said.

"Modernizing isn't necessarily bad," Doug shrugged. "When I was younger, I was darker, more Asian-looking. Kids used to call me 'rice paddy boy,' and teachers used to ask me if Koreans were dumb slant-eyed peasants like in M*A*S*H. It's kind of nice now to see Americans driving Hyundai cars and drinking OB beer in fancy restaurants."

"This place is wonderful, though," I said.

"You know that little town we just passed? The one with WEDDING TOWN? I believe that's the village my mother came from. It has the same name, at least."

"She never took you there, in all that time you were in Korea?"

He narrowed his eyes at me.

"No," he said coldly. "You can't go back to a place like that, when you've become what my mother became."

I knew enough to stay quiet, until he wanted to talk again.

We ate a dinner of rice mixed with mountain vegetables, side dishes of dark-brown *mook* made from acorns. Bitter with tannins, it quivered like jello, but I didn't foresee Bill Cosby endorsing it anytime soon. Next to the restaurant was a rice wine house. We sat outdoors on a raised wooden platform papered with that yellow oilpaper they used on the floor. The waitress brought us some of those grassy pancakes that Mrs. Lee had made me, plus a big pot of milky white liquid that we shared using a hollowed-out gourd as a dipper. Doug said it was a traditional farmers' rice wine called *mac'oli*. It didn't taste like milk at all, it burned like a shot of tequila. A few of the village men were drinking and smoking from long pipes next to us, the breeze carrying the smoke and their voices away from us.

The rice wine went straight to my head. The moon was rising into a flung-out sky, and shy stars were emerging, one by one, to keep Venus company.

For dessert, the waitress brought us some irregularly shaped rice cakes, steamed on a bed of pine needles, which gave them a resiny taste-smell that brought me back to many summers ago.

"We used to rent this cabin on Sand Lake," I told Doug. "In northern

Minnesota, there are so many lakes, they just give up and name half of them 'Sand Lake.' "

Doug leaned forward, sleepily interested.

"The cabin was nothing special. It didn't even have indoor plumbing. I used to have to tell Christine when I needed to go to the bathroom at night, and she would go out with me."

I was afraid of spiders, so Christine would whack around the privy first with a broom, then she'd wait outside. Sometimes I could hear her gently singing, her voice carrying through the crescent-moon ventilation cutout on the door.

"The lake smelled like pines, exactly like these cakes," I said.

"I keep forgetting you grew up in the sticks."

"Well, we would go *up* to the sticks, from Minneapolis. Ken was originally from the north country. He remembered a lot of stuff from growing up, like how to take the bark off birch trees without killing them. He used to make little birchbark boats down in the basement."

"When was the last time you were there?"

"I was seven or maybe eight," I said. "They later bought a place on Bass Lake, closer to the Cities. That lake, ironically, is a 'dead' lake, without fish in it. I think there's some movement afoot to change its name to Lake Gitchigumee, you know, the whole Hiawatha story."

"You fished?"

I nodded, recalling my child-sized Zebco, its clear filament, the red-and-white bobber, lead sinker shaped like a tear. Like any true Minnesota child, I caught sunfish by the stringerful. Even the ones hardly bigger than my child's palm, Christine prepared. I admired her courage as she slit open the fishes' bellies and pulled out their soft, silvery guts, scaling and cutting until she had a row of neat white filets which she would dip in a mixture of cornmeal, flour, and black pepper and pan-fry.

We would sit on the deck at twilight, squeeze slices of lemon over the crunchy-coated fish and watch the sun go down, while in the background, mosquito coils burned like incense. When the mosquitoes donned their teeny-tiny gas masks and made their way through the smoke, we would go back into the cabin, shut the screen door, and Christine and Ken and I would play endless games of Chutes and Ladders or Parcheesi, as many times as I wanted.

"I like hearing that," Doug said. He was smoking again, and he exhaled a cloud that remained for a few seconds like an apparition before fading into the sky.

It became too late to secure a taxi back, but a passerby showed us to a place where a woman would rent us a room in her house. The room had a clean wooden floor and bedding that smelled like rice starch and sunlight. We lay down, naked, then realized there was only one pillow. Doug gave it to me.

After making love, he fell asleep. I, as usual, stayed awake. I stared at him in the muted light from the moon. He looked like an angel when he slept, one arm protectively around me, the other curled under his chin, fingers extended as if he were secretly waving at me.

I gently worked the pillow under his head. He gave a sigh, rubbed his eyes in a childlike gesture, and I saw the baby he had once been in the adult he was now.

The idea of escape was a fiction, I realized. You could travel to the other end of the earth in an airplane, but you wouldn't get too far from yourself and your accretion of all your secret histories, the sins and curses and mercies that ever touched you. People entered and disappeared from your life, but they irrevocably left parts of themselves, the way that soft candy prayerfully pressed by Korean mothers onto the gates where their children were taking their college entrance exams eventually hardened and became part of the gate itself.

Perhaps I'd finally learned, from this strange twisted language, the answer to my question, *Why am I I?* In Korean you rarely used the "I," *nae-ga*. Instead of "I'm going to the store," you just said "Going to the store." You only needed to say "I" in situations where you needed to distinguish yourself, "I—not Doug, not Bernie, not Jun-Ho, not Jeannie—am going to the store." I felt too insecure, however, about when an "I" was truly needed, and so I sprinkled *nae-ga*s all over my sentences the way a desperate cook keeps adding salt, even as *Sunsengnim* kept scolding me, saying, "Sal-ah-*ssi*, we know it's *you*."

I am I, not anybody else. The subject is understood.

For our morning rice, the *ajuhma* presented us with a full country breakfast: bean-sprout soup, a pile of sesame leaves washed in the morning dew, searingly hot chili peppers she expected us to dip in hot pepper paste before eating, cubes of radish kimchi, fried tofu, a bundle of wild onions, bowls and bowls of rice. And from somewhere, she had procured a warm bottle of FAIRY orange soda.

"*Eat a lot*," she told us.

We took the bus back to Seoul, the subway back from the Express Bus Terminal. Doug held my hand the whole way. I couldn't stop smiling at him. The subway doors opened at our stop, *Cho-Dae*—short for Chosun Daehakyo. I jumped out the door ahead of Doug, and we almost clotheslined a countrified *ajuhma* running past, bundle in hand, head wrapped in a towel. She burrowed into the crowd on the platform to bemused cries of *Hey, what's your hurry, Auntie?* She was a strange, almost anachronistic vision, as if we had inadvertently brought her back from the River Circle Village with us, a seed hidden in our clothes.

We took the long way back to the Residence so I could stop for an ice cream. It was a Sunday, with shoppers, young families out in force, giggling junior-high girls crowding two, three at a time into photo-sticker booths. As we strode along, me chewing my General Yi's Turtle Boat Ship ice cream, I found myself starting to look, that hopeful gaze, again. I looked at the shape of eyes, the curve of bone, the way hair fell off a part. I looked and looked. For chocolate-chip-colored moles and thick hair. At every woman *d'un certain âge* who walked by, all the way until we entered the Chosun campus.

KYUNG-SOOK
Enduring Pine Village
1993

Chosun University.

That had been her real destination all along, of course. The place where they said the girl would be.

But how to get there, the other side of the city? There were no trolleys anymore. Instead, buses in all sorts of colors and numbers went every which way. A kindly passerby told her that the "underground-iron-train" was the best way to go to the Chosun neighborhood, and he pointed out that the station was right there, under their feet!

Kyung-sook descended stairs that gave way to a long corridor that ran under the street. A faded, neglected sign said "Emergency Shelter"—it must have been part of the network of old bomb shelters from the 6.25 War. She followed the corridor to the end and found herself in the middle of a clot of people, whooshing trains, shoe stores, newsstands, underwear places, seaweed-roll vendors, machines spitting out money. The posted map revealed a jolly knot of bright-colored worms, the names of the stations unfamiliar. Great East Gate Stadium? Air Port? South of Han River? Poyang Satellite City?

When she bought her ticket, she asked the ticket ajuhshi how to get to Chosun University, but the man, bathed in a haze of smoke from his cigarette, mumbled a contemptuous reply and waved at the next person in line to step forward.

Clutching the colored bit of paper she had received, Kyung-sook wandered among the different lines: green, purple, red, yellow. Everyone seemed to know where they were going and were in a rush to get there.

Ironically, she ended up asking a whiteman for directions. There seemed to be a goodly number of foreigners in Seoul now. The Westerners were sauntering around with bulky rucksacks and short pants that shockingly bared their furry legs. They looked like nothing in their lives had ever troubled them.

But since none of the Koreans had stopped to help her, she tried a man leaning against a pillar, reading. He had a warm, brown face-hair and he smiled and answered in perfect Korean, "I would be pleased to help you."

He pulled out a book that had a map of the subways in its center, and he showed her which line to take, where to get off. He even marked the stop *Cho-Dae* with a pen, then tore the page out and handed it to her.

"You're very polite for a foreigner," she said, wondering about the meaning of a station called *chodae*—"invitation." An auspicious sign? "A thousand times, thank you."

"A thousand times, you're welcome," the man said, nodding his head the Korean way before returning to his magazine.

Kyung-sook watched the other riders feed their colored bit of paper into the little machine, and she did the same, and boarded her train.

❁ ❁ ❁

"Lady, what do you think you're doing?" The policeman gripped her roughly by the elbow.

"I-I—" Kyung-sook had arrived at the correct station with no difficulty. But at the exit marked "To Street," she hadn't known what to do at the machine on the way out. Everyone else was putting in those little scrips of paper again, which the hungry machine gobbled up and let them pass with a green light. She didn't have her ticket any more—hadn't the first machine "eaten" it? Then it was the ticket ajuhshi's fault for not giving her enough tickets. She had shrugged and started to crawl under the bar.

"It's illegal to jump the turnstile," he said. "Really, you should know better, ma'am, especially since you know we're instituting a strict new crackdown policy on farebeaters like you."

"I-I—"

"I'm sorry, but I'm going to have to bring you to the police station."

The police station!

She knew what happened at Seoul police stations from watching *The Dark Yushin Era*—people sat tied up in dark rooms under a single harsh light and were beaten and tortured with electric shocks. Some of them never were seen again. She couldn't do that to Il-sik!

Kyung-sook yanked her elbow with all the strength gained from years of slogging heavy barrels of shrimp, and she ran pell-mell back down to the platform.

The policeman was speechless for a moment, then he yelled, "Halt! You!"

Kyung-sook ran on. Another train had arrived, and waves of people poured onto the platform and up the stairs, tangling the policeman in the crowd. Kyung-sook could hear the man swearing, but then his voice was swallowed up in the rest of the din of the station.

...PLEASE DON'T SMOKE. PLEASE USE CAUTION WHEN THE TRAIN COMES INTO THE STATION. PLEASE DON'T SPIT ON THE PLATFORM. LOST ITEMS...

She pushed her way through the people, almost breaking up a couple holding hands—holding hands! She couldn't stop to look back and marvel at such a scandalous sight. Instead, she ran on.

Thank goodness she had brought only the smallest bundle with her!

She made it to the end of the platform and through another corridor. It led to a different train, the signs were a different color. Was the man still in pursuit? As she stood, trembling, among the people waiting, she tore off her headscarf—she noticed no one in Seoul wore those. She looked at herself in one of the large mirrors mounted on the wall. She was still so terribly conspicuous. That policeman was going to find her and cart her off to be tortured and Il-sik would never know what happened to her. He might even think she had found her daughter and then abandoned him!

"Oh Dear Heavenly God," she prayed. Could he hear her up in Heaven when she was praying from so far under the ground? "Help me! What should I do? Please give me a sign."

Down the tunnel came the sound of the train. Without looking up from their newspapers or pausing in their talking into their little boxes, the people moved to the designated yellow-painted areas that said "The Doors Will Open Here."

Kyung-sook glanced over her shoulder. She would have to take this train, wherever it was going, just to get out of this station.

The doors opened with a *whoosh*, and she boarded, pushing, shoving with everyone else into the crowded car. A man with heavily oiled hair seemed to be leaning a little too close into her chest, so Kyung-sook pinched his arm, hard, through his suit that was shiny and gray like fish scales. The man swore and moved to a different part of the car.

"Where is this train going?" she asked a student in a navy middle school uniform. The girl was grasping the pole with one hand, holding her English textbook up to her face with the other.

"Toward Seoul Station, Grandmother," she said.

Seoul Station, where the train would be waiting to bring her home to Enduring Pine Village—to safety, away from the ills of this horrid city. She wasn't meant to find the child, was she? God had given her an answer, Kyung-sook thought, although she couldn't help being a little peeved that the student had called her "grandmother"—she wasn't yet even fifty years old!

KYUNG-SOOK
Enduring Pine Village
1993

"You've been gone a few days," Cooking Oil Auntie observed.

"Only a day," Kyung-sook said, and added, "It was just a little kamgi, a sniffly summer cold. I feel better now."

"You were gone somewhere," Cooking Oil Auntie repeated. "I saw Song Grandmother go to take care of the house."

Kyung-sook hummed, pretended not to hear her. She became very interested in watching the machine press the dark sesame oil out of the roasted seeds, drop by bulging drop.

"You know, the Mothers' Association started their own general store," Kyung-sook said. "They have sundries, even an electric freezer for ice cream—the little kids go wild for that kind of stuff."

"I said, you were gone somewhere," Cooking Oil Auntie repeated, a bit louder. "Where?"

"Oh? Oh yes, I also had to go to Seoul for some business."

"What business could *you* possibly have in Seoul?"

Kyung-sook blinked. There was a spot, exactly round like a changgi chess piece, covering Cooking Oil Auntie's face. Not unlike the one that had appeared before the cook-owner was killed.

"Oh, I went to see my imo."

"Your imo is still alive and well in Seoul?"

Kyung-sook nodded and blinked some more. Maybe it was this bright sunlight flooding the morning market that was making her eyes play tricks.

"Well, while you've been gone, it looks like Okja is going to marry Sun-Woon after all."

"Okja?"

"Unh, it seems that her rich girl rival had one big deficit . . ." Cooking Oil Auntie paused dramatically. It took Kyung-sook a second to remember she was talking about characters from her soap opera, *The Date Tree*.

"Eun-ju, that little vixen, couldn't conceive! Her frantic parents tried everything: deer antler, breath-holding, prayers to the Birth Goddess—but she's barren as a rock, *hee-hee*! Of course Sun-Woon, being a first son, must fulfill his filial duty. So remember how Okja found out she was pregnant and had decided to kill herself? Well, Sun-Woon's parents gave him permission to divorce the vixen and marry Okja because two *separate* fortunetellers predicted he would have a son by the next Autumn Harvest Moon festival—that's exactly when Okja's due to deliver!"

"Oh, yes?" Kyung-sook said.

"Well, after all that waiting for those two to get together, now I'm sad this soap opera's going to end—" Cooking Oil Auntie began to cough. One cough bled into another, and then another. She spat on the ground. A spidery tentacle of red floated in the mucus. Kyung-sook sighed.

"You said your son is planning to come visit you soon?" she asked.

"*Haaaargh,*" Cooking Oil Auntie said, wiping her mouth on her sleeve. "These damn summer colds are the worst, I need to get some tonic from the Chinese herbalist—he was out of Siberian ginseng last time I was there. My son? He just started a new job—Samsung Incendiaries and Explosives—he certainly couldn't take any time off for at least a year."

"You might want to have him come up as soon as he can," Kyung-sook said, and she sighed again.

SARAH
Seoul
1993

Choi *Sunsengnim* stopped writing on the board.

"We will have free-talk today," she gasped.

Our classroom's air conditioner, which never worked well in the first place, had given up the ghost. Smack in the middle of the *sam-bok,* the thirty hottest days of the lunar calendar.

Bernie, hot and irritable, began needling Jeannie about her eyes, which were finally starting to look more normal, so to speak.

Absent a week, Jeanie had returned for the last days at school with tiny, Frankensteinian stitches on her lids, which were swollen and red as if she'd been attacked by bees.

"*Mein Gott!*" Helmut had practically jumped out of his seat when he'd seen her. "You had the *ssan kop'ol* surgery!"

Jeannie nodded, even gamely answered some questions—no, it didn't hurt, no it wasn't dangerous—but then declared the subject off-limits.

Now healed into their more-or-less permanent shape, her eyes did look different. She reminded me of Katharine Hepburn in *The Good Earth*; Hepburn's eyelids, fixed with tape, had looked neither Western nor Eastern, only strange.

"Free-talk in Korean," Choi *Sunsengnim* said weakly.

"Did you go to a real doctor?" Bernie continued. "Or to a *tol p'ari* surgeon? I've seen their ads, for boob jobs, hymen-restoring surgery, too."

"Shut up, Bernie," Jeannie said, from behind clenched teeth.

"Just tell me, Jiyoung-*ssi*," Bernie said, leaning almost longingly toward his former lover. "Why did you do it?"

"My aunt kept bugging me—okay?" Jeannie spat. "She kept saying, you'll look better with *ssan kop'ol*, you'll look better with *ssan kop'ol*. She even paid for it—I had it done at HanYong University Hospital—the best hospital in Seoul. It's not the big fucking deal you're making it out to be. I had droopy eyelids before, I felt like a fucking Shar-Pei dog. So now I can *see* better—okay? Even Gloria Steinem's had plastic surgery on her eyes."

"I read in the paper," said the nun (and we knew she meant the real Korean paper, like the *Dong-Ah Ilbo*—those Chinese-character skills of hers!—and not the *Korea Herald*), "that one awful aftereffect of such a surgery is that sometimes, the lids do not close completely, when it is time for sleep."

"Please," said Choi *Sunsengnim* in desperation. "Speak in Korean."

That was when the word *ddong* was brought up in class. It started when Helmut finally said something in Korean. He spoke of eating something called *boshin-tang*.

"*How novel for you!*" said Choi *Sunsengnim*, in relief.

"*What is poe-sin-dang?*" I was reduced to asking, still the worst student in *ill-gup*.

"'Health tonic stew,'" said Helmut. "*Sunsengnim*, why do they call it that?"

"Because of tourists," Choi *Sunsengnim* said, inadvertently slipping back into English. "During the Olympics, the president, he makes all the restaurants put up signs that say 'health tonic stew' over the ones that say 'dog stew.' If you go out in the country, though, sometimes you can still see the signs that say 'dog soup' or 'dog meat.'"

Koreans, modern Koreans, eat dogs.

"Koreans eat dogs?" I ventured. Fluffy? Spot?

"Don't you know anything?" said Bernie. "It's a fucking sacred tradition. My uncle and I do it every year during the *sam-bok*."

"I don't like the eating of dog," I said.

"But you eat cow-meat, right?" said Choi *Sunsengnim.* *"American* hambuh-goo?"

"Neigh."

"So what is the difference? Meat is meat."

"But dogs are different," I said. *"They're—ah—"*

"Pets," said the nun, obviously pleased with her knowledge of this English word.

"Oh-moh! We don't eat personal dogs!" Choi *Sunsengnim* said with horror and offense. *"We only eat* ddong-*dogs."*

Ddong-dogs?

"That doesn't sound very appetizing," Bernie commented, once again shifting the class back to English.

"No, *ddong*-dog means like no one's dog, like—"

"Stray," said Doug, although later he would tell me that the best-looking dogs on the army base—the big, beautiful German shepherds in particular—had a habit of mysteriously disappearing.

"That's it, stray. *Belongs to no one. See, no one eats another person's dog! But stray dogs, they are the most delicious."*

"Ddong *kae*," I said, marveling. Stray dog.

"Sal-ah-ssi, your pronunciation has gotten quite a bit better," Choi *Sunsengnim* commented. The others nodded.

KYUNG-SOOK
Enduring Pine Village
1993

The cicadas were back.

The end of a seventeen-year cycle already. The buzzing would go on for days without ceasing until some people would swear the insects were nesting in their brains, others would be lulled to sleep by the steady hum. The government had begun a program of spraying poison on the trees in Seoul, saying that the noise disturbed the foreign tourists.

Mengmengmengmengmengmengmengmengmeng.

She went to the Three Peaks Lake so she could be among the gentle sounds of the water, the cooling color of summergreen oaks and white pine, where she could let the buzz-sound of the cicadas fill her veins with their unending thrum. She had been not-so-old the last time she heard that sound. Seventeen years was time enough for a tree to grow tall, for a baby to grow into an adult. Those years had just washed away like silt.

Il-sik's look of utter relief when she returned safely from Seoul had touched her to the core. Somehow, during the time she was gone, he had found a way to take his anger and disappointment and bury it like a pot of kimchi. It was true that in a marriage, each spouse knows exactly where the other's tenderest, softest secret spots lay, and that words could be sharper than a policeman's worst torture instrument.

But then also, resisting the temptation to use secrets as a weapon, that was the truest kind of love.

Knives cutting water, the saying went, referring to these marital mercies.

The child, her flute, had been lost to her. But she was able to see how she had gained things as well—her life, the one she had built for herself, Il-sik, her dear father living in her marital home, cared for by her own hands. She had to admit, she loved this life.

My daughter, I want to tell you about your mother, and I want to say this prayer for you ...

She had begun this letter, and it had run to many pages, until her hand had knotted up so painfully it looked like her husband's. At the market, she had purchased sheets of the nicest pounded mulberry-bark paper, brought those pages all the way to the lake.

She cleared a small space in the grass, drew a ring of dirt as if she were a geomancer, and put the papers in the middle. In the background, the mountain peaks waited. She did not know the child's name. The girl on TV had been called "Sal-Ah," which she was sure was a mistake on the part of the translator. Kyung-sook knew in her heart, the girl's American parents would not have given a baby a name that meant "child to buy" in their country's tongue.

She put a match to a corner of the papers and stood back as the flames consumed the small pile. The edges of the bark paper writhed and danced joyfully as the smoke swirled up into the sky. Soon, all that was left were a few silky ashes, which Kyung-sook rubbed into the earth with her hand. Part of the prayer for her daughter would remain in the earth, the rest gone up to Heaven.

SARAH
Seoul
1993

The time to go had crept up and pounced like a stealthy animal. We Motherland Programmers were packed and ready to leave.

I had been tempted to stay with Doug, who had decided to extend his Korean stay for a few more months—it was easy to get English-language tutoring jobs anywhere in the city. For me, all it would take to refresh my visa for three months would be to follow him down to Pusan, hop on a ferry to Fukuoka, Japan's closest port, and return to continue things as they had been, in Seoul, the two of us. *Pudae chigae* and karaoke bars, watching the lavender-pantsed men at T'apkol Park, eating *samkyupsal,* the three-layers-fat pork that you wrap in a lettuce leaf and stuff, whole, into your mouth.

Yet something was pushing me away from Korea. Jun-Ho had written a hastily scrawled letter in which he said,

> *Sarah, Jun-Ho Kim is here to say that I wish for you that you will make a beautiful future. I know you will come back to Korea so that our minds can meet again in happy intercourse uninterrupted. Post crypt: every Lee in Korea claims they are descended from the famous Chunju Lees. The paterfamilias could not possibly have sired so many descendants. But ask your* Omoni. *Who should know?*

Choi *Sunsengim* gave me a gift wrapped in bright purple Mylar. I didn't open it until later, when Doug and I were killing time in the TV room.

Underneath the wrapping was a skinny metal object, cigar-sized. Fake glass gems glued onto it. At first I thought it was a very ornate pen, but when I took off the hidden cover, I saw it contained a small blade, notched at the top, like a bowie knife.

"That's a strange gift to give someone," Doug commented.

"What?" I said. "A letter opener?"

"You're supposed to use it to kill yourself."

"Excuse?"

"Don't you remember it from the Cultural Treasures Museum in Taejon?"

I had been there, another class trip. But after seeing so many gold crowns, jade chopstick holders, and replicas of the Turtle Boats, I'd become too dizzy with Korean things to remember them all.

"This is the chastity knife. The one women wore on the blouses of their *hanbok*. If you were ever raped, you were supposed to kill yourself to preserve the family honor."

"Uh huh." I tested the point of the blade on my finger. It made a dent, but didn't break the skin.

"But see, the blade is very short. You *seppuku* yourself, but you can't hurt someone else with it."

I looked at the veins running under the thin skin of my inner wrist, the color suddenly inviting. "You sure remember a lot from that museum visit."

"Some things are more memorable," he shrugged.

I put the whatever-it-was into my bag. Its jaunty red tassel glowed in the darkness of the interior of my purse.

Bam-BAM-BAM!

On the TV, Sylvester Stallone, bullet bandoleers X'd over his chest.

"Rambo says, Elephant Ice Cream is number one!"

"*Lambo,*" the voiceover translated. "*Numbah wang.*"

Another commercial. Meg Ryan in a white nun's outfit, patting a horse. Hawking SEXY-MILD.

Then the crude graphic of the spinning globe. The nightly news.

The big story: a bank holdup. Grainy security-cam footage of a bank. The perp—identity disguised not by the usual nylon stocking or hood but by a surgical mask, as if he were a doctor running amuck—wielding a gun (although Korea has very strict gun-control laws). While the male employees cowered behind chairs, a beslippered *ajuhma* jumped over the counter and started wrestling with him. He awkwardly pointed the gun, seemed confused as to how to use it, then gave up and hit her on the head with it. They showed her later getting some kind of citation from the mayor of Seoul, a white bandage wrapped around half her head.

Then, familiar music.

Michael Jackson!

"Michael Jackson will be in Korea with his friend, Liz Taylor!" Doug translated. He was going to be in Cheju Island, relaxing, looking to perhaps establish an Asian outpost for Neverland.

"The Korean people have always been very gracious to me," he said, in his wispy little-girl-man voice.

"I heard Liz Taylor is getting married again," said Doug, who kept up on American goings-on by going to the USIA to read *People*.

"I'm hungry," I said. "Let's go to one of those noodle-salad places."

We were about to finally summon the energy to shut off the TV. But then we both recognized the word *adoptee*. And the word Minn-ah-soh-ta.

Footage of a young Korean guy arriving at the waiting area at Kimp'o Airport.

"My name is Brian Muckenhill," he said, in a familiar Midwestern voice. He was from Blue Earth, Minnesota, population five hundred and three.

"I'm here to try to find my birth family."

Shock.

"Because of *ahm*," Doug said. "Cancer of the blood. He needs a bone marrow transplant and no donors could be found in the States. A biological relative would have the best chance."

Thousands of Koreans had come out to help, plastering posters of his picture in the crevice of every tiny hamlet. Makeshift marrow testing centers sprang up everywhere. Entire military units came out. I strained to see the screen, as if I might see Jun-Ho within the masses, which looked so alike, short haircuts and uniforms. Like a set of toy soldiers.

"The Koreans are impressed," said Doug, translating a reporter's words, "that a non-Korean family could love this boy so much, someone who is not of their own blood. So Koreans want to come out and help, to get their marrow tested and help him find his family."

A young woman was on the screen, eyes large as a doe's.

" 'He is, after all, Korean. And Koreans have to help each other.' "

"He's a cadet at West Point, so the U.S. government's paying for the best treatment. But if he doesn't get a bone marrow transplant, he'll most likely die by the end of the year. He was a quarterback on his high school's football team. That blond girl you just saw—that's his girlfriend back in Blue Earth, Minnesota. Man, how come you Korean adoptees all end up in Hicksville, Minnesota?"

"Something to do with the churches. The adoption agencies all have some kind of name like Catholic Charities or Lutheran Services," I said, distracted. "So how about his birth family, did they find them?"

"Mm, they went to the orphanage and searched the files, like you did, and they found a baby picture, so next they're going to broadcast it on TV and in the newspapers."

I found myself unexpectedly weeping, throwing myself against him.

"Hey, take it easy," Doug said, but his eyes were soft.

I wanted to claw and rend, hear the scream of fabric tearing. I stretched out the neck of Doug's T-shirt until it hung down like loose skin. I was aware that Brian Muckenhill had terminal cancer, but all I could think of was that *he* was going to meet his birth mother—and I would never, ever know mine, never have that hand to touch. It occurred to me suddenly that I didn't even know if my birthday was September third, the day I was found, or September second—today. Jun-Ho said that the exact time and date of one's birth was very important in Korean astrology, that fortunetellers could tell you your entire destiny from those two pieces of information, which most people have. Christine and Ken managed to skip that thorny issue by doing the cake and presents on the anniversary of the day I arrived in Minnesota, my "Gotcha day" they called it, March 17.

Gotcha meant nothing. A human-set date chosen by others. Not like my birth, the date and time that I, by that eternal and mysterious baby instinct, decided to leave the womb. No one should be without this knowledge. But it wasn't forgotten, or unclaimed at the bottom of some dusty file. It was, simply, gone. Like her.

I wanted to scream so loud that every person in Korea, in America, in the world beyond would cover their ears and grimace.

KYUNG-SOOK
Enduring Pine Village
1993

On Saturdays, when she was done with her time in the market, she went over to the church to prepare it for the next day's service. Small Singing had left her stall with a smile because Kyung-sook had mentioned that the bone-shaped birthmark on her son's neck was an auspicious sign.

Shrimp Auntie works so hard, said some of the observing villagers. She takes care of a husband and a father, her business, and the church.

Do you remember her mother? She had the best singing voice in the village. No one could sing "My Hometown" like she could—she wouldn't leave a dry eye in the place!

The daughter didn't inherit any of that singing voice, now did she?

Oh my, no. The girl was tone deaf—her singing voice was like a couple of cats screeching.

But she was smart, I remember. Didn't she go to college in Seoul for a while?

Shrimp Auntie? I don't think so. She's just been a wife and daughter, for all I know.

I seem to remember she left the village to go to college.

You're getting too old to be the village gossip—you can't keep your facts straight. It's a pity Cooking Oil Auntie has passed on—now, *she* knew what was what. You're getting Shrimp Auntie mixed up with her childhood friend, last-one daughter of the five daughters of Kim the junkman. That girl ran off to North River County to the Yankee army base, not Seoul.

Oh, perhaps you're right. Aigu, but these old bones ache! But probably not as much as Shrimp Auntie's are going to, after she spends all evening bent under those benches. Then on Sundays she plays on that Western pi-a-no so the parishioners can sing their Christo ballads—she has that much musical talent, at least.

She loves her God, that's why she does it.

Kyung-sook opened the door to the church, its familiar woody, slightly musty odor rushed to greet her.

Saturday nights she cleaned, all by herself. Her soft cloth would slide noiselessly across the pews, in perfect rhythm to her breathing. She would quietly straighten the things on the humble pulpit, all the while receiving her peace in this walking meditation.

September third had come again. Her daughter's coming-out-to-the-world day. This time, she did not force her mind to other things. Instead, she merely moved about in gloomy silence, shed a few bitter tears during the lull time in the market. Soon it would be Chu-sok day, the day she needed to make obeisance to her mother and her other ancestors for three generations back. She would thank her ancestors for her profitable year at the market, she would tell her mother, again, *I'm sorry for what I did to your dreams of having a college-educated daughter. Please forgive me.*

Il-sik, as he did each year, would rebuke her for her adherence to these ancient rites. In his sermons he preached that the Korean people needed to move away from ancestor worship, fortunetelling by the chom chengi, shamanism, and Buddhism—these things were all sent by Satan to distract people from the True Way, Christo. Il-sik encouraged churchgoers to even physically restrain their friends and relatives when they headed out to the chom chengi or to the Buddhist temple.

But old ways are not so easily changed. He had to know that even the most fervent churchgoers had their prophecies read, made offerings to the mountain gods "just in case." And no one Kyung-sook knew would make a marriage match for their children without having an astrologer make sure their zodiac signs and blood types were compatible.

For her part, honoring her ancestors through the Chu-sok rites were something she could not, would not, end. It was something she had done all her life, her mother had done it all hers, all the way back through the many generations delineated in the pages of the chuk-bok. She would again, on the preceding day, leave her market stall and spend the whole day shopping for and cooking a feast of her mother's favorite dishes. This she would spread out in front of her esteemed mother's burial mound, and she would implore her mother's spirit to return and enjoy this repast made by her daughter's hands.

Thus, the cycle of life. She had left the village and come back, and to some eyes, it was as if she had never left—she was the same.

But because of Il-sik, her husband, she had become a Christo-follower. Because of that other man, she had borne a child, one that she had not raised, one whose fate was—and would be—unknown to her.

In many other ways she had come back to the village changed, and she would continue to change. All people did, like a snake that sheds its skin: at some point the new skin becomes old, the old becomes the new.

Yet life was not a circle, as the Buddhists and Confucius thought. She would not be reborn at sixty to start a new life. No, her life was winding, winding, following the coil of a spring. At each point she was able to see behind her to what her experiences had been, but at each point, a little further up the coil, her perspective was a little bit different.

It would be like this until she reached the end of the coil, the time when she would go up to Him, if He has deemed her faithful.

She moved her cloth along the wood of the pews. The rough-hewn wood was slowly, slowly taking on a bit of a burnished glow, and this pleased her.

The coming of Chu-sok would also mean the night of the fullest autumn moon. The night of the Harvest Moon Festival, where all the village women would gather for the kangkang sullae. Girls, women, and grandmothers would all join hands, they would become an expansive circle that would slowly unwind. Then, one by one, each dancer would be lifted toward the sky for her chance to sing out her story, framed in the light of a luminous moon.

SARAH
Seoul
1993

"Hello, you've reached the Thorsons. Sorry we can't take your call but we'd love to talk to you, so please leave your number and have a wonderful day!" There were various noises of the bird and the cats and the dog in the background. *Yip. Arf. Meow. Skrrech.*

At the beep, I informed them only of the day of my return. I didn't want Ken and Christine and Amanda to meet me at the airport, to rush back into my life. I would make my way home, make a gradual adjustment back through the layers of my Minnesota life: English words, greenbacks, Viking-ish faces. Slowly, slowly I had to be debriefed, depressurized, to avoid a fatal case of the emotional bends.

Doug and I rode in silence to the airport. In the rice fields on the way, bareheaded men drove motorized harvesters, spewing blizzards of straw in giant arcs toward the sun. The big yellow billboard that greeted me almost a year ago, HYUNDAI — FOR BETTER LIFE had been corrected to HYUNDAI — FOR A BETTER LIFE.

At Kimp'o Airport, I saw some program-mates debarking from sleek black cars aptly named Princes. People kept coming out the doors endlessly: grandmas, uncles, cousins, aunts, like in the cartoons.

The airline people said to come two hours early, and we did. There was nothing to do but wander around a huge oval-shaped, arched-ceilinged room that reminded me of a hockey arena—I almost expected to hear the drone of a Zamboni.

At the center of the room, people slumped on the plastic-and-metal chairs, KNN blaring from TV monitors above their heads. Doug returned from a gift shop with a keychain that had a bell with a drawing of Hodori, the Olympic tiger mascot on it. A smiling neonatal tiger—in a land where all the native tigers had been killed for their penises (a supposed aphrodisiac)—Hodori wore a traditional Korean cap with the long propeller-like ribbon on it. Tae *Sunsengnim* had worn such a hat at the music performance for her group, Sa-mul Nol-I, to which she had invited me. Even though the *kaenguri* position was traditionally reserved for a man, she had been the one to play the shining gong. While keeping perfect time with her *chang-chang*ing, she had spun her head around so fast that the twirling white ribbon eventually formed a perfect, breathtaking circle.

The bell tinkled in my hand as we settled onto the uncomfortable chairs. Something smelled like old, ripe kimchi.

The departure board trembled, like leaves catching a breeze, and the *flap-flap-flap* revealed a BOARDING sign next to my flight, a red light blinking urgently next to it.

"This is it?" I said, rising.

Doug didn't say anything. He grabbed my bag and carried it to the line. He had assembled a collection of my favorite snacks: an ear of midget corn, *ddok* rice cakes, squares of roasted seaweed, and yes, *o-jing-o*, dried squid—I'd developed a taste for that salty, smelly, leathery stuff after all. I'd better finish everything before I landed, he advised, or customs would probably take it away. He had also written the address of his new boarding house in Seoul.

It was at once easy and hard to think of leaving Doug. The way his eyes could look so deeply into my truest self. His angular face, with that sweet spot under his chin, the little frog's belly of softness that perhaps only I knew about. I would miss him. But now that we'd found each other, we could go on, no matter where we were. I looked at him, my Doug, the features of his long-gone American father impudently pushing to the surface of his face.

"I love you," he said. "And I *will* see you again."

I laughed, wondering how he could think otherwise.

I showed the attendant my ticket, my passport with the eagle stamped on it in gold. She gave it a cursory glance, then handed it back, put her hand out for the ₩ 10,000 "departure tax."

Then there was only Doug's hand on my arm holding me to this place. In just a step, Korea would be receding to that place where my Korean mother was, the place just inside my eyelids, on the cusp of a dream, where we could not speak or touch.

I moved. His hand fell away.

I looked back into the waiting area, past Doug's shoulders. The fantasy image I'd had of my mother—the long black hair, rosy lips, slender hands—those varied pieces flattened out and joined together to form a paper doll, its edges curling as the form caught an invisible breeze and went twirling, twirling, up to the high, domed ceiling of the airport, then out into the sky beyond.

"*Um-ma, anyong-hi kae say yo,*" I said. Stay in peace.

"Goodbye, Sarah."

I waved one more time to Doug, then entered the long tunnel. Because it curved, ten steps in I saw only wall when I looked back. In front of me, a large Caucasian man, a jarhead, toted an overstuffed Adidas bag, the counterfeit logo looking like marijuana leaves.

"Never coming back!" he said, to no one in particular. "Never coming back to this stinking country. The U.S. Army can fuck this country!"

❀ ❀ ❀

In the plane, the stewardess spoke to me in Korean, asking me if I wanted something to drink.

"*Neh,*" I said. "*Coke-ah col-ah chu sae yo.*" She didn't blink, poured me a Pepsi from its red-white-and-blue can.

The guy across the aisle looked familiar, Korean American. Military crewcut, slightly pale, thin, a Confederate-gray uniform banded in black.

"Excuse me," I found myself saying. "What's the uniform?"

He looked over at me.

"West Point."

I stared at the ice in his Coke. Where had I seen him before? I needed to say something more to him, before the hole of cordiality closed and we became strangers once again.

"What were you in Korea for?" he said, instead.

"To learn Korean on the Motherland Program."

"And where are you going?"

"Minneapolis."

He smiled.

"You're adopted, aren't you?"

I sat bolt upright, sloshing some of my drink. He laughed. "I can always tell. I am, too."

A heavyish blond woman strode up the aisle, smiled at me, then carefully navigated herself through the narrow airspace between the young man's lap and the seatback, to dock in the middle seat.

"My mother," he said, and I saw the pieces of the puzzle falling together.

"Gretchen Muckenhill," the woman said. Now seated, she leaned over him to shake my hand. Our fingers could barely meet over the distance.

"An adoptee, too, Mom," the guy said.

Mrs. Muckenhill's face softened, like warmed wax. "And what are you doing in Korea, all by yourself?"

"Studying Korean," I said. I remained quiet a few seconds more, then asked the young man, "Did you find your family?"

He laughed. "Wow, your Korean must be great if you can understand Korean TV," he said. Then he shook his head. "No, we had some leads, that was it. There was someone who thought she recognized my baby picture, but no dice. But geez, we met so many nice people while we were here."

His mother nodded in agreement. "Oh, for sure. The Koreans are the most warmhearted, generous people, really. So many people gave blood. Such a shame there wasn't a match in all that."

Now he was going to die, wasn't he?

"I'll get my marrow tested, if it will help," I said. I stared at him. There was always the chance, I supposed, that we were related. Maybe my birth mother's sister also had a pregnancy she didn't tell anyone about, and then this guy and I were cousins. Maybe I was related to any of a zillion Koreans I saw. Maybe I had been related to Doug, whom I had slept with. Or Jun-Ho.

"That'd be great," the guy said. "I'll give you the number of the Cammy Lee Foundation, a marrow registry for Asian Americans, where you can get it done."

There were no outward signs of the cancer cells ravaging his body. Except for his thinness, which wasn't exceptional, he looked untouched by disease. I wondered how many cancer cells, lurking in secret, somatic places, would mutate and divide on this twenty-hour flight home.

❁ ❁ ❁

In Seattle, at Customs, someone must have broken a jar of kimchi, because the kimchi smell was oddly worse than it had been at the airport in Korea. I imagined the smell swimming through my hair, dusting my skin like DDT.

I noticed that Brian, the West Pointer could not lift more than a small flight bag. The thick wool of his uniform made up for the heft he must no longer have. His mother stacked their bags onto one of the few luggage carts around.

She said *uff-da!* as she pushed hard to get the cart rolling. I followed behind, somewhat less burdened because Doug had helped me ship my heaviest things home.

In front of me, two Korean ladies had two very sticky and very unhappy babies between them. One of the babies had hair that stood straight up, making him look cartoonishly frightened, the other had downy black fuzz that circled a bald spot at the top of her head like a monk's tonsure. The women were loaded with multitiered luggage, tipping on flimsy wheels, and an overstuffed diaper bag.

I ended up in line behind them. I tried to amuse the babies by making faces as we waited. The tonsure-headed baby rewarded me with a gummy, drooly smile.

One of the ladies smiled at me in weary gratitude.

"Beautiful baby," I said.

"Oh, they're not ours," said the woman, who was short and chubby and had an easygoing smile. "These little ones are going to meet their new families. We're just their escorts."

"We get to fly at a discount this way," said her companion, who had a stronger Korean accent. She was wearing a sleeveless shirt and I could see the scar from a vaccination, big and round as a mushroom cap, on her upper arm. "Say, are you Korean?"

I pretended to need something from deep within my bag. I didn't want to explain to them that I was one of those babies, grown up.

Then my hand touched *o-jing-o,* smooth and dry and somehow set free from its plastic wrapper. I had completely forgotten about the food: ear o' corn, *ddok,* seaweed. Suddenly, I wanted to cache it away, to have something of Korea when I was back on American soil. Now I needed a plan, an excuse for why I checked "no" on the box that asked if I was bringing any food or food products, fruit, soil, etc. into the country.

The low-tide odor of the *o-jing-o* was starting to seep out of my carryon.

A yellow light went on, urging me to step forward. A man with hard, buckshot eyes faced me. His expression suggested that he was looking for ways to keep me out of *his* country.

I handed him my American passport and my form.

"That your real name, Sarah Thorson?"

"Yes," I sighed.

"What were you in Korea for?"

"To learn Korean."

Tendrils of squid-smell were gently swirling around us.

He hoisted my Samsonite onto a stainless steel table like they have at the vet's. He asked me to unbelt it and open it. I sighed, again.

He pawed through my clothes, fingers probing my underwear and the presents I'd brought back: a silk tie and an OB beer ("Korea Best Beer") T-shirt for Ken, a lacquered box for Amanda, a very well done fake Chanel bag for Christine, and some traditional Korean green tea that I'd gone all the way to the Buddhist neighborhood of Insa-Dong to get. It was a special, uncured kind of tea, the leaves loose in a decorative wooden box, which, I noticed for the first time, said GLEEN TEA.

"What's this?"

The man pulled out Choi *Sunsengnim*'s present, exposed the blade.

"A souvenir letter opener."

"It's a knife. You could hurt someone with this, young lady," the man said.

"Not you," I mumbled.

"What did you say?"

"I said it's just a souvenir."

"There's a prohibition against bringing weapons into the country," he said.

I thought of it as a letter opener, but Doug proclaimed it a knife, as did this man. A chastity knife. I was reminded of one of the cultural field trips I didn't go on, the Puyo Festival in July: it celebrated the three thousand court ladies in ancient times who committed mass suicide rather than face the penises of oncoming Mongol and Shilla armies. Not unlike ancient Rome's Lucretia, raped, then driven to burying a sword in her viscera to "preserve" her honor. Women's lives cut short because of things men did, or even just threatened to do.

"Okay, keep it then." There was something fitting to all this. Let me leave this totem behind.

He dropped it in a plastic Ziploc bag, as if it were already evidence for a murder case. He closed my bag and waved me on.

I hoisted my carryon onto my shoulder. Now I smelled like an open tin of sardines. I walked away, careful not to look back, careful to hide my smile.

We landed, finally, in Minneapolis. Outside the window, planes waited patiently as livestock at their jetways; other jetways gaped empty as loneliness. The gray of the airport matched the smudged color of the clouds, floating brains in a washed-out sky. The exact scene from the day I left.

Had I actually left and come back? Or had I nodded off and begun dreaming, my Korean trip yet to begin?

The pilot cut the engines. Everyone rose at once, as if to give him a standing ovation.

"Good luck." The guy, Brian. His mother began to gather their bags.

"I'll go to the marrow center," I promised, touching the slip of paper in my pocket. Something jingled from inside. It was the Hodori keychain.

Brian nodded, smiled, but he looked incredibly tired, as if it took all his strength to lift the corners of his mouth. I was at once sorry I had imagined the cancerous cells in his body dividing and dividing as we flew, as if I might have inadvertently caused it to happen.

Outside, the glare of camera lights. WCCO. WMIN. *The Pride of the Northland.* Balloons, signs, open-mouthed Minnesota grins and whoops. People in Vikes shirts. All for Brian, I imagined.

Or maybe those babies. Twenty years ago, I was aware, Ken and Christine had movie camera'ed every minute of my "birth"—my passing from the womb of my Northwest Orient flight, through the tubular jetway, into the cold, bright blaze of the terminal.

Dazed and seeing spots, I stepped into the gate area.

To my left, a blond woman, tanned legs in pink shorts, held the tonsure-monk-baby in her arms. The short Korean woman was nowhere to be found.

I had this thought that the new adoptive mother might look up and see me, that we might exchange secret smiles as I passed. But no, she was gazing at her baby, to the exclusion of everything else in the world. New baby, new life.

But what was this baby's life going to be? Was she going to grow up psychically untethered as I had, a tiny, brave astronaut floating in that airless void of uncertainty? To become an adult and not be able to know what parts were biological legacies, what was the result of habit and environment, what part of the self sang as pure, free improvisation?

But we humans are resilient. We're programmed to be able to pick things out of the rubble and make something new, aren't we? Something possibly beautiful and lasting. Or edible. *Pudae chigae*, for example.

Baby-girl, I wish you luck, I whispered as I passed. *You're going to need it.*

"Sarah!"

The *famille* Thorson: mother, father, and biological daughter—shared genetic clay—were waiting, leaning on the gate's railing.

For the better part of a year, I had been among "my people." Suddenly, this trio of Caucasian faces.

This family has nothing to do with me.

They are just some random, suburban Minnesota family.

WELCOME HOME, SARAH! said the posterboard sign Amanda was holding. It had a Korean flag drawn on one side, the Stars and Stripes on the other. How irretrievably corny: Korean, yet American.

"You're here," I called.

"Of course, silly," Christine called back. "We wouldn't miss it for the world."

She detached herself from the crowd to take a picture with her expensive autofocus camera. Amanda was smiling at me, waving, as she clutched the sign with her other hand. Ken looked, somehow, proud. His lawyerly eyes were watery, his mustache trembled.

My legs suddenly became ionized. I walked faster, faster, closing the distance between us.

Author's Note

I started writing the Sarah stories in 1992 and amassed a good number of them, but no matter what I did, the stories didn't gel as either a collection or a novel. Slowly, I began to realize that another voice was struggling to be heard: Sarah's birth mother. I ignored this call for quite a while, because I knew inevitably that I'd need to go to Korea. And beyond the usual hassles of planning and funding such a trip, finding a place to live, etc., I'd also somehow have to find some birth mothers, get them to agree to talk to me about the most traumatic experience in their lives, and I'd have to learn Korean well enough to talk to them! At the time I also had many urgent things occupying my mind: I was getting married, and my mother-in-law-to-be was dying of cancer.

But the voice kept calling to me. Without much hope, I applied for a Fulbright Fellowship, calling my project *Silent Mothers: The Story of Korean Birthmothers*. Practically on the eve on my wedding, I found out that I had actually won it—funding plus other support for a year in Korea. My husband encouraged me to go, even if it meant we'd spend our first year of marriage apart. Three weeks later, I was in Seoul with little more than my Fulbright credentials (which gave me access to the U.S. Army bases) and some leads from my friends Brian Boyd and Mrs. Hyun-Sook Han, which eventually led me to Mrs. Sang-Soon Han and the Ae Ran Won home for women.

Doing research for a fictional work is always tricky—what to leave as the real fact, what to fictionalize? For this project in particular, taking oral histories of the various birth mothers who agreed to be interviewed was both inspiring and heartbreaking. None of the birth mothers who spoke to me imposed restrictions on what I could ask, and they all freely offered so many brave and unsparing glimpses into their hearts (one woman even let me read her diary) that I can never thank them enough for this gift. They all said—independently—that part of their motivation for agreeing to speak with me, despite the stigma and secrecy that still exists, was that they hoped some fragment of their love would pass into the book and be understood by their birth children.

The deepest hearts of these mothers, then, inhabits this book, and I send these women my everlasting love, gratitude, and admiration. Everything else is fiction. Kyung-sook is entirely my creation, as is Enduring Pine Village.

❀ ❀ ❀

So many people and institutions aided in the writing of this book that inevitably I'm going to forget to thank some very important people—and I apologize in advance.

For financial support and research opportunities, I want to thank the J. William Fulbright Foundation, Yale University, Brown University, the Hedgebrook Writers' Colony, and the Money for Women/Barbara Deming Memorial Fund. The O. Henry prize panel gave me a lift by bestowing an honorable mention for one of *Somebody's Daughter*'s original seed stories when I needed it most.

Thank you to early readers Edward Bok Lee, Dean Jacoby, Michelle Lee, Ed Hardy, and especially Professor Heinz Insu Fenkl—mentor, *oppa*, all-around great guy. I am also thankful to Brian Boyd, Mrs. Hyun-Sook Han, Mrs. Sang-Soon Han, and of course, my mother, for opening doors for me in Korea, and to Professor Ok-Ju Lee of Seoul Women's University for taking excellent care of me while I was there.

The Sinunus—Karen, Mike, Chris, and Matt—for giving me a beautiful space in which I wrote the final pieces of this book. Quang Bao and the Asian American Writers' Workshop have always been there for me whenever I needed a shoulder, or a little shove.

Thanks to the awesome folks at Beacon, Helene Atwan, my editor extraordinaire, and the rest of Team Beacon: Kathy Daneman, Tom Hallock, Joy Kim, Pamela MacColl, Lisa Sacks, Christopher Vyce, and all the hardworking sales reps. Lots of love to Charlotte Sheedy and Carolyn Kim—thanks for keeping the faith over the long haul.

Thanks always to my family, Lees and Jacobys, to Karl, my first and last reader, partner in crime, keeper of my heart.